ELK GROVE VILLAGE PUBLIC LIBRARY
3 1250 011
W9-ATT-700

Vines of Entanglement

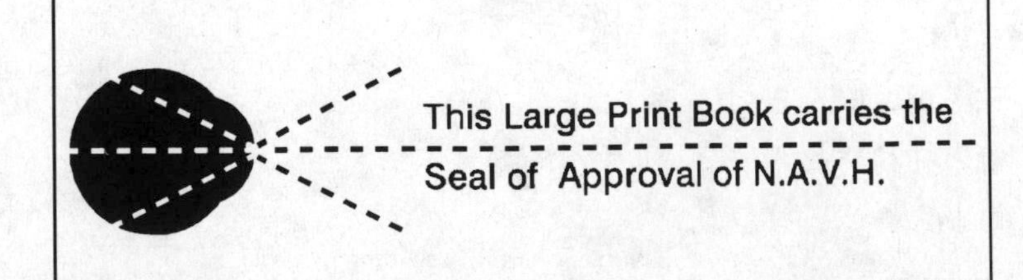
This Large Print Book carries the
Seal of Approval of N.A.V.H.

VINES OF ENTANGLEMENT

LISA CARTER

THORNDIKE PRESS
A part of Gale, Cengage Learning

GALE
CENGAGE Learning

Farmington Hills, Mich • San Francisco • New York • Waterville, Maine
Meriden, Conn • Mason, Ohio • Chicago

Thorndike Press, a part of Gale, Cengage Learning.

Thorndike Press® Large Print Christian Mystery.
The text of this Large Print edition is unabridged.
Other aspects of the book may vary from the original edition.
Set in 16 pt. Plantin.

LIBRARY OF CONGRESS CATALOGING-IN-PUBLICATION DATA

Carter, Lisa, 1964–
Vines of entanglement / Lisa Carter. — Large print edition.
pages cm. — (Thorndike Press large print Christian mystery)
ISBN 978-1-4104-7944-0 (hardcover) — ISBN 1-4104-7944-7 (hardcover)
1. Widows—Fiction. 2. Detectives—North Carolina—Raleigh—Fiction. 3. Murder—Investigation—Fiction. 4. Large type books. I. Title.
PS3603.A77757V56 2015b
813'.6—dc23 2015009210

Published in 2015 by arrangement with Abingdon Press

Printed in Mexico
1 2 3 4 5 6 7 19 18 17 16 15

To my father, James W. Cox —
I love you.

For those who've found themselves ensnared in entangling sins and encumbrances. For all who've struggled to overcome fear, loss, and guilt. For all who need to hear that no one is beyond God's grace and mercy.

The Christian life is not a sprint.
It is a marathon.

Each of us has our own, individual race to run. My race will be different than your race. But each race will be full of peaks, valleys, bends, and pitfalls in the road. And there are no shortcuts in life's amazing journey of faith. Detours will only derail and delay us from reaching the stadium of faith's crowning hope.

I'm thankful for the cloud of witnesses who've lined my path, cheering and encouraging me along life's journey. I'm thankful for Jesus, beside me every step of the way.

Readers — Thank you for reading my books and being a blessing to me along this stretch of my race. When we cross life's finish line I pray we will each hear Jesus say, "Well done."

Until then . . .

Because of the joy that lies ahead if we — if I — endure: **let's throw off what weighs us down; run the race; and fix our eyes on Jesus.**

ACKNOWLEDGMENTS

Thanks to **David, Corinne, and Kathryn,** who are always there for me when life — writing and edits, too — gets crazy. Over the years, it's been fun riding and biking our portion of greenway trails. Thankfully, our most exciting encounter — unlike Laura's — has been spotting bunnies and the majestic blue heron.

Grant — Thanks for letting me borrow your name.

Laura Jackson — Thanks for allowing Aunt Velma to use Aaron's nickname for you, Laura Lou.

Thanks to **Hope,** my friend and first reader. I look forward to monthly get-togethers. True friendship — to quote Miss Lula — is a rare and precious thing.

Ramona Richards — You are not only a great editor, but also a wonderful teacher. I continue to learn so much from you.

Cat, Mark, Teri, and all the marketing, sales, and editorial team members — I feel blessed to work with you.

Tamela Hancock Murray — You are simply The Best.

Jesus — You are the beginning of life's amazing journey of faith. And You will be waiting to welcome me at life's finish line. You are the ultimate prize.

So then let's also run the race that
is laid out in front of us,
since we have such a great cloud of
witnesses surrounding us.
Let's throw off any extra baggage,
get rid of the sin that trips us up,
and fix our eyes on Jesus,
faith's pioneer and perfecter.
He endured the cross, ignoring the
shame,
for the sake of the joy
that was laid out in front of him,
and sat down at the right side of God's
throne.

Hebrews 12:1-2

1

Would this ever get any better?

Laura Mabry swallowed past the lump in her throat. "Why didn't you tell me this was a father-son fishing trip, Ian?"

She gave her ten-year-old son The Look in the rearview mirror. "Garrett would've gladly —"

Ian's full lips twisted. "Exactly why I didn't tell you."

Switching off the ignition, she wheeled around in the driver's seat. "I don't know what you have against Garrett. He's been nothing but a godsend since your dad . . ."

Ian's deep chocolate eyes flashed. "Helping himself is more like it."

Her eyebrows rose at his insinuation. Where had he learned about — ?

She bull's-eyed Ian with one of Aunt Velma's Frozen Looks, which had skewered her often enough during her own adolescent years.

Adolescence.

Was this what she had to look forward to as a single parent for the next ten years, give or take a few? Mouthy, teenage angst? Where had that sweet boy who loved Mom and baseball gone?

But she knew.

Into the grave with his father, a year ago this past February.

A wave of humid air enveloped her through the open window. She sighed.

Welcome to Memorial Day weekend. Temps still in the nineties as late afternoon drew a veil over the hazy Carolina sky.

"Garrett and I have known each other since we were children." She gentled her tone. "He understands what it's like to grow up without a dad. He wants so much to be there for you, Ian."

His mouth tightened in a thin, straight line, his lips disappearing into a grimace. He swiveled at a movement at the top of the driveway. Gangly limbed, sixteen-year-old Justin Monaghan hauled cases of Gatorade out of the Prescotts' brick colonial.

Ian reached for the door. "Justin's going to buddy with me on the trip. He lost his dad, too, a few years ago."

Despite the lurid publicity surrounding his father's murder, Justin, his sister, Claire, and their landscape architect mother, Alison, emerged intact. Better than intact.

A smile flitted across Laura's face at the thought of Alison's new husband and the children's adored new stepfather, Mike Barefoot, recently promoted to lieutenant within the Raleigh Police Department homicide unit.

Ian swung open the door. "And I don't need no . . ." He muttered something, too soft for her ears to catch fully, but without a doubt uncomplimentary regarding various aspects of Garrett Payne's lineage.

She placed a restraining hand on Ian's duffle. "You wait one minute, young man. We don't talk like that in this family."

Dr. Stephen Prescott, a colleague and friend of her late husband at Rex Hospital, emerged from the cavernous depths of the garage. Twelve-year-old Trey and ten-year-old Dillon followed like frisky puppies.

"Gotta go. They're waiting on me. We're the last to arrive," Ian huffed. "As usual."

Stung by his unaccustomed sarcasm, she let go of the bag. "Don't you sass me." Traces of Velma echoed in her voice.

When had she started sounding like her seventy-five-year-old maiden aunt?

She pursed her lips. "With that attitude, you may not be going at all."

Ian clenched his teeth. "Don't embarrass me, Mom." The guys drew closer. "I need this trip. I need to get away from . . ."

From her.

Since Holt died, she'd smothered him. Afraid she'd lose Ian the way she'd lost everyone else she ever loved.

But like she'd fixed everything else, she'd make this right. She'd get herself and Ian past this crater in life's road if . . . if it killed Ian?

No, killed her. Killed her.

"Honey . . ." She laid her hand atop his shoulder.

He jerked at her touch, his face like obsidian. "Whatever."

"Mr. Flint Face," Holt used to joke.

His stubbornness. So like his . . . Holt, never was . . . She stuffed the memory of his other —

Ian scooted out, clutching the black duffle to his chest. "Wouldn't want to mess up your weekend with your boyfriend." He slammed the car door behind him.

Stephen rested his hand on the open window frame. "We'll take good care of him, Laura." He smiled. "Val's already gone to open the beach house."

Dillon, Ian's best friend, punched him in the arm. "Our base camp."

Ian punched him back. They grinned at each other, Dillon's big baby blues and fair complexion so different from Ian's more exotic looks.

Trey popped up between his father and the car. "We'll bring you some of our catch."

Stephen laughed. "Or not." He gestured toward his sturdy black Expedition. "Why don't you boys finish stowing the gear?"

"And the snacks." Dillon tugged at Ian's arm. "Mom bought Oreos."

"We'll be back Monday, Laura. I'll drop Ian off at your house." Stephen flicked a glance toward the crew headed for the SUV.

Except for Ian, who, although seemingly anxious to be rid of his mom, lingered.

"Val will make sure we don't starve. We're going to have fun, aren't we, bud?" Stephen slapped a hand across Ian's shoulders. "Tell your mom good-bye for now." Stephen waved good-bye, his long-legged strides eating up the distance toward the garage.

Ian huddled next to the window. Her stomach knotted. They'd been inseparable since the freak winter accident claimed Holt's life.

She swallowed. "Did you pack your underwear? Got your cell phone charged? Aunt Velma, Garrett, and I are a speed dial away. Call me, night or day if you need —"

Ian shoved away from the car. "Stop babying me." His eyes narrowed, a dangerous glint surfacing. "I hate Garrett 'Payne in the —' "

"Ian . . ." Hot tears prickled her eyelids.

His breaths came and went in short spurts. "And if you marry him, Mom, I'll hate you, too."

Jon Locklear slipped the key into the lock of his apartment. He entered, slinging his duffle bag onto the lumpy seen-better-days couch borrowed from his sister Yvonne. His long, slightly hooked nose — like a bird dog his other little sister, Kelly, teased — wrinkled.

The elders on the swamp might've wondered at the pungent scent. Wondered if a toten — an evil spirit — wandered about. But he knew better.

After a week of well-earned vacation time, the apartment had a closed-in, musty smell.

He'd taken out the garbage before leaving town to spend time with his mom, hadn't he?

Maybe . . .

He approached the silver bin in the kitchen with trepidation. His foot clamped down upon the pedal, swinging open the trashcan lid. He flinched.

Maybe not . . .

"Oh, Jonny boy." He covered his nose in a futile gesture of self-preservation. "You're an idiot." And, a terrible housekeeper.

Not much house to keep while he'd been in the Marines at either Camp Lejeune or overseas. But after deciding not to re-up, his feeble attempts to keep house — first in Baltimore and then after landing this gig with the RPD Homicide Unit — hadn't amounted to more than pirating towels and sheets from his mother's linen closets.

As for dishes?

Nah . . . Not necessary. Not as long as McDonald's continued to thrive on these here American shores.

One of the things he loved most about America — a Starbucks, a fast food joint, and a church on every corner.

He fumbled for an errant clothespin in the closet of his one bedroom walk-up. He opened and closed it on the end of his offended appendage. Taking a deep breath — not unlike the posture he assumed when his sisters pressed him into changing a diaper or in defusing an IED outside Kabul — he gathered the edges of the garbage bag and headed for the dumpster in the parking lot.

With a mighty, overhand swing worthy of his lacrosse-playing ancestors, he heaved the bag into the rank confines of the puke-green bin. He backed away from the garbage bin across five empty spaces until he leaned against the still-warm engine hood of his golden-hued Ford F-150.

Exhaling in a loud gust of air, he glanced about feeling sheepish, wondering who else might've observed his bizarre behavior from the building's wall of windows. Realizing the clothespin still rested like a figurehead on the prow of his nose, he removed it and stuffed it in the pocket of his cargo pants.

Jon shoved off from his truck and returned to his apartment. He stopped on the threshold, his nose testing the air for any more malodorous smells.

Not great. He sniffed again. But better.

He pressed the message button on his wireless phone. Grabbing his duffle, he carried the phone with him into the bedroom. The first, Yvonne's home number.

"Uncle Jonny?" A pause. "It's me." Another pause. "Cami."

He smiled at the voice of his six-year-old niece. He placed the phone on the bureau to listen while he unpacked.

"My toof came out. All I had to do, like you said, was bite into one of Gram's apples. Mom says if I put it under my pillow tonight, I'll get a surprise." Her voice fell to a whisper. "You think she means money?" A sense of awe entered her tone. "I got four more loose ones I can wiggle with my tongue. Four," she added in case he hadn't caught it the first time. "I'm going to be rich."

He laughed, breaking the stillness of the apartment.

"We miss you already. See ya, Uncle Jonny. Bye."

"I miss you guys already, too." He dropped onto the bed, the edge of the mattress groaning at his weight.

Message two. His mother, Florence Oxendine Locklear, recuperating from hip replacement surgery. "Jon, call and let me know you got home safe."

He grinned. Never know he was thirty-three. She treated him like he was still a mischievous child, a *yerker* in the English-Southern-Lumbee way of speaking.

"Lots of crazy drivers in the big city. Don't know why you couldn't have found a nice job with the sheriff's department in Robeson County or with the local Mimosa Grove police."

He rolled his eyes.

Maybe because there were no career opportunities in good ole, one-stoplight Mimosa Grove, North Carolina? The back end of Nowhere.

"Did you eat yet? You were as skinny as a corn stalk when you got here last week."

He'd eaten. In the truck on the way to Raleigh. Everything his sisters packed in containers from a week's worth of family barbecues and get-togethers.

"I wish . . ."

Here it comes.

"I wish you'd find a nice girl . . ."

His mom and sisters had done their best to introduce him, over the last week, to every available female under the age of forty.

"I know I should've had the courage to say these things to your face, son. But somehow over the phone is easier. You need to find you a good, Christian woman and settle down. Preferably a good, Christian, Lumbee girl."

This again. Same song. Stanza ninety-five in her quest to pair him with a real Lum woman.

"It's not right you being alone so much. If your dad were here, he'd say the same thing."

A picture of his hard-working dad perched atop his red Farmall tractor rose in his mind. Jon's mouth pulled downward.

His mother cleared her throat. "You got to get over her, honey. What's done is done.

No going back. You got too much life and love in you to waste on something never meant to be." She murmured her love and hung up.

If only.

He sighed.

If only he could. If only his mother knew . . .

He wondered sometimes how much his never-miss-a-trick mother did know. Or, suspected.

Iraq and two tours in Afghanistan. A string of failed relationships between here and every Marine base he'd been stationed at over the last decade. Including the police academy and as a rookie on the mean streets of Baltimore.

But nothing had ever erased an image of china-blue eyes and the sweet smell of honeysuckle from his heart.

The best and the worst days he'd ever known. He'd tried over the years not to think of what might have been. Only pain lay down that path.

Now, a second chance career-wise. An opportunity to make a difference on the home front. To protect and serve.

A chance to see his long-neglected family on the weekends he wasn't on duty. A chance to start over.

His mom was right. Time to move on.

A beep. Message three. Ana Morales's strong confident tone. "Hey, handsome. You back in town? Great news. The paperwork came through transferring me from Narc to Homicide. We're colleagues now."

He smiled into the phone.

"The guys are meeting at Leo Loco's for a game of pool and drinks. Wondered if you wanted to grab dinner first and keep me from eating alone. Again." Her voice, throaty, sexy, and inviting, rumbled across the phone line. "Call me if you're available."

The skin on his forearms tingled.

He glanced at the pile of dirty laundry. The silence engulfed him, broken only by the tiny ping of a water droplet hitting the basin of the bathroom sink. He rubbed at his jaw, shadowed with stubble.

Was he available? Was this call from Ana so soon after his mother's a sign from God?

Taking a deep breath, he reached for the phone.

2

Feeling superfluous, Laura headed toward her own Woods Edge neighborhood. She heaved a sigh of relief as she entered the peaceful, tree-shaded lanes of her mother's childhood home. And as an added bonus, underneath the towering canopy of oaks, the temperature dropped ten degrees.

Stately colonials, Tudor Revivals, and Craftsman bungalows boasted large, leafy lots bordering a set of intertwining naturalized trails. The greenway meandered through Woods Edge, paralleling Crabtree Creek and Raleigh's more exclusive neighborhoods.

Driving into her cul-de-sac, she curled her lip at the decorative ivy vines suspended from the peaked roofline of her storybook Tudor cottage. With the vines embedded into the stones of the house, contractors advised her to leave the vines alone or risk damaging the integrity of the structure.

In the garage, she rested her head on the steering wheel before her sense of duty prevailed. Buggsby waited for their daily afternoon stroll.

Her bare thighs below her black Nike running shorts stuck to the hot leather seats. As if ripping a Band-Aid off skin, she tore herself free. Way too early for temps like these. Felt like July or August.

In the kitchen, she helped herself to plenty of ice cubes in a glass of her summertime favorite: peach tea. Her hand wrapped around the glass, she paused. Goose bumps prickled her arms. Something wasn't right.

The air had a disturbed feel in her home since she'd taken Ian over to the Prescotts'. Cocking her head, she listened for noises that didn't belong to the creaking house. Her eyes darted around the kitchen, but nothing appeared out of place. She forced her hunched shoulders to relax.

Taking a deep, welcome swig, she gazed out the window at her weed-infested backyard. After Holt died, she'd bought the family home. The home Aunt Velma insisted she couldn't vacate to join her friends at Stonebriar Assisted Living until someone trustworthy — that is, Laura — took it off her hands.

With gratitude, she accepted her aunt's

generous terms, opened the needlepoint shop she'd dreamed of, and made a new life for herself and her son. In the nine months since the remodel, Ian succumbed to his night terrors only twice. And those she traced to the first day of a new school year and the other, the first ice storm of winter.

Aunt Velma, quilter extraordinaire, never had the time or inclination for gardening. But years ago, Laura and her mom, Louise — on the good, pain-free days — sat together on the screened porch and dreamed verdant dreams. Dreamed of replacing the overgrown azaleas and camellias with newer plants more suitable in scope. Envisioned the gardenias they'd plant for hot summer blooms. Planned the pruning and shaping of the wild wisteria blanketing the back of the property adjacent to the greenway.

The sight of those purple clusters during her mother's final spring brought tears of joy to her mother's eyes. And when the last petals had fallen to the pine-needled lawn, so too, had her mother's spirit. Laura set the glass upon the counter with a decided clunk.

The vines had to go. Atmospheric? Sure.

If you were into creepy and parasitic.

Make that grasping. Predatory.

She hated vines now. Hated how they devoured the soul out of the tree. Choked life from everything they touched. A draping mantle of slow death. She much preferred the order of the rose bed she'd planted.

But the contractor hired to install the waist-high white picket fence, Zeke Lowther, was nowhere to be seen. Her lip curled. Not that she enjoyed any more encounters with him than necessary.

She shuddered, picturing the scruffy, roving-eyed fence builder. He'd come recommended by needlepoint aficionada, socialite Patti Ogburn. And, most important, he was cheap. But then again, you get what you pay for.

Her eyes flicked toward the wall clock. Four o'clock. Early to call it quits, but maybe not considering it was Memorial Day weekend. Two hours from Raleigh to the nearest beach. The highways jammed.

Thinking of Ian and the guys on the road to the beach house, she contemplated sending a prayer for protection on their behalf. It's what Holt would've done. Her mouth twisted.

But Holt wasn't here anymore. And she and God hadn't been on a first-name basis for a long time. To be fair, her fault. Not His.

She'd tried to be the good wife that prominent oncologist Holt Mabry deserved.

And how abysmally she'd failed in that respect, too.

But no point in following that depressing rabbit trail again.

She speed-dialed Tapestries. The phone rang. "Pick up, Renna. Where are you?"

Laura tapped her running shoe against the hardwood floor. "We're not supposed — you're not supposed to close the shop until five o'clock."

Voicemail, Laura's own voice, kicked in with, "Hello. You've reached Tapestries Needleworks. Our hours —" She clicked Off.

Guess everybody but her had plans for the holiday.

Correction.

Garrett was coming over with Thai takeout to discuss his election campaign and her participation in tomorrow's Memorial Day Parade in the small-town suburb of Garner. The first of many campaign stops over the summer leading to November's big day.

Laura reached for the dog leash and risked a peek at her appearance before wishing she hadn't. She made a face in the mirror.

Laura tucked an erstwhile strand of blonde hair behind one ear and smoothed her pale-pink jogging halter over the waistband of her shorts. But as Aunt Velma had often reminded Laura during her image-obsessed teen years, life was too short to waste it in front of a mirror.

Stepping onto the screened porch, she nudged her dog with the toe of her sneaker. "Wake up, Buggs. Time for our walk."

Buggs opened one baleful eye, embodying the stereotype of the lazy basset hound.

"Some watchdog you are. Lowther's come and gone with nary a peep from you, I'm sure. Up and at 'em. Garrett will be here in a few hours."

Buggsby opened his jaws as wide as a hippo on the Congo and yawned until Laura almost swore she heard them crack.

"This century would work great for me, Buggs, if you don't mind."

Buggsby lurched to his feet, stretching wiener dog–like. "Whatever" written across his ponderous features. Every boy — and every dog — seemed to have an attitude these days.

She clipped the leash to his collar. The air, heavy with moisture, hit her like a fist in the face. She maneuvered past the piles of stacked pickets and tools scattered throughout the grass. Her brows drew together.

What craftsman neglected his tools, the implements of his livelihood? What kind of project had Lowther completed for Patti?

Laura supposed his redneck charms attracted some kinds of women. But not her. No matter the sizzling, come-hither looks he sent her way.

He gave her the heebie-jeebies, and Aunt Velma had always taught her to pay attention to her instincts.

With a long weekend ahead, she resolved to do her part to help speed Zeke Lowther on his way. Starting with hacking down this jungle of vines so he could enclose the perimeter of her yard.

A greenway footpath ran alongside her property. A path used by generations of Woods Edge residents as the most convenient shortcut to the greenway itself. Her mother had grown up in this house. And to this house, her mother had come home to die. Aunt Velma had retired from teaching to care for her dying niece when Laura's father couldn't or wouldn't —

Laura bit her lip.

Don't go there.

Just another scabbed-over wound in her life. Problem was, she tended to be a scab-picker.

Laura muscled her way through the tangle of vines. Kudzu, one of the two imported curses of the South, snaked around several trees, creating a virtually impenetrable wall. Buggsby foraged his way through the undergrowth, his bloodhoundlike nose sniffing out the trail on the hunt for his sworn enemy, the jackrabbits.

With a sudden burst of energy, Buggsby gave an excited bark and lunged out of the green darkness onto the leaf-carpeted path. Scrawny young saplings boomeranged into Laura's face.

Panting, she trotted to keep pace. "Warn me next time, Buggs, when you feel like playing greyhound."

The tree canopy of river oaks, maples, and pines arched above the trail. Only shafts of light penetrated the interlocking branches. Dust motes danced on sunbeams. A spider web sparkled like a prism in the refracted light. She jogged past a late-season cluster of grape wisteria, its ropelike vine intertwined among the trees.

Her mama would've drawn Laura's attention to the goodness of God. Some goodness. She snorted, recalling the repeated doses of morphine unable to blunt the edges of her mother's pain.

Leaves from winter's final hurrah

crunched on the ground beneath her feet. A lush carpet of green moss dotted the path. Crabtree Creek gurgled below the embankment, visible here and there through gaps in the foliage.

The greenway stretched for three miles until it reached the Village, a small shopping center where Tapestries was located. Maybe she'd venture there, check on the store, and jog home. She and Buggsby could use the exercise.

Allowing her mind to drift, she eased into a rhythmic stride. When life got to be too much, Laura ran.

Inhale . . . Exhale . . . Inhale . . .

Her running shoes pounded over the wooden bridge spanning a smaller artery of the creek. The sweet scent of honeysuckle tickled her nose. Her nostrils flared.

Skidding to an abrupt halt, she released Buggsby's leash. She whipsawed, trying to locate the source of the perfume. She hadn't imagined it this time, had she? Sometimes she did, but no —

Yellow blooms looped through the rails of the bridge. Trumpet-shaped flowers in pockets of sunshine cascaded down the embankment. Laura closed her eyes.

A long sigh trickled out from between her lips. She was so tired. Soul-weary.

Just once, please God.

She'd expended a great deal of effort over the last eleven years trying not to imagine the might-have-beens. Fighting not to indulge the traitorous longings of her heart. Best to leave those memories in the past where they belonged.

Or so she told herself. Over and over and over.

But Holt was gone. Wouldn't hurt anyone but herself to breathe deeply and savor the honeysuckle now, would it?

To pick at this scab. To let it bleed and — maybe once and for all — flush out this particular infection. Just this once to take out long-buried memories from the forbidden place Laura never allowed herself to revisit.

Was it better to have loved once, truly loved, than never at all? In her experience, having known a love like that only served to emphasize the bleakness of her existence after she lost it. She squeezed her eyelids tighter.

Inhale . . . Exhale . . . Inhale . . .

Her senses sharpened and attuned to the rushing stream. The water bounced and reconnoitered over the rocks and fallen logs. She listened to the skritches of the squirrels playing tag in the brush. Her pulse thrummed in tempo with the cicadas.

She drifted to another time. Another body of water not as lively as the creek.

To a place where the water undulated around her bare arms. Where tiny minnows nipped at her legs. To where her toes sifted the sandy pond bottom as he closed the distance between them.

His face, smiling. Those chocolate-kiss eyes. Where the sweet tangle of honeysuckle encircled the grove, heady in its promise of love.

A place where she'd weighed the risks and chosen to gamble more than her heart. Though at age twenty, she'd neither the experience or knowledge to count the cost of love. Where she'd turned her back on all she knew of God, and in the choosing, lost all hope of redemption.

Buggsby bayed, a foghorn shattering her dream world.

Jolted, Laura stuffed her memories down deep, where she'd stored them for over a decade. "Buggs?" She'd lost the leash.

Fixated at the other end of the bridge, his nose sniffed at the wooden trestle, half hidden under blackberry brambles. Growling, Buggs crouched, his tail thumping the ground. Between his teeth, a purple Converse shoe.

In two strides, she caught up with him. "Buggs, let go of that nasty old thing . . ." Edging closer, her eyes widened.

The shoe wasn't empty. A streak of crimson zigzagged across the stark white laces. The rest of the attached, female leg disappeared into the eye-level underbrush. The hair on the nape of Laura's neck rose.

"Let go, Buggs," she whispered. "Come here, boy." She tugged at his collar.

Buggsby shook his head with the shoe clamped in his jowls. A scattering of pebbles ricocheted farther down the slope. The brambles rustled. Her head jerked and shivers of fear crawled up her arms.

They weren't alone.

Ian flashed through her mind, and she released Buggsby. She needed help. She had to get somewhere safe before —

A black-clad arm snaked out, wrapping around her throat like a vise. She let loose a cry of sudden terror. Flinging her arms wide, she grabbed hold of the bridge railing, but the coiled arm dragged her backward toward the creek below. And once he wrestled her to the ground?

Raped? Certainly murdered, like the poor woman —

"No!" She clawed at his arm. And back-kicked, connecting with his shin, though not what she'd been aiming for.

He grunted in an expletive of pain. His rancid breath brushed against her cheek.

With her shoulder blades pressed into his chest, Laura bit back a sob as her futile defenses ebbed, giving way to his inexorable strength.

He squeezed his hands around her windpipe, kneading her air supply. She pummeled her elbows into his torso. If she lost consciousness . . . *Oh, God!*

Snarling, Buggsby dropped the shoe and chomped on the attacker's leg. Locking his teeth with a sickening crunch of bone. Cursing, the man loosened his grip around her throat.

Laura twisted to break free. His big ears flopping, Buggsby shook the man's leg from side to side. Strings of drool dribbled from his mouth.

She writhed. The man flung out his hand, ensnaring her ponytail. Laura screamed as he yanked her closer by the hank of her hair.

Laura groped for something, anything behind her to cushion her fall. Anything to use as a weapon. She cranked her head to ease the strain, and for the first time caught a glimpse of her hooded attacker.

The man smacked his other hand across Buggsby's head. Howling, Buggsby fell over, stunned inert. Freed, the man shoved her forward, pitching her face first onto the path. Her lips open to scream, she sucked in a mouthful of rotting leaf mulch.

Sputtering, Laura scrabbled for the cover of the vines on the opposite side of the trail. She belly crawled through the labyrinth.

"You little —" His hands pawed at her legs.

Beyond coherent thought, she wormed deeper into the shelter of the vines. The scratching thorns tore at her skin.

But today, the vines saved her.

Above the echo of her cries, another voice, another man arose on the trailhead. "Mrs. Mabry? Mrs. Mabry?"

Her attacker released his stranglehold on her ankle. Laura curled into a fetal position. His footfalls clambered away down the embankment toward the creek. Through the tangled vines, the edge of a saffron garment at ground level met her eye. Brown toes peeked from brown Birkenstock sandals.

"Mrs. Mabry?" The Buddhist priest offered a hand. "What has happened here?"

Shaking, she allowed the small Thai man to hoist her out of the choking undergrowth. Laura coughed. "A woman . . ." She gestured off the trail.

"And then he grabbed me —" Laura burst

into tears.

"We shall call the police, I think." From the folds of his robe, Mr. Wangchuk, owner of the Village florist shop, whipped out his cell. His face scrunched with the effort to speak precise English as he relayed the nature of his 9-1-1 to the dispatcher.

Disoriented, Laura sank to her knees. Whimpering, Buggsby nestled next to her, his cold, wet nose sliding up her arm.

She wrapped her arms around his thick neck, averting her eyes from the skinny, too-pale leg the dog had dragged out of the thorn bushes. "Buggs, you saved my life."

Buggsby licked her shoulder.

"You and Mr. Wangchuk."

Mr. Wangchuk removed the phone from his ear. His shaved head glistened, the humidity heavy as a blanket. "Help is on the way."

Her gaze returned to the leg tapering into one of those skimpy blue jean skirts the younger girls favored. The purple sneakers teased with familiarity. Her eyes widened.

No, oh God, no.

Leaning between the railings, Laura gagged and vomited.

His finger curved over redial, Jon's cell rang in his hand. Startled, he dropped it on the bed beside him. Ana again?

He checked Caller ID. Mike. His longtime friend and new boss at the RPD. What was he — ?

Jon's hand fumbled. He grabbed the phone from the folds of the bedcovers on the last ring before routing to voice mail.

"Mike?"

"Jon? Are you there?"

"I'm here. What can I do you for?"

Static crackled across the line. "Are you in Raleigh yet, bud?"

"Yeah. Just got back."

"I hate to ask this of you. I know your rotation doesn't resume till tomorrow, but we got ourselves a murder vic on the greenway. Morgan's out with the flu. Chavis is away with that training conference till next week. Dispatch is sending you the coordinates. I'd go myself but Alison —"

"Everything okay with Alison?" Worry sharpened Jon's tone.

The love of his lieutenant's life was five months pregnant with their first child together. Make that their first two children. Twins. A widow and the mother of teenagers before she met Mike, Alison was older than your average mother-to-be.

"Hope so." But Mike's voice sounded low and urgent. "She's in pain. Braxton-Hicks, she claims. Nothing to worry about. But you know Alison isn't a complainer and when she gets pale and —"

An audible gasp reverberated through the phone. The skin goosebumped on Jon's arms.

"Deep breath, Alison. Gotta go." Panic laced Mike's words. "Just a few blocks from Rex."

"No problem, Mike. I'll deal with everything on this end. You take care of Alison."

"Thanks, man." Mike's voice wavered. "And if you wouldn't mind, we'd also appreciate prayer for Alison and . . ." Mike faded out. "The babies."

"You got it. Anything else I can do for you guys?"

"Catch the killer for me."

"Roger that, Lieutenant."

3

Jon drove his truck into an empty parking space beside a bevy of flashing blue-and-whites at the Village Shopping Center. According to his coordinates, the crime scene lay halfway along a park area between the shopping center and the upscale Woods Edge neighborhood. The horseshoe-shaped strip mall contained a florist, an antiques shop, a post office, and other assorted businesses.

One of the uniforms waved him toward the forest behind the storefronts where a trailhead emerged. His nose twitched at the smell of something delicious in the air.

Pizza?

The swift turn of his head as he approached the greenway revealed a crowd of curious onlookers, drawn by the police activity, in front of a mouthwatering place called Mambo's. His stomach growled, thinking about the lost dinner opportunity with Ana. With a homicide investigation, it promised to be a long night.

Five minutes out of the air-conditioning and already his shirt underneath his blazer clung to his back. His eyes scanned left and right as he entered the hushed environment, not unlike the pine forest of his Sandhills home. The greenway was another world, located within the heart of bustling Raleigh, yet set apart, peaceful, and unsullied.

Except for the inconvenient fact of murder.

Maybe a good thing he hadn't eaten first. Mike hadn't had time to brief him on the particulars. But he'd been insistent it was murder and not an accident. Though a veteran of war, both foreign and domestic — if you counted the drug wars he fought in Baltimore — Jon was well acquainted with grisly, blood-drenched crime scenes.

As the newbie in the platoon and on the force in Baltimore, he'd learned not to allow his stomach to give way to his feelings. Learned to condition himself, switching his mind and his heart to off. Pity paralyzed.

Jon had a job to do. Feelings only clouded the issue. And the issue was to catch a killer and prevent him or her from wreaking their evil upon another innocent — or not-so-innocent, as the case might be — ever again.

Finding justice for someone gave Jon the next greatest thing to a purpose in his life since serving his country. Doing his part to put things right. His calling — to impose a semblance of order on an otherwise chaotic world.

Hokey ideals. Not cool or popular in this culture. But the way his dad had raised him.

Rounding a curve in the trail, he was startled to find Ana on-site. Slim and well-proportioned in skinny jeans and a hot-pink blouse, she waited for him against a back-drop of the curled fronds of lady ferns. Bees droned in the distance.

She flashed him a toothy smile. "Fancy meeting you here, Locklear."

He grinned. "I was about to take you up on your invitation when Mike called." He ran a hand through his short-cropped hair.

She sidled closer. Her shoulder grazed his with the barest of touches. "Rain check?" She swished those impossibly full lashes at him.

His chest broadened.

Deep-throated croaking frogs chorused, breaking the silence of the forest.

Jon licked his dry lips. "You got it."

Her generous, fuchsia-slashed mouth curved. "Mike's got the entire team working the case. Nothing like on-the-job training." She fondled the gold crucifix dangling around her neck, giving him a sideways glance.

At a sudden cacophony of birdsong, he wondered what the RPD and Mike's policy was on office fraternization. A hint of patchouli teased his nostrils.

He stepped back to clear his head. "What are we dealing with here?"

Wearing a half-smile, as if she understood exactly the effect she had on him, Ana reached into her jean pocket and whipped out her notebook. "First responders arrived after a 9-1-1 from a Mr." — she flipped a few pages — "Wangchuk. Owner of the Village florist shop. He rescued a woman who claimed she stumbled upon our vic while the killer was still on scene."

Jon's gaze sharpened. "The witness attacked? Hurt?"

"Attacked, yes. Hurt? Not so much. Scratches and bruises. Paramedics checked her out and released her on her own recognizance when she refused to go to Rex for further tests. The M.E. is working the body."

He nodded. "Assault vic get a good look at the attacker?"

"Do they ever?" Ana fluttered her eyelashes. "Wouldn't want to make your first big homicide in Raleigh too easy for you,

Detective."

Jon resisted the impulse to banter. He was on the clock now. "Wangchuk get a look?"

" 'Fraid not. I've got a uniform standing guard over him at his shop. An old man. Weird man."

"Weird how?"

Ana smirked. "Wait till you get a load of his getup. Orange bathrobe. Looks like Gandhi. Not from around here."

Jon bit back a small chuckle, forbearing to remind the second-generation Latina that to the folks of this Old Raleigh enclave she wasn't either. He'd found out the hard way — years ago — how they viewed his own illustrious First American ancestors.

Ana pointed down the trail. "Patrol secured the crime scene. Waiting for you as lead investigator to interview the witnesses."

"ID the vic yet?"

Ana tilted her head. "You bet. Interesting, little coincidence. Our other victim — the assaulted one who lived to tell about it — says she knows the murdered vic. The younger girl worked in her needlepoint shop at the Village. Has no idea what the college student was doing out on the greenway at this time of day when she was supposed to be minding the store. Lady went for an afternoon run with her dog and discovered her murdered employee's body."

His eyes narrowed. "I never have put much faith in coincidences."

"Me and you both, cowboy."

"Victim's name?"

Ana consulted her notes. "Renna. Renna Sheldon. Political Science major from the University of North Carolina. Part-time sales person at Tapestries Needleworks. We found Miss Sheldon's car still parked behind Tapestries, locked and undisturbed, as was the store."

"We'll need to run a check on everything in Renna Sheldon's personal life. Her family. Her school friends. Who she hung out with. Any enemies. What she ate today. Her previous whereabouts."

The 24-24 rule clock had begun to tick. A basic law enforcement creed contended the last twenty-four hours of a victim's life and the first twenty-four hours of the investigation were the most crucial in solving a murder.

He peered over his shoulder toward the Village. "See if the shopping center had any security cameras in place. Maybe we'll get lucky and get photos of Miss Sheldon headed for the greenway with or without her assailant."

"Will do."

"Family?"

"Unmarried. Only child. Widowed mother. Well-to-do. As is our other" — irony threaded Ana's tone — "victim."

He glanced at Ana. Like him, her background was working-class poor. Like him, she put herself through college, fighting her way with guts and intelligence to her current rank.

Not surprising she'd have a slight chip on her shoulder regarding the more fortunate. He'd had one, too, especially after . . . Jon frowned.

He'd grown weary of the load of bitterness he was never meant to carry and given it over to God. But he'd learned to lean the hard way. As did most people.

After a lot of hard knocks and bloodied knuckles.

He cocked an eyebrow. "Not much good either one of 'em's overprivileged lifestyle gave them today."

A muscle ticked in Ana's jaw.

"I'd like to interview this one." He jerked his head at the trail. "If you'd do the honors with Wangchuk?" He placed a hand on her shoulder.

Her body uncoiled and a smile returned to those fabulous black eyes. "Sure thing. And I could also take an officer and notify the mother."

"You don't have to do that. As lead, it's my responsibility. A rough job."

"No worries. Can't tell you how many parents I've had to inform of their teen's OD. Unfortunately, I'm a master at it."

She swiveled toward the Village. " 'Sides, I'll do anything to get us to the station sooner rather than later. This way, too, I get the air-conditioning. Meet you over a cup of awful department joe and a box of stale doughnuts?"

He stroked his chin. "You got it. Maybe get patrol to canvas the Village and neighborhood to see if anyone observed anything suspicious this afternoon."

She waved the air behind her, already trudging up the path. "See you whenever."

He'd taken two steps before he realized he'd forgotten to get the assault victim's name. He shook his head. Sloppy.

Focus on the job, Locklear. Not your hormones.

No matter. He'd easily get them from the uniform standing watch over the assault vic.

Still thinking of the pleasures of powdered doughnuts — among other things — he nodded as he passed the forensic team from the City-County Bureau of Identification. Outfitted in white bodysuits, one snapped photos of the crime scene. Another stretched a measuring tape while a third copied exact distances between points of interest.

Dr. Randall, on his haunches over the body, extended a hand. Reaching down, Jon heaved the portly professional to his feet. Dripping, red flecks dotted the undergrowth. A metallic, coppery smell — blood — hung in the air. A tech waded through the waist-high thistles, collecting and labeling miniscule droplets of blood in plastic vials.

"What've we got, Doc?"

"From the spray pattern of the blood, the murder occurred where her body lies. Head bashed in with something round. Wooden splinters in the wounds. Violent struggle."

The doctor's hand swept across the trampled trail leading down the embankment. "My guess? The attacker waited underneath the footbridge. Seized her from behind, wrestled her to the ground, and then proceeded to beat the living daylights out of her skull."

Jon winced. "Never had a chance, did she?"

The doc shook his grizzled head. "Preliminary findings, mind you. But the depth of those wounds? The attacker was strong, highly motivated, or crazed. Take your pick."

"Random or premeditated?"

"Your call, Detective." Dr. Randall slid his owl-like glasses up his bulbous nose. "Can't do all the work for you." He gave Jon a lopsided smile to show he was kidding. "The angle and trajectory of the blows suggests the assailant's right-handed."

"A woman able to do this?"

"Footprint left in the mud says a man-size sneaker. Witness" — Randall tilted his head toward the other end of the bridge — "says male attacker. But in my experience, an athletic woman, if properly ticked off, can do as much damage as a man twice her size, if you get my drift."

Jon's experience, too.

"Dead how long?"

"From the state of the body, factoring the heat and the lack of," the old man flicked a glance around them, "lack of predators and amount of insects on the body . . ." He glanced at the sky, mentally calculating.

Jon took a good, hard look at the ravaged form that had once been a living, breathing human being. A form upon which flies feasted. His stomach rumbled.

Maybe the stale doughnuts weren't such a good idea. Outdoor crime scenes were investigators' worst nightmare. Give them a nice, enclosed, contained indoor murder every time.

"Your witness says she last saw the vic at the needlepoint shop around three, right before she left to drop off her son for a fishing trip. Gives me a starting point to narrow the parameters. I'll get my report to you ASAP. My boys —" The head of one of the white-clad suits popped up, with distinctively female features, from the tangle of vines.

Randall growled. "Sorry. Forgot this is the Age of Political Correctness. My *crew,*" he amended, "will be finished in a couple of hours."

Thanking him, Jon ambled toward the bridge, leaving the team to sketch the body and surrounding area. They'd bag and tag any evidence. Time for him to interview the witness.

A tantalizing aroma of a long-buried memory wafted past his nose.

Honeysuckle.

Jon scowled at the vines entwined around the railing.

He glanced through the tree canopy as he crested the bridge. Even with the extended light of a Southern, almost-summer night, he'd better get a move on and get this portion of the investigation wrapped up before darkness shrouded the crime scene.

At the sound of his tread upon the bridge, a tri-colored basset hound lazing at the feet of a female officer raised his head. The uniform peered in his direction. As did the attack vic.

Sunlight dappled the woman clad in exercise clothes. Her eyes widened. A smile flitted before her lips tensed.

Jon's heart — and feet — froze.

Gripping the railing, his fingers curled around a fistful of honeysuckle blossoms. The sweet smell of a long-ago summer flooded his senses. A splinter of wood sliced into his palm.

It couldn't possibly . . . His gut clenched.

No way. Not here. Not now.

What was it the Bogart fellow said? Of all the crime scenes in all the towns in all the world, she had to walk into his?

Or something to that effect.

Please, God. Anybody but her.

Laura gasped.

This couldn't be happening. Standing not two feet in front of her was her worst nightmare come true.

And, her fondest dream.

Just like that, her world — the one she'd so carefully constructed and lied to protect

— groaned, tilted, and slid off its axis with a crash.

Her knees buckled.

Jon's hand shot out, grabbing hold of her forearm.

She jerked, fried by his touch on her bare skin. Her heart skipped a beat. "What are you — ?"

"I never expected —"

Then, silence roared between them.

She closed her eyes. Hoping Jon Locklear was an illusion, an unwelcome hallucination of an overactive imagination.

Opening her eyes, her pulse skittered. He was real. Too real.

A rosy flush mounted from beneath the collar of his white Oxford shirt. His sensuous lips parted.

The policewoman shuffled her feet, breaking the spell. "Detective?"

His Adam's apple bobbed as he swallowed.

"CCBI has already obtained samples from underneath her fingernails in case . . ."

He removed a small, black notebook from his coat pocket. "Thank you, Officer Schultz. I can handle things from here." The policewoman nodded, patted Bugg's head, and headed toward the Village.

"Lau . . ." Shaking his head, he moistened

his lips. “Laura Bowen . . .”

She blew out a breath. “Laura Mabry.” She hated how her voice quavered.

A spasm of something flickered across his broad, high-planed face before disappearing so quickly she wondered if perhaps she imagined it.

His forehead creased. “Right.” He scribbled, his head bent over the paper.

Two thoughts occurred to her so simultaneously as to be one unified cohesive chain.

First, why in the name of all that was holy hadn’t she bothered to put on mascara or at least lipstick before she went for her run? She smoothed her hair and fished out a stray leaf. Great.

And two? She needed to think fast, prepare for major damage control, or everything she and Holt had done would be for nothing.

“Tell me what happened here.”

His probing gaze traveled to the region of her mouth. With the speed of heat lightning on a stormy summer evening, his eyes looped to hers before dropping to his notepad. He clutched his pen, his knuckles white.

Laura’s gaze fastened onto his hand, hard with calluses.

Those slender, brown fingers . . . had once

caressed and . . .

She bit her lip and fought to keep from revealing how the familiar timbre of his voice affected her.

Achieving a deceptive measure of normalcy, she recounted her movements from the time she leashed Buggsby, to finding Renna, interrupting the killer, to the assault and her rescue by Mr. Wangchuk. A carefully edited account — no more no less than he ever need know — rendered to the close-cropped black curls on the top of his head.

The locks he kept short, she recalled, or risked getting teased by his sisters as being too girly. As if anything about Jon Locklear had ever remotely resembled girly.

She remembered a lot of things. Things she'd spent a decade trying to forget. Like the ply of those curls between her fingers, the . . .

Laura shook herself like Buggsby after running through the water hose.

His head snapped up. "What about before? Last time you saw Miss Sheldon? How did she seem?"

She crossed her arms over her chest. "Renna seemed like she always seemed. I opened the shop at ten this morning. Renna came in about one o'clock, and I left. She was supposed to close the shop at five."

"Why did you leave this afternoon?"

Laura pinched her lips together. "Errands."

Suspicion darkened his eyes. "Go on."

Laura explained her attempt to reach Renna by phone and her plan to jog by Tapestries.

His eyes bored into hers. "What made you think something might not be okay?"

Laura dropped her gaze, unable to field his intensity. "She'd been kind of . . ."

"Kind of what?"

"I don't know. Crabby lately."

"Crabby like how?"

Laura knotted her fingers. "Coming in late. Wanting to leave early. Questioning every request."

He scribbled again. "So there was trouble between you two."

Laura's spine went ramrod straight. "No." She frowned. "Not at all. Until . . . recently." Sweat trickled between her shoulder blades.

Had she become a suspect?

"Why the change?"

"I don't know. I asked about a week ago, when I first noticed her attitude toward the customers. But she told me to butt out of her private life. And then, I said —" Laura flushed.

Jon's mouth flattened. "I can imagine

what you said." His voice dropped a degree. "Having been on the receiving end of it myself a long time ago."

The image of herself hurling hateful words at him in a parking lot in Jacksonville flashed across her mind.

And Laura recalled why she hated Jon Locklear.

She clenched her fists. "A long, long time ago."

Not long enough, apparently.

"Why the third degree? Are we done here? I've told you everything I can about what happened today. Buggs and I need to get home."

He slapped his notebook shut.

She jerked.

A muscle ticked in his cheek. "Fine. For now."

He retrieved the leash lying at their feet. "I'll have further questions for you as the investigation proceeds. I'll need a formal statement."

Laura lifted her chin. "I need to check the shop. Make sure it's locked for the night. I'm not sure how Renna left things."

She reached for the leash.

"No need. Officers found it locked tight as a drum." He held onto the leash. "I'll escort you home. Make sure you don't get into any more trouble."

Laura pulled harder. "Not necessary."

His rugged profile hardened. "I insist."

A brief tug of war ensued. But Jon proved, as usual, an irresistible force.

Feeling ridiculous, she let go. He staggered a few paces.

She smiled. Which she wiped off her face as his lips clamped tight.

Never having met a stranger, Buggs waddled to Jon, wiping his drooly jaws down the length of his khaki-clad thigh. Jon made a face.

She smirked at the memory of how fastidious the athletic boy had been. Still was.

Looping the leash over one arm, Jon took firm hold of her elbow. He marched her and Buggsby toward Woods Edge. Buggsby trotted ahead, his tongue lolling out of his mouth, glad to be on the move again.

What a traitor. She kicked a loose pebble with her sneaker as Jon frog-stepped her along. If Buggs hadn't just saved her life, he could've kissed any more bacon treats goodbye for a week.

Jon's hand rubbed at the five-o'clock shadow on his jaw. "Didn't realize you and your husband lived in Woods Edge."

Her skin tingled with remembrance of the scratchy feel of his stubble sandpapering her cheek once upon a time.

She fought the urge to spill her guts, to unload eleven years' worth of pain onto the sender of the pain. But the picture of a voluptuous blonde clad only in his Marine shirt froze the words on her tongue.

Jon tucked one hand into his trouser pocket. "Last I heard you lived in Chapel Hill."

Didn't know you were keeping track . . .

She chewed the inside of her cheek. "Didn't realize you lived in Raleigh, either. Figured you for a career Marine. Heard you were in Iraq."

He kept his face pointed straight ahead, his features inscrutable. "Old news. Several armed conflicts ago. Been with the RPD a few months. Things and people change."

And some things, Jon Locklear, are long past changing.

"One of the officers told me your son was away."

She tripped over a tree root.

He clutched her arm as she regained her balance. "Your husband is probably getting worried."

Laura's heart pounded. She might as well tell him. A little homework on his part and he'd find out soon enough. "I'm a widow."

This time, he stumbled.
"Oh," he rasped. "I didn't know."

4

Jon stole a look at Laura's shuttered face as they trudged up the path toward her home. He'd not allowed himself a good look before, sensing his own weakness. But something about the thread of vulnerability in her voice when she told him about being widowed . . .

Almost like the innocent, younger Laura he'd known — and loved beyond reason — all those years ago.

Different from the woman at his side, cold and remote, who found herself involved in a homicide. His homicide.

Her skin glowed as fair as he remembered, though crisscrossed now with a mixture of welts, bug bites, and scratches from her attack on the greenway. Her figure still girlishly slim, but the innocence gone.

What he couldn't ever let himself forget, to his eternal shame, was his part in destroying her innocence.

And those beautiful, china-blue eyes . . .

Never seen another pair of eyes that color. But lines radiated out like crow's feet from the corners. Lines, from the stress marks bracketing her mouth, he suspected had nothing to do with laughter and everything to do with a world of hurt.

"How long ago?"

"About a year and a half." Her voice crisp, she pursed her lips.

Lips he once delighted in, now curved in a permanent twist. Bitterness? He'd hoped — despite his own pain at the time — Holt Mabry would be good to her.

Jon clenched his fist around Buggsby's leash to control the sudden tremors in his hand. "How?"

She fretted the hem of her shirt, her eyes on the forest. "Ice storm. Responding to a call about one of his terminal patients. Lost control of the car and crashed head-on into a tree." Her mouth pulled downward.

He stopped where the trail dead-ended. "I'm sorry, Laura." And in those words, he tried to convey his regret for so much more.

She pointed through the vines. "My house. I'll be fine from here on out."

After a decade of famine, he wasn't ready to let her go just yet. He drank in the sight of her like April rain soaking into the dry desert sand of the Afghan hill country. Shafts of sunlight dappled her hair.

His fingers remembered its texture.

Like cornsilk.

If he buried his face in her hair, as he'd done so often that summer, would her hair still smell of strawber— ?

He was losing it. Losing control of himself and this investigation.

Jon took himself, his thoughts, and his heart in hand. "How old was your son when it happened? Your other children?" His voice sounded gravelly to his own ears.

She angled away. "No other children. Good-bye, Jon." She tugged at the leash.

"Not so fast, Laura." His hand shot out, capturing her arm again. "I need you to take your clothes off for me."

She gasped. "Excuse me?"

Jon flushed.

That hadn't come out the way he'd intended it.

She glared at his fingers curled around her wrist.

"I'm going to need to bag the clothes you're wearing so forensics can test for anything our murderer might've left behind, DNA-wise." He released her, lifting one slow finger at a time. "I can wait in the living room while you change."

A funny look crossed her face.

"Can't I drop them by your station tomorrow?"

She could, but he'd prefer not, for so many reasons. "No."

His well-honed instincts — which through several tours of duty had kept him alive up to now — shouted she was hiding something. He hadn't missed her earlier remark that she'd told him everything she *could* tell him. Doubt ate away at his stomach.

She squared her shoulders. "Oh, all right, then." She let go of the leash. Buggsby slithered through the dense foliage into the clearing beyond.

Jon stepped in front of her, lifting and parting the tangle, opening a briar-free path for her to follow.

Eyes averted, she glided through. He followed on her heels, his eyes dazzled by the intensity of the sun, although low on the horizon. Buggsby disappeared through an opening at the bottom of a screened door.

But she bypassed the screened porch. She led him instead past the closed garage toward the front, and down a flagstone path to stone steps. The cop part of his brain documented the two-story half-timbered cottage with its steep-pitched roof and assorted gables. Tendrils of ivy draped the chimney.

The house reminded him of the *Sleeping Beauty* tale he read to his niece, Cami, *ad nauseum* last week. As the fanciful notion overtook him — Laura Bowen had that effect on him — Jon wouldn't have been surprised to find an enchanted princess enshrined within its honey-colored stone and stucco walls. The house slumbered in a storybook way, as if time had stood still, awaiting its awakening.

But time stood still for no one and nothing. Not for him. Nor for Laura.

She reached underneath a pot of pink impatiens and held up a key.

His eyebrows rose. "Really, Laura? First place a burglar looks. Hiding a key in back would be prefer—"

"I never keep the back door —" She whirled and turned the key in the lock.

Then why hadn't they gone in from the back?

Opening the door, she pivoted and placed a restraining hand against his chest. The heat of her hand through his shirt sizzled his flesh.

She retracted her hand as if burned. "Wait here while I change."

"Not going to offer me a cool drink or respite from the heat?" His lips quirked.

"I'm underwhelmed by your hospitality, Laura."

Those beautiful eyes flickered. A below-the-belt verbal punch, violating the cardinal rules of Southern politeness engrained in male and female from birth. A hospitality extended even to enemies.

Did she view him as her enemy?

His heart panged at the thought. "Don't you trust me?"

Blue fire flashed from her eyes. "Do I have any reason to?"

Guilt surged through him, followed by a swift current of anger.

"Still not good enough to enter through the front door of Laura Bowen's house? How 'bout I go stand at the back while you hand it to me through the doggie door?"

Laura reared and grabbed for the door. He stuck his foot across the threshold, and blocked her attempt to slam the door in his face.

She scowled at him. "Your words. Never mine."

Jon's chest heaved.

"Do you have a search warrant to enter my home, Detective Locklear?"

His eyes narrowed. "Do I need one?"

Brakes squealed as a black Corvette convertible shuddered to a stop at the curb.

A thirty-something professional in suit and tie flung open the driver's door. His boy-next-door face puckered. "Laura!"

Gripping a white takeout bag, the man hurtled across the lawn toward them. A man Jon recognized from countless television ads. Garrett Payne, U.S. congressional candidate, deep-pocket attorney, and kisser of babies.

"Garrett . . ." Her voice broke and she pushed past Jon.

Dropping the bag, Payne wrapped his arms around her. "What's going on? Are you all right? I noticed the police cars at the entrance to the Village."

"Oh, Garrett . . . I'm so glad you're here."

She buried her face in his shoulder. Garrett's arms tightened.

As did Jon's jaw.

"There's been a murder. Renna's —" She choked back a sob.

Garrett jutted his chin. "Who's he?" He shuffled Laura behind his back, shielding her from Jon.

Jon bristled.

And Laura — he noted — didn't release her hold around Payne's waist.

"The detective investigating Renna's . . . It's so awful. Her body . . ."

"Why is he here, Laura?" Garrett's blue

eyes bored into hers, his well-manicured hands grasping her shoulders.

Jon stiffened at Payne's hands on Laura. A pang of jealousy? Of course not. He took a breath.

Because . . . because Payne was corrupting the chain of evidence.

"Jon says he needs my clothes for evidence."

"You know this man?" Garrett whipped around. "Is she a person of interest, Detective?"

Forcing himself to relax, Jon lolled against the doorframe. "Everybody remotely connected to this case is a potential person of interest right now, Counselor."

Garrett sheltered Laura against his body. "You're not to say another word to him or any RPD officer without me or another attorney present."

She darted a frightened look at Jon. A look that jabbed his heart. "You think I'm a . . . You think I could've — ?"

"Come, darling." Garrett shepherded her into the house. "You change, and I'll make sure the *detective*" — sarcasm dripped — "gets what he came here for." He shouldered Laura past Jon over the threshold, forcing Jon to shuffle and straighten.

Garrett's lip curled. "Be right back."

And before Jon could whistle "Dixie," Garrett slammed the hunter-green door in his face.

Jon smacked the iron railing with his fist.

That sanctimonious, overprivileged . . . politician. Should've seen that one coming.

When it came to Laura Bowen — *Laura Bowen Mabry* — Jon was definitely off his game.

He had a job to do. His first big chance to prove himself to Mike and the unit. Now was not the time to let his emotions cloud his judgment.

The door opened. Garrett, a self-satisfied smile greasing his face, thrust a brown grocery bag at him.

Payne loosened his knotted silk tie and opened the button of his starched blue shirt at the collar. "The clothing you asked for, Detective. You do your investigating. I'll take care of Laura. You have any questions for her? Schedule an appointment with my secretary."

Jon bit back a retort that could've cost him his job as Payne once again slammed the door in his face. The temper he'd struggled to master, since it had cost Jon everything he'd ever wanted, threatened to consume him.

How true to form Laura Bowen was.

Mrs. Mabry, he corrected, his teeth clenched.

Jon stomped around the side of the house. Payne probably watched him from some vantage point within Sleeping Beauty's abode. He snorted, but kept his back straight as he retraced his steps toward the greenway.

And when he reached his truck and laptop, he'd run a check on the too-squeaky-clean-to-be-real congressional candidate. Because first rule of staying alive in the Marine corps?

Know Thy Enemy.

Jon's gut roiled.

Husband dead a little over a year and already she'd found a replacement. Had to give the woman credit, though. She always kept a spare, a backup, in reserve. Women like her couldn't operate without a man propping them up.

Just like after the summer with him, when she'd reverted to her own kind. Her I-do-own-this-entire-state, thank-you-very-much, kind.

Jon remembered in vivid detail why he hated Laura Bowen.

He clenched his fist.

Laura Bowen . . . Mabry.

■ ■ ■ ■

Laura leaned against the cool, wet travertine tile. Raising her face to the showerhead, she closed her eyes and allowed the water to trickle down her face. Of all the crazy things she'd conceived Jon doing over the years, never in a million years would she have guessed cop. Straightening, she stuck her entire head under the spray of the nozzle. She hunched her shoulders, her nerve endings flayed.

A close call.

She'd been desperate to keep him out of the kitchen.

Away from the refrigerator.

Stalling, she'd taken him around front, panicking when she remembered she couldn't let him into the front parlor, either. Saved by Garrett.

Garrett, retrieving the squashed Thai bag and putting supper on the table while she showered, wasn't going to be put off so easily. She better come up with a good explanation. After his years with the D. A., Garrett was too sharp to be taken in by liars.

And that's what she was. A liar.

Laura squeezed her eyelids shut. The weight of her lies overwhelmed her. Tore at her conscience. Suffocated everything good.

Inhale . . . Exha— But she'd never lied to Holt.

He'd known. Every sordid thing.

A rap on the door.

She jerked.

"Laura?"

Garrett.

"Are you okay? You've been in there a long time."

The steamy water leached the tension from her muscles.

Dear, dependable Garrett. What would she have donc this last year without him?

She swallowed. Time to face the music. Questions Garrett had every right to ask.

"I'll be right there," she called through the etched-glass shower door. Sudsing her hair and body, she scrubbed off every last trace of the greenway and him.

Him, the attacker.

The essence of Jon Locklear had long ago soaked deeper than her skin. Penetrated the marrow of her bones — her heart — and would be less easily excised.

Because God knows, she'd tried.

Toweling off, she grabbed a white T-shirt and khaki shorts. Running her brush through her hair, she gathered it out of her face and secured it with a scrunchy. She didn't bother with makeup.

She ventured downstairs to find Garrett putting the finishing touches on their meal. He'd removed his coat, hanging it on a chair. He'd unbuttoned his blue Oxford shirtsleeves and rolled them to his elbows. She paused in the doorway, grateful for Garrett's friendship these last sad months.

Far too often, she'd taken their relationship for granted. She admired the adorable shock of light brown hair that refused to stay in place and hung across his brow. His white-toothed grin fluttered every female constituent's heart from Murphy to Manteo.

Including her own?

Maybe it was time to move on to something new. Something for herself this time.

Life with Garrett would be . . . pleasant. She'd grown up with the thrill of the campaign chase. And, once elected, together they'd experience the intoxicating adrenaline rush of life in the nation's capital.

But what about her shop?

Not to mention Ian's inexplicable attitude. Maybe not so inexplicable — a threat to his beloved father's memory. The final nail in the coffin of reality that screamed Holt was never coming back.

She and Ian both needed time. Ian would

come around. Once he got to know Garrett like she knew Garrett.

If only Garrett would be patient a while longer. He'd been urging her for weeks to marry him so he could make the announcement before things got too crazy as the November election heated up.

She'd spent most of her childhood helping Mom and Dad navigate the murky waters of politics, Carolina-style. Politics remained a good-ole-boys' club in this state. The astute learned to play by the rules or go home.

Garrett glanced across the table. "Hey, babe." He gave her his trademark lazy smile.

His blue eyes radiated pure Southern charm. "I've salvaged enough Thai to feed us." His head tilted toward a pile of envelopes on the counter. "Brought your mail to save you a trip. I fed Buggsby —"

A pair of dark black eyes swam before her vision.

Stop it . . .

Garrett, like Holt, deserved so much better than what she had to give.

Something must have crossed her face.

"Laura?"

Garrett opened his arms and she flew into the shelter of his embrace. The food growing cold, she told him about finding Renna.

"And you know this detective how?"

She winced. Not a question she wanted to answer. "We met a long time ago during college."

Almost the truth.

He gazed at her, a silent, probing look, the wheels turning in his mind. Garrett was nobody's fool. But to her relief, he abandoned the topic.

Perhaps, like her, he preferred not to confront the truth head-on.

Later, she picked at her reheated food. The strong spices inflamed her stomach as she tried to block out the images of Renna's battered skull, the blood, and tissue.

"You've had a shock." Garrett wove his fingers through hers. "Let me stay the night."

She snatched her hand away.

He bit his lip. "On the couch. With Ian gone, I hate to think of you spending the night alone in this old monstrosity."

She scooted her chair across the hardwood. "It's my home. I'll be fine. I have the new security system."

He touched her sleeve. "I wasn't thinking of outside terrors as much as those that might haunt your dreams tonight."

She edged out of his reach. "I'm tougher than I look. I have the Weathersby needlepoint project meeting at Tapestries in the morning."

He frowned. "Can't you cancel?"

She eyed the clock over the breakfast nook. "Too late. And with Renna out . . ." She swallowed past the lump in her throat.

His mouth drooped. "You won't be able to attend the parade with me tomorrow."

"I'll be there if I have to close the shop. I'll try Alison Barefoot's daughter and see if she can handle Tapestries for the afternoon."

Laura dumped the Styrofoam plate in the trash. "Don't worry. I'll be there." Shifting, she startled to find Garrett inches away.

He leaned forward, swaying on the balls of his feet. "I want to be there for you, Laura. Every day, every hour, every night." He closed the distance, his lips hard against hers. Hungry.

The curve of her spine pressed into the granite counter. Her own loneliness rose, meeting and matching the innate loneliness she'd sensed in Garrett since he was a boy. Her arms drifted around his neck.

"Laura . . ." he whispered. "I've always loved you. With Ian gone, let me . . ."

He groaned. "Just once. I'd make you so happy. Let me be the one to comfort you. Love you . . ." His hands groped at the hem of her T-shirt.

Laura dropped her arms, holding back from taking the next step sealing their relationship in stone forever. A progression she knew Garrett viewed as inevitable since his mother had become her father's executive assistant and their paths crossed as children.

She pushed him away and took a deep, steadying breath. "I'm not ready, Garrett."

Gripping the counter, Garrett closed his eyes.

She'd hurt him. Again.

He opened his eyes and started for the door.

"Garrett —"

"I want to see you set the alarm before I go."

"Garrett . . ."

He cupped a hand under her chin. "I'll see you at headquarters about eleven. Ride with me to Garner?"

She nodded.

Garrett pointed at the security panel on the wall. "Be a good girl." He watched until she punched in the numbers. Garrett blew her a kiss, and shut the door behind him.

Her eyes brimmed with tears.

Why did she always hurt the men who loved her?

Restless, she drifted into the kitchen,

disposing of the remains of their uneaten dinner. She scoured the sink until her hand ached. If only she could scour her heart as easily. She was so tired of being afflicted with the disease called Jon Locklear.

Searching for anything to distract from the what-ifs, she scooped the mail off the desk and sank into the damask chair next to the mullioned bay window. She yanked at the tasseled cord of the porcelain lamp on the side table and sorted through the pile.

Junk. Bills. Her bank statement. An invitation to a Weathersby function. A small, square envelope.

No stamp or postmark. She flipped the envelope in her hand. No return address.

Maybe one of the neighbors placed it in her mailbox. Aunt Velma had mentioned something about an annual cul-de-sac get together.

Using the stiletto edge of the paper cutter, she pried open the envelope and removed a note of thick ivory stationery.

I know what you've done. I'm here to make sure you don't get away with it.
The Accuser

She gasped and drew her legs under her as a single, solitary dried petal floated out of the envelope to the Aubusson rug. A trumpet-shaped blossom. Faded to a mere shadow of its once-vibrant yellow hue.

A whiff of honeysuckle stirred her senses. Her heart thudded.

How? Who?

Only she and Jon . . .

She flung the note across the room. Burying her face in her hands, her body shook with sobs. Darkness crushed against the window.

And her safe, ordered world, like an unbound tapestry, unraveled around her.

5

Jon spent a sleepless night wrestling with the if-onlys. The worst one he'd struggled with over the years was if only he'd been a better man. So early Saturday morning, as he pulled outside Mambo's per Ana's request, he wasn't in the best of moods. He also hadn't heard from Mike. He hoped — prayed — Alison and the twins were okay.

By force of habit, he assessed the parking lot, empty save for a few service vehicles and Ana's unmarked Chevy. He glanced at his watch. Only eight. Except for the coffee shop, way too early for the other stores to open.

Leaning against the hood of her car, arms crossed, Ana waited for him outside the restaurant. Her white jeans hugged every curve of her body, her hair in a twist at the nape of her neck. Looking more Narc than Homicide, Jon had a feeling Ana was overdue for a little dress code chat with the sergeant.

She sounded excited over the phone. She'd uncovered a new development. But she wanted Jon as lead investigator to conduct the interview with Mambo's owner, Pete Scorelli. He appreciated her sensitivity to any semblance of stepping on his professional toes.

Unwinding, she strolled over to his truck, rapping on the windowpane. "Hey there, cowboy."

He pressed the roll-down button before shutting off the engine. "How many times I have to tell you, Morales, my loyalties lie with the other side?"

Laughing, she folded her arms. "Got results for you. Doc narrowed Renna Sheldon's time of death to between three and four-thirty p.m. The Mabry woman have an alibi for the time frame?"

He frowned. "Haven't gotten up with the Prescotts to verify exact time she dropped off her son. They're probably sailing the Sound and off the grid. Neighbors, however, corroborate her testimony that her car pulled away around three-thirty."

"But no alibi afterward until Mr. Wangchuk rescues her, so she says . . ."

He bristled. "Which he approximates at being around four-thirty."

"No need to get so testy, Locklear. You up all night or what?"

He forced himself to take deep, even breaths. What was the matter with him? Snarling at his drop-dead gorgeous colleague, for heaven's sakes? Wasn't like Laura Bowen deserved any loyalty on his part.

"Sorry." He tried again. "Cause of death yet?"

Ana shot him a penetrating look and cleared her throat. "Bludgeoned to death, as we suspected. Size 10 running shoe from the print in the mud at the creek's edge. We matched the tread to a pair of ECCO men's footwear."

"Expensive?"

She lifted a thin, penciled brow. "Yeah, way beyond our pay grade. Over three hundred dollars a pop. A model — and I quote — 'of Teutonic engineering. The leather uppers are made from a Himalayan yak.' "

"A yak?"

"You heard right. Only a few stores in the area sell them. I've got uniforms on the ground checking, but until we narrow the suspect pool . . ."

"The killer could've bought them online."

She sighed. "I've got the computer nerds working that angle." Her voice dropped to a seductive whisper. "But don't tell them I called them that."

He chuckled. "I got your back, Morales."

She cut her eyes at him. "I'd like to have yours, too, Detective."

Patchouli assaulted his senses.

Jon dropped his eyes. Unlike the women in Mimosa Grove, this Latina was nothing if not direct. Maybe it was how she'd succeeded thus far in the macho world of law enforcement.

He figured the steamy summer air had risen at least ten degrees between them. Time to change the subject. Ana Morales made it difficult for him to concentrate.

"Besides Scorelli, any other persons of interest from our interviews around the Village?"

She shrugged. "Early days. You may want to probe further. Best I can figure, the killer made his getaway across a shallow point in the creek where we found the print. Sloppy. Lots of dry places he could've made a crossing. But I guess if criminals were as smart as they think they are, we'd never catch 'em."

"You said 'he.' " He cocked his head. "So it eliminates Laura Mabry?"

"Why so interested in clearing the elegant Mrs. Mabry, Detective?"

He cleared his throat. “Just trying to get to the truth. But when you said the killer probably crossed the creek . . .”

“Perhaps the Mabry woman was the decoy, and lured Miss Sheldon to that isolated spot so her accomplice could finish the deed.”

He refused to wrap his mind around that scenario. Instead, he envisioned the twenty-year-old Laura who’d driven into his mother’s yard in Mimosa Grove to start a summer internship with Florence Locklear, well-known Lumbee textile artist. The Laura who listened as if hearing the gospel for the first time in his mother’s white-framed church.

Images rosc of tlie swimming hole. Him and her . . .

Ana rapped her knuckles on the metal frame. “Hey. Where’d you go?”

He shook his head. “Sorry.”

Struggling to maintain his professional detachment, Jon reminded himself Laura *Mabry* was a person he didn’t know at all.

Ana pointed. “Mr. Scorelli’s arrived. Interesting tale he told me. Thought you should hear for yourself.” She stepped aside as he swung the door wide.

“Results back from the material you gathered from Mrs. Mabry? Match anything from the vic?"

Ana chewed her lip as they ambled over to Mr. Scorelli. "No. Appears Mabry didn't lay a finger on the vic. Fibers and DNA are from an unknown."

His mouth curved. "The killer who assaulted Mrs. Mabry per her testimony yesterday."

"An unknown for now." Ana flicked a glance at him. "Killer or accomplice yet to be determined."

She stuck out her hand at the short, balding proprietor. "Mr. Scorelli, Ana Morales again." She nodded at Jon. "Detective Jon Locklear, lead investigator on this case."

Mr. Scorelli hung his head. "All my fault pretty girl die." He wrung his hands.

"Go on," Ana encouraged. "Tell the detective what you told me last night."

Scorelli raised his eyes heavenward. "I do decent thing. Who knew?" He muttered something in Italian.

"Who knew what, Mr. Scorelli? What did you do?" Jon made a determined effort to relax, placing both arms behind his back.

Scorelli raised his shoulders in an elaborate, helpless shrug. "The homeless guy who lives on the greenway, I feed him. We usually have a few leftover pizzas. Can't serve next day. What the harm, I think?" He dropped his face into his meaty hands. "Oh, the harm to the young miss."

Jon's brow creased. "I'm not following you, Mr. Scorelli."

Pete lifted woeful eyes, bringing Buggsby to mind. "You feed a stray, they never leave." He made a circular motion with his finger next to his head. *"Pazzo."*

Jon cut his eyes at Ana. "Huh?"

She pursed her lips. "Like we say *loco* in Spanish. Crazy."

Pete nodded, his double chins wobbling. "Drugs fried his brain like TV commercial."

At Jon's blank look, Ana sighed. "Don't you watch TV in Lumbeeland?"

Her voice went TV announcer-like. "This," she intoned, "is your brain on drugs." She play-punched his bicep. "Eggs, Jon."

"Anyway . . ." He angled to Pete. "A name?"

Pete thumped his chest. "Me Mambo Pete. We call him Texas Pete."

Jon's eyes widened. "Like the hot sauce made in Winston-Salem?"

Pete jabbed a finger in the air. "You got it."

"Is he from Texas?" She retrieved her notepad from her back pocket.

Though how she could've squeezed a

nickel, much less a pad of paper, in that curvaceous place . . .

"No," Pete shook his head. "But his name is Pete." He spread his hands, palm up. "That's all I know. Oh," Pete frowned. "He wear army clothes. A patch on his jacket. Like guys I see jump out of planes over Vietnam. Two A's."

For the first time since he topped the bridge and came face-to-face with the one who got away, Jon allowed himself a smile. "Morales, check military records for a Pete, circa late 1960s / early 1970s from Fort Bragg."

At her incredulous look, he added, "Eighty-second Airborne in good ole Fayettenam back in the day. And get the department sketch artist out here and see if he and Mr. Scorelli can compose a fair likeness of our mysterious hobo."

She reached for the cell phone tucked in the other pocket of those oh-so-tight jeans. "You got it, partner."

Forcing his gaze to the CLOSED sign on Mambo's door, Jon repeated his vow to himself, made years ago to God and Chaplain Grant, about the covenant with his eyes.

Ana wasn't officially his partner. Off the clock?

Maybe . . .

But a pair of china blues dancing with laughter blinked across his vision.

Sweat broke out on his forehead.

Jon twitched, pretty sure that girl no longer existed. "I'm going to make the rounds as the shopkeepers arrive."

Shooting him a strange look, Ana held the phone to her ear. "Try The Java Jolt while you wait." She waved toward the adjacent café. "Serves a great cup of joe, and they make their own cinnamon buns."

He grinned. "And you know this how?"

Ana gave him an insolent wink. "I do my homework. I'll meet you there when Mr. Scorelli and I are finished."

"Sounds like a plan."

As Jon left them on the sidewalk and meandered his way among the near-empty wrought-iron tables and chairs to the coffeehouse, he prayed at last they had a viable suspect in the case.

Someone other than Laura Bowen.

And as for Laura, he still had a few more questions. Questions he wouldn't allow her to evade this time.

Laura was hiding something. And, above all things in his line of work, he'd learned to pay attention to what his gut tried to tell him.

■ ■ ■ ■

Laura parked her car in the alley behind Tapestries. Renna's car was gone. Probably impounded by the police as evidence.

Her hands fumbled with the key that unlocked the service entrance. Her eyes scanned the deserted alley behind the row of shops. A breeze sighed through the treetops of the greenway. Not even a birdcall broke the ominous stillness of the forest. She shivered despite the ever-mounting humidity promising another scorcher of a day.

At dawn, she'd given Buggsby a vigorous walk around Woods Edge after a long night huddled in the chair, lights blazing. It'd be a while before she'd be able to force herself to face the greenway again. Her dreams were haunted by bittersweet memories of her too-short time with Jon, interlaced with faceless shadows plucking at her hair and skin like thorny vines.

In her nightmare, the vines snaked closer and closer. Wrapping green death around her throat. She couldn't breathe. Could somebody, anybody, help her? She cried out for God, but a mocking, hateful voice suggested she was getting what she deserved.

Drenched in sweat, Laura awoke, grateful Ian was away until Monday.

Gaining the sanctuary of her shop, she flipped on the overhead lights. Her fingers couldn't resist stroking the fabric panels. Vibrant taffetas for her crazy quilter clientele lined the shelves.

Thread spindles of every imaginable hue beckoned like silk rainbows. Patterns, frames, books. Shop samples tacked to the walls. A refuge of creative beauty in a world of loss and chaos —

She jumped at the staccato rap on the glass-fronted door. Aunt Velma, her hands cupping the sides of her wrinkled face, peered bug-eyed into the shop.

Velma mouthed, *Open up.*

Retracting the deadbolt, Laura unlocked the door.

Aunt Velma, all skinny five feet of her, looked Laura up and down. "What ails you, Miss? You look terrible."

Laura gestured for her aunt and Tayla — the college kid hired to drive her aunt around for the summer — to enter. Her hand shook as Laura returned the ring of keys to the pocket of her white linen capris.

Velma's face tensed. Seventy-five and counting, with her sharp blue eyes the same shade as Laura's, she missed nothing.

"What's wrong? Is it Ian? Has something happened?"

Laura moistened her lips. "No, Ian's fine." She beckoned them beyond the cash register to the casual sitting area she'd created for needlework groups to mingle.

Velma allowed Laura to take her bony elbow. Laura steered her aunt toward a brocade-covered lady's chair, just the right size for someone of Velma's diminutive stature.

"You don't look fine. Something's happened."

She eased Velma into the cushiony upholstery. "I'd rather not say till everyone gathers." Earning another shrewd appraisal from Velma.

With Laura's mother dead, Aunt Velma knew her better than anyone alive. Knew all Laura's secrets she'd long suspected, though the old woman had never broached a word of recrimination.

"Haven't got the coffee going yet? You're moving mighty slow this morning, Laura Louise. The ladies will be here directly." Velma darted a glance to where Tayla sprawled, boredom etched across her ebony features. A picture of hipness in her booty shorts and skintight T-shirt.

Tayla straightened. "I was hired to drive.

Do I look like a secretary to you? I do not do coffee." She mumbled something under her breath.

Velma's lips pursed.

Laura scurried toward the mahogany sideboard where she kept the silver coffee urn. She set out the violet-studded china cups and saucers. "I'll make the coffee, Tayla. I always do."

She eyeballed her aunt and the teen. Those two weren't exactly hitting it off after two days together.

Velma's face assumed the imperious English-teacher look she'd worn teaching high school imbeciles — Velma's word for the hormonally challenged — how to read and write the Queen's English. And Tayla resembled a red sky on a summer morning, a promise of trouble brewing.

Laura busied herself measuring scoops of the specialty Carolina Coffee she served customers at Tapestries. Rain or shine, snow or heat wave, Aunt Velma wanted her morning Tapestries' caffeine pickup as usual.

Flustered, Laura scooted to the sink in the storage area to fill the coffeepot with water. Aunt Velma asked Tayla to retrieve her pocketbook — Southern for "purse" — from the Crown Victoria. A dramatic, much maligned groan followed. The bell jangled as Tayla departed.

"Come here, Laura . . ." hissed Aunt Velma. "Quick! I want to talk to you about the black girl you've got driving me around town."

Laura hurried into the sitting area. "African American, Aunt Velma. Af-ri-can American. It's the preferred appellation used now."

Velma waved a blue-veined hand. "You know who I mean. I can't keep up with all this political correctness." She drew herself up. "And I never used that offensive N-word. Demeans speaker and recipient."

Laura sighed. Aunt Velma didn't mean anything by it. Just her generation's way. Maybe better to let that sleeping dog lie.

Velma peered out the front. "I'm referring to Tayla, Lula Burke's granddaughter. The one you sprung on me since you took my driver's license away."

Laura poured the contents of the water into the coffee dispenser. "The license the State of North Carolina took from you after you sideswiped a police car, Aunt Velma."

Velma harrumphed. "Whatever."

Whatever?

Laura cut her eyes over to her aunt and pushed the coffeemaker button on. Some days Aunt Velma and Ian sounded so much alike.

"That grape bubblegum wad in her cheek is about to drive me crazy. You know how I feel about gum-smacking, cud-chewing teenage . . ."

"I know. I know."

The percolating aroma of *A Carolina Morning* filled the room with its hint of velvet chocolate creaminess. Velma took an appreciative sniff.

You could take the high school teacher out of the classroom. But you could never take the classroom out of the high school teacher.

Her aunt settled her bottom in the seat cushion. "Daddy always said . . ."

In the South, grown women called their fathers "daddy" until the day they — not their fathers — died.

Laura tried not to smile. Would only rile her aunt.

Velma drummed her fingers on the curved mahogany arm of her chair. "Are you listening to me, Laura Lou?"

"Yes, ma'am."

"My daddy always said, 'Gum-smacking women and cackling hens, neither 'tis fit for God nor men.' "

"I thought he said, 'Whistlin' women and

cackling hens,' Aunt Velma."

"Same difference." Velma's voice lowered to a conspiratorial whisper. "The girl wants to sign me up for something called Twitter. Tells me I got to learn to tweet."

Velma exhaled a loud breath. "At first, I thought she was talking about joining a bird-watching club, and I was all for it. But this 'twitter' business?"

Her aunt's eyebrows rose like two question marks. "Like I need to twitter, tremble, or quake any more than I already do. What's she trying to do? Give me Parkinson's?" Velma gave a ladylike snort. "But then I realized it had something to do with the computer and you know, Laura, how I feel about that sort of thing . . ."

The bell jingled.

Tayla stomped through the door carrying Aunt Velma's quilted purse. She paused on the threshold, holding the door open for her grandmother, Lula Burke, even though they were arguing, it appeared, about Tayla's attire for a day on the job. About the same as Velma, Lula was stooped like Laura's aunt, but there the resemblance ended.

Not in her usual housedress she wore as the Housekeeping Supervisor over at Weathersby Historic Park, today Lula sported one of her Sunday-go-to-meeting dresses, lilac purple. Her tight gray curls peeped from underneath a matching wide-brimmed hat. After the goings-on at Weathersby — multiple murders, including Alison Barefoot's first husband, and scandal — Lula had been promoted and others hired to assist her in the cleaning duties required to keep the antebellum home an architectural gem.

Lula threw up her hand and waddled over to the low-slung couch. She sank amidst the cushions, laying her matching purse beside her. After handing Velma her purse, Tayla slouched next to the case of decorative buttons.

Velma's eyes twinkled at her friend. "I like your shoes."

Lula's seersucker face broke into a mischievous grin, her dentures gleaming. "I knew you would. You like anything purple. It's why I wore 'em."

She extended her feet, straight out in front of her, her ebony legs studded with varicose veins. Lula gave a small moan in her deep contralto. "Though these heels are killing my legs. What we women do suffer for fashion."

Laura handed her aunt a cup just how Velma liked it. Strong and black.

Miss Lula scrunched her nose in the air like a bird dog scenting quail. "That your special coffee I smell, Laura Lou?"

"Yes, ma'am, Miss Lula. Can I pour you a cup?"

"Certainly." Lula's second chin bobbed. "Real reason I come to sew with you fancy-schmancy society ladies."

Velma lifted the bone china cup to her lips. "You come to hear the gossip, Lula Rae Burke."

Lula favored Laura with a sphinx-like smile as she accepted her cup and saucer. Cream mostly, with a dash of coffee for flavor.

Velma, the undisputed leader of the committee restoring the needlepoint cushions at the Weathersby Plantation Chapel, set her cup on the saucer where it gave off a tiny ping. "Where's the rest of the crew? We're only two weeks away from the Festival, and our goal was to have the cushions in place for the concert."

Both ladies rummaged in their bags for their current needlepoint creation in the ongoing project. Each canvas was secured in a wooden hoop, the tapestry needle docked in place, its eye threaded with dangling strands of silk embroidery.

Velma fumbled in the bottom of her bag for her crane-shaped embroidery scissors. "How's that African headdress art quilt coming, Lula?"

Her aunt tilted her head in Laura's direction. "Beautiful shades of orange, green, and brown."

Laura opened a bag of Pepperidge Farm Milano cookies and plated them on a matching violet-fringed saucer. She knew where this was headed.

"Fine. Fine." Lula fixed her tiger-striped reading glasses on the bridge of her nose. "Where's your glasses, Vel?"

"Guess I left them in the side pocket of the car." Velma's eyes cut to Tayla. "Would you mind — ?"

"I'm studying pre-med. Not day care worker to Velma Louise Jones." Tayla jutted her jaw. "This isn't some remake called, 'Driving Miss Velma.' "

Laura gasped. Velma gripped the arms of her chair. Lula's eyes widened.

And hardened.

"I got this one, Velma." Lula shot her granddaughter a warning look, her brows furrowed. Lula moved faster than Laura expected from a woman of her age. And girth.

The old woman got in Tayla's face.

"If you'd learn to keep your mouth shut and your ears open, you might surprise yourself and learn something from a woman

I happen to respect and admire. I'm on the Board at Weathersby now. How dare you embarrass me in front of my friends?"

"These people aren't your friends. They're your employers, Grandma."

Lula didn't back down. "They're your employers, too, or did you forget that? You're Velma's driver, and that means a lot more than sitting your rear in that seat and steering. It's about making sure she gets where she needs to go, properly, completely. And you do not know what you're talking about, with this attitude. Don't you disrespect *me* either, thinking you know what's best for *my* life. Velma and me go way back. Maybe one day you'll understand that true friendship, white or black, is a rare and precious thing. Not to be scorned or taken lightly." Lula took a breath. "Now. Why don't you do part of your job and get my good friend's glasses?"

Tayla stared at her grandmother a moment, anger still clear on her face. Then she swung around and headed out. The service door creaked. Swung wide and smacked the frame.

Silence.

Laura reddened. Aunt Velma sipped her tea. Miss Lula lowered her substantial rear onto the seat, smoothing her skirt. "I apologize for my granddaughter's behavior. That Tayla's never minded work." A wicked gleam shone from Lula's black bean eyes. "Never minded lying down right beside it."

Laura fought the urge to smile.

Velma laid down her cup. "You should show Laura that wondrous orange-and-red quilt we're showcasing at the festival, Lula."

"Why? You think she'd want to display it in Tapestries on consignment for me? Maybe . . ."

Lula cut a sly look at Velma. ". . . maybe one of those rich, ole —"

"White women might decide it's perfect for a sunroom," finished Aunt Velma.

The two geriatrics grinned at each other.

Miss Lula jerked her head toward the parking lot. "No offense?"

"None taken. It's this ADD generation, Lula."

Lula's chins wobbled in agreement. "Gotta have everything now. No work ethic to speak of. Knows it all."

"Sense of entitlement," chimed in the hitherto silent Doris Stanley, standing on the threshold at the front entrance.

All three, Laura included, swiveled. In the commotion, no one had heard the bell.

Lula fist-pumped the air. "Preach it, sister. They gonna single-handedly eliminate poverty and usher in world peace."

Velma stabbed her needle into the tapestry. "They can have their crack at the world. We certainly had ours, didn't we, Lula?"

Lula tossed her head. "Had? I can still do a mean shimmy, I'll have you know, Velma Louise Jones."

"You ain't lived," former English teacher Velma Louise Jones lifted her chin, "till you've seen me shake, rattle, and roll."

Truer words on God's earth were never spoken.

Puzzlement creased Doris's face. "Like Elvis?"

With that image of her aunt stuck forever in her mind, Laura cleared her throat. "I think we should —"

The front door bell jangled again.

Patti Ogburn poked her head inside. "Let the party begin." She propped her hands on her hips at the gales of laughter from the blue hairs.

"What? What did I miss?"

6

Gathered at Tapestries, the ladies sat stunned at Laura's news of Renna Sheldon's death. Tayla rejoined them, returning with Velma's glasses and a mumbled apology. The teenager sank onto a crewelwork footstool. Hilary Munro put an arm around the girl's shoulders. Velma fixed a cup of strong coffee for Tayla, who took a fortifying sip.

"The shattered myth of youth's invincibility." Velma clasped her liver-spotted hands. "Always a shock to the young how fragile life is."

Lula nodded. "How death is no more than an elbow's length from all of us, all the time."

More confusion than normal drifted across Doris Stanley's patrician features. Laura cocked her head at Velma. Surely the police had already informed Doris of the murder. Renna had been living for the summer with her great-aunt Doris and the General.

But perhaps she'd forgotten. Alzheimer's lay heavy on Doris's once cover-girl features. Perhaps the General had hoped to distract his befuddled wife today with the reassuring routine of the needlepoint group.

Forty-something, Patti fingered her tennis skirt. Her hair flamed in the slant of the sun's beam through the plate glass. "I bought yarn from Renna about three-fifteen yesterday."

Laura's eyes widened. "Did she seem okay to you? Agitated?"

Patti shrugged. "She rushed me. I asked her if she had a date."

"What did she say?" Velma's voice quavered.

"Nothing. Handed me my receipt and practically ushered me out the door." Patti frowned, but smoothed away the parallel lines between her brows with a glossy, copper-colored nail.

Worried about ruining the expensive Botox treatment?

As to be expected, bubbly Hilary, her heavy black eyeliner rendering her more like a near-sighted raccoon, recovered first. "What can we do to help you, Laura?"

The former beauty queen — at the half-century mark with her “jacked up to Jesus” bouffant heavy on the hairspray — was renowned for her kind heart and sunny disposition.

“I appreciate the offer, Hilary. But I’m going to try Claire Monaghan first. See if she can help me out this afternoon while I attend Garrett’s rally.”

Velma clanged her cup in the saucer. “Thought it was a Memorial Day parade in honor of heroes who gave that last, full measure of devotion.”

Laura picked up the cell phone behind the counter. “Course it is. That’s what I meant.” She speed dialed the Barefoot residence, an old two-story fixer-upper that Mike had gotten for a song before marrying Alison and, to his eternal joy, acquiring his two teenage stepchildren, Justin and Claire.

The shop would be in good hands with the poised high school senior, who headed off to the Savannah School of Art and Design next year. Claire often helped out in the shop before Renna had taken the job for the summer.

“Claire? I have a favor to ask —”

Laura listened. “I had no idea your mom was having trouble. Is she okay? Is she at home or did they — ?” She nodded as if

Claire could see her across the telephone line.

"Bed rest till her due date? Alison's going to hate that." She laughed. "Yeah, I can imagine Mike threatening to tie her to the bed if she doesn't behave. Don't worry about Tapestries. I'll find —"

Laura paused. "You can? Thanks so much, Claire. I'll see you soon."

She hung up as the bell jingled. Glancing up, panic laced her heart. Jon Locklear framed the doorway.

Her pulse staccatoed. "What're you doing here?"

Jon's pleasant expression vanished. "I'm here to do my job. Investigate the last place Renna Sheldon was seen alive."

His mouth twisted. "Unless you have a problem with me trying to solve Renna's murder."

"No, I just have a problem with you."

A flush of anger darkened his face. The chatter behind Laura died away as all eyes fixated on the drama at the door.

Brushing her sleeve, Aunt Velma stood at Laura's elbow.

"Velma Jones." Her aunt extended her hand to Jon. "I'm not sure you'll remember me." Her vivid blue eyes, sharp as a tapestry needle, ping-ponged between them.

"I spent a summer, about ten years ago, in Mimosa Grove clearing out our family's homeplace and grieving after the loss of my —" Velma swallowed. "Laura's mother. I remember your mother's kindness to Laura and me then."

A look of pain — and regret? — crossed the wide planes of his face.

Laura tensed.

This couldn't be happening. Might as well wave a banner in the sky announcing the lies she'd told. She skimmed a strand of hair out of her face and behind her ear.

Velma gave Jon's hand a squeeze. "I hope your mother is well."

He ducked his head, his eyes on the floor. "Yes, ma'am. Recovering from hip replacement surgery, but doing well."

Velma patted his hand. "If I remember your mother aright, Florence won't let that stop her for long. She's got enough spirit for two people."

Laura stationed both hands on her aunt's shoulders. "Something we could say about you, too, Aunt Velma. What do you want from me, Jon?"

She blushed.

That could've been phrased better. A piercing glance from Jon ripped at her scabs.

Velma nodded, as if imminently satisfied

about something. "He wants to interview anyone who knew Renna."

Her aunt gestured toward the group. "And it's your lucky day, Detective Locklear. We all knew Renna. Some better than others."

Velma drifted to her chair. "I've continued to follow your mother's groundbreaking work. The art quilts. The gallery showings."

He smiled. "And she's gone viral these days, too. Her website portfolio. The YouTube demonstrations. Got her first computer after I left for Lejeune and now she's a certified Facebook maven."

Velma's eyebrows quirked. "Really? At her age?"

Laura moved to block his view of the ladies. "Interview or interrogate my customers, Locklear?"

She'd not forgotten the hateful note with its insinuations. Information possessed by only two people — herself and Jon Locklear. What mind game was he playing?

He leaned closer, his nose inches from her own. "Do you think they'd prefer to answer my questions at the station, Mrs. Mabry?"

A collective gasp from the women.

Velma gave an exasperated huff. "Laura Louise, get out of the man's way and let him do his job."

Her hand proverbially slapped, Laura

retreated behind the counter. From a distance, she watched him gently lead the women through a round of questions. Answers he inscribed upon his notepad. She especially noted the sensitivity he displayed toward a frightened Doris.

With her elbows on the display case, Laura indulged herself for the first time since encountering Jon yesterday. She drank in the sight of him, a sight Laura never stopped longing for since the terrible moment she discovered Renna . . .

Her gaze flickered.

The day Laura walked away forever from love. But despite his betrayal, she couldn't help comparing the boy he'd been with the man he'd become.

Self-conscious, she straightened and sucked in her belly. So unfair how childbirth altered a woman's appearance.

He'd fulfilled the promise of his gangly teenage physique, his shoulders broad under the navy sport coat tapering to a narrow waist. His face had matured from a good-looking boy to a handsome man. The firm chin. The thick, straight brows.

If Laura lived to be a hundred, she'd never forget the first day she met him in the yard of his mother's tin-roofed farmhouse.

Taking apart something mechanical from

his prize Camaro, he leaned over the hood, greasc staining his white T-shirt, streaks on his high cheekbones. And straightening at her approach, he favored Laura with a smile she'd never been able to erase from her heart. He'd wiped his hands, those dexterous long-fingered hands, on an oily rag and introduced himself with a special something in his eyes. Something Laura — for that golden summer at least — believed meant something special for her alone.

A promise of possibilities.

Her knuckles whitened. She forced herself to let go of the display case and practiced taking steady breaths.

Don't go there . . .

She willed her heartbeat to settle.

Feeling eyes on her, Laura turned. Velma caught her gaze, grinned like a barracuda, and offered Jon the plate of Milanos.

He snagged a few off the tray. "Thank you, ma'am." He popped one into his mouth.

Always the polite Southern boy. And he'd always had a sweet tooth, too. She remembered so much about him . . .

He inhaled. "That coffee I smell?"

The much-married Patti leaped off the couch. "I'll get you some."

He had that effect on females, young or

old. Another, more unpleasant fact, Laura recalled. Probably caused preschool girls to swoon, too.

"Laura's signature specialty." Another pointed look from Velma.

He took a sip from the cup Patti handed him. The corners of his mouth perked. The deep-set brown eyes Laura once drowned in crinkled at her across the room.

"She always —" He flushed. "That's good coffee, Laura." He gulped. "I mean, Mrs. Mabry."

Mollified for no practical reason, she nodded.

This was the Jon she remembered. The goofy, funny, sweet boy. A barrier crashed around her heart.

Jon rose. She accompanied him to the door.

He paused, his hand grasping the door handle. "I'll need to come by and get that formal statement from you. Would this afternoon work?"

If only . . . But just in time Laura remembered her prior obligation. "No. I'm attending a rally with Garrett at the Memorial Day parade."

He drew up and glared. "Then I'll have my people contact your people to arrange a more convenient time."

The moment passed.

She stiffened.

In truth, their moment had long since passed.

She was a fool of the first order.

"You do that, Detective."

Grim-faced, he barreled out of her shop, sideswiping Claire Monaghan.

Auburn-haired Claire stared after his rapidly departing figure. "Was that — ?"

"It was nobody," Laura growled.

Claire's azure-blue eyes widened. "Whatever. I'm here for the duration. But Mom let me come on one condition."

Laura walked Claire to the storage room to stash her purse. "What's that?"

"Mom says you have to come to church tomorrow and eat dinner with us afterward."

Claire's Sunday dinners were legendary. But Laura hadn't darkened the door of Jesus Our Redeemer since Holt died. Unbeknownst to Ian, after dropping her son off at his church class each week, Laura sat out the service at the local Starbucks.

Laura bit her lip. "I don't know . . ."

Claire reached for the dupioni silk panel on the floor. "How did this get here? Mom says she hasn't seen you in so long. Feels bad her pregnancy has kept her from making sure you and Ian were doing okay."

Nothing would ever be okay again, but the phone lines worked both ways. Laura had gone out of her way to avoid encounters with old friends. And some friend she'd been to Alison. Maybe it was time to stop wallowing in her own guilt and be there for her friend going through a difficult pregnancy.

"Okay." She took the panel from Claire. "I'll be there."

"Great." Claire headed for the front.

Bidding her aunt and compatriots *adieu,* Laura gathered her purse and went out the service entrance. The rest of her day would be about Garrett. The time and attention he deserved on this big day. But a small, square envelope rested on the windshield of her Lexus, trapped between the glass and the wipers.

Not again . . .

A knot of dread formed in the pit of her stomach.

With shaky fingers, she plucked it from its nest, ripping it open.

You've deceived others but be you not deceived. Fornicators and adulterers will not inherit the kingdom of God.

Falling against the car, she crumpled the

note in her fist. This wasn't anything like the boy she remembered.

This malice, this . . . evil.

Why was Jon doing this to her? What did he hope to gain?

A thought shook her to the core. He didn't know, did he? He couldn't.

Oh, God, not that.

Her eyes shot to the patch of sky, a hazy blue in the humidity. "Anything God," she swallowed. "Please . . . anything but that."

Sunday morning, Jon crumpled *The News and Observer* in his hand. His gut did a slow burn at the headline on the front page.

HOMEGROWN HERO TURNED
CANDIDATE USHERS IN MEMORIAL
DAY

Jon snorted.

"Hero?"

Just because the guy successfully litigated the sensational case of a serial killer who stalked prostitutes and prosecuted a high-profile drug kingpin didn't make him anybody's hero.

What truly got Jon's morning off to a grand start, however, was the accompanying photo of Payne — shirt collar open, blue-collar casual in his chinos and Sperry's — at a podium and beside him, Laura's adoring gaze.

Blue collar, Jon's eyeball.

That slick spin-meister wouldn't know clean, honest, hard work if it bit him in the — *sorry, God* — most delicate place where supreme pain can be felt.

Jon willed his heartbeat to slow. Things seemed to be going in a positive direction with Laura yesterday until . . . He shook his head.

Until they didn't.

Something was eating at her. He fought to maintain his objectivity and lost. No way she was the killer.

Jon caught Laura staring at him with those big baby-blues while he interviewed Hilary Munro.

For a moment, her look had taken his breath. It'd taken everything in Jon not to take Laura in his arms and demand to know why she'd walked away from a future with him.

Laura Bowen, the only woman he'd ever contemplated marrying. The Laura he once knew was still there, although hidden beneath the barbed layers of the Laura Mabry she'd become.

His cell rang. Ana.

"Good news. We've got footage from the Village's security camera of Renna leaving Tapestries and heading for the greenway. Alone, but carrying something we haven't been able to identify in the crook of her arm. Patrol found Texas Pete's deserted campsite under another footbridge not a quarter-mile from our crime scene."

"That's your good news, Morales?"

She laughed. "Wait for it, Locklear. I had a hunch our suspect had moved on to less, shall we say, active territory. I had the boys search other nearby stretches of the greenway on the other side of the Village and bingo."

His heart leaped in his throat. "You got him? Got him in custody?"

"You bet, partner. At headquarters as we speak, awaiting your interrogation."

He shoved the paper off his lap. "I'll be there in ten. With bells on."

Finally, a break.

He'd miss church this morning, but potentially eliminate Laura from the suspect list. "You're the best, Ana Morales."

A deep, throaty chuckle.

It didn't stir his blood, though, the way it had Friday.

"And don't you forget it, mister." She signed off.

Jon frowned.

Ana's undisguised interest in him — colliding with his never-quenched yearning for Laura Bowen — was a professional disaster waiting to happen.

7

Seated between Mike and Alison — allowed out only for church — Laura endured the curious glances. One reason she'd avoided church since Holt's death. Not the main one, though. Alison, her figure willowy despite her protruding belly, smiled at her as they shared a hymnal.

Holt had been a fixture at Redeemer. A deacon, a teacher in the men's Bible study. She'd been along for the ride, coasting on the coattails of his faith. But after his death, her hypocrisy proved more than Laura could stomach every Sunday.

With a father like hers, Laura was well acquainted with the inviolate rules of law and its consequences to those who trampled them. She didn't need reminding — despite Jon's little notes — God would judge her for breaking His Law, too. And one day, her reckoning would come.

Laura only hoped it'd be later rather than sooner.

Mike kept glancing over his shoulder at the church foyer. Beside him, Claire reposed, coiffed and outfitted to perfection as usual. Dinner simmered in the Crock-Pot at the Barefoot residence.

Justin, Ian, and the Prescotts returned on Monday. Was it a lifetime ago Laura bid them good-bye?

She muddled through the songs, but with no spirit behind the words. Laura tuned out the gentle words of Pastor Fleming, who every fortnight or so, continued to call and inquire about her and Ian's well-being. But the Scripture reading from First Corinthians snagged her attention.

It was a long list of the unrighteous who wouldn't inherit the kingdom of heaven.

She fiddled with the bulletin. Might as well add her name to the list.

The next verse Fleming read surprised her. "That is what some of you used to be! But you were washed clean . . . you were made holy to God . . . and you were made right with God in the name of the Lord Jesus Christ and in the Spirit of our God."

A glimmer of hope?

Laura squashed the bulletin in her fist. Just a bunch of big church words. Not for the likes of her.

If Bryan Fleming knew . . . She cast an uneasy glance around the congregants. If any of these good people knew what she'd done . . .

The words of The Accuser floated back to her.

No possibility of redemption. Not for someone as unworthy as Laura.

Pastor Fleming wasn't a podium pounder, and the service ended with a gentle invitation to come forward. She kept a tight grip on the pew in front of her as they rose to sing the closing hymn.

Whew . . . that was done.

Mike extracted his phone from his trouser pocket, his close-cropped hair cut on the sides and back like the state troopers. "Ah." He nodded to his wife. "Just as I thought. Called in to work, but he says if he gets done in time he'll try to make dinner."

Mike laughed, his face stretching into a grin emphasizing his high Cherokee cheekbones. "A man after my own heart. Not going to miss a home-cooked meal if he can help it."

Alison used the armrest to hoist herself to her feet. Mike caught her elbow. "Good. I can't wait to meet your friend. At last, maybe our schedules will coincide."

Laura followed the Barefoots home, only a few streets away from her cul-de-sac. Once inside, Alison rested on the sofa while she and Claire bustled in the cherry-red kitchen. Laura volunteered to set out flatware and dinner plates. This place was so unlike the palatial lifestyle Alison and her kids enjoyed while married to her first husband.

But the happiness that shone from Alison's brown eyes more than compensated for any financial reversal of fortune. For indeed, Mike's love made her, in Alison's view, the most fortunate of women. Mike topped an ice-filled glass with a lemon and carried the beverage over to his wife.

"Sweet tea for someone sweet."

Alison pushed herself into a more comfortable sitting position. "You know how I like it." The corners of her mouth turned up.

His hand caressed the top of Alison's silver-blonde pageboy. The look Alison winged Mike's way brought tears to Laura's eyes.

Laura pivoted, stabbed with envy and regret. She'd lost so much to the lies. She didn't deserve to find happiness like Mike and Alison.

The image of Garrett intruded into her thoughts. Did her only chance for future happiness reside with Garrett, her old childhood friend? Laura hunched her shoulders and busied herself folding the napkins. Claire shuffled upstairs to change out of her Sunday dress.

At the sound of a vehicle, Mike hurried to the front window. "Jon made it."

"Jon?" Laura whirled. "Jon Locklear's coming here?"

But Mike hadn't heard her. He rushed out, his greeting followed by a low-voiced rejoinder. The voices grew stronger and the front porch creaked. Alison, unhindered by her watchdog husband, swung her feet to the floor. "You know Jon, Mike's friend?" Laura swallowed hard and nodded. Alison heaved herself off the sofa and over to the window. She lifted her hand to wave, but her smile faded.

"And that's Jon Locklear? Oh, Laura . . ." Alison gripped Laura's arm. "What have you done?"

The door opened.

Mike and his friend, Jon Locklear, strolled inside.

His heart hammering in his chest, Jon allowed Mike to draw him into the room. Was God trying to tell him something? Once again at the sight of Laura, Jon had trouble remembering to breathe.

Laura stepped back, her eyes wide with shock. She obviously hadn't expected to see him, of all people, here. He'd have retreated, but Mike stood between him and the exit.

Mike's forehead wrinkled. "Do you two know each other already? I didn't realize . . ."

Jon sent Laura a sideways glance. "We're old . . ." His lips craved the touch of hers.

She nodded like a tightly strung marionette. "Old acquaintances," she whispered.

Clomping down the staircase, Claire broke the awkwardness. "Hey, Jon. We didn't get a chance to speak when you rushed out of Tapestries yesterday. Big case?"

Without waiting for an answer, Claire motioned for them to take their seats. She continued to chatter as she served generous portions of coleslaw, her own secret Crock-Pot chopped pork barbecue recipe, and sweet tea.

Jon found himself across the table from Laura. Tugging at his tie, he longed to touch her, just once to hold her in the circle of his arms.

She refused to meet his gaze, finding her napkin fascinating.

He should go home. He'd make this

miserable, not only for her, but for everyone else.

Claire plunked the biscuits on the table. "How do y'all know each other?"

At the head of the table, a spark of recognition dawned in Mike's slate-gray eyes. His mouth opened into a big *O.* Closing his lips like a fish, he cast his wife, at the other end, a troubled look.

Laura rubbed a wisp of her hair between her thumb and forefinger before tucking it behind her ear. "The summer my mother died, Aunt Velma and I went to Mimosa Grove to clear out the family homeplace. My textile professor secured me an internship with Jon's mother, the famous Lumbee textile artist. Jon was spending his final days at home before reporting to boot camp. We became . . ." She blushed.

His eyes never left her face. "Friends."

Something stirred inside him.

And between them.

Laura's lips trembled.

"Wow." Claire swiped a dishtowel at an imaginary speck of dirt on the immaculate counter. "That's funny. Never made the connection before, but you wouldn't believe how much Laura's son . . ." Claire snagged a photo from the fridge.

Laura closed her eyes.

"Claire —" Alison struggled to scrape back her chair.

Too late.

". . . resembles you, Jon." Claire handed Jon the photo.

His brow furrowed, he scanned the picture.

Jon knew Justin and Claire Monaghan from an afterschool visit to the station one day. The lanky, ginger-headed man in his thirties — Holt Mabry? Beside the man, a sturdy, compact-sized boy with milk chocolate skin. Short, wiry black hair. And dark, obsidian eyes.

Like his own.

His head snapped up and he blinked.

Claire rattled on. "They say we each have a twin somewhere. More like a little twin in this case. Oh —" Comprehension followed, and she clamped a hand over her mouth.

Jon leveled a glance at Laura, who'd shrunk into her chair, her eyes averted. "What's she talking about, Laura? Is this" — he pointed to the photo — "your son, Ian?"

Mike leaped to his feet. "Jon." He placed a hand on Jon's shoulder. "Let's —"

"Did you know about this, Mike?" Jon shrugged him off. "Is this why you hired me? Brought me to Raleigh?"

"No, man. No way. I never realized you and Laura Mabry had a prior relationship."

Jon's mouth tightened. "Is this your son, Laura?" His voice rose a notch. "Answer me."

Laura's face had gone ashen.

"For once in your life, tell me the truth."

Alison signaled Mike. "Come on, Claire. I think they could use some privacy." The trio tiptoed out and disappeared upstairs.

Jon banged his fist on the table. She jolted. The dishes rattled.

"Look at me, Laura."

The sick feeling of her utter betrayal gnawed at him. A blinding flash of anger seared the back of his eyelids.

"Is Ian my son?"

Her eyes welled with unshed tears. "Yes."

Stunned silence.

He gaped at Laura. "Why didn't you tell me? I wanted, I dreamed of . . ."

The rush of words she'd held in for eleven years poured out of her lips. Truth, at last. The weight of the lies far eclipsed this long-dreaded moment. Why had she waited so long?

Laura perched on the edge of her chair. "I'd planned to tell you. After boot camp at Parris Island, you were waiting for your orders to come through as you finished your specialized training at Lejeune. I'd returned for fall semester before I knew for sure. I had it out with Daddy. Told him my intentions. Packed my bags. Burned my bridges."

She choked on the memory of her father's rage and his parting shot that if she chose to lie down with the dogs, she could get up alone with the fleas.

His face contorted. "Why would you hide this from me? I believed I meant something to you, Laura. We talked about you joining me wherever I was stationed." He shook his head. "And then that day at Lejeune, your crazy accusations."

She'd been crazy that cold, rainy afternoon in November. Crazy with hormones and jealousy. Her mother's death and the discovery of her father's affair coupled with the voluptuous form of Jon's betrayal had proved too much.

Finding the peroxide-blonde in one of his misbuttoned shirts lying on rumpled sheets in the motel room sent Laura over the edge. A note — Jon's note — had instructed Laura to meet him in Jacksonville near Lejeune. To stop by the room he registered in her name, to drop off her bags before their appointment with the Marine chaplain.

When Laura arrived on the heels of her

confrontation with her dad, she discovered the woman. But no Jon. Bolting from the room, Laura ran into him in the parking lot. She'd erupted, irrational. Her anger spewed, scalding and lacerating them both.

How like Jon to lay the blame at her door. Righteous indignation swelling, Laura stuffed the guilt of what she'd done, stirred the embers of the old fury to life, and fought fire with fire.

"You have the nerve to question anything I've chosen to do after what you did with that woman?"

"Like I told you then, I never sent you a note to meet me at a motel room. You sent me a note to meet you there. You said you'd broken your engagement with Mabry and your father threw you out. There was no woman. Just an empty room."

He scrubbed his hand across his forehead. "Never another woman once I met you. My heart — God help me — has always been true to you."

"I know what I saw." She scrambled to her feet. "I'm not the only one who lies."

Jon surged over the table, his countenance raw with anger. "I want to see my son."

"He's Holt Mabry's son. Never yours."

She plucked the photo from the table and jabbed her finger at Holt's image. "Holt adored Ian. A better man than you could ever be. I won't let you destroy what Ian has left of his father."

"I'm his father," Jon growled.

"Holt is his real — in every sense of the word except for sperm — father."

Jon grabbed the picture out of her hand, holding it inches from her face. "This is my boy. My son. And I will not allow you to take him away from me again."

She knocked his hand out of her face.

"Why would you keep him away, even if you despised me, from my family who'd have loved him, who loved you, so much?"

She flinched. "I couldn't trust you anymore. I wanted to be as far away from you as I could get." She raised her shoulders in a helpless, futile gesture and dropped them.

His hand trembled, holding the photograph high. "And you got a living reminder of me every day, didn't you? I only have your word you and the *good* doctor treated my son well all these years. Maybe you took out your anger against him."

Laura's nostrils flared.

His brow furrowed into a *V*. "The same Dr. Holt Mabry you were secretly engaged to the whole time you were cavorting" — he said the word like one said *vomit* — "with me. Did you tell *him* the truth about Ian?

Did you lie to him, too? Or were both of you part of this sick conspiracy to rob me of my son?" Jon flung the photo on the table.

She clenched her fists. "I came to him, broken and weeping at your betrayal, Jon Locklear. I told him I was pregnant. I never told him who Ian's father was. He never asked. After we married and Ian was born, I don't think he ever wanted to know."

Jon sneered. "Then he was a fool." He laughed, a barking mockery of mirth. "Just like me. You stringing Garrett Payne along to take Mabry's place?"

She slapped Jon hard across the face. "What I choose to do or don't do has nothing to do with you. Never has had anything to do with you."

His eyes darkened.

She drew back.

His features morphed into something predatory, vulturelike. Into a man she didn't know. "I think you'll find, in this case, you are very much mistaken, Mrs. Mabry."

A coldness and the dread of what she'd so long feared overwhelmed her. Laura fought the urge to crumble. Any sign of weakness and this man, this monster, would take everything that was life itself to her.

She jutted her jaw. "Are you threatening me?"

He cocked his head. "I don't threaten. This is a promise."

Snatching the photo off the table, he stormed through the living room, flinging open the door.

"I hate you, Jon Locklear," she screamed as this time he walked away from her.

The only person Laura hated more was herself.

She jerked as the door crashed behind him. An engine roared and tires squealed out of the driveway. Her knees buckled, and she crashed against the wall. A shiver crawled the length of her spine. Laura squeezed her eyes shut.

Oh, God . . . Oh, God . . . Oh, God . . .

Her real nightmare had begun.

Jon made it about two blocks before the shock hit him. With the photo in his hand curled around the steering wheel, he wrenched his truck to the side of the road, rocking to a standstill.

A son.

Something right and beautiful shot through him. An incredible joy flooded his senses. He lowered the window, taking deep draughts of breath from the pine-scented air.

His lips curved into a smile. A son. His

mother, his sisters, Cami would be thrilled . . .

Jon frowned. But not yet. He'd tell them later. He had things to settle with Laura first. He'd left the Barefoot house before he did something he could never undo.

His head throbbing, he swallowed. Rage battled with the pain. The rage won, licking at his insides like a consuming flame. A fire mixed with ice as the coldness returned. The clinical detachment he'd cultivated as a survival mechanism in the hills of Afghanistan.

Jon's heart pounded, frightened.

The pounding made him afraid of what he was capable of doing if Laura thwarted his efforts to connect with his son.

A gentle wisp, a Scripture, floated through his mind. An urge to pray.

Jon shook his head. He'd handle this situation his way. He wouldn't let Laura Bowen keep his son from him. He revved the engine.

Whatever he had to do to get his son back, he'd do.

His stomach clenched. How he'd loved that girl. A frigid emptiness threatened to engulf him. She was his enemy now.

He steeled his resolve. Putting the truck into motion, he wondered how expensive a good attorney would be.

But no matter how expensive, his son was worth any price.

8

Wearing an old, baggy T-shirt of Holt's, Laura spent Sunday night, her head hung over the toilet, sick to her stomach and overcome with fears for herself and most especially, Ian. Physically spent, her mind refused to quiet. She agonized over whether this outcome could've been avoided if she'd told Jon the truth so long ago.

Perhaps. Perhaps not.

She replayed every conversation with Jon over the last several days for clues as to how she might've sidestepped this ugly scenario. The scorn — the disgust — she'd seen in his eyes when forced to tell him the truth — gnawed at her insides.

The queasiness returned. Gagging, she leaned over the commode until the dizziness and nausea subsided.

What would Jon do? He didn't make idle threats. What could she do to keep her son safe from him? Her stomach refused to settle.

Pray . . .

No, that wouldn't work for her. God wasn't interested in a messed-up sinner like her. Her mind whirled, unable to wrap itself around the idea Jon could — would — take Ian from her.

Something Jon said at Tapestries nagged at the fringes of her memory. And with it, the memory of that fateful encounter in Jacksonville. But what he said to Aunt Velma regarding his mother going twenty-first century tugged at Laura.

What was so compelling about Florence Locklear's computer? Laura crinkled her forehead, trying to capture the elusive fragment of thought.

She groped for the tissue box. Yanking out a tissue, she wiped her face and, planting her hands on the seat, pushed herself upright. Wadding the tissue, she hurled the missile into the trashcan and her thoughts coalesced.

The note from Jon, eleven years ago, directed her to meet him in Jacksonville. The note, which had arrived via her dorm mailbox.

Behind her back, her father had dropped the bombshell on Jon that she'd been engaged to someone else the whole summer Laura spent in Mimosa Grove. She'd been eager for a chance to explain her pseudo engagement with Holt Mabry to Jon. And she had wonderful news to share. News, though unexpected, she hoped he'd welcome.

News of a child, their child.

So why had Jon been caught out when he'd been the one specifically who invited her to work things out?

Driven by an urge, she flung open her walk-in closet. She shoved aside her cocktail dresses and formal wear, looking for one cardboard box in which she'd sealed away her memories of that summer.

As if a sealed box had a snowball's chance in a Carolina August of actually sealing off memories.

Flicking on the overhead light, she wrestled out the cumbersome carton. Squatting on her heels, she stared at the duct-taped Pandora's box. Drawing a breath, she ripped at the seams, heedless of her nails. Propping open the folds, she rummaged, refusing to become distracted by tokens of a bittersweet time. Deep in the bowels of her past, her fingers closed over the square contours of the paper she sought.

Yes, she'd saved it. Why?

Because she was a scab picker.

Holding the elegant, ivory envelope to the light, she examined it. Postmarked Raleigh. She rocked on her heels.

Not Jacksonville.

She had been so relieved to hear from Jon after his well-deserved anger at her deceit, she'd not been observant of this crucial particular eleven years ago. Removing the note, she scanned the contents once more, as if, hope against hope, the message had somehow changed.

Nerving herself past the pain, she kept her perusal clinical, like Holt would have performed a diagnosis. Detached, objective. Thorough. Her hands analyzed the note. She flipped the vellum stationery front and back, side to side.

Typed, not handwritten.

Not truly typed, though. Printed. Laser-printed.

Expensive paper. Unlike what a Marine would employ. More like what lawyers — her mouth went dry — like judges used.

Laura's breath caught. Had Jon been telling the truth?

Had they both been the victims of a cruel manipulation that changed the course of their lives forever?

Laura didn't bother asking herself if her

father would stoop to such a dirty trick to prevent his only child from making the biggest mistake of her life — his words. From the rough and tumble of Carolina politics, she knew the retired judge — the betrayer of his own wife in those heart-rending days of her mother's illness — had done far worse already.

She buried her face in her hands. She'd been wrong about Jon. She should call him, try to work something out about Ian . . .

But what about those other notes? Was Jon the accuser? Was he capable of such venom? Who else would've known those details?

She'd loved the boy from Mimosa Grove. This man — this cop — the one whose eyes glimmered at her across the table at Alison's, he frightened her. Him she didn't know. Him she couldn't trust with the tender heart of her son.

Laura glanced at the clock. Just before midnight, but this couldn't wait. She reached for the phone on her nightstand.

And dialed Garrett's number.

He answered right away, not a hint of grogginess in his voice. As if he'd been waiting for her call.

In a way, she reckoned, he had. All his life, he'd said over and over this last year, he'd loved her.

Steeling herself, she plunged into a detailed account of what had transpired between her and Jon over the last few days. His threats regarding Ian.

But not of the more distant past. She'd never spoken of that stolen-out-of-time summer in Mimosa Grove with another soul.

Not Aunt Velma. Not Holt. And she wasn't going to start now with Garrett.

She plowed ahead, somewhat incoherently, but to give Garrett credit, he never once interrupted. He never so much as made a single sound. When she ran out of words, she stopped.

And waited for him to respond.

"I'd like to say I'm surprised by this, Laura. But I always wondered at the haste you and Holt married the year he got his residency." Garrett took a breath. "And then the other day when I met Locklear . . ."

She swallowed.

"You'd have to be a fool not to see the resemblance between Ian and that cop."

Garrett would never be anyone's fool.

"If you'd come to me then, you know I'd have done anything —" He broke off, choked.

"You're my oldest friend, Garrett."

"I'll do anything you want, Laura. I won't allow him to take your son."

She closed her eyes. She'd known he'd help her. She'd counted on Garrett.

He had connections. Influence. If anyone could fight Jon Locklear and win, Garrett Payne could.

She broached the topic that lay like an unwieldy boulder between them. "We'd have a stronger case if you and I were married, wouldn't we, Garrett?"

Silence stretched taut like a rubber band.

"We would. But I'd never want you to feel pressured to —"

"I'm only suggesting we do now what we've contemplated for months."

"Are you sure? Absolutely positive you want — ?"

"Let's do it. Soon. Make it happen." Before she lost her nerve and Ian.

"I'll need to make an announcement first. I can call in a favor the newspaper editor owes me."

Of course he would. Wouldn't hurt his ranking in the least. His numbers in the polls would soar.

Reality was catching up to his squeaky-clean family-values image. A wife and a ready-made son in the wings before election day.

That would've been her dad's spin on things. And if there was anyone on the planet she wanted to resemble least, it was her father.

Laura winced. She sounded more like her father every day. Another by-product of the lies.

Who was she kidding? She'd become exactly like her lying, scheming father.

"This weekend?" Garrett brought her out of her reverie. "A quiet, little —"

"Not quiet." In for a penny, in for a pound. "Soak it for every ounce of publicity you can get."

"Laura . . ." he exhaled. "I've always loved you."

Bile rose at the back of her throat. She found it difficult to breathe. This one particular lie she'd never been able to utter.

Not to Holt. She'd respected him too much for that. Nor could she find it within her to do so now to Garrett.

"I know, Garrett." She sighed, her voice on the verge of tears. "I know."

As she clicked the phone off, she didn't miss the irony of her situation. Holt hadn't been the man of her choosing eleven years ago. And history, sadly, tragically, had a funny way of repeating itself.

■ ■ ■ ■

Wisps of Laura floated through Jon's semi-conscious dreams. His failure to protect her from himself. His selfishness.

How he pushed her into something she'd been uncomfortable with. How he violated his conscience and her innocence one afternoon by the pond in the pine barrens.

Laura was grieving the loss of her mother. He was reeling from his father's accidental death on the farm. For a heart-stopping, unforgettable moment he looked up at the sound of a car in his mother's gravel drive.

And fallen for a girl he'd not realized until then he'd been dreaming of his entire life. A girl who embodied golden sunshine, sweet tea, and the scent of honeysuckle.

They bonded over their shared losses. Long walks. Church ice cream socials.

Laura spent her mornings learning his mother's textile artistry. They chaperoned the youth group inner-tubing on the Lumber River one afternoon. Watched fireflies each evening and talked on the front porch of his mother's home.

Two souls that recognized, despite their outward differences, a kindred spirit in the other.

He'd not finished growing up when they met that summer. Feeling duty's call to his country and his family, he wrestled with becoming the man of the house after his father's unexpected passing.

Maybe like Ian after Holt Mabry's death?

Pain stabbed at how another man occupied that special place in his son's heart. Jon still missed his dad after all these years and so much mileage in between. An unexpected bond he now shared with his son.

Jon tossed on the mattress, punching and stuffing the pillow under his head as he rolled, trying to flee the recriminations of his sin. And he'd long since repented of his impetuous foolishness. He'd loved her. She said she loved him.

But they'd gotten God's order all wrong, assuming a license for something intended for married people. He'd wanted to marry her. Make things right. Not because of what they'd done. But because he loved her. Always and only loved her.

True repentance had only come after he lost her, as he fathomed the loathsomeness of his iniquity before a holy God. In the sands of a foreign land, he rededicated his life, washed symbolically clean in his first public baptism in the waters of the Euphrates by his good friend Chaplain Grant.

He'd lost Laura, but Jon had gained a brand-new understanding of his Comforter. He spent the intervening years becoming the man God intended him to be.

And now this . . .

He was blowing it again with her. He'd not been the man Laura deserved eleven years ago or the father Ian had needed.

Forgiven certainly. But there were always consequences. And the consequence of his anger and the miscommunication between them made his heart shudder at the loss of ten never-to-be-regained years with his son.

A plan formulated in his mind. He sat up and pushed aside the bedcovers. Swinging his feet to the floor, he stumbled into the kitchen.

Time to apologize to Laura for everything. Beg her forgiveness. Work out an arrangement, with Ian's welfare at the forefront of their negotiations.

His good intentions lasted only as long as it took him to retrieve the morning edition of the paper. In his shock, the soles of his feet barely registered the coolness of the concrete on his stoop.

GARRETT PAYNE, CONGRESSIONAL CANDIDATE, TO WED RALEIGH SOCIALITE, LAURA BOWEN MABRY

This weekend?

Something flew, as his mother would've said, right into him.

It'd been a long, long time since that summer in Mimosa Grove. Too long. They'd both moved on. Taken different roads.

He crushed the paper in his hands. He'd tried to move on with little apparent success. She, obviously, had.

But marry this excrement and give Payne control over his boy?

His mouth tightened.

Not while he had breath in his body. Or, better yet, custody of his son.

That scumbag, Lowther, hadn't shown for work. Laura pulled on her gardening gloves. Never could count on a man to do what needed doing.

Except for Holt, she amended. And now, Garrett.

As she extracted the long-handled loppers from the rack on the garage wall, she remembered it was Memorial Day. Lowther had probably taken the holiday. Ian would be home later.

She'd cut down those noxious, parasitic weeds herself if it was the last thing she did. She didn't need a man to do anything for her.

Except for Holt. She grimaced. And now, Garrett.

Fighting mad at the corner she'd stitched herself into — again — she dragged the clippers to the back line of her property where the vines entwined as thick as her arm. She glared at the twisting roots.

She'd whack them off at the bottom. Kill them at the source. Deprived of nourishment, the rest would die. Painful and agonizing, she hoped.

Like she deserved . . . according to The Accuser.

She gritted her teeth and took a swing at the vines as if she wielded a machete.

For a good part of the morning, she hacked. Her Wolfpack red T-shirt drenched in sweat and her shoulders burning, she stopped for a breath. Only to sense a stealthy presence behind her. A feeling of eyes boring into her back.

She stiffened in gut-twisting terror. Her grip tightened on the loppers.

How could she have forgotten what happened only a mile from this spot just three days ago? She was too close to the greenway. A murderer lurked somewhere out there.

Laura inhaled, bracing and ready to propel the cutting tool like a javelin. Her muscles bunched. Tightening her grip, she hefted the loppers, spun and —

"Jon!"

The shears clattered to the ground. One hand over the erratic beating of her heart, she slumped against a tree.

His face livid, Jon shoved a crumpled newspaper in her face. "What's this, Laura?"

Laura shielded her eyes from the glare of the noonday sun. Squinting as her eyes adjusted, she focused on the offending article in question, an old grainy photo of herself and Garrett. And the headline.

Garrett — the editor a poker buddy — hadn't let any grass grow under his feet.

Dread turned into defiance.

She set her jaw. "I don't answer to you, Jon Locklear."

The scowl on his face deepened. "You're telling me this isn't some ploy to keep my son from me."

"Ian's not your . . ." She bit her lip and tried again. "Garrett and I have been toying with the idea for months." She snorted. "Only someone as egotistical as you would assume our engagement had anything to do with you."

His eyebrows arched. "Oh, really? If you two are so hot and heavy, what's been the holdup till now?" He waved the paper.

"Clue me in on what constitutes a decent interval between a funeral and wedding in your world, Laura."

She was *not* going to let this Neanderthal bully her.

Laura was sick to death of being bullied by her father. By Garrett. By everyone . . .

She crossed her arms. "We were waiting for the right moment to announce it in the hectic pace of campaigning. Not that it's any of your business."

"You mean announce it when it would serve Payne's agenda the most."

She winced, his guess shooting not far off the mark.

He threw the paper to the ground. "And Ian, my son, makes everything you do my business."

Jon's lip curled. "If you think for one minute I'm going to let my son be raised by that talks-out-of-both-sides-of-his-mouth cockroach, you have another think coming, Laura Bowen."

Her eyes narrowed. "When Garrett gets through with you, you won't be allowed within spitting distance of *my,* not *your,* boy."

Jon closed the distance between them so quickly she didn't have time to react. His chest heaving, he backed her against the vines. The prickly thorns tore through the thin cotton of her tee.

He jabbed a finger. "Your daddy and his cronies don't run the North Carolina courts like they did a decade ago when he threatened to clean my clock if I didn't get out of town and leave his precious debutante alone."

"What did you say?"

"You heard what I said. My attorney is ready to file a petition tomorrow for temporary custody and an injunction preventing the RPD's main suspect in the murder of Renna Sheldon from access to my minor son."

She gasped. "No, Jon. It's not true. You can't believe I'd ever —" She flung out her hand and grasped his forearm.

The muscles of his arm tensed, rippled, and jerked away. Her fingertips tingled.

"I believe the evidence, Mrs. Mabry. Means?" He ticked off one finger. "I'll have a search warrant by the end of the day for your house and store."

A second finger. "Opportunity? Like a firebug, some murderers like to hang around to witness law enforcement process the crime scene."

She threw her hands in the air. "What motive? What possible motive could I have for murdering Renna?"

Jon scrunched his eyes into black-banded slits. "Some love triangle going down between you, Payne, and his young political science intern, Renna Sheldon. A fact you so conveniently neglected to mention."

Her eyes widened. "Love triangle? She worked there two afternoons a week. Garrett was in court or on the campaign trail most of that time. It's not true. Lies. It's all lies."

"A topic at which you excel," Jon sneered. "When my lawyer gets through dragging your name and Garrett's through the mud, he won't be able to get elected dog catcher."

"You haven't one iota of evidence of any inappropriate conduct on Garrett's part. You'd destroy a man's career, his life, over your insane — ?"

"Oh, I'll have proof all right. The M.E. found evidence Renna Sheldon was pregnant. We've got tissue samples from the fetus. Won't take much to match DNA to the father."

She reared. "What?"

Renna, pregnant? That explained the surly attitude and so much more.

But Garrett? No way. He deserved her loyalty, her trust, after all he'd done, was doing, for her and Ian.

She lifted her chin. "Your case is nothing

more than circumstantial. Trumped up by a man with a vendetta. A good lawyer will have the charges dismissed within a day."

Jon leaned in so close his breath warmed her cheek. The vein in his neck throbbed with a pulsing beat. She clenched her fists, wanting to strangle him with the vines.

The way the vines of her lies strangled her all these years.

But the treacherous Laura — the one she'd never been able to quell — desperately wanted him to kiss her. To feel once more his lips upon hers and his arms around her. She found it hard to take a breath.

The essence of Jon tugged at her heart, filling her senses. Her lips parted at the tremor of desire that coursed through her veins. An odd look entered his eyes, an utter awareness that turned her insides to liquid.

Her body swayed.

Jon took hold of her shoulders gently. And her skin soaked in the warmth of him like spring absorbed winter's ice.

Had her emotions given her away? Did he guess her feelings for him?

She flushed. And lifted a trembling hand to smooth back a tendril of hair.

His hand caught the tangled lock first, finger combing it in place. Out of habit. A habit born eleven years ago.

Jon's hand froze. His fingers lingered and cupped her ear.

She stilled. Afraid to breathe, afraid of losing this moment, her pulse jackhammered.

His face changed. Something incredible, on the cusp of wonderful, sparked in his eyes.

Jon angled his head as his hold on her tightened. "Laur—"

"Mom! Mom! Are you back there? I'm home."

Jon's hands dropped. He rocked back.

Her heart lodged in her throat, she stepped around him as Ian rounded the corner of the house, dragging his duffel in the grass.

"Mo— Oh." Ian came to an abrupt stop. "I didn't know you had company. Dr. Stephen dropped me off." Ian's gaze traveled between them.

With every nerve ending tingling, she placed her hand over her ear, still feeling Jon's caressing touch. Her fingers instead found a stray leaf, which she plucked out of her hair. Swallowing, her eyes followed the leaf's slow descent toward the ground.

"Mom?"

She jerked and met Ian's darkened eyes. Laura crossed her arms over her chest.

Frowning, Ian moved closer. "Are you okay, Mom?"

She nodded, unable to speak.

Her son inserted himself between them and pivoted, forcing Jon to step back a pace. Squaring his shoulders, Ian extended his hand. "I'm Ian Mabry. Don't believe we've met."

Jon shook his hand, his brown fingers wrapping around Ian's. "I'm . . ." His voice quavered.

Please, God, don't let him say it. Not here. Not this way.

She held her breath.

Jon darted a look at her. His eyes dropped before returning to Ian. His shoulders slumped. "I'm Jon. Jon Locklear."

She released the pent-up breath.

"Your mother and I are old" — Jon cut his eyes at her — "friends."

Ian relaxed his stance. A smile lit his face. He pumped Jon's hand. "Nice to meet you. We stopped at McDonald's for lunch, Mom."

Her son tilted his head with a studied gaze that hopscotched between her and Jon.

Then he grinned at Jon. "But I'm hungry again. Can you stick around for a sandwich or something, Mr. Locklear?"

Jon couldn't seem to tear his eyes from Ian.

She tensed.

"Mr. Locklear?"

Jon blinked.

"Not this time, but thanks, Ian. Maybe another time." Jon pursed his lips. "Your mom and I still have unfinished business to settle."

He placed his hand on Ian's shoulder. "I hear you're a tremendous first baseman."

She bit the inside of her cheek. How had he — ?

Duh, he was a cop with access to databases and he'd done his research. She shuffled her feet.

Her son gestured at the baseball cap stuffed in the back pocket of Jon's jeans. "Durham Bulls. I love the Bulls. You a baseball fan, too, Mr. Locklear?"

"I played a lot of baseball in high school. Please call me . . ." He swallowed. "Call me Jon."

"Maybe we can talk teams next time. My dad was a basketball player."

His dad . . .

She closed her eyes. How long before Jon exploded with the truth?

"Unless I get a growth spurt I'll never be tall enough to be any good like my dad, but who knows what could happen, right, J-Jon?"

In Texas, football might be king. But every born-and-bred North Carolinian lived and breathed Atlantic Coast Conference basketball. March Madness wasn't just a figure of speech.

This had to end. Before Jon lost it and devastated Ian. Hoisting the strap of Ian's overnight bag, she moved toward her son.

Ian wrapped his arms around her, almost knocking Laura off balance. "Missed you, Mom." He buried his face in her shirt and whispered, "I'm sorry for everything I said."

Her sweet, loves-baseball-and-Mom boy. Her and Jon's boy.

She folded Ian in a tight embrace and kissed the top of his hair. He smelled of sun and sea salt.

Jon's mouth wobbled before hardening.

Barking and with his tail in a wagging frenzy, Buggsby bounded out of the screened porch at the sight of Ian. Buggs pranced between them, begging for his ears to be scratched.

"Bye, Mr. Jon." Ian waved and ran forward, roughhousing with his dog.

Jon whipped around. "Who knows what could happen, right, Laura?"

He stalked toward the driveway. "You'll

be hearing from my attorney."

And she knew this wasn't over. Not by a long stretch.

The next time he came to her door, he'd come armed with either a search warrant —

Or a warrant for her arrest.

9

The ache in Jon's heart refused to budge as he drove away from his son and from Laura. White-knuckled, he grasped the wheel. He caught a look at himself in the mirror, at the scowl embedded on his face.

He hated the things he'd said to Laura, how he'd threatened her. And in failing to master his anger — the weakness he'd struggled to control since renewing his commitment to Christ — he'd spewed confidential information that could compromise the investigation.

What was wrong with him?

Had he lost what little mind he had left? But one minute with Laura Bowen and every barrier, every defense mechanism, much less every bit of good sense, flew out the proverbial window. She could make him madder than anyone he'd ever met in his life.

She also, once upon a time, made him the

happiest.

God, what do I do? How do I get my son back?

An answer came. Not one he liked.

"No," Jon ground his teeth. "She's gonna pay for keeping my boy from me."

His cell phone buzzed. He veered into the parking lot of the Village and glanced at the caller ID. Mike.

A text that ordered him in no uncertain terms to get his butt to Mike's house pronto, or else. He texted his ETA.

Jon shoved the gearshift into drive and retraced his route into the Woods Edge neighborhood. The poorer section, as Mike joked. Where people who worked for a living dwelled.

After his performance at Mike's house yesterday, Jon prayed he still had a job. Anxiety gripped his chest. His reflex was to pray, but today he didn't seem to be getting the answers he hoped for.

The peace he'd experienced since that day on the riverbank of the Euphrates eluded him. Scared him by its absence. As if a vital organ had ceased to function.

He shook his head to clear his mind.

Too much going on right now. A murder. A lost son.

He and God would get right after life

slowed. As Jon pulled into Mike's driveway, he found the lieutenant waiting for him. Seated on a bench under the shade of a stately oak, Mike's eyes skewered Jon through the windshield.

Jon's feet dragged as he left the safety of his truck and slogged through the grass. Mike wasn't smiling.

Mike crossed his arms over his black T-shirt. "Finished reading the brief you sent updating me on the latest developments in the Renna Sheldon case. That homeless guy didn't pan out as a suspect?"

Okay . . . This was an official summons.

Jon tensed. Mike hadn't invited him to take a seat. So he stood, feet slightly apart, hands behind his back as in his time with the Marines.

"No, sir. Texas Pete had an ironclad alibi, courtesy of Wake County Sheriff's deputies who were, at the time frame of the murder, processing him to a holding cell in the county jail. Texas Pete awaited a hearing for vagrancy and panhandling without a license."

Mike's chin sank to his chest. "Sorry to hear about that. He was our best lead so far. Your interview yield any results?"

"He claims to have heard an argument in the alley last week between the vic and an unknown male. He was dumpster diving. Didn't bother to crawl out and get a look-see."

"Therefore, no way to ID said male. Could he identify a voice if he heard it again?"

Jon nodded. "He thinks so. But the voice-print he listened to wasn't the guy he heard arguing with Renna Sheldon."

"Garrett Payne."

Jon pounded his fist into his other palm. "He's as dirty as cow manure. I feel it in my gut, Lieutenant."

Mike's eyes narrowed. "Why? Because Payne had the gall to become engaged to a woman you're still in love with?"

"I'm not still —"

"Every time she enters a room you occupy it's obvious how you feel about her."

Mike rose, getting in Jon's face. "You're using my unit as your own personal lynching mob instead of following the trail of evidence and using the brains God gave you. You've lost all objectivity over this woman. A woman you not only have a prior relationship with, but with whom you share a son."

Jon kept his eyes trained on a space slightly above the lieutenant's right shoulder. "Yes, sir — I mean, no sir — uh, yes —"

Mike's steel-gray eyes glinted. "A woman who is a person of interest in this investigation. The minute you recognized her you should've recused yourself from this case as a conflict of interest."

Jon shuffled his feet. "I-I —"

Mike poked him in the chest. "You. You. You. This is not about you. This is about solving the murder of a college coed. Justice. Not your version of revenge on a woman you believe wronged you."

Jon clenched his fist. "Believe? She lied about my son. What else is she lying about? Lying's second nature to this woman."

The lieutenant exhaled, a long breath of air. "Not excusing the lying. But how have you responded to this situation, Jon?" Mike stepped back. "I'm speaking now as your friend. Have you made things better or worse? Have you taken the time to ask God what He wants you to do? Ponder maybe He has a bigger purpose in all this between you and Laura and Ian?"

Jon tightened his jaw.

Mike took a long, hard look at his face. "Your actions have left me no choice in the matter, Locklear." He straightened. "You are hereby put on administrative leave, and you can consider yourself off this case."

Jon swung his gaze toward the lieutenant. "You're firing me?"

Mike shook his head. "No, I'm extending your vacation, unpaid, for the next two weeks. But if I so much as catch a whiff of you interfering in Morales's investig—"

"You gave my case to Ana?"

"Not your case, Locklear. The State of North Carolina's case against the killer of Renna Sheldon. Ana's the most up to speed anyway."

And she'd probably jumped at the chance to prove herself, Jon suspected, a sour taste in his mouth. Had Ana planned that all along? Or just given him enough rope to hang himself with his unprofessional conduct?

Either way, more his fault than her ambition.

Mike clenched his jaw. "I've found a judge this holiday weekend who 'knows not,' as the Scripture says, Judge Bowen. We've got probable cause to search Laura's home. Ana's on her way there now to carry out the warrant."

Jon jerked. "So you think Laura killed Renna Sheldon?"

A smirk twisted the contours of Mike's mouth. "To hear you rant, Locklear, I thought you did, too. I don't want to believe Laura Mabry is guilty of murder. She, Alison, and Val Prescott have been friends forever."

Mike ran a hand through the top of his close-cropped hair, leaving it standing on end like a mohawk. A sure sign of frustration with the lieutenant. "Holt Mabry was one of the finest Christian men I've ever known. My first mentor, besides Stephen Prescott, when I came to the Lord."

He sighed and speared Jon with a look. "But I've got a job to do. A higher calling that I answer to. And I'm not talking about the RPD. Get my drift?"

Loud and clear. Jon gave a terse nod.

Then his gut twisted. "Ian's home from his trip with the Prescotts. Searching the house is going to scare him."

Mike stared off into the distance.

Silence tiptoed between the men.

A neighbor's lawnmower hummed. A robin lighted on the branch above their heads. A nearby magnolia bulged with blossoms, perfuming the air.

The grass grew . . .

"I'll give you this, Locklear — go over to the Mabry house. You tell her the warrant's on its way. Get Ian and her out of there, but don't allow her a moment alone to dispose of or tamper with any potential evidence."

Jon grabbed Mike's hand, pumping it. "Will do. I promise by the book this time, Lieutenant."

"You betcha you will, Locklear. I'm going out on a limb for you and yours. One more unprofessional slip up on your part, and I'll ask for your badge."

Stuffing Ian's beach towel into her canvas bag, Laura heard tires squeal and brake on the street.

Ian rocketed down the stairs three steps at a time. "It's Jon Locklear. He's back." Her son had the front door open before she could get around the center island of the kitchen. Her stomach knotted.

Back meant trouble. Jon never brought her anything but trouble. She slipped her feet into a pair of hot-pink strappy flip-flops.

Not true, her conscience chided. He'd brought her Ian, after all. Remorseful over the way she violated God's law, she'd never regretted the gift of Ian in her life.

Was he here to arrest her for Renna's murder? She tried to swallow past the yarn-ball-size lump clogging her throat. She entered the foyer to find Ian regaling Jon with a recent fish story.

Jon glanced up as she approached, a quick studied appraisal that brought a blush to her cheeks. She crossed her arms over the white coverall that upon hindsight did too little to conceal her blue tankini. She tucked a strand of hair behind her ear.

Why did she always look like something Buggs had dragged through a boxwood hedge every time Jon Locklear paid her a call?

And in a swimsuit at her age?

Belatedly, Laura remembered the creamy white sunscreen she'd forgotten to rub into her face. Her hand flew to her cheek. What a hag she must appear to him in contrast to the last time he'd seen her in a swimsuit.

If he remembered things like ponds and honeysuckle.

But his bemused expression didn't read disgusted. More like . . .

Laura cleared her throat. "We were on our way to the neighborhood pool." She wrapped an arm around Ian's shoulders and drew him against her.

Jon's eyes glinted. "You'd think he had enough sun after a weekend at the beach."

"It's a tradition." Ian wrestled free of her grip. "We always spend the Memorial Day afternoon at the pool potluck. Last year with Aunt Velma." He extended his arm next to

Jon's for inspection. "I've got a natural tan. I don't need much sunscreen. Mom has to slather gallons on her skin." He snickered. "And she still doesn't tan."

Jon smiled at Ian and rumpled his hair. "She freckles." The smile almost extended to his eyes as he glanced over to Laura.

Her face flaming, she massaged the remainder of the sunscreen into her skin. Her eyes lifted to meet his and locked.

A shared look of memory. His lopsided smile reached his eyes this time. She'd always liked the way he smiled at her.

Electricity between them, sharp and clean, crackled. Her heart turned over. A temporary truce? A cease-fire of hostilities?

Ian laughed. "I'm the most tanned in my class. 'Cept for the black kids."

"African American," she muttered to no one in particular.

Jon squeezed Ian's shoulder. "Does it bother you that you're different from the other kids, Ian? Where I come from everybody had skin pretty much the same color as me."

Ian shook his head. "Not really. My dad told me once to be thankful I don't burn like him and Mom. Said with skin like mine when I grew up I'd be a natural-born lady killer." He made a face. "Whatever that means."

Jon gave Laura a sheepish look. "Well, I don't know if I'd go that far . . ."

She squared her shoulders. "I would." She crossed her arms again. "What can we do for you, Detective Locklear?"

He shot a glance at Ian.

"Mom told me about what happened to Renna. I think it's cool you're going to find her killer." He hung on to Jon's arm. "Could I see your badge? Do you carry a gun? Could I — ?"

"Whoa, there." Jon held up both hands. "Yes. Yes. And whatever else you were about to ask, I can guess, and the answer is no."

Jon flicked a glance at her. "I wasn't sure if you'd told him about Renna."

Ian nodded. "She kept grape Dum Dums for me in her purse."

At Jon's bewildered look, Laura translated. "Grape-flavored lollipops."

Jon cleared his throat. "I'm glad you were on your way out."

Laura's heart beat faster.

"One of my colleagues is coming by in a few minutes with a warrant to look for any evidence that might pertain to the Sheldon case."

A search warrant. She allowed herself to breathe. Not an arrest warrant.

Thank you, God.

She'd offered more heartfelt prayers since the murder than she had since Ian's birth. Starting to become a habit. Once she married Holt, Laura hadn't needed God.

"Why?" Ian's eyebrows bunched like tiny caterpillars. He glared at Jon. "Why search our house?"

Ian placed his hands on his small hips. "Do you think my mom killed Renna?" He took a step — a menacing step — toward Jon.

Jon retreated, his back against the doorframe. He shifted his gaze over Ian's head to Laura.

Laura said, "Good question, son. Well, do you, Detective?"

A muscle twitched in Jon's cheek. He stared at her.

Her eyes prodded him to answer the question.

Jon broke eye contact with her and dropped his gaze to Ian. "No, Ian. I don't believe she did."

Laura averted her face, lest Jon see the sudden, unexpected pool of tears. She hadn't realized until now how much his earlier accusations hurt. How much she longed to hear his vindication of her.

Ian lifted his shoulders. "Then why?"

"Because we need to eliminate any innocent people who have a connection with Renna."

"So you're going to prove my mom didn't kill Renna."

Laura touched Ian's sleeve. "I don't think Jon meant —"

"Yes, Ian." Jon's eyes never wavered from his son's. "I think that's exactly what I'm going to do."

Relief washed through her. She groped behind her for the strength of the wall. "We should leave so you can get on with your search."

At the sound of car doors slamming, Ian peered out the sidelights of the door. "Here's your police friends, Jon."

Jon shook his head. "Not my search. Conflict of interest. I've been officially taken off the case. Officer Morales's investigation now."

Ian got that stubborn look in his eye. Mr. Flint Face, Holt used to call him. Reminded Laura of a certain detective standing not a foot away. "They're going to mess with my stuff?"

Jon folded his arms. "Absolutely not, Ian. You and your mom head to the pool. I've been cleared to stick around and make sure my friends put everything back where they find it."

"Really?" She and Ian asked, each canceling the other out.

"I promise."

Ian grabbed Jon's hand. "Can I show Jon my room, Mom? So he'll know how I like to keep my stuff?"

Jon's lean, chiseled features transformed at the touch of Ian's hand on his.

Guilt pierced Laura's heart.

Jon's eyes pleaded for her answer. As did her son's.

She couldn't fight them both.

"Go ahead," she gestured toward the stairs. "But hurry."

Jon hesitated until Ana Morales's frame filled the open door. A tense look passed between them.

Envy gutted Laura. Those two had a relationship. Whereas she and Jon —

She mocked herself. Had she truly believed a man like Jon would go ten years without someone in his life? She was the fool now.

"We'll be right back, Detective Morales." He motioned with his free hand to the stairs. Morales's gaze hardened on his other hand, entwined through the boy's fingers.

As soon as they disappeared to the second

story, the detective lasered Laura with a scathing glance at her scant attire. The Latina extricated a piece of paper from her cotton blazer. Identical to the small, cardboard circle also held by the two uniformed officers on the front porch. A circle, approximately two inches in diameter, a template of some sort.

Laura wasn't the daughter of a former judge for nothing. "The shape of the murder weapon, Detective Morales?"

If she had to defend herself against future charges, better to know what she faced.

Morales's fuchsia-tinted lips curled. She jerked her chin at the men. "Start the search around the perimeter of the house. The garage. Any outbuildings. Anything with an end shaped like that, I want bagged and tagged. I'll wait here with Mrs. Mabry."

The look she threw Laura's way could've sandblasted paint off a building.

Laura tucked the coverall about her body.

"I'm only going to say this one time, Mrs. Mabry. Leave Jon Locklear alone. You've managed to do a number on his head. Almost destroyed his life. I'm warning you. I won't let you destroy his career, too."

"And this is where I keep my baseball card collection. And here," Ian's arm swept the shelf above his twin-size bed. "The airplane models my dad helped me build."

Jon tore his gaze away from the quilt on Ian's bed. "You like airplanes?"

"Yeah. I want to join the Air Force and fly faster than the speed of sound." Gripping one of his fighter planes, Ian raced it across the dormer room accompanied by gender-appropriate zooming noises.

Jon drank in the telltale signs of his son's blossoming personality. The UNC/NCSU "House Divided" banner — Laura and Holt's separate alma maters. Posters of exotic animals, the books on the Wild West. A well-used children's Bible on the nightstand.

In his anger, Jon never once stopped to consider his son's spiritual state. At least one thing Laura had seen to. Or had that been Holt Mabry's doing?

A grudging respect for the late Dr. Mabry grew.

He cleared his throat. "You like cowboys and Indians?"

Ian grinned, revealing strong, white teeth. "I like pretending I'm one of the Indians." He poked his two fingers in a *V* behind his head like a feather. "Mom says I make enough noise to be a war-whooping terror."

Jon fought the urge to grin back. And lost.

"Oh really? Why Indians?"

Ian shrugged. "Don't know. Always have. I'd like to learn to hunt and track deep in the wilderness. If I don't fly planes, I plan on becoming a biologist and studying the creatures God made in their natural habitat."

Jon nodded. "My dad taught me to hunt and track. We killed only what we intended to eat." The last bit Jon threw in, because as a father, he felt duty-bound to say it. Like his dad once told him.

Ian's eyebrows rose. "Say, maybe Mom would let me invite you to come with my Boy Scout troop this weekend." His eyes fell to the Berber carpet. "That is, if you're interested. It's a father-son thing." He shrugged to show his disdain one way or the other for however Jon responded.

Jon swallowed. "I'd be honored to go, Ian. If your mom thinks it's okay."

Maybe while Laura frolicked on her honeymoon with the Pain?

Jon's lips tightened.

Ian's eyes flickered. "Did I say something wrong?"

Loosening his collar, Jon sank onto the edge of the mattress. "Tell me about this quilt, Ian. Did your mom make it for you?"

Ian flopped down on his back, his arms

spread-eagled. "Yep. I had one in my crib, too. She makes bigger ones as I grow to fit my bed."

Tears misted Jon's eyes. His finger traced the red, black, white, and golden swirls of the pinecone pattern.

"Do you know the name of this pattern, Ian?"

Ian arched his body, undulating like the waves of the ocean, rocking the bed. "It's a pinecone. She's got earrings like it that she wears."

Jon's gaze swiveled to his son's bouncing legs. "Why these colors?"

His son threw himself off the bed, a study in motion. "Mom always does my quilts in these colors. She likes yellow a lot. I know."

"Yeah, I know, too."

The red, black, white, and gold were the official colors of the Lumbee tribal logo. The Pinecone quilt, a traditional Lumbee pattern. A pattern Florence Locklear had used in textiles and jewelry to make a name for herself in the art world.

"We should go now, Jon. Mom gets grumpy when she waits."

He herded Ian downstairs past an officer pawing through the contents of Laura's roll-top desk. Ian stiffened. Jon soldier-marched him out to the front porch.

Laura turned an overly bright smile on their son. "Everything okay?" A wide, straw-colored hat shaded her eyes.

Ian grabbed the tote. "I'm going to the pool." He hurtled down the drive, waving good-bye over his shoulder.

Laura hollered using a mother's voice. "You wait for me at the street." She shifted toward Jon. "Everything all right?"

Uncertainty and fear clouded her face.

Fear he put there. A growing shame at his behavior gnawed at Jon. "Beautiful Pinecone quilt."

She licked her lips and stared after Ian. "Not as good as your mother's quilts."

"His grandmother."

She nodded. "But I wanted him to have something of his heritage . . ."

Her eyes glistened. "Holt and I were going to tell him about his background when he was old enough to understand."

Laura raised and lowered her shoulders, a sad, defeated gesture. "We just ran out of time. Holt and me."

Holt.

Taken aback, Jon fought to keep his arms at his side. To not caress her face. To not offer the comfort he so —

Something tore inside him. Raw, fresh pain gouged his soul.

Garrett Payne he could fight.

The memory of Saint Holt he'd never be able to touch.

Jon's chest ached. "I'll find you at the pool when they're done here."

She shouldered the canvas beach bag. "We'll be waiting." And set off after Ian.

Jon's eyes followed her until the stand of trees obscured her from his sight.

He'd see her again. See her and Ian again. Soon.

Not everything he wanted. Not by a long shot.

But it was a start.

10

Lounging poolside, Laura arrived at the unhappy conclusion Ana Morales would pin Renna's murder on her, for lack of a better suspect, unless Laura did something about it. And soon.

She waved at Ian poised on the edge of the diving board. He bounced on the balls of his feet, once, twice, three times, the board springing. The fourth time — with a decisive twang from the board — his body arched. And he performed a perfectly executed flip before breaking the water's surface with only the teeniest of splashes.

As his head topped the ladder to see if she'd been watching, Laura broke into a round of muted applause. Enough to show her approval. Not enough to draw unwanted attention from the older guys he headed off to join at the Ping-Pong table.

She knew the drill.

Heat shimmered on the concrete. The heat

rebounded and slapped those not fully immersed in the blue chlorinated water with the double whammy of a one-two punch. Removing a notepad, like Jon employed, she created a list of everyone she could think of who knew Renna. Laura could conduct her own private interrogations, with questions a stranger — and a member of the male gender — might not think to ask.

A short list.

1. Doris Stanley

Renna had been staying the summer with Doris and the General while her mother enjoyed her seventh honeymoon in the Mediterranean.

2. Aunt Velma

Velma knew everybody. And she knew everything about everybody. But seldom told everything she knew unless she had a mighty good reason. Her aunt could be a cagey old bird.

3. ?

Her attacker and Renna's killer, Laura'd bet the shop, was a man. Renna spent time at Garrett's campaign headquarters. Maybe it wouldn't hurt to ask Garrett a few questions, see what he remembered about the political science intern.

Laura flushed, recalling Jon's lurid suspicions about Garrett.

Which were absolutely untrue. And she'd prove it. But she added Garrett's name to the list.

4. Garrett Payne

She'd have to be subtle. He'd be infuriated at what Jon suggested — and hurt — if he believed Laura put any stock into those lies. But he'd have to understand this was for his own good. Better to clear the air and have nothing damaging hanging over his career.

An aroma of coconut oil, chlorine, and sun wafted across the breeze. A shadow loomed over Laura, blocking the light.

Startled, Laura craned her neck, pushing up the brim of her floppy hat.

"Oh, Patti." Laura put a hand over her heart. "I didn't hear you."

Sunshades as big as sunflowers, Patti dragged a lounge chair alongside Laura's. "My husband says I have the sneakability of a ninja."

Patti reclined, her white string bikini reflecting her toned, muscled body. "Useful I say for keeping track of my tomcat husband." She kicked off a pair of mannish navy-blue deck shoes, probably Woodrow's, and pointed her toes sunward.

Her marital escapades were the stuff of legend — Old Raleigh legend.

"But what's good for the goose is good for the gander." Patti snatched at the paper lying in Laura's lap.

Too late, Laura made a grab for it.

"What's this? The beginning of a wedding guest list? I sure hope my name will be included."

Having given no thought to any such thing, she gave Patti a weak smile. "Of course," Laura hedged. "Soon as Garrett and I finalize the details."

Like whatever Garrett's campaign fashion stylist ordered her to wear to the photo-op wedding.

Patti laid the paper on the arm of Laura's chair. "I hate to think of losing my favorite shopkeeper to the intrigues of the Capital Beltway."

A humid breeze fluttered the paper. Laura paperweighted the paper with her fist. "Garrett will be an asset to our government, and I try to remember the opportunities it will bring Ian, too."

Patti stretched like a sleek Siamese. "Garrett brings a lot of assets to any table. You're one lucky woman."

A good fifteen years Laura's senior, Patti had the shape of a much more youthful woman. More youthful than Laura, whose assets didn't stack quite so well as Patti's.

Laura's eyes flicked to Patti's incongruous pedicure, misplaced on the older woman's ploughboy feet.

Laura was lucky to have someone in her corner like Garrett, who'd proved his devotion over and over. But she didn't like the tone in Patti's voice, her inference unmistakable.

Often the best defense was a good offense.

"I know you and Renna's mother are good friends. Did you know Renna was pregnant?"

Patti chuckled, like gears grinding. "You don't say? Well . . ."

"Any idea who's the father? I thought I'd ask Doris if Renna had been dating someone."

Patti's mouth went razor sharp. "I could hazard a few shot-in-the-dark guesses."

Laura waited for the effusive Patti to elaborate.

Patti didn't.

"Like who?" Laura prompted.

A palpable fury seeped from the usually laid-back socialite. "Like maybe that no-good scumbag I married."

"Surely not, Patti." Woodrow Ogburn, attorney-at-law?

"Woody likes 'em young." Patti's sensuous mouth rounded. "Though he usually prefers blondes. But he's got the attention span of a dragonfly when it comes to the fairer sex."

The rotary cutter calling the needle sharp . . .

"But how would they — ?" Laura bit her lip.

Patti smirked.

"I mean when . . . ?"

Laura lapsed into silence.

Southern Belle 101 didn't cover how to ask such a question.

Patti leaned closer. "Last winter, Hilary Munro's husband, Woody's partner in the firm, taught a law class at the university. Renna spent a lot of time at the office doing research for a paper." The older woman snorted. "You believe that and I've got some nice property in the Great Dismal Swamp I'd like to sell you."

An ugly look contorted Patti's features. "You need any DNA to tie Woodrow to that dead girl and her baby, you give me a call. I'll give you enough DNA from that louse — from where it hurts — to nail his sorry hide to the wall."

There was your mental picture.

"Speaking of hides," Laura changed the subject. "I haven't seen hide nor hair of Zeke Lowther since Friday. He left his tools, too." Laura frowned. "Exactly what project did he do for you, Patti?"

"Oh, this and that." Patti smiled like the cat that swallowed the cream. "Whatever I needed him to turn his hand to do."

"Well, I need him to finish the job I hired him to do. To build that fence."

"I'm sure your yummy Lumbee detective could work something out."

Laura stiffened. "He's not my —"

"Honey, the sparks between you two the other day at Tapestries could've lighted the entire Raleigh Memorial Day fireworks show."

The veiled innuendos had gone way past distasteful.

Laura stuffed the list in her tote, making excuses about needing to get her casserole for the potluck ready.

"And looky here. Speak of the devil." Patti licked collagen-pouty lips. "A handsome devil."

Laura swiveled. Patti pushed her shoulders back — and other portions of her anatomy forward in Jon's direction.

Scrambling to her feet, Laura snagged one of her flip-flops on the towel lining her recliner. She and the chair tumbled. Her arms flailed.

The chair hit the pavement with a clunk

of metal. Jon grabbed her around the waist just in time to keep her from landing on her butt. Laura sagged in his arms.

Of all the klutzy, inelegant moves . . . it had to happen in front of Jon Locklear.

Her cheek against his shirt, she felt his heartbeat moving at a furious clip. Hammering to a beat that matched her own. She fought the urge to tuck her face into the curve of his neck.

But Jon brushed his lips across the top of her hair and inhaled.

Her breath stutter-stepping, she found herself hoping, wishing —

With a grunt, Jon settled Laura onto her flip-flopped feet.

She searched his face, but dark glasses obscured his eyes.

Jon gave Patti, however, a white, even-toothed smile. "Miz Ogburn," in that country boy drawl of his, "Laura . . ."

A drawl, which came and went according to his own ulterior purposes. The drawl — combined with a faint aura of recklessness — that drove women wild. A drawl that once sent shivers down Laura's pearlescent painted toes.

That still —

Stop being an idiot.

Men — Laura reflected not for the first

time — were too often, at the sight of an attractive female like Patti, rendered hormonally stupid.

Settling her bag on her shoulder, she yanked Jon out of earshot of Patti. Patti waggled her fingers good-bye.

"Your police buddies gone yet?"

A muscle jumped in his cheek. He pushed the sunshades onto the crown of his head. "They're gone."

"Good." Pleased to see the vapid look wiped right off his too-handsome face, she stuffed her sunglasses into the bag.

"Hey, man." A dripping, shivering Ian sidled up beside them.

Jon grinned. "Hey, man, yourself." His eyes flickered over Laura before he turned his body away. He muttered something under his breath that sounded like the word *covenant* and inserted space between himself and Laura.

She slung the tote on the ground.

Ian and Jon stepped back to save their toes.

Flushing, she gathered the cover-up over her tankini. "We're leaving, Ian. I need to stop by and see Grandpa this afternoon."

Ian's eyebrows rose toward his wet, slicked-back hairline. "Can't I stay and hang out with Jon?"

"Jon probably has a dozen things he needs to be doing. Not baby —"

"I'm not a —"

Jon cleared his throat. "I can think of nothing I'd rather do than spend time with Ian. Maybe try out that ice cream shop at the Village, Sugardaddy's. If that'd be okay with you, Laura?"

Ian steepled his hands as if in prayer, bobbing on his tippy-toes. "Please, Mom? Please?" Water from his swim trunks dribbled onto the concrete.

The longing in Jon's eyes was no less intense.

She waffled. This was exactly what Garrett had told her not to do.

Give Jon an inch, she was deathly afraid he'd take a mile. But what she had to say to his father was best done without Ian's inquisitive presence.

"All right."

Ian sprang in the air to high-five Jon.

She held up her index finger. "One hour and I want you both back at the house."

Their heads, so alike, nodded simultaneously. Like two little boys willing to promise anything to escape.

"Got to get my goggles," shouted Ian. Running to the other side of the pool, Ian's feet slapped the pavement as if he feared she'd change her mind.

The lifeguard blew a short blast on his whistle. "Slow down, mister."

Ian slowed his pace to the legal limit.

Silence ticked between her and Jon.

Wishing in equal parts to be away from Jon Locklear *and* to throw herself into his arms, she struggled to fold the towel.

"Here," he reached for the other end. "Let me help."

Laura watched him fold his half and enjoyed the play of his muscles along his bicep.

"Sorry about . . ." She fluttered one hand toward the upside-down chair. "Always so ladylike."

Their fingers touched as he brought his end even with hers.

An electric current tingled the tips of her fingers.

She wondered if she had the same effect on him as his touch had on her.

Maybe so . . . he thrust the towel at her and backed away.

Maybe not.

She retrieved the tote. Adjusting the strap sliding off her shoulder, she scuffled a stray pebble from the parking lot with her flip-flop. "Not quite the girl you remembered, huh?"

Jon's eyes went opaque.

He brushed an errant wisp of hair from her face. "You're still the most beautiful woman I've ever known." His voice ended on a husky whisper, and he jammed his hands into the pockets of his jeans.

"Uh, guys?"

At their elbows, Ian studied them, his brown eyes alert, a funny look on his face.

She and Jon drew back as though stung.

"Can we go get the ice cream now, Jon?"

Sitting outside Sugardaddy's on one of the umbrella-topped wrought-iron tables, Jon watched Ian's tongue work its way around the gigantic waffle cone in a vain attempt to capture every last morsel of the blue-and-red Spider-Man Delight.

A son.

Jon tilted back in his chair. And here he was, on a fine Memorial Day afternoon, eating ice cream with his new favorite kid.

"Umm, Jon?"

"Yeah, champ?"

"Would you mind if I ask you something?"

Jon took a quick swipe of his melting Cookie Dough Dream cone. "Sure. Go ahead."

"You and my mom knew each other before she married my dad, didn't you?"

His earlier elation abated. "Yeah . . ."

Murky waters. And a neon sign shouting Caution.

"Exactly how long ago was that?"

Flashing — Dangerous Currents Ahead.

This line of questioning could end nowhere good. Despite wanting to burst with the truth, Jon forced himself to honor Laura's wishes.

For now.

"A while back."

Calculation gleamed in Ian's eyes. As if he knew Jon wasn't giving him the straight up and up, but as if he'd give Jon the benefit of the doubt.

For now.

"You like my mother, don't you?"

Hunching, Jon gripped the fragile cone. "She's a fine woman."

The cone cracked. Cold oozed between his fingers.

"I heard you say you think she's beautiful."

This one didn't miss a trick. Maybe a career as the next 007.

He decided not to comment.

"I know she likes you, too."

Jon wasn't about to let that one go. "What makes you think that?" He took a big bite of what was left of his cone.

The cold hit his teeth like a sledgehammer.

"Way she gets all flustered when you're around, turns red, looks at you the way I feel about an orange sherbet push pop on a hot day."

Jon sputtered dairy globules over the sidewalk. When he regained his breath, he wiped his mouth. "And you'd be an authority on these things how?"

Ian shrugged, focusing on his neglected cone. He swung his feet under the chair. "That's the way Justin gets when Sandy Fleming from church comes around. Claire explained it."

Jon grimaced. "I bet she did."

Claire Monaghan, expert on all things.

Seeing Ian's sticky hands, he handed the boy a stack of napkins. Jon wrapped his mouth around another portion of the cone.

"I'm not some stupid little kid."

Ten going on twenty-five . . .

"I can see that."

"Anyway, would you consider marrying my mother?"

The ice cream slid down Jon's windpipe in one large gulp. He choked.

Ian pounded Jon's back. Tears leaked from underneath Jon's eyelids.

Tears due to a lack of oxygen.

"I-I have your p-permission then?" Jon's voice sounded strangled to his own ears.

His son handed him a clean — semiclean — napkin. "Finding out about Renna's murder wasn't the only bad news I got today from Mom."

Jon's tooth ached from the coldness of the ice cream. He clamped a hand over the spot. "Weally?"

Ian's nose crinkled. "Told me she's decided to marry that Pain."

Jon would've laughed at Ian's bulging lower lip that made the Grand Canyon seem small, but a headache had developed over Jon's left eyeball.

"Course I already knew about it, but I didn't let on that I did."

"You did?" Jon gave his head a vigorous shake in an attempt to blunt the pain. "Or didn't, I mean?"

Ian snorted. "They got newspapers at the beach, too, you know."

Anger tugged at Jon. "You shouldn't have had to find out that way, Ian. I'm sorry."

Ian shrugged. "At Dr. Stephen's, after I got over my fit —"

"Your what?"

"Hissy fit is what Aunt Velma calls them. Temper tantrum. Anger management issues. Mom says I get it honest."

Jon reddened. Between his temper and Laura's, the boy hadn't stood a chance in that gene pool department.

"But Dr. Stephen explained nobody could make me mad unless I chose to be mad. And how as a Christian, I was a terrible witness to others when I gave in to those feelings instead of handling them the right way, God's way."

Jon swallowed. "What else did Dr. Stephen suggest?"

Ian sighed. "He asked me if my mom had been sad since Dad died."

Did he want to hear the answer to this?

Jon took a deep breath. "And what did you say?"

"She cries a lot. Did cry a lot," Ian amended, "till she got busy opening her shop. But I can tell she's still sad. Dr. Stephen asked me if she seemed better when she was with Garrett."

Jon closed his eyes. "And is she?"

At the silence, Jon opened his eyes.

Ian tore off a tiny square of the napkin. "Some. But my dad didn't like Garrett Payne."

"Do you know why, Ian?"

"Heard him tell Mom once, Garrett was like a teensy bit of dog poop sticking in the sole of your shoe no amount of scraping or cleaning shakes free." Ian squinted at Jon. "You know what I mean?"

"Can't get rid of it, but it sure stinks up the house till it wears off?"

Ian smiled. "I think you and my dad would've liked each other. Had a lot in common."

Jon bit the inside of his cheek, the truth of that hitting too close for comfort. If ever an understatement . . .

Ian plucked off another square of the napkin. "I think Garrett was waiting on the sidelines, on deck like in baseball, hoping my dad would drop dead, and then he could step up to bat. He doesn't like me, you know."

Jon's chest tightened. "Oh?" His voice went soft.

That dangerous softness when he caught the target in his crosshairs. "Why do you think that?"

Ian stacked the squares and added more. "Just a feeling I get. I think he can't wait to rustle up with Mom a set of blue-eyed, blonde-haired little Garretts to add to his Christmas cards."

Jon's forehead creased.

"I give it a year." Ian started a second pile. "He'll have me shuttled off to reform school like that evil almost-stepmother in *The*

Sound of Music."

Jon clenched the edge of the table. "I will do everything in my power to make sure that doesn't happen."

Ian — his son — smiled. "I thought you might say that. I was worried when I came home from the beach till I saw you and Mom pressed against the vines."

A flush mounted from beneath Jon's collar.

"But I prayed over the situation with Dr. Stephen before we left Carolina Beach. I knew it wasn't right to keep my mom from finding true happiness."

Rolling another napkin into a spyglass, Ian held one end up to his eyeball. "I couldn't see Garrett being the answer, but I left it in God's hands and voilà!"

Voilà?

Ian slugged Jon on the shoulder. "Sometimes God works fast."

Jon stared at Ian. The corners of his mouth turned up.

He'd never met a boy like Ian Mabry before. His son, Jon reminded himself with a flicker of pride. A strange, interesting, infinitesimally wonderful mix of him and Laura.

Ian grabbed the watch on Jon's arm and peered at it. "Now you've got to work fast.

We've only got till Friday to change her mind."

Nothing like a little pressure to motivate.

11

Laura changed into a pair of lime-green capris and a pale-pink blouse. Feeling contentious, she declined to add the *de rigueur* pearl earrings and strand at her throat. She pointed the nose of her Lexus toward downtown and the affluent neighborhood where she'd grown up.

Pulling alongside the two-story Colonial Revival, she lingered, trying to compose herself. Mr. Smoke and Mirrors had some answering to do.

Getting out of her car, she strode up the flagstone path leading to the white-columned porch. Fire truck–red geraniums and trailing ivy spilled out of black marble urns on either side of the door. She rang the bell.

It was no longer Laura's home. Not since her stepmother, Barbara, had wiped the house free of all traces of Laura's mother.

As if Louise never existed.

The housekeeper opened the door. At the sight of Laura, her smile crinkled her eyes. "Miss Laura, how good to see you." She gestured Laura into the spacious entrance hall.

Mrs. Andrews's welcome always warmed the cold places of Laura's heart. Especially since the day she'd run over from Aunt Velma's to retrieve the Bible her mother left in the upstairs master. A day Laura discovered her father had found other ways to console himself pending the imminent loss of his devoted wife.

A consolation found in the arms of his secretary, Barbara Payne, Garrett's mother.

That perchance encounter, which she suspected had been engineered by the devious Barbara, had staggered Laura, already reeling from her mother's rapid decline. The affair had probably also prompted Louise to spend her last days in the Jones home at Woods Edge with Aunt Velma.

Laura shoved aside the painful memories. "Is my dad awake, Mrs. Andrews?"

"Indeed, he is. And where he is most days after the nurse gives him his bath, and we get him settled in his chair."

"The library?"

Mrs. Andrews nodded. "He'll be so glad you came. He looks forward to you and that sweet little boy coming. Like a ray of sunshine, your visits perk him up."

Guilt stabbed for not visiting more. But she struggled to forgive the man who betrayed not only her dying mother but also their life together as a family.

As for Barbara . . . ?

Distaste twisted Laura's mouth.

Waiting in the wings for Laura's mother to die, Barbara weaseled her way into marrying Judge Emerson Bowen six weeks after they laid Louise to rest at Oakwood Cemetery.

Mrs. Andrews drew Laura past the magnificent circular staircase. "You've missed Mrs. Bowen. She's with her son this afternoon." The housekeeper's mouth quirked.

And with any luck — Laura finished the unspoken joke they shared — she'd be gone before the Dragon Lady returned from doing her filial duty at Garrett's campaign appearance. Garrett made sure his mother's and Laura's paths seldom crossed.

Mrs. Andrews left Laura at the partially closed door. Squaring her shoulders, Laura rapped lightly. "Dad?" She pushed it open.

Time to deal with yet another act of malfeasance on her father's part.

She stepped into the room that had been her childhood favorite. Here, Emerson had put his foot down with Barbara. No remodeling. Time stood still in this place, if none other. Laura didn't have to look to take in the details. In this room, her mother's presence remained.

Louise's colorful gardening books lay scattered across the coffee table as if she'd stepped outside to return any moment. Her father's judicial books lined the oak-paneled shelves. His law degree and awards hung on the wall behind his desk. As did the gavel first used by a Civil War–era Bowen mounted on pegs below the framed honors.

Her father slumped in his chrome wheelchair.

Parked behind the mahogany desk where he'd spent hours researching judicial decisions, these days the contrast between the symbol of his ambition and his shrunken shell of a body was stark. A stroke one month after Holt's accident had left the once all-powerful legal arbiter broken and helpless.

Emerson's white head raised at the sound of her soft footfalls across the hand-knotted Persian carpet. His dark, ocean-blue eyes took on a glow. Pleasure lifted his face, except for the drawn right side. He worked his mouth, but only garbled noises came forth.

Laura wondered sometimes if that would be her fate one day, too — the fate of all liars — before a righteous Judge. To be rendered incapable of uttering any more lies.

She sighed. Her big head of justifiable steam vaporized at the sight of the husk that contained his formerly brilliant personality.

Emerson's twisted hand clawed at an open Bible. Laura's brow furrowed. Her mother's Bible?

"Dad, it's me, Laura."

Unnecessary, but it filled the silence. The stroke hadn't robbed him of his quick mind, only eradicated his powers to communicate.

"E-E —"

Ian.

Funny, how her father had despised Jon and the Lumbee neighbors in the rural county where both had risen to manhood. But, to give her father his due, Emerson adored her son.

Their son, hers and Jon's.

People, herself included, were such an inexplicable mixture of contradictions.

"No, Dad. I didn't bring Ian with me today. He's having ice cream with —"

She took a deep breath. "With his father."

A look of confusion.

Then, Emerson's eyes narrowed. "J-J-n."

"Yes, Dad. Jon's come back into my life."

With a bang.

"Is it true you threatened him that summer if he continued to see me?"

She braced for the superior look by which Emerson judged most of the world, especially his social inferiors in Mimosa Grove. Instead, his lined face crumpled. He dropped his shaky, gnarled hand into his lap and hung his head.

Tears pricked Laura's eyes. She crossed the room and fell to her knees beside his chair. "Oh, Dad. How could you? You know how I loved him. He made me so . . ."

Laura turned her head, blinking away the moisture, and gazed hard at the wall behind them. She frowned. Something wasn't —

"So-o-o-rrreee."

His weak hand, featherlight, brushed the crown of her head.

Laura jolted.

Sorry?

Maybe she hadn't understood him. Emerson Sterling Bowen the Fourth didn't apologize.

"Jon swears he doesn't know anything about the woman I discovered in his room. I never believed him before. If I had . . ."

Her voice broke. "Why, Dad? Why hire someone and hurt me like that? Your pride cost me everything."

Emerson's face contorted. His lips puckered, wheezing with the effort. "No-oo, Laaa—"

"What's going on here?"

Laura's head jerked to the doorway where Barbara stood, hands on her Ann Taylor-clad hips. Emerson shrank into the chair.

Her ash-blonde stepmother advanced into the room like a mother lioness defending her cub. "If all you can do — when you deign to favor us with your presence — is upset your father, I will have to establish boundaries. Such as visiting only when I am present."

Laura rose, though the statuesque Barbara towered over her petite frame. Emerson groped for Laura's hand.

Not in a forgiving mood, Laura snatched it out of his reach.

Barbara rounded the desk and crooked her arm around Emerson's frail shoulders. "I simply will not allow you to upset your father this way. Sets him back for days."

Nothing and no one — not even poor Garrett — ever took precedence over Emerson with Barbara.

Laura swallowed. "I'm sorry." She fought to keep the tears at bay in front of her stepmother. "It won't happen again."

"La-La—rrrraaaa."

Hardening her heart, she wheeled toward the door.

"Oh, Laura, dear?"

She paused, her hand on the doorknob.

"Let me be one of the first to wish you and my son all the happiness in the world." Barbara's mouth stretched in what passed for a smile. "May you both be as happy together as your father and I have been."

Emerson choked.

Her stepmother's mocking lilt followed Laura out of the house. And for the first time since discovering Emerson's affair, Laura experienced a stirring of sympathy for her father.

Laura shuddered, thinking of her father trapped in a vise of his own making. But as she contemplated her estrangement from Jon and the lost years Ian might someday come to hate her for, Laura realized there were all different kinds of bondage.

Some chains you forged yourself.

Ian took a gander at the clock. "We ought to start that casserole for Mom. She's running late. You'll go with us to the potluck, won't you, Jon?"

Jon studied the renovated 1950s retro kitchen. "I don't know, Ian. Your mom may have other plans."

This house was so Laura. The outside, refined and elegant. The inside, the kitchen in particular, revealed her quirkiness.

"We could help her." Perched on the island stool, Ian kicked the wooden base with his feet.

Clunk. Clunk. Clunk.

"The *Bible,*" Ian eyed Jon. "Says we're supposed to help others."

Jon added TV evangelist to his running tally of future occupations for Ian.

Ian pantomimed a layup. "Do you have any slam-dunk meals?"

Jon rolled his eyes. "Ian, my man, I don't even do a mean microwaveable dinner."

He fingered the silver hardware complementing the mint-green glass backsplash. "My mother would love this kitchen. Your mom must spend a lot of time here."

Ian shrugged. "I guess. She made lots of fancy stuff when Dad was alive. Lots of parties every weekend in our other house."

Jon ran his hand over the built-in drain board on the counter space next to the deep farmer's sink. "Do you miss your old house?"

Rocketing off the stool, Ian nudged him aside to wash his hands. "Nah. Got to stay at the same school. That's all I cared about. The old house made us too sad. We always had good times here when we visited Aunt Velma. This place made Mom feel . . ." He reached for the hand towel. "Safe. Mom always loved old houses better than new ones. I haven't had as many nightmares here, either."

Jon frowned. "Nightmares?"

Ian opened the fridge. "Bad dreams after Dad died. Kept seeing Dad's car crashing into that tree like the test dummies do. I keep screaming for him to stop. Sometimes I'm in the car. Sometimes I just see it." He shook his head. "But I can't ever stop it from happening."

Jon draped an arm across Ian's shoulders. "I'm so sorry you and your mom had to go through that."

Ian returned his hug. His head just topped Jon's chest.

Jon wrapped both arms around his son. He relished a moment that might never come again. A gift. A grace he didn't deserve.

"Yoo-hoo! Anybody home? Spotted the truck parked out front."

Velma poked her blue-rinsed head through the kitchen door. The screened porch door banged as Tayla sashayed in behind her.

"Aunt Velma." Ian released him so quickly Jon staggered against the picture-clad fridge.

Velma stood on tiptoe to receive Ian's exuberant hug. Her china blues twinkled. "What're you guys up to? I take it my Laura isn't home."

"She will be anytime." Ian bounced. "We were about to make something for the potluck. But Jon," he jabbed a finger in Jon's direction. "He doesn't do food preparation."

"I'm right glad I caught you here, Jon."

Jon dragged his attention from the photos of Ian at school, Ian the Boy Scout, Ian's fourth grade art project, et cetera, that adorned the refrigerator. No wonder Laura had blocked his entry that first day.

A look passed between Velma and her young attendant. "Tayla's taught me about something called Facebook. She helped me create a website for our Weathersby Quilters."

Velma patted Ian's head. "I expect you know about Facebook," pride at her techno-lingo evident in her voice.

"Sure, Aunt Velma."

But Jon could tell Velma had something on her mind other than the joys of social media.

"Ian, I sent your Mom a friend request. Maybe you could show Tayla her profile on the computer, and if you think she'd like to be friends with me, hit confirm. Got to build my followers."

Velma cocked her head like a pert Carolina wren. "Or is that a tribe?" She threw up her hands. "I forget."

Ian laughed. "Of course, Mom'll be your friend. She already are." He winked to show her he was kidding.

She gave his bottom a swat, shooing him. *"Is,* young man. *Is."* He and Tayla departed for the front room.

Jon leaned against the counter, feet crossed at the ankles, feigning a nonchalance he didn't feel. "I take it you want a moment alone with me."

Velma laid her voluminous pocketbook on the island. It clattered as it landed.

What did she have in there? A brick? With Velma, you never could tell.

Velma attempted to hitch her leg onto the stool. She frowned and arched an eyebrow.

Taking the hint, he offered a hand. Soaking wet, Velma Louise Jones would only weigh ninety pounds. A pleasant old lady smell, of talcum and lavender, floated past his nose.

Settling her derrière on the cushion, she cleared her throat. "I decided I'd enlighten you as to what's been happening in Laura's life since you two parted ways."

Jon scowled. "Not my choice. And if I'd

had any idea —"

She shushed him, her bony white finger over his lips.

Velma darted a glance toward the front of the house. "That boy's got ears like a hawk. You copy that, Locklear?"

"Yes, ma'am."

"No need to be yes ma'aming me. Makes me feel as old as Methuselah."

She waved a tiny hand in the air. "I figured I needed to tell you some things — about Holt Mabry — Laura will never tell you herself. Things she'll never, out of an undying sense of loyalty to a good man, ever explain to you."

Jon bristled. "Here we go. Saint Holt Day."

With a glare, Velma fixed him like a bug on the end of a pin. "Now don't you go and take that attitude with me, mister. You get right off that high horse you're riding these days, and let me tell you a thing or two about what's what."

Jon tamped down his resentment. Perhaps he might learn something that could turn things to his advantage with Laura regarding Ian's situation.

"Any of your people called Ian?"

Jon blinked, thrown off guard by her apparent change of topic. "No, ma'am. Not to my knowledge."

Velma sighed at the ma'am part. "Didn't think so. Ian, in case you didn't realize it, is a Welsh name."

Jon nodded slow, not sure where she was going with this. "Lots of Welsh and Highland Scots settled near Mimosa Grove alongside the Lumbee. Like the Bowens."

"And the Joneses," Velma added for good measure.

Velma splayed her fingers across the surface of the island. "Holt Mabry grew up the boy-next-door to Laura here in Raleigh. His parents were killed in a plane crash over Liberia when Holt was in high school. My Louise — Laura's mother — she died before you two met that summer . . ."

A sheen of tears peppered Velma's eyes. She blinked rapidly.

Jon kept still, giving Velma a moment to recover.

"Holt had been in love with Laura since junior high. He was a few years ahead of her in school. When his parents died, my Louise semiadopted him, and he became a large part of Laura's life. Louise — and I excuse her 'cause she'd just discovered she had stage-four breast cancer — pushed Laura into accepting an engagement ring from Holt when Laura went to college."

"You don't have to tell —"

"I taught Florence Oxendine and Clarence Locklear high school English, and I'm pretty sure they taught you to not interrupt your elders."

"Yes . . . ma'am."

She winced and flicked a pointed look at him to let Jon know his barb wasn't lost on her.

"Louise, like all the Joneses, was tougher than she looked, and she hung on till dying the spring of Laura's junior year."

He shuffled his feet.

"You know some of this. Emerson threw that engagement announcement in your face the day you reported to Parris Island. An engagement Laura hadn't bothered to share with you that summer."

His face flushed with remembered anger.

She held up a hand. "But hear me out. Laura and Holt both went into that engagement as a means of putting a dying woman's concerns to rest. I think Louise already knew that Emerson and Barb— well, that's best not spoken of at this late date. Neither Laura or Holt thought it anything more than a meaningless gesture, though I'm sure Holt always hoped . . ."

"Always two — sometimes three — deep in admirers, isn't our Laura?" He gave an ugly, hopeless laugh. At himself. "Always keeps a spare. Better prepared than most Girl Scouts." Jon crossed his arms. "And when Laura believed I'd betrayed her, she turned to him, and Holt was more than willing to accommodate. Even another man's child." He bit his lip until he tasted the salty tang of his own blood.

Velma tucked her chin into her chest. "Holt was the man Laura needed when she needed someone the most."

"And I wasn't that man?"

Velma's eyes clouded. "No, Jon. You weren't. But she never forgot you."

Jon braced his hands against the contours of the sink.

"Laura tried. God help her, she tried. I witnessed the pain she lived with. Ten years of pain. Her heart belonging always to you, the guilt she suffered for failing to be the wife Holt deserved."

Jon closed his eyes.

"You may choose not to believe this. That is your right. To go on being angry. To blame Laura for everything that happened. But I hope — I pray — the two of you will work out a way to share Ian and maybe even . . ."

Velma sighed, the sound like autumn leaves rustling in the wind. "This meddling old woman has interfered enough for one day, I reckon."

She slid off the stool and let gravity have its way. Smiling, she landed her dismount in the fine tradition of world-class gymnasts.

"You think on what I said."

He nodded.

"And Jon?"

"Yes, Miss Velma?"

"The name Ian is Welsh."

She laid a papery thin hand over his cheek. "But in English, it translates to *John.*"

12

The sun had begun its slow, summertime descent from the sky when Laura drove up to her house. Pink, orange, and lavender streaks needled the treetops. She noted Jon's F-150 and her Aunt Velma's Crown Vic alongside the curb. Raising the garage door, she slid into her usual spot, parked, and flung herself out of the car.

Emerging into the kitchen, Laura blinked. At the chopping block, Jon deftly sliced bananas. Was he wearing — ?

Couldn't be. But he was.

"Are you wearing my apron?"

Jon's eyes lit at the sight of her.

Causing her heart to skip erratically.

"I believe the correct term is *frock-saver.*" A grin bracketed his mouth. "Not every guy could pull this off, you know."

And pull it off he did.

He managed to make the ruffled pink polka dot apron seem manly. Could be the

Maui Jim shades hanging around his neck. Or perhaps the well-tapered Levis that —

"Hey, Mom."

Ian's voice tore her fascinated gaze away from where Jon gripped the knife, his muscles bunching and releasing. She battled to keep her eyes focused on Jon's face. The hard, high cheekbones. The strong white teeth and chiseled lips —

Actually, that wasn't too good an idea, either.

Her eyes scanned for a safer spot to linger.

Was it just her or was it hot in here? Why was it always so hard to breathe in any space Jon occupied?

She fanned herself with her hand.

His lips tilted upward, wolfish, amused. He crooned a tune under his breath. A wicked gleam sparked in his eyes as if he —

Laura's cheeks flamed.

This thing between them — he always seemed to know and feel what she knew and felt.

Embarrassing for a woman of her age. School-girlish. But that's what Jon Locklear excelled at — reducing her to a quivering mass of emotional Jell-O.

Could she continue to fight against her attraction — not just physical, but also her feelings — for him? Would it be safer for

Ian's sake to forge a friendship? Did a small part of Jon want to stop fighting, too?

"Hey, Mom," her son repeated, breaking Laura's trance.

Perched on a stool, Ian gave her a mischievous, one-sided smile. His contribution, to whatever was going on, appeared to be licking something gooey off the mixer paddles. Beside him, Tayla waved a hand and returned to layering a row of bananas, topped by an equally precise row of vanilla wafers.

"What's going on here?"

Velma stood at the sink, her arms elbow deep in sudsy water. She pushed her white bangs off her forehead with the back of her soapy hand. "Jon remembered his mama's famous banana pudding recipe, and we're giving you a head start on the potluck."

Laura licked her lips at the memory of Florence Locklear's Not Your Grandmother's Banana Pudding.

Velma wiped her hands on the towel. "Laura, let's leave the rest of the preparations to the food crew. I brought something you might like to have." She grabbed her purse and headed for the living room.

Following, Laura lowered her voice. "You and Tayla appear to be getting along better these days."

Velma made a piffling noise as she released

the catch on the purse. "We've come to a point of mutual respect. We're trading areas of expertise. She's getting the quilters into the twenty-first century."

Her aunt eased onto the ottoman at the foot of Holt's recliner. "Did you know you could find free quilt patterns on the Internet?"

Laura sank down beside her. A bird took up more space than Aunt Velma. "And your contribution to this mutual love fest?"

Velma drew several leather-bound journals from the cavernous depths of her bag. "I convinced her learning how to do fancy stitches like the Lazy Daisy and a French knot would only increase her chances of impressing her professors at medical school. Not to mention strengthening her fine motor skills. We're working on a surprise birthday sampler for Lula."

"Speaking of surprises, do you happen to know how my father got hold of Mother's Bible? He was . . ."

Laura fought to keep incredulity from coating her voice. "He was . . . reading it."

"Certainly, I do. He asked for it, and I gave it to him."

She stared at her aunt. "You visit my dad?"

"No need to look at me like I've grown horns." Velma shifted in her seat. "Scripture gave your mother a great deal of peace in her darkest days. Since the stroke, I believe Emerson Sterling Bowen the Fourth has had a great deal of time to reflect on the way he's lived his life. The good and the bad choices."

Laura pursed her lips.

"Don't you give me that look, missy. I wouldn't deny any hurting creature the comfort that can only come from its Maker."

Velma peered at her sensible tan orthopedics. "A comfort I found only recently through reading Louisc's Bible and these." She thrust the stack of journals at Laura.

Laura flipped the pages of the one on top. "Mother's prayer journals. I'd forgotten about them."

Velma sighed. "Louise's personal thoughts as she grappled with the Enemy."

The Enemy, her mother's term for the disease tearing her body to pieces. Faith had been her mother's bedrock in those last months. A faith Louise embraced as, little by little, life let go of her.

Velma pressed Laura's hand. "I've always wondered if I'd read sooner, understood for myself the journey through which Louise found the One who is always faithful and true, if that summer, you . . . If I could've . . ." Velma's voice broke.

Laura's eyes widened. "Oh, Aunt Velma. Don't blame yourself. Jon and I both knew better."

Velma took a deep breath. "Thing is, Laura. I couldn't share what I didn't possess."

Laura wrapped her arms around the frail woman.

Velma gave her a one-armed hug. "But I did read finally. I asked Holt questions I knew he'd know the answers to from the Holy Scriptures. He showed me the way. The way back to Louise one day."

Tears streamed unheeded down the old woman's cheeks. "I showed Emerson." She shook her head. "Don't know if he took that course, or not."

Velma squared her shoulders. "Time I shared with you what I now do possess. Start with your mother's own words. Take baby steps with one of Holt's big Bibles. And Lord knows I'm no theologian, but I'll do the best I can to launch you on your way."

Her aunt gave herself a shake. "There's other things I want you to know, but with a houseful of company, tonight is not the time for further revelations."

"We're done," yelled Ian.

Laura swiped at her eyes. "That boy is a megaphone." She fingered the journals. "Thank you, Aunt Velma. This is a treasure."

Velma cocked her ear toward the front door at a furious rapping. "Who's that bozo trying to beat down your door?"

Laura rose, peeking out the blue brocade curtain. Her heart sank. "It's Garrett."

Velma muttered something under her breath about fools and angels.

Laura flung open the door, catching a red-faced Garrett with one hand upraised. Brooks Brothers casual, he reeled, startled. Recovering, he grabbed her forearm. She tried jerking free, but his hold was implacable.

"Stop, Garrett. You're hurting me."

"What's he doing here, Laura? I told you —"

"I'm telling you" — Jon's deep voice sounded from the arched doorway between the living room and kitchen — "get your hand off her."

Garrett's face hardened. But he let go.

Rubbing the spot where his fingers had dug into her skin, she spun around. Tayla gripped Ian's shoulder. Velma stood and smoothed her linen skirt. A dangerous glint in his eye, an apronless Jon leaned against the piano.

Garrett brushed past Laura, knocking her off balance. She caught the door to steady herself.

A muscle in Jon's cheek twitched before he went rigid. His eyes, the scariest eyes she'd ever seen, beaded on Garrett.

Laura was glad Ian stood behind Jon, unable to see his expression.

Garrett must have perceived something there, too, for his brown-tasseled loafers stopped dead in the middle of the room. A flicker of uncertainty crossed his choirboy features. "Get out of this house." His nostrils flared. "I'll call the Chief of Raleigh Police again if I have to."

Laura gasped. "You got Jon taken off the investigation?" She angled. "Jon, I'm sor—"

"What's going on, Laura?" Garrett's blue eyes shone with fury.

Ian broke loose from Tayla. "Jon's helping us make dessert for the potluck."

Garrett wrenched his gaze from her to Ian.

Laura didn't like the way his eyes narrowed at her son.

"How cozy." Garrett's mouth twisted. "Now get out, Locklear."

Jon must not have liked the way Garrett glared at Ian, either, because he stepped in front of Ian again, blocking Garrett's view. "Didn't realize the name *Payne* was on the title of this house."

Pounding his chest, Garrett snorted. "My title is on —"

"Garrett!"

Scrambling, she inserted herself between the men.

Garrett barreled forward, forcing Laura, arms rammed to her sides, against Jon's hard-packed torso.

"Stop it this instant," boomed the diminutive septuagenarian. "You're both behaving like schoolboys. And," Velma added, "scaring Ian."

Way too much testosterone in this room.

Laura squeezed out of the deadlock and placed a hand on each man's chest. Stretching her arms in both directions, she forced the men apart.

"Get out, Locklear. You're not wanted here," Garrett growled.

"*I* invited him to stay for the potluck." Ian grabbed hold of Jon's hand. "We wanted to surprise Mom."

Brows low and furrowed, Ian tugged at Laura's hand, too. "Mom, tell him."

Unsure which "him" Ian referred to, Laura feared Garrett would burst an artery but said, "You did work hard, it's not fair for you not to —"

Garrett's shoulders slumped. "Laura?" He

took on that look she likened to a hurt puppy dog. "It's me you don't want here?"

She bit her lip at the awkward silence.

Garrett's chin dropped. "I'm . . . we're . . ."

Jon released Ian's hand. "I'll go."

Ian pulled at his arm. "No, Jon, no. I invited you . . . I want yooou . . ."

Laura's eyes lifted to Jon's. Something visceral passed between them.

The yearning in Jon's eyes jolted her. An unspoken caress, his eyes speaking a language his lips did not.

Breaking contact first, Jon gave Ian a quick hug. "I'll be seeing you, don't worry, son."

Garrett exploded, shoving Jon's hand off Ian's shoulder. "Don't bet on it, you red-skinned, trailer trash tomahaw—"

Jon drew his fist, his muscles coiled.

Garrett froze. Ian cried out.

Laura's breath hitched, and she clutched Ian. Shame passed over Jon's face.

Confusion and torment filled his eyes. With a ragged breath, he dropped his fist. Pivoting on his heel, Jon stalked out the door.

Ian yanked free and ran up the stairs to the landing. "I hate-hate-hate all of you." His bedroom door slammed.

Garrett quivered with rage.

With a sinking sense of dread, Laura knew she'd pay for not rushing to Garrett's defense and taking his side against Jon and Ian.

Aunt Velma took Tayla's arm. "Let's see what we can do to calm Ian." She darted a look at Laura. "Should we convince him to escort us to the potluck and give you two some time alone?"

Laura swallowed past the lump in her throat.

Velma's features pinched. "Laura Lou?"

Laura nodded.

One hand clutching the railing, Aunt Velma ascended with Tayla's assistance. Giving Velma a chance to catch her breath, Tayla paused, a befuddled smile on her face. "You rich white people are more entertaining than watching *The Young and the Restless* any day."

Jon slammed the door after he climbed into the truck. He buried his head in his hands. Light from Laura's home spilled into the dusk. He watched her as, head bowed, she gently closed the door against the coming night. And him.

The desire to cradle her engulfed him. But a gesture she'd made clear she didn't want.

Not from him.

He banged the steering wheel, his blood roaring. What was wrong with that woman? Why couldn't she see that self-important weasel for what he was? See how Payne manipulated her feelings? See what marriage to Payne would do to her — and to their son?

A glimpse of the anguish in his son's eyes at the confrontation between him and Garrett forced Jon to retreat for the moment. But he'd return, Jon vowed, to fight another day for what belonged to him.

For *everyone* who had always belonged to him.

"Sorry, God," he whispered into the twilight. "I'm the one who knows better. You've told me to turn the other cheek."

Jon didn't want to be a man who couldn't control his temper. A brawler. Not how he wanted Ian to remember his father.

Remember?

Who was Jon kidding?

He was a nobody. The Paynes of this world controlled the destiny of nations. In this case, his, Laura's, and Ian's destinies.

Garrett Payne would see him dead before he'd allow Jon within a mile of Ian because within a mile of Ian meant too close to Laura for Garrett's peace of mind.

A small thrill shot through him as Jon recalled her reluctance to side with Garrett against him. The wistful look on her face that betrayed Laura's desire. Or was he reading too much into it? Deluding himself over something never there?

He groaned. The thought of Garrett "comforting" Laura, his arms around her, his hands touching her . . . made Jon want to puke.

Was there any use in calling an attorney? Jon wasn't a quitter, wasn't one to give up, especially with something as important as his son. And Payne raising his boy sent Jon's blood pressure through the roof.

But was dragging his son and Laura through a heated custody case and paternity suit the right thing to do?

He slipped the key into the ignition. He needed to do something he should've done yesterday when he'd first realized he had a son. Before he let his self-righteous anger take over.

Take it to His Father and seek wisdom for what would be best for Ian. Not just satisfy his own pride.

If ever there was a head-in-your-hands moment, this was it.

With a heavy heart, Laura watched Aunt

Velma and Tayla escort a sniffling, mutinous Ian out the door to the clubhouse. She sighed as the red taillights of the Crown Vic disappeared into the shadows of the night.

She doubted, noting Garrett's loaded-for-bear expression, she and Garrett would be joining them anytime soon.

As the door closed behind the trio with a decisive thud, silence thickened like whipping cream into stiff peaks.

Her arms rigid as if straitjacketed to her sides, she sat beside Garrett on the sofa. His mouth taut, he made no attempt to touch her.

In truth, she was a little afraid of Garrett right now. In his dealings with Jon, she'd glimpsed a side of Garrett she'd never seen before. And more important, never seen before in regard to Ian.

Garrett shifted his weight. She held her breath.

"Does this mean you don't want to marry me?" His voice quavered.

Garrett — nor Holt — had ever deserved this from her. Everyone who loved her got hurt in the end. She was like a lovelorn Typhoid Mary.

He fumbled with a box in his jacket. "I brought this with me tonight, hoping to surprise you with an engagement ring under the stars."

Garrett popped the top of the box. Diamond studs encircled the velvet-encased sapphire. The sapphire itself was the width of a dime.

She gasped.

He pressed closer, his knees touching Laura's.

"I'm sorry I lost my temper with Ian. I'll apologize. I'd hoped we'd form a bond. I'd never try to replace his father . . ."

Garrett grimaced. "Holt, I mean."

She swallowed. "Things are going too fast. With Renna's death —"

"Is that what this is about?"

Garrett fell to his knees, thrusting the box into her folded hands.

His face blanched. "You believe Locklear's lies about Renna and me?" Garrett's jaw jutted. "Whatever it takes. I'll prove it to you and the police. I'll give them a DNA sample tomorrow." He gripped her wrists, his eyes probing her.

A twinge of pain traveled up her arms. She winced.

"I swear to you, Laura. I never so much as looked at that girl." A glimmer of the old vote-winning twinkle sparked in his eyes. "You know I prefer more mature women."

He ran his hand along the length of her thigh.

She shivered.

Not with desire.

She focused on the box.

He stiffened at her knee-jerk reaction. "We've made announcements . . . plans."

You made announcements . . . For the first time, Laura resented his campaign.

"I never imagined you'd treat me like my mother —"

"I'm nothing like Barbara." Laura glared.

"Aren't you afraid of losing Ian to that man?" Garrett's tone harshened. "You lied on the birth certificate, Laura. You never bothered to inform him of his parental rights. You fight him alone, I'm not sure in whose favor a judge will decide. I hear through the grapevine that Morales woman is itching to slap a warrant for your arrest. You go to prison, you'll never see your son again. Locklear will turn him against you. You've seen how he holds a grudge. Ian will be taught to forget you ever existed."

Her father's voice about lying down with dogs and getting up with fleas echoed. And flitting through her mind, images of Emerson in the library chained by the lies of his own making.

Like her.

She broke into a cold sweat. "No . . ." Her stomach knotted.

"Laura," Garrett's eyes pleaded. "Let me help you. Help Ian. Please . . ."

The smile on his face went dead.

Garrett folded his arms, his voice clipped. "Think of Ian. I'm the only one who can save you from the monster who'll snatch your child away. Not Holt. Me, Laura." He thumped his chest. "Me. Don't do this to Ian. I'll keep you both safe. Never let anyone hurt you again."

Hating her helplessness, her fear for Ian stronger than anything else, Laura extended her left hand.

Garrett's eyes lost all movement, all expression. "Say it, Laura. Tell me what you want so we're clear."

"I want . . ." She trembled. "I'd be honored to marry you, Garrett. Please. If you'll still have me."

Much later, after he departed with a promise to pick her up in time for Renna's funeral tomorrow, Laura slipped the weighty stone off her hand. Before Ian and Velma returned from the potluck. She couldn't handle any more anger from Ian tonight or the disapproval she'd receive from her aunt.

Bringing Ian home, Velma and Tayla exited without a word, though Laura could see the unasked questions fairly burning a hole in her aunt's tongue. Ian, simmering with resentment, didn't exactly go gently into bedtime. Laura carried her mother's journals upstairs after securing the doors and quenching the lights downstairs. She undressed, reaching for her nightgown in the lingerie drawer.

An overpowering fragrance of honeysuckle perfumed the air.

Frowning, she drew the silky shift closer to her nostrils. Within the folds of the lingerie, something crackled.

Her breath hitching, she withdrew a square envelope. Another hateful missive. Her third. The tips of her fingers after touching the nightgown stank of honey-suckle. She dropped the garment to the floor.

> All liars end up in the lake of fire. For you, Laura Bowen, Judgment Day cometh. Soon.

Her skin crawled. Someone had been in her things. But who?

She replayed the events of the day. The police search. Tayla. Aunt Velma. Ian.

And unable to fathom a motive for the notes except for sheer revenge, her mind settled on Jon.

Jon, who'd spent a lot of time alone in the house with Ian this afternoon.

Crumpling the note, she sank onto the edge of the bed. This couldn't be happening. Not again.

They'd seemed to grow closer today. Some barriers eroding. Trust rebuilding.

Wishful thinking on her part?

Not Jon. She shook her head. He wouldn't do that to her.

Would he?

She couldn't — didn't — want to believe this of Jon. But who else? The hardness in his face, the barely suppressed rage, was nothing like the gentle boy she'd known in Mimosa Grove.

Nor was Laura the wide-eyed innocent she'd been, either.

She had to start thinking with her head and not her heart. Her hands clammy, she skimmed her hair from her face.

Means? She ticked off one finger.

Jon.

Opportunity? She ticked off another.

Jon.

She wanted to weep.

And motive?

She'd supplied Jon Locklear with lots of motive.

Ten years of motive.

13

"Morales?" Jon spoke into the phone at his apartment. "We need to talk."

A long sigh on the other end.

"Jon, I'm sorry about Mike's decision."

His brows constricted. *Were you truly, Morales?*

"But, if you want to talk about the case, I can't."

"Laura Mabry did not kill Renna Sheldon."

"And you know this how? Based on the residue of adolescent hormones?"

He clamped his mouth shut, afraid the angry retort that rose to his lips would permanently alienate Ana, whose cooperation he needed if he hoped to learn any vital evidence to clear Laura.

Was Ana's animosity toward Laura truly about his breach of professional ethics or about jilted feelings? He decided to apply more honey than vinegar this time in his dealings with Ana. "As you've guessed, Ian's my son."

"The son she kept from you all these years. Doesn't that make you furious, Locklear? I don't get why you're so determined to prove our murderer is anyone but her."

Yeah, he was furious with Laura. And Jon wasn't sure why he was convinced the killer wasn't Laura, either.

"My gut's telling me Laura's too obvious, too easy. Something else is going down here. As cops, we learn to rely on those feelings."

Ana snorted. "Sure it's not a feeling emanating from another part of your anatomy?"

If she'd been a guy standing in front of him, Jon wasn't sure he could've resisted the urge to punch her.

He took a deep breath. Humility — eating crow or whatever you wanted to call it — would be a new experience for him.

An unpleasant experience.

He kept his voice soft. "Ana, please? You were my first friend, besides Mike, in Raleigh. I promise I won't interfere with your case. If you had a kid, wouldn't you look out for his interests, too? And like it or not, his mother is vital to his well-being."

"Problem is, Locklear, I don't believe you.

This is not completely about your son's interests. This is about your interest in his mother."

Jon knew enough to be quiet. He'd said his piece. It was up to Ana whether she'd bite or not. Ana let him twist in the wireless wind for another minute.

"All right," she huffed. "What do you want to know?"

He took a steadying breath, glad she couldn't see the smile that enveloped his face. "Any connection between who bought those expensive running shoes and Renna?"

"We're working those leads now."

"Names, Ana."

A puff of air on her end. "Garrett Payne does not own a pair, if that's what you're asking. That's a dead horse you're beating."

"Garrett Payne is about six foot. Based on the shoe print, he could be our killer."

"I got a text from Payne saying he was coming into the station for a voluntary DNA cheek swab tomorrow. Hardly suspicious behavior from a murderer. We'll soon know one way or the other if Garrett Payne is the father of Renna's baby or not."

"Garrett's got the perfect motive. Knocks up an intern. He's running for political office. Renna threatens to expose him, and he kills her."

"Why would she threaten to expose him?"

"To ruin his chances at the congressional seat and his chances with Laura."

Ana sniffed. "You turn that around and you've also got the perfect motive for the merry widow Mabry, too."

Jon exhaled, letting the air trickle out through his mouth. "Come on, Ana. Don't you have any other male suspects on your shoe list?"

"Despite your insinuation that I'm trying to railroad your girlfriend, Locklear, I happen to know my job. I do have a few names I'm not sharing with you. And before you get patronizing on me, you can bet Garrett's not going to be the only one I request DNA from."

"Mind if I attend the funeral? Two eyes better than one."

"Jon . . ." Ana muttered something under her breath he didn't catch. It wasn't complimentary to his heritage or his mother.

"I promise to stay out of your way. In the back. Way in the back."

"Okay. Don't make me regret this, Locklear."

"Those other men on your list don't have to cooperate with your DNA dragnet, you know."

"I know, but I'll keep everything nice and

legal. I'll inform them that even though they're persons of interest, they're not required to provide their DNA."

"Make sure you also let them know that to refuse makes the police real suspicious."

"Are you telling me how to run an investigation now, Locklear? 'Cause I'll tell you how to —"

"Thanks, Ana. I owe you one."

"You owe me more than one, Locklear. And don't you think for a minute I don't mean to collect."

And with that threatening promise, she hung up on him.

Jon scrubbed his hand across the back of his neck. Collapsing against the pillow, he sorted the pieces of evidence — the players he knew about — in his mind. He was surprised about Garrett's offer to yield his DNA.

Had to be a bluff. A magician's trick to obscure the real reason for Renna's death.

Jon's nose wrinkled. He wouldn't trust Payne as far as . . . As far as he could throw that proverbial tomahawk with which Payne ethnically slurred him. His frustration mounted. Jon sensed he was missing something vital.

Lying in the darkness, he expelled a long breath. At the end of each day since that gut-wrenching day ten years ago in Jacksonville, whether in Iraq, Afghanistan, or Baltimore, it always circled round to Laura.

An olfactory memory conjured the scent of honeysuckle so perfectly, he sniffed the stale air of his bedroom. Jon swallowed. Just his imagination remembering.

Again.

Twisting, he buried his face in the pillow. Morales was right about his fury regarding Laura. She'd taken — she'd stolen — ten years of his son's life from him. Moments forever lost. Memories made with another man, another father. Never his to reclaim.

He'd behaved like the back end of a horse. But nothing excused what she'd robbed him of. Robbed Jon's mother and family of. Robbed Ian of.

But making Laura pay didn't offer the satisfaction he'd envisioned upon first learning this revelation. Making her pay would also mean making Ian pay. How could Jon ever form a relationship with his son if he wounded Ian's mother, Laura?

A court case and the publicity would damage not only Laura but his precious son, too. His anger at Laura and the wrongs she'd done to him were getting harder and harder to hold on to, like holding water in your hand. It trickled out as if between his fingers every time he was near her. Every time she looked at him.

Jon groaned.

"What do I do, God?"

A whisper in his soul.

Jon switched on the bedside lamp and grabbed his Bible. His name, Jon Locklear, was engraved in gold on the cover.

His mouth quivered at the memory of Ian's smaller Bible. Engraved for all time as Ian Mabry. Not Ian Locklear. Jon's gut clenched.

Jon raked his hand through his hair. "Okay, God. Do Your thing. Here goes."

He flung the Bible open on the sheets and squeezed his eyes shut. Jon winced as if he expected lightning to strike his insolence toward the Creator of the universe.

Nothing happened. He raised his eyes to the ceiling, thankful God delivered grace, instead of what he deserved.

An uncomfortable thought arose about his failure to do the same with Laura.

His God-fearing mother would be ashamed of his treatment of his Savior and of Laura. He was ashamed, too, of his childish pettiness.

Sheepish, he glanced to where the Book had fallen open. Philemon.

He reclined against the headboard. Jon

wasn't a Bible scholar, but wasn't Philemon something about a slave? Nothing to do with his situation.

And best thing about Philemon?

One of the short books. He'd read a few verses, check daily devotion off his to-do list for today, and go to sleep.

The first verse gave Jon pause, though. Grace and peace.

Peace would be much appreciated, God.

A hint of how peace arrived floated through his mind.

Forgiveness?

Not ready for that yet, Lord.

Then an intrusive thought. *Perhaps not ready for peace yet, either.*

His mouth went as dry as desert sand. He frowned, focusing his eyes on the printed page, determined to plow through until the end.

The next few verses stopped Jon cold. "I would rather appeal to you through love . . ."

Laura's face rose so strongly in his mind's eye, he blinked for a moment picturing her on the blank wall of his bedroom.

"What about what she did to me?"

He shook the Book. Just a little. He'd been taught to fear lightning.

No answer.

His eyes returned to the page. "I'm sending him back to you . . ."

Jon gasped.

Did he have the eyes of faith to comprehend how God had indeed sent Ian back to him?

". . . sending my own heart."

Jon winked back the moisture creeping into the corner of his eyelids. His son. Jon pondered God's Son.

God the Father knew about losing and receiving back.

He read on about Paul's entreaty to the slave master, Philemon, to receive back with much grace the runaway slave, Onesimus, who'd so wronged his master.

The apostle asked for Philemon's mercy. Not by force . . . but by petitioning Philemon's own free will.

Paul and God didn't threaten.

God wasn't going to make Jon drop his lawsuit. God wasn't going to make Jon forgive Laura.

His choice.

Jon flushed, thinking of the hateful words with which he'd speared Laura. His finger traced the next sentence where Paul offered the supposition that there existed a divinely ordained reason for the situation that separated Philemon from Onesimus.

". . . separated from you for a while so

that you might have him back forever."

A sob broke from Jon's clenched throat.

"If he has harmed you in any way or owes you money, charge it to my account. I, Paul, will pay it back to you . . . I won't mention that you owe me your life. . . ."

An image of a sheep he'd come upon in the hill country of the Taliban rose in Jon's memory. Another animal had ripped the sheep's flesh. Wounded, the sheep had staggered across the rugged terrain, until Jon's squad came across the dying creature. The gashes in the sheep's flesh swarmed with maggots. Jon put his revolver to the animal's head in a gesture of mercy.

Jon recalled his wild days at army bases all over the world after he and Laura had split apart. He remembered the cleansing that came when he poured out his heart first to Chaplain Grant and later when he bowed his knee to his Savior. The baptismal water of the Euphrates symbolized how Jesus flushed the maggots of sin from his life.

He'd been Onesimus, who'd greatly wronged his Master and desperately needed forgiveness.

Philemon was a book about God's grace and forgiveness. Tonight, Jon sat in Philemon's seat, wronged by another.

Forgiveness or not, his choice.

"I can't!" he yelled, a primal cry at the silence. "It will cost me my son. Again."

But I can. And it cost Me my son, too . . .

Propelled by a need stronger than any he'd known since the call of salvation, Jon rolled off the bed and went to his knees. Clutching the bedclothes in his fists, he lowered his head and with wrenching sobs allowed the blood of Christ to flow through his wounds of bitterness. Toward peace and forgiveness. At last.

14

Laura rose at dawn to walk Buggs around the block. The neighborhood appeared peaceful in the early morning light. She'd arisen twice during the night to check on Ian. He slept undisturbed, but tear tracks stained his dark cheeks.

It required threats of imminent violence to get Ian out of bed this first school day after Memorial Day. Sullen, he crunched his cereal at the island counter. He kicked one foot against the wooden base until Laura thought she'd scream. Which was exactly what he wanted her to do.

Which was exactly why she resisted the urge.

Molasses ran faster than Ian Mabry this Tuesday morning as he stuffed his sack lunch into his book bag. He dug in his heels at her suggestion to run a comb through his hair, and generally tried to be as disagreeable as a deer tick in her efforts to get him to the school bus on time. Once he slammed the front door behind him — indicating his continued and eternal ire with his mother — she sagged against the countertop. Laura reached for the coffeepot.

Eight a.m. And already eighty-two degrees. But it was either coffee or a stiff drink.

She wasn't a drinker, so she fixed her drug of choice. Measuring a scoop of Carolina Coffee's *Coastal Blend,* she wished she could sail away from her troubles. She had a funeral to attend — on the arm of Garrett — and the continuing dilemma of proving her innocence. That plus raising her son — a thankless job today — and running the store.

As the aroma filled the room, her nostrils flared as she inhaled the promise of a caffeine jolt. Chilled despite the unseasonable temperatures on this first day of June, she poured the brew into a mug and wrapped her hands around the warmth. She took a satisfying draught and leaned over the sink like a hungover drunk.

Out the window, the red, pink, and yellow hybrid tea roses lifted their second flush glorious faces to the sun and reveled. Garden expert Alison Barefoot had suggested Laura plant an English cottage garden more in keeping with the architecture of the house. But cottage gardens were so . . . so deliberately chaotic.

And while nature detested straight lines, Laura craved them.

She relished the row after row of soldier-straight roses. How their velvety petals drank in the sunlight. Alison warned of black spot and powdery mildew. To expect aphids and a Japanese beetle invasion. These demanding, delicate divas of the plant kingdom needed constant attention.

Laura lifted her chin and toasted the rose bed with her mug. Just let a pesky bug decide to chew on her prize Mr. Lincolns.

She made a mental note to weed the bed and deadhead the roses. Probably needed to check for bugs. Forget the sprays. Normally a live-and-let-live kind of person, today she could use some bug-squashing therapy.

Metal glinted in the sunshine.

She set her cup upon the counter with a thud. Tools lolled in the grass. Lowther should've been here by now. He'd been prompt the last two weeks, reporting for work by seven to get an early, cooler start to a long, hot day.

But no Zeke.

Well, that just tore it.

Zeke had gone AWOL, as had her plans

to enclose her yard in the foreseeable future.

She massaged her forehead and sighed.

Ian was furious with her. She'd damaged her relationship with Garrett. She was about to be arrested for murder by that Latina woman and Jon was . . .

Jon was like Jon always was with her.

Stomping up the stairs, Laura showered and changed into a simple navy-blue dress with three-quarter-length sleeves. Her only other funeral attire was the black dress she'd worn to Holt's funeral. She couldn't face that one again. Yanking the offending garment off the hanger, she wadded it into a ball. She'd send it to Goodwill at the first opportunity.

Texting Garrett to pick her up at the store, she slipped her Lexus out of the garage and headed toward Tapestries. There, she placed a hand-lettered sign in the door.

CLOSED For Funeral.

For the second time in days, her skin prickled. Laura glanced about the shop, overcome by a strange feeling. Had someone been in the shop over the holiday weekend? The doors had been locked when she arrived. Laura spun in a slow three-sixty in an attempt to pinpoint the source of her unease.

Nothing appeared out of place. But in the

air there hung a faint trace of . . . ? She puckered her brow, unable to identify the scent.

It'd come to her eventually. Her daddy used to say she had a nose like a dog, and Aunt Velma was always quick to point out that she had — not to her credit — a memory like an elephant.

A memory that couldn't let go of what should be relinquished. A memory that couldn't forgive herself when God already said He would. A memory that fueled an already unforgiving nature.

Garrett was nothing if not punctual, and at ten o'clock sharp, he arrived to escort her to the funeral.

Or was she escorting the political candidate to the funeral?

He gave her a tight smile as she eased into the passenger seat of his Corvette. His smile widened when he caught the flash of the sapphire on her hand gleaming in the midmorning glare of the sun. Parking behind a line of cars, he gripped her arm as they climbed the stone steps of the church the General and Doris attended.

She elbowed Garrett for wiggle room, but he dug his fingers into her skin as if he feared she might bolt upon the slightest provocation. The General, ramrod straight, held his frail wife upright beside the casket. Renna's honeymooning mother a no-show.

Thankful for the closed coffin, Laura whispered a somber hello to Patti behind them in the receiving line. Barbara — minus Laura's dad — slipped into place a few paces farther down the line from Patti. The church pews filled with mourners come to offer their respects, not only to Renna but also to her prominent godparents.

Garrett released Laura's arm to grasp the General's hand. With a slight nod to Laura, the General pulled Garrett aside to speak in a more confidential tone. Confusion clouded Doris's features. Laura bent to hug the elderly lady.

"Who died, Laura?" Doris whispered, her lips featherlight against Laura's cheek.

Laura's eyes cut to the General, engrossed in an intense discussion with Garrett. She gulped. "Miss Doris —"

Doris's face cleared. "Oh, yes. Renna. Renna was going to tell you."

Laura blinked. "Renna had something to tell me? What, Miss Doris? Do you know what Renna wanted to tell me?"

Doris squeezed Laura's hand. "Only if you promise to pinky swear." Her face scrunched. "No, that's not right. She gave me the finger."

"I don't understand."

Doris extended her liver-spotted hand, palm out. Her eyes narrowed, studying each digit. Dropping her hand, she sighed. "I can't-can't remember. Come see me and we'll talk about —" The old woman pinched her lips. Anger, strange in the usually gentle soul, replaced the blankness. "Renna wasn't a good girl. She hurt babies. She killed my baby."

Laura reared.

Doris's voice rose. "Killed my babe — eee . . ." Her wail blared before dissipating into the rafters.

The General reached for his wife as an unnatural disquiet settled over the congregation.

Aunt Velma muscled her tiny frame between the General and Doris. "Let me."

Velma wrapped her arm around Doris. "I think we should let her sit this one out. Don't you?"

The General's bottom lip trembled. "I'll handle the rest of the guests."

Aunt Velma nodded and led Doris to the reserved family pew.

Garrett soldiered up beside the General, shoulder to shoulder. "This is no time for you to stand alone, sir." He snaked his arm around Laura. "We wouldn't dream of letting you go through this alone, would we, Laura?"

And though she longed to dash out of the church and back to the peace of her roses, Laura stood transfixed in place. With a waxen smile, she went through the same horrific motions that a year and a half ago, she and Ian endured at Holt's burial. Utilizing the same perfunctory responses, she allowed her mind to drift. Laura scanned the congregation. A gaggle of twenty-somethings, male and female. Probably Renna's college cohorts.

The father of her child, perhaps, among them?

She spotted Tayla and her grandmother. Lula's sharp black eyes darted, missing nothing. What Aunt Velma didn't know about Raleigh society, Miss Lula or one of her friends, who worked in various capacities for the rest of the Old Raleigh families, probably did. A photographer stepped out of the shadows of the sanctuary.

Garrett shoved Laura between himself and the General. "Put your hand on top of my arm."

She gaped at him.

"Now," Garrett hissed in her ear.

An intimate gesture artfully done, which appeared as nothing more than a playful nibble upon her earlobe to an observer.

She laid her forearm on top of Garrett's, Princess Diana style.

A flash blinded her.

Garrett worked his face into an expression of moral outrage, genuine enough to fool the General and draw murmurs from the congregation. Garrett motioned to an employee of the funeral home who hastily ushered the photographer outside.

A good act, but she wasn't buying it, not after the terse call he placed to his campaign manager while wheeling out of Tapestries parking lot earlier.

When her pupils returned to their normal size, she returned to her survey of the audience.

Patti and her husband, Woodrow, took their seats. Hilary Munro and her husband slid into the pew beside them. Elderly grande dames from the Weathersby Quilt Guild. Older gentlemen whose stiff-as-a-loblolly-pine bearing identified them as military contemporaries of the General. And on the back row —

Her breath caught. Ana Morales occupied the farthest pew. Staking out suspects?

Or maybe, in Ana's eyes, *she* was the suspect. Laura teetered on her four-inch pumps, glad for the support of Garrett's sturdy right arm.

Swallowing, she forced her gaze away from the detective. A movement at the massive oak door diverted her attention. A man in a white shirt and black suit stepped across the threshold. Her pulse leaped.

Perhaps her arm flexed. Garrett flicked her an annoyed look, not bothering to pause in his effort to solicit goodwill, funds, and votes — not necessarily in that order — from the distinguished business investor in the receiving line with whom he conversed.

At the back of the church, Jon looked as bad as Laura felt. Dark circles bruised his eyes. Shadows hollowed his cheekbones. He assumed a stance with his feet shoulder-width apart and pressed his back to the wall of the sanctuary.

With a stark longing, Jon watched her watch him.

And something broke in Laura's heart.

Entangled in the snare of her own making, she yearned to touch his face. To connect and bridge the lies standing between them. To clasp his hand and allow him to lead her to a place she needed to go, a place only possible with him.

She made as if to move, but a glimmer of light from the ornate chandelier bounced off her hand and threw a blue sparkle onto the sidewall, capturing Jon's attention for a split-second before his gaze returned to hers. The flash of pain in his eyes crossed the expanse and seared her heart.

Laura dropped her arm from Garrett's, but it was too late. Jon had disappeared out the door. Abandoning Garrett, she dashed for the pew behind Aunt Velma. His mouth tight with anger, Garrett stomped in beside her.

The service was brief. The pallbearers, the General's former comrades, escorted the coffin toward the waiting hearse. Garrett jerked Laura to her feet as soon as the aisle cleared.

Her fiancé dragged Laura like Buggsby on a leash toward the parked cars. Laura's high heels skittered across the pavement. She stumbled.

"Get. In."

He threw the door open to the Corvette, barely giving Laura time to get her feet inside before he slammed the door. The small sport coupe rocked. Garrett revved the engine once the tires hit the main thoroughfare.

She'd embarrassed him in front of his constituents. She threw Garrett a wary glance.

Rage simmered below the surface of his

flushed skin and frightened her. Garrett gunned the car down Glenwood Avenue. This was a man capable of murdering anyone who stood in the way of his objective.

Had Renna?

Laura's heart thudded.

Too fast, Garrett wheeled around a curve. She fell against the side of the door. Crossing the double yellow line, he floored the vehicle and passed a slower-moving car. A FedEx truck crested the hill ahead.

Gasping, Laura grabbed hold of the dashboard.

She screamed and squeezed her eyes shut. Laura tensed for impact.

With a lurch, Garrett wrenched the car into his own lane. Horns blared from the frightened truck driver. A Ford Escort slammed on his brakes to avoid rear-ending them.

She cringed in the passenger seat and clutched her seat belt. The Corvette shuddered to a complete stop at Tapestries.

Ominous silence reigned.

She gritted her teeth and waited for the explosion.

Garrett whirled in the seat. "I don't know what to say to you right now."

But his voice was once again under the

tight control he maintained when grilling a hostile witness on the stand.

Cold, remote, deadly.

Garrett took a steadying breath. "Since that" — he uttered a racially charged word meant to demean; and if push came to shove, could also apply to her son — "came into your life, you've changed. I don't know you anymore."

He reached across her.

She flinched.

He shoved open her door.

"I won't play the fool for you, Laura. After he succeeds in dragging your son away and you're ready to be the wife I deserve, call me."

Wresting the ring from her finger, she clambered out of the car. Leaving the stone on the seat, she shut the door. He threw the gearshift into reverse and roared out of the parking space.

And out of her life?

Laura checked her heart for any vestiges of sadness.

And found only relief.

Off duty not by choice, Jon returned to his apartment to change out of his suit and tie and into a more comfortable golf shirt and khaki cargo pants. Something Ian said over ice cream surfaced in Jon's mind like flotsam in the swamp after a storm. Driving past the station where he was persona non grata these days, he wended his way toward the medical examiner's office, and the domain of Doc Randall.

Doc, his salt-and-pepper head hung over a microscope, glanced up when Jon entered the laboratory. He held up a hand to forestall Jon. Realizing the doctor held a recording device, Jon took the hint and remained silent while the doctor finished a physical description of a victim.

He listed the victim's height, the approximate weight, hair and eye color, clothing found in, jewelry, and any distinguishing marks like tattoos or piercings. The defensive wounds were noted.

From the amount of sheeted corpses, the Doc was backlogged. Murder never took a holiday. Memorial Day weekend often kept the medical examiner even busier.

Doc pressed the button to off. "Heard you were . . ." He cleared his throat and averted his eyes. "What can I do for you?"

Jon took a breath. If Doc Randall refused, his options were limited. "Wondered if you'd call up a file for me. A traffic fatality from about a year and a half ago."

Doc regarded him from underneath

grizzled brows. "Who?"

"Holt Mabry. Dr. Holt Mabry."

Doc thrust his hands into the pockets of his white lab coat and rocked on his heels. "Why?"

Unconsciously mirroring Doc's stance, Jon shoved his hands into his pockets. "A hunch. A loose thread that begs to be unraveled."

Doc nodded and motioned for Jon to join him by the computer monitor. After giving Doc the pertinent details, a few keystrokes later, Doc pulled up the accident report filed by a highway patrolman for the night of February 3. They scanned the document together.

"Icy road conditions." Doc shook his head. "You weren't in Raleigh then, as I recall, but no one from around here has forgotten that storm. We don't get snow like that more than once in a lifetime. And then the weather worsened, if that was possible, when the temps rose and an inch of sheer ice fell, entombing the two feet of snow on the ground."

Jon leaned closer to the screen. "The car went off the road. No other vehicles involved. Mabry ran head-on into a tree." He angled. "No autopsy?"

Doc sighed, exasperated. "Sheets of heavy

ice fell off roofs and treetops. Crashing with pops like shotgun blasts. Power lines collapsed. Electricity out for days. Hot wires set houses on fire. As I remember, over one hundred vehicular accidents were reported during that three-hour stretch. Five other fatalities besides Dr. Mabry. Law enforcement and emergency personnel were stretched beyond thin."

Jon winced at the Doc's description, hurting for the sounds that surely reverberated through Ian's nightmares. "Why in heaven's name was Holt Mabry out on a night like that?"

Doc shrugged. "A lot of medical people were encouraged to report for duty." The M.E. nudged his glasses farther up the bridge of his nose as he clicked the document to page two. "Wife said in the police interview he got a call about a terminal patient at the Rex Emergency Room."

He adjusted the lapels of his lab coat. "Doctors of the dead, like me, or of the soon-to-be dead, like him, we've got obligations we swore to uphold."

Doc darted a glance at a white-sheeted gurney off to the side. "A duty to that teenage boy who believed he could defy the laws of gravity and the effects of alcohol in his brand-new muscle car." He sighed. "Why do parents give hormonally addled teenagers loaded weapons on the highway?"

Jon didn't bother to answer Randall's rhetorical question. "So when Mabry failed to arrive at Rex, his patient died?"

Doc studied him over the top of his glasses. "A question you want me to answer?" He shuffled over to a phone. "Guess I better or you'll never leave me in peace."

Randall barked questions into the receiver and waited, his foot tapping. He hung up twenty minutes later. "No page to Dr. Mabry was sent out that night. My wife's cousin checked the records. No patient of Dr. Mabry was admitted that night." He quirked a shaggy eyebrow at Jon.

"Somebody lured Holt Mabry out into that storm."

"Appears so."

"Was his vehicle checked for mechanical malfunction?"

"Not according to the accident report. The highway patrol had their hands full that night. Who'd have thought it necessary?"

"Who indeed, Doc? Maybe a murderer thinks he's scot-free after a year and a half."

"Now don't jump the gun, son. Not before we have all the facts. The slope of that hill down Glenwood to the intersection is steep enough in good weather. With ice?

An accident waiting to happen."

Jon clenched his teeth.

Doc scribbled an address on a notepad. "Police impounded the vehicle. Pruitt Brothers towed it to their junkyard at the south end of town, where I imagine it still sits." He tore off the page.

Jon reached for the slip of paper.

"Be careful, Locklear. Nothing so enrages a complacent killer as being found out after all this time."

"I hear you, Doc. I'll watch my back." He pivoted on the threshold. "And, Doc? Thanks."

Thirty minutes later, Jon stood dwarfed beneath a towering megapolis of twisted steel. Glinting in the noonday sun, the dead carcasses of man's quest to challenge the force of inertia spread as far as the eye could see.

A paunchy, weather-beaten man in a faded pair of grimy once-blue overalls pointed in the general direction of Tennessee. "What's left of that bronze Expedition is in that quadrant over yonder."

There was a quadrant? A method to this madness?

Jon hefted the flashlight and toolbox out of his truck.

"Take yer time, young feller."

Jon heaved a sigh, glancing once more over the miles of rusted steel. At this rate, that wouldn't be a problem. Saying a quick prayer for wisdom — and direction — he headed west. The owner of the junkyard spray-painted each of the vehicular remains with a numbered code. On the fourth row, he hit the jackpot.

His heart fell to his toes at the sight of the smashed automobile. He contemplated the person once contained in the wreckage, the mangling of skin and bone. Not just any person. Ian's stepfather and Laura's husband.

With the crowbar, he jimmied open the hood. Ten minutes later, Jon had his answer. He rubbed his hand across the back of his neck. His scalp tingled like in Kandahar when he sensed evil lurking just outside the periphery of his vision. Waiting.

Someone had gotten under the hood of Holt Mabry's SUV and manually disconnected the hose that connected to the power booster and controlled brake pressure. Normally secured by two clamps, one clamp was missing. Hoses didn't wiggle loose on their own. Probably the vibrations of the vehicle eventually jiggled the remaining clamp free while Holt was driving.

No other way for the clamp to have disconnected. Holt's SUV had been tampered with for murderous intent. The storm, the fake page from the hospital, the missing clamp. Holt Mabry's death was no accident. Holt Mabry had been set up to die.

For what purpose? Who benefitted from robbing Laura of her husband and Ian of the only father he'd ever known? Jon re-packed his tool kit.

One obvious answer.

And one more stop to make. He'd say his good-byes forever. But though Jon might never see his son again, he'd make sure Holt Mabry received the justice he deserved. Nobody hurt someone Laura and Ian loved and got away with it.

15

Unable to face opening Tapestries, Laura left the *CLOSED* sign in place and headed home. She remembered a new member of the Weathersby Quilt Guild Aunt Velma had befriended. An avid Tapestries shopper, the retired former State employee had an empty nest and too much time on her hands. An idea emerged for filling Renna's now-vacant position.

Once home, Laura telephoned Aggie and offered an employee discount if she'd consider becoming her afternoon assistant. And after explaining job responsibilities, Laura was thrilled to welcome the grandmotherly figure onboard and glad to have solved one of her looming problems.

Laura shed the clingy navy-blue dress and donned more suitable summertime attire. Perfect for tending to the rose bushes before Ian returned home in a few hours. Cooler in her blue jean Bermudas and turquoise tee, she sliced a tomato and slathered mayo on two slices of whole wheat. Layering the tomatoes, she sprinkled salt and pepper on the juicy red wagon wheels and ate her lunch at the white wicker table on the screened porch.

Buggs lolled listless at her feet, his droopy eyes shut. His body jerked spasmodically with doggy dreams. Pleasant ones, she hoped. Laura spread out her mother's journals on the table, and opened the last one her mother penned before succumbing to the Enemy.

On one side of the page were listed prayer requests for: Laura, Emerson, Louise's mother. Louise's requests for strength. Better white cell counts.

And on the opposite side of the page, the answers.

Laura discovered tiny, jotted answers to prayer over issues she didn't recall. Such as "Laura's sociology exam" followed on a corresponding line with "95."

Prayers prayed. Answers received.

Except for the biggest one — to be cancer-free.

Her mother hadn't lived to see Laura pregnant with Jon's baby.

Small mercies.

Louise also hadn't lived to see her wedding to Holt. The birth of a much-longed-for grandchild. Another Christmas. Another sunset over the Outer Banks. Laura closed her eyes.

Stop picking the scabs.

But she couldn't resist reading the rest of the notations. Her mother's elegant when-penmanship-mattered writing looped across the pages. Throughout the journal, Louise's spirit grew at the same pace the cancer ravaged her body.

Statements like, "If God calls, He will equip."

Or, "Delays in our Father's hands are never without purpose."

The one that got Laura, though?

Emerson's name coupled with Barbara's.

Barbara's?

Laura blinked to make sure.

With an arrow drawn from their names to the other side of the page. A blank line. As if Louise died waiting for the answer.

Laura's lip curled.

One final post at the bottom.

"No one," Louise Jones Bowen wrote, "is too far removed for God's mercy and grace." And underlined it three times in blue.

Laura cast her eyes to the sky.

"No one, Mama?" she whispered to the

breeze ruffling the trees. "Dad? Barbara? Even me?"

If only Laura could truly believe that.

She left the journal and went in search of one of Holt's big Bible dictionaries. Hoisting the volume, she rifled pages until she came upon the word *mercy.*

Not getting something you deserved.

The notes from The Accuser had been explicit as to what Laura deserved.

She flipped to the G's.

Grace — getting something you don't deserve.

Like mercy and forgiveness.

The doorbell rang. She bit her lip.

God, I don't know if You care about someone like me. We never really got to know each other that summer. Holt and my mama, now Aunt Velma, say You do care. I've got no right to ask, but please don't let this be Garrett. I can't take another round of him today.

The bell buzzed again.

Taking a deep breath, Laura flung open the door.

Jon stepped back, his usual stony expression replaced with . . . grief? His jaw clenched, he widened his stance and clasped his hands behind his back.

Inexplicably reminded of the night the highway patrolman had rung the bell,

Laura's throat tightened. This was it. The end of the road.

Jon had come to claim her son.

A bleak expression in her eyes, she stood frozen in the doorframe and stared at Jon. Just . . . stared at him.

Unsettled, Jon shifted his feet, assuming a more relaxed posture. "Laura, we need . . ."

He swallowed. "I need to talk to you."

The color drained from her face. Falling back inside the cool interior of the house, she gestured to the sofa. Her hand trembled as she shut the door behind him.

He'd caused that fear. Him and his loud-mouth threats.

She sank into the wingback and splayed her hands across the armrests.

Jon's hands gripped his knees and sat. No easy way to say it. Better to get it done.

He dropped his eyes to the coffee table between them. Where to start?

At the beginning . . .

"I want to apologize for that day at the pond in Mimosa Grove. The last week of our summer when I pressured you . . . pushed you into doing something I knew was wrong. Something beyond your comfort zone and the boundaries God established. I'm sorry for not being the man I should've been. And though I don't deserve it, I'd like to ask for your forgiveness."

He held his breath.

A clock ticked.

Scared of her silence, his eyes cut to where Laura's fingers clawed into the fabric of the armrests. Her left hand, he noted with irrational joy, without the gaudy engagement ring from Garrett.

Laura squared her shoulders. "We both knew what we did wasn't right."

His eyes found hers.

She shook her head. "You didn't push me into anything I didn't already want to do. I won't let you take the blame for more than that."

"I'd still like your forgiveness." He tensed. "If you can. If you would."

She sighed. "We need to forgive each other."

Jon nodded. "I didn't . . ." Distaste filled his voice.

He flushed. "I didn't hook up with that . . . that woman in the motel room."

"I know. I believe you."

His head snapped up. "You do?"

She gave a hoarse, mocking laugh. "Always a day late and a dollar short, but I eventually get there. My father set us up."

Laura wet her lips with her tongue. "And

then I went off halfcocked and . . ." Her broken smile tore at his heart. "The rest is history."

Jon screwed up the remnants of his courage. The next part would be even harder to say.

"I had no right to threaten you. I won't be filing a custody suit. I don't deserve to be part of Ian's life. I respect your wishes, and I will never contact our —" He bit his bottom lip to stop the tremor. "Never contact your son again."

She released her death grip on the chair and exhaled. The sound of her relief at his leave-taking like a hammer blow to his heart.

"I do have one request."

She stiffened.

This, the shakiest of ground.

"You are in no way obligated to comply." Jon leaned forward. "Before I leave Raleigh —"

"You're leaving Raleigh?"

"By now Mike has filed the paperwork with IA — Internal Affairs — and my employment with the RPD is a matter of days."

"What will you do? Where will you go?"

He gave her a crooked grin. "Now you make me sound like a male version of

Scarlett. 'What will I do? Where will I go?' "

The teensiest of smiles flickered across her face. "I'm not going to play to Rhett's parting line."

He smiled. "I'll do the honors. Frankly, my dear, I don't have a clue. Make my mama happy maybe and apply for a deputy position within the Robeson County Sheriff's department."

"Oh." Her face shuttered. "What's your one request?"

"I'd like, if you'd allow me, to see . . ."

A heartbeat. Four more.

"What, Jon?"

"I'd like to see Ian's photo albums since his birth. The years I missed and then, I promise you, Laura —"

He caught and held those fabulous baby blues of hers. "Then you'll never have to lay eyes on me again."

She'd won.

Why did she feel like weeping?

The birth-to-twelve-months period spanned two albums. The rest of the preschool years in two more. Ian's current elementary status contained in another.

Laura brought the photo albums to the coffee table and spread them out in front of Jon. And she left him to his private perusal of the lost years of his son's life.

She went out through the kitchen and raised the garage door. Donning garden gloves, she grabbed the clippers from the workbench. Rounding the house, she attacked the black spotted leaves of the hybrid teas with a vengeance.

He'd never bother her or Ian again. It was over. Jon Locklear was many things.

A liar, unlike her, he was not.

Instead of the rush of joy she'd expected at his capitulation, Laura couldn't shake a disquieting feeling of sadness. Sadness for Jon at the loss of any chance to know his son. Sadness for Ian.

Jon was a good man. A man worth knowing. Despite the pain they'd caused each other, she wouldn't have given up that summer she spent with him for all the sapphires in the world.

And she'd never see Jon again, either.

He'd disappear forever out of her life as suddenly as he'd dropped into it less than a week ago. She was doomed never to reach a satisfactory answer to the saddest of questions — what might've been.

Sunlight arched vertically in the sky. She'd forgotten to put on a hat. Sweat dripped — elegant as always — down the tip of her nose. Could she risk tiptoeing inside to retrieve her garden hat?

Laura squinted at her watch. He'd been in the house for over an hour. Had Jon finished sorting through the memories of his son's young life?

Her pulse quickened.

Or had he already taken his leave, never to return again?

Dropping the clippers, she slung her gloves as she ran. Pounding up the garage steps, Laura seized the doorknob and froze.

Why was she so panicky? A quick look revealed his truck still parked out front. No need to act like a fool.

Her heartbeat slowed. She'd get a drink of peach tea and her hat. Laura winced remembering her lack of hospitality — the hardwired curse of Southern culture. Where were her manners? She'd offer some tea to Jon, too.

Laura tiptoed through the kitchen and into the front room. And a sight she'd never forget — or ever speak of — halted Laura in her tracks.

Jon had sunk to his knees beside the coffee table, where happy pictures of his son's first Christmas, first Easter basket, and first day of kindergarten lay scattered across its surface. His head bowed, Jon's shoulders heaved with silent, bone-jarring sobs.

Laura backtracked the way she'd come and fled toward the beauty and order she'd created with her roses. Gripping the shears, she opened and closed them, slashing the black-spotted leaves.

She'd done this to Jon. Done this to them with her lies.

Clipping the leaf at the stem, she sliced at her lofty attempts to control.

She'd done this. Not Dad. Not Barbara. Why? Why had she done this?

Laura worked the clippers up the stalk.

Not for Ian's sake. Not because of her mistrust of a man she believed betrayed her. No room left now for anything but truth.

She'd kept Ian from Jon because of her own hurt, for the sake of her own pride. Out of a primal need to hurt Jon the way he'd hurt her.

Clip, clip.

At a terrible cost to Jon's own well-being, he'd given Laura back her son. He'd given her forgiveness and a gift of mercy in not tearing her apart in front of a courtroom. An act of grace giving her far more than Laura ever deserved.

While grappling with death, her mother understood life was about grace and mercy. Neither of which she nor Laura nor Jon could ever deserve or earn. It wasn't about deserving.

It was about God. His grace. His mercy.

Tears streamed down Laura's face, burned and scalded. Precious years of Ian's life forever lost to Jon because of her selfishness and lies.

Forgive me, God. Forgive my lies. My attempts to control circumstances and people.

Clip. Clip. Clip.

Why Jon didn't hate her she'd never understand. But instead, he'd come asking for her forgiveness. Asking for one small gesture on her part.

Her heart thudded in her chest. One day Ian would learn the truth. And he'd hate her for what she cost him and his father.

Clip. Clip.

Oh God, help me —

"Laura!"

She jerked.

Jon wrenched the shears out of her hand. "Stop, Laura. Stop."

The shears clattered to the ground.

"What're you doing?" His arm around her waist, Jon pressed Laura's shoulders against his chest. "Laura, honey? What's wrong?"

Pink, red, and yellow petals showered her flip-flops. And through the curtain of her tears she beheld the decapitated remains of her prize roses.

Laura sagged into the shelter of his arms. "I'm so sorry, Jon. For keeping Ian from you. For the years you lost with him." Her voice caught. "For the years we lost. I should've trusted you. Listened to you. Never believed . . ."

Sobbing, she sank to her knees in the petal-littered mulch.

Jon dropped to his knees. Hugging her, rocking her as she cried out a decade of accumulated pain.

"I don't want you to leave, Jon. I want Ian to know you're his father." She gripped his shirt with both fists. "Don't leave us again. Don't —"

Her body shuddered with hiccupping sobs. "P-p-please don't leave me again."

"Laura . . ."

Her name on his lips rocketed into the marrow of her bones.

She lifted her head. Hope warred with fear in her heart.

A breeze, with a sweet hint of honeysuckle, floated between them.

He cupped her face, his eyes searching hers. "I never want to leave."

She quivered at the longing in his voice. An aching need swelled in her soul.

Laura's arms slipped around his neck, and she knotted her fingers. He crushed her to his chest with such force, she gasped. But she tilted her head and his lips closed the distance, traversing the barriers separating them. At the touch of his mouth, she moaned.

His kiss . . . warm, inviting. Like the gentle ripples of a secluded pond outside Mimosa Grove one long ago summer. A lingering kiss that sought to burn away the pain of lonely years.

Cradling the crown of her head, his fingers tangled in the strands of her hair. "Corn silk," he whispered. His lips brushed against her ear.

"Jon . . ."

She guided his mouth back onto hers, tasting him, claiming him. His body jolted, shuddering as his hands explored the curve of her spine. As she gripped and caressed in turn the broad planes of his shoulders. Deepening her kiss, her veins pulsed with desire. Alive again after a decade of numbing purgatory.

Jon groaned and his mouth plumbed the sweet hollow of her throat. Drowning. Devouring.

Heat coursed through her body. And like a never-forgotten song, she pressed into him, molding her shape into his. Promising — begging this time — for forever.

But suddenly, he wrenched away. Scrambling to his feet, Jon staggered. Shock, pain, and regret stared back at her through his eyes.

Had she disgusted him? Disappointed him? Demanded what he no longer wished to give?

An image of Ana Morales flashed into her mind. And the notes . . . ?

She closed her eyes. She wouldn't — couldn't — listen to the lies of those insidious notes. Not Jon.

Had her body and her good sense betrayed her once more? No one else could have known about — Laura bit her lip.

And tasted him again.

No, not Jon. Please God, never Jon.

Laura placed her hand over her chest in a vain attempt to control the wild beating of her heart. She swallowed past the boulder lodged in her throat. If Jon didn't do something, say anything, she was going to shatter . . .

Trembling, he held his hand out to her. Like her, he appeared to have difficulty maintaining a steady breath. "We need to go slower this time. Do things the right way."

Relief washed through her.

Jon pulled Laura to her feet. His fingers

squeezed around hers.

She brushed pink petals from her wobbly legs. "We always seem to end up on the ground, don't we?"

He flushed. "Not this time." He ducked his head. "I mean to give God's commands and you the respect you deserve. It's just every time I'm near you . . ."

Pleasure fluttered her belly like the gentle stroke of a butterfly's wings that she still had that effect on him. "This time we'll have a built-in chaperone."

"Do you think he'll be okay with me as — ?" Jon gulped.

"Let's get out of the heat." She tugged Jon toward the screened porch. "Ian already thinks you hung the sun and the moon."

She smiled at him as Jon held the screened door open for her. "Like mother, like son. We do need to decide how and when would be the best time to tell him, though."

Leading the way into the kitchen past Buggs, who raised bored eyes as they passed his pallet, Laura withdrew two glasses from the cupboard.

Jon leaned against the counter, his hands stuffed in his pockets. The way she'd seen Ian do countless times. "Whatever you think."

She pressed one glass under the ice dispenser. "We'll tell him soon. I'm done with the lies." The cubes clinked against each other.

"I want you to know I think you and Holt have done a fine job of raising him. Any man would be proud . . ." Jon looked away.

She set the glasses on the counter. "Thank you, Jon. Holt was good to both of us. And I —" Her throat constricted.

Her hand on the refrigerator handle, Laura pressed her forehead to its cool exterior. "Holt deserved so much more than I could ever give him."

She closed her eyes. "There was so little left of me to give him after I'd given everything to you."

His shoulder brushed against hers. "You never had more children. You said that summer you wanted a house full." He curled a tendril of her hair around his index finger.

Laura laughed. "I said I wanted three." Her smile slipped. "Holt had leukemia as a boy. The bone marrow transplant, the chemo, and the radiation gave him a great ability to empathize with his patients. What he endured propelled him into that field, but it also robbed him of the ability to have any children of his own. We both knew that going in. I know it's hard for you to hear this, Jon, but he truly adored Ian. Ian, in every sense but the biological, was Holt's son."

Jon turned Laura to face forward. "I owe a debt of gratitude to Holt Mabry for being the father I wasn't worthy to be. I don't ever want to take that away from Ian." He leaned his forehead against hers.

"Did Ian say anything to you about a Boy Scout campout this weekend?"

Humor sparked in Jon's eyes. "He might have mentioned it. Why?"

"Ian's been hounding me about you two going together." She gave him a sad smile. "He's so desperate for a male figure in his life. Stephen Prescott, Mike Barefoot, and Justin Monaghan have tried to be there for him."

She shrugged. "He doesn't think I know, but it's supposed to be a father-son camping trip. I think Ian may've nominated you for the position."

"I'd love to go camping with Ian this weekend, but what about . . . ?" A funny look crossed his face. "We seem to be getting ahead of ourselves again."

Her cheeks reddened. "Chemistry's never been our problem."

"No, I mean, yes." He shook his head. "I meant what about Payne?" Jon wrinkled his nose. "Won't you be on your honeymoon this weekend?"

His jealousy, though unfounded, curled her toes in delicious ways.

She touched his mouth with her finger. "That's one wedding that's never going to happen."

He released a gust of air that ruffled her hair. Taking her hand, he brushed his lips against her bare ring finger. "I still have the ring I planned to give you before your father told me about your engagement to Holt. I kept it with me in my footlocker at basic. And then when I got what I thought was your note, I brought it to Jacksonville hoping . . ." He sighed.

Tears pricked her eyelids. "Oh, Jon."

Her lips parted. Jon tightened his hold on her and lowered his head —

Brakes groaned from the street and a bus door opened with a whoosh.

With a wry smile, she planted a quick peck on his cheek and shooed him away. "Our chaperone." She headed for the front door.

Ian, book bag slung over one shoulder, raced up the lawn toward the house. He barreled through the door. "Is Jon here? That's his truck, isn't it?"

"Hello to you, too, son." She stepped aside. "Yes, it's —"

Ian brushed past her. "Jon?"

Jon leaned against the arched frame between the living room and kitchen. "Hey, buddy. How was your day?"

Ian halted midway between them. He tossed his bag on the sofa. "Why're your eyes red, Mom?"

He pivoted to Jon. "Why're you grinning like Buggs when he thinks he's treed a squirrel?"

Jon's laughter boomed.

Ian's grin lifted his cheeks. His eyes swirled upward into half-moons.

"Mr. Eloquence." Laura mouthed over Ian's head at Jon, *our son.*

Ian's gaze ping-ponged. "Okay, you guys . . . What did I miss?"

16

Jon and Laura talked of many things on the screened porch after supper while Ian chased Buggs around the backyard.

Make that, Buggs chased Ian around the backyard.

Jon couldn't remember when he'd last been this happy. One summer ten years ago, maybe?

Insects whirred as he shared some of his experiences on tours in Iraq and Afghanistan. But he muted the violence for Laura's ears. Those worry lines he'd noticed on her forehead relaxed as Laura related how she fulfilled a lifelong dream by opening Tapestries. With the heat gentled by the setting sun, Jon proposed they venture to Sugardaddy's for ice cream.

Wanting to face her fears — with Jon by her side this time — Laura suggested they give Buggs his evening stroll and take the shortcut through the greenway to the Village. Ian blazed the trail ahead of them on his bike. Swirls of pink and blue strands of cotton candy flossed the horizon.

Jon's hand closed around Buggsby's leash. "Stay in sight of us, Ian."

Ian crested the footbridge and waited half a football field ahead. Laura tucked her hand in the crook of Jon's arm.

A quick pleasure registered at the touch of her hand. He relished the play of sunset burnishing her golden hair. Squirrels scrabbled on the bark of trees.

Laura tightened her grip as they passed the flattened underbrush at the site of her attack and Renna's murder. Yellow police tape fluttered in a sultry breeze beneath the river oaks. The song of birds belied the horror of a life snuffed out.

Ian got off his bike to examine an overturned, abandoned turtle shell. The luminescent glow of fireflies tempered the humidity. Perhaps in an effort to erase the bloody images from her mind, Laura breathed deeply of the fragrance of night-drenched blossoms.

Past the police tape, Jon slowed, careful to keep out of Ian's extraordinary earshot. "I have reason, good reason, to believe someone tampered with Holt's Expedition, causing his death the night of the ice storm."

She tripped over a root. "What did you say?"

Jon caught her elbow.

Laura's eyes widened. "You think Garrett had something to do with it, don't you? And with Renna's death."

"He had the most to gain by Holt's death. And the most to lose if revelations about her baby came out."

"The most to gain? Gain what?"

Jon pursed his lips. "You, Laura. To gain or lose you."

"Oh, Holt . . ." Tears welling, her eyes drifted toward the tangled undergrowth lining both sides of the path. Her face inscrutable, the lines creased her face once more.

Jon's heart nosedived.

Velma had been right. Laura had said everything to him she ever intended to say about her late husband. Their relationship — hers and Holt's — would forever remain taboo.

"Even with Garrett's offer to provide the police with his DNA, you think he's the father?"

Jon shrugged. "DNA results take a long time. Garrett Payne is the master of spin doctors. I think Garrett believed you'd be married to him by the time the truth came out and his campaign, his ego, and whatever he calls a heart would be safe."

"According to Patti Ogburn, Garrett may not be your only suspect regarding Renna's unborn child."

"Come on, you guys," yelled Ian. "We'll be Thanksgiving getting ice cream at this rate."

As they moved forward, she told him about Renna's "research" with the Ogburn-Munro law firm, and Patti's accusations against her husband, Woodrow.

Jon gave a low whistle. "No love lost between those two, is there? I'll contact Ana and give her a heads-up."

She bristled. "Are you and Ana in a off-duty relationship, too?"

Jon allowed himself a small smile. As if anyone could ever come close to his feelings for Laura. "Almost, but nothing ever amounted to much, not once you and I found each other again."

His lips brushed her cheek. "There's never been room for anyone else besides you, Laura."

She relaxed, a quirky smile on her face. "Well, no wonder she hates me. I'd hate me, too, if someone stood between me and you."

"Ana's a good cop. She'll find out the truth about Renna's murder."

Emerging into the parking lot at the Village, Jon joined Ian, already in line, at the takeout window of Sugardaddy's. On a sweltering day where the temps would only drop to the mid-eighties come nightfall, Raleigh residents came alive and outdoors after five o'clock.

"Butter pecan still your favorite?"

She flushed with pleasure. "You remembered."

"I remember a lot of things."

He'd spent years of lonely nights under the stars of Afghanistan replaying every detail of their short time together. Jon placed the order and shuffled off to wait. Ian occupied himself by doing doughnuts around the parked vehicles.

She pressed her shoulder against Jon's.

A joy shot through his body. A joy he'd never tire of.

She tucked her head against the curve of his neck. "Oh, I forgot to tell you what Doris said to me at the funeral."

He reached for two of the cones, handing her one and waving Ian over, while he listened. They moved to a wrought-iron bench. He looped Buggs's leash over the back.

Buggs roosted on the pavement, tongue extended and ready to catch any errant plops of ice cream. Laura waved at her neighbors and fellow customers on this lazy, almost summer night. Ian headed for neighborhood pals on the sidewalk.

Even the ice cream tasted better with Laura at his side. How right and good that he, his son, and Laura were together at last. Good didn't begin to describe his euphoria.

Thank you, thank you, Lord.

He struggled to bring his mind off the future and to the case at hand. Doris Stanley. Laura was telling him about Doris. "Baby? The finger?"

"You've met Doris. The Alzheimer's leaves her in and out of it."

"Ana could —"

"Morales would scare her to death." Laura shook her head. "Better let me see what I can get out of her. Let's hope she's having a good day tomorrow. I'll pass any info along to you."

"Don't hold anything back she tells you, no matter how nonsensical. You never know when something useful will emerge."

"Promise." She swiped her tongue across her melting cone.

He gazed into the distance. "Renna may have been trying to catch you at your house after you dropped Ian off for the fishing trip. Something important she wanted to tell you that couldn't wait."

"And she took the shortcut?"

Jon nodded.

"Did the police discover anything when they searched my house yesterday?"

He settled back. "No, they didn't, as I knew they wouldn't."

"What were they looking for, or can't you tell me?"

"They were looking for the murder weapon." He straightened. "Hey, why the carpentry tools lying around the yard? Did Ian leave them out?"

"No, it was that no-account handyman I hired to build a fence. Zeke Lowther was gone when I returned from the Prescott's Friday, and I haven't seen him since." She blew out a breath. "Probably still sleeping off a drunk."

Jon's eyes narrowed. "Friday the last time you saw him? The Friday Renna was murdered?"

She put a shaky hand over her mouth. "You don't think he . . . ? Why would he kill her? Did he know Renna Sheldon?"

Jon tossed the empty cup into the nearest receptacle. "Interesting coincidence he's dropped off the face of the earth since then. Who's to say he killed her? You left him working at the back of your property off the greenway. Maybe he heard Renna scream.

Saw something. Maybe he paid for his curiosity or good citizenship with his life and he's . . ."

"He could be dead, too." She cast a glance toward the forest. "Out there."

Jon reached for his cell. "The greenway continues on the other side of the Village toward downtown. We didn't check that far when we canvassed the crime scene. Ana can tap into any DMV records and pull his vehicle tags. She can issue a BOLO —"

A blank look from Laura.

He hit speed dial.

"Be on the lookout. The RPD can lift his picture from his license. She can also get the record for the make, model, and plates of his vehicle. Then issue an all-points bulletin so every law enforcement officer in the state will start the hunt for this guy."

Ana picked up on the other end. He edged away, his tone terse.

Waiting for Jon to finish his extended conversation with Detective Morales, Laura shivered despite the heat, wishing they'd driven to the Village. Now they faced a long, creepy walk home through the greenway. She gestured to Ian across the shopping center as a black sedan, windows tinted, surged into the parking lot.

Ian waved good-bye to his friends and nosed his bike toward her.

The car sped up and swerved.

With the quickest distance between two points being a straight line, Ian was halfway across the parking lot when the sedan's engines revved. His eyes widening, Ian froze, one foot on a bike pedal. With his other foot on the ground for balance, Ian shrank against the rear bumper of another vehicle. His mouth worked, but no sound came out.

And Laura realized her son had become the sedan's target.

Raw fear churned in the pit of her stomach. "Ian!"

Oh, God. No. No. Don't let —

The vehicle lurched forward.

Laura rushed past the startled diners at Mambo's. Her feet pounded the pavement. Leaving the sidewalk, she darted between the parked cars in front of Mr. Wangchuk's florist shop. Her heart in her throat, she knew she wouldn't, couldn't possibly reach Ian in time.

Her precious son . . . He'd be crushed. Killed . . .

Like Holt.

Some woman screamed like a crazy person for God, for Jon . . .

For Holt.

In a blur of motion like a sudden gust of wind, Jon passed her as if she were standing still. Launching himself like a rocket-propelled grenade, he clambered over the top of the car where Ian remained paralyzed. Metal crunched and dented beneath his high stepping treads. He slid head first, as if approaching home plate, down the back end of the car.

Arms extended over his head, he grabbed Ian around the waist. Jerked him up. Plucked the boy from his bike.

Digging his feet into the sleek steel of the automobile, Jon scrambled for traction, away from the murderous grill of the sedan. A heart-stopping moment. He and Ian slipping. The black sedan charged, grinding the bike into the bumper.

The resulting collision sent Jon and Ian flying over the roof of the car to land with a bone-jolting bounce onto the sidewalk. The sedan reversed. Tires smoking, the sedan spun a one-eighty and peeled out of the Village.

Chaos erupted. A rush of people stampeded toward Jon and Ian. The mangled metal of Ian's bike glinted in the fiery rays of the setting sun.

The mangle that could've been Ian's body.

Laura began a slow descent toward the pavement. A neighbor caught hold of her arm. Laura dropped with a thud onto her behind and placed her head between her buckled knees.

"Mom! Mom!" Springing up, Ian hovered over her.

"I'm okay." She grabbed hold of his shirt, scanning for bruises and cuts. "Are you okay, honey?"

He helped Laura to her feet. She encircled Ian in the shelter of her arms.

"I'm fine." Ian shot a glance over his shoulder. "Thanks to Jon."

Jon unwound slowly. He tested his arms and legs for functionality. "The resilience of youth." He swallowed as color leached from his face.

She ran her gaze over the angular line of his jaw to where the asphalt had shredded his shirt. An angry cement burn marked Jon's cheek where he'd done a face plant on the sidewalk. He'd taken the brunt of the impact on his body.

Wincing — she could tell he was trying not to groan out loud — Jon stiff-legged his way over to them. A crowd gathered, shocked and shaken at the violence.

Jon's eyes darted around. "Anybody see my cell phone? I think I lost it when . . ."

He swayed.

One of Ian's buddies stepped forward. Broken bits of plastic and wires dangled in his hand. "Uh, dude? I think this is what's left of your cell when you tossed it and ran." He whistled, giving Ian an appreciative look. "Man, that was something else."

The teen fished his own phone out of his baggy pants, strapped with a belt at the level of his thighs. "Here. You can borrow mine to call the police."

Jon smiled. His face twitched with pain at the effort. "Thanks. I am the police, but you're right. I could use some backup." He tried to whistle back, but his busted lip contorted. "Cooler phone than mine anyway."

Ruffling the top of Ian's head, Jon nuzzled the undamaged side of his face against Laura's bare shoulder. Holding on to her son, she looped her arm around Jon's waist. Like Jon, she just needed to touch them both.

To reassure herself they were okay. With the three of them together, she felt complete. Safe. She sent a prayer of gratitude to God.

Squaring his shoulders, Jon dialed 9-1-1. "We're going to be okay," he mouthed to her.

A promise.

But somebody somewhere, Laura knew, would not be. Not after going after Jon Locklear's son.

Staring into the gathering twilight, the look in Jon's eyes changed to cold fury. The same look he'd directed at her across Alison's dinner table in what seemed an eternity ago. That Marine trained to be a lethal weapon was back. His face hardened as the operator picked up. "Officer needs assistance," he barked.

Renna's killer — if indeed this assault upon her son was tied to Renna — had made his first mistake.

17

Jon stood, hands in his chino pockets, beside Ana on the shore as the grinding coil of the wench hauled Zeke Lowther's paint-peeling red pickup out of Glen Lake. They'd already run the license plate. Jon rubbed a hand across the back of his neck.

This morning, a scuba-training certification class made the grisly discovery. RPD divers verified the find and snapped underwater photos to document the evidence *in situ* before summoning the tow truck. Doc and his team waited nearby, ready to perform their part in the investigation. Usually the victim and the crime scene weren't disturbed until the M.E. officially declared the victim dead, but in this case, it was a moot point.

A dozen blue-and-whites blocked access to the local fishing hole. An ambulance wasn't among them. The divers reported the corpse's hands were tied to the steering wheel, legs bound at the knees. Gray duct tape slathered the occupant's mouth. Zeke Lowther, if the corpse was indeed the former handyman to Raleigh's glitterati, was beyond the help of human intervention.

ID'ing the body would be problematic. The vehicle had been found with the windshield smashed, side windows rolled down. The body had been submerged in the water long enough for the water creatures to feast at his expense. Doc would determine cause of death — drowning or whatever.

Jon pictured the man floundering against the seat cushions. And if Lowther had still been conscious, panic growing as the water rose. Tugging at the knots as the water rushed in. In the realization of imminent death, the man was unable to cry out, to be heard.

A feeling of futility? Regret? And finally, the soul's departure for a reckoning with the eternal.

Jon stifled a shudder. He moved back a pace lest Ana see him in a moment of weakness and despise him. She'd called him to the crime scene, returning the favor for his tip regarding the AWOL carpenter.

Ana strode to the beached vehicle and opened the door. Water gushed out onto her brown leather flats and puddled on the sand. Backpedaling, her feet squelching in her shoes, she grimaced.

Jon waited for her signal. Her case. Her call.

"Get over here, Locklear." Ana gestured. "Tell me what you think." Her shoes ruined, she wouldn't be in a good mood.

Unbuttoning his shirtsleeves and rolling them to his elbows, he poked his head inside. His nose scrunched more from a mental aversion to the mortal remains than from any smell emanating from the body.

Floaters.

Death and submersion in water were the worst. Hardest to collect evidence from. Water possessed a deleterious effect on fingerprints and errant fibers.

Jon craned his neck over the body, examining the far side of the cab. Squatting on his heels, he scrutinized the floorboards for evidence. Fast food debris had floated out onto the sandy soil when Ana opened the truck door.

"Heck of a dent in the frontal quadrant of his skull," Jon commented over his shoulder. "Coincidentally similar to Renna Sheldon's death wound."

Ana smirked. "You noticed that, too." In a tell-me-something-a-rookie-wouldn't-know tone.

Maybe the guy had been unconscious or dead already when the water flooded in.

Small mercies.

"I'm no Doc, but the condition of the corpse suggests he's been dead a few days."

She nodded. Her black eyes continued her studied perusal of the waterlogged crime scene. "Rained last night. Any tire tracks washed away."

He loosened the tie at his throat, opening the button on his shirt, though why he bothered to dress official when he was no longer official, he didn't know. Force of habit. "If this is Lowther, you figure him for seeing something he shouldn't have, like the murder of Renna Sheldon? Or was he a murderer and/or accomplice silenced for his trouble?"

"Sure wasn't suicide. Somebody stuffed him into his own vehicle, bound him, beat in his head, shifted into neutral, and gave his truck a mighty shove. Probably believed he'd never be found."

"The assailant either had another car stowed nearby or somehow managed to walk home afterward."

Ana jerked her head at Doc. "All yours."

Doc and his team ambled forward for photos. They'd draw the crime scene in context and do measurements. Anything left in the truck would be bagged and logged.

Jon stepped aside to the partial shade of the pine trees that dotted the perimeter. A feeling of déjà vu, or somebody walking over his grave, as his Lumbee grandmother would've said, seized him. Water, pines, Laura.

Only the fruity smell of honeysuckle was missing.

His son had been attacked. It had been a late night as the police interviewed the handful of witnesses to the hit-and-run. Ana responded, too, though a hit-and-run wasn't officially tied to her murder investigation. But only a stupid person would believe the death of Renna on the nearby greenway and the attempted murder of first Laura and later his son at the shopping center weren't connected.

Jon's mother hadn't raised any stupid children.

He glanced at the hard profile of his colleague. Ana Morales's mother hadn't raised any "all-gas-no-bean tacos" — her words — either. He appreciated Ana's kindness toward his frightened son as she questioned Ian that night. Her switch from aggression to compassion toward an undone Laura allowed him a glimpse into the woman Ana was when off duty. The woman he might've grown to love if murder and Laura hadn't intervened.

"Unless you've got a problem being under a woman, Locklear . . ." Ana's voice was brusque, her cop persona firmly in place.

What she actually said hit them both at the same time.

He kept his face purposefully blank.

"You know what I mean, Locklear. Working under the authority of a woman."

He so hoped there was a good man in this woman's immediate future.

She darted a snarky look at him, ready to smack any hint of sarcasm into Labor Day. "I've been keeping the lieutenant updated on how you've fed us leads and not held back. He's impressed at your professionalism. I could use your help with this case."

Jon gulped. She'd gone out on a limb for him and his career.

"The lieutenant thinks you could handle partnering with me in an unofficial capacity on this investigation as long as we're clear on who's the lead detective. I think between us we've managed to avoid involving Internal Affairs."

She flicked a hand. "Dates? Who can remember? You were a first responder for the homicide unit, but there was a conflict of interest. So the case was turned over to me with Mike's blessing and your acquiescence."

Not so acquiescent on his part. "Ana, I —"

"Are you trying to create more paperwork for the lieutenant and me, Locklear?"

"No, but —"

She blew air between her lips, a gust. A hurricane. "Stop being such a Boy Scout. Can't remember what in the world I ever saw in you. I prefer my men more . . ."

His brows rose.

She placed a well-groomed hand sans polish against his mouth. "What are well-raised Southern boys taught to say when a female authority figure in their lives issues an order?"

His mouth quirked. "Yes?"

She planted a fist on her hip. "Say it like you mean it, Locklear. Don't shame your mama."

He laughed this time, right in her face. "Yes, ma'am."

The front bell jingled and Hilary Munro swept — no, not today, Laura noted with quick concern — skulked in for the weekly needlepoint gathering.

Hilary didn't look so hot. Her makeup haphazard, she was a disgrace to Southern beauty pageant wannabes everywhere. The usually effervescent Hilary struck Laura as worried, like she hadn't slept in days. And the final mint in the julep — Hilary's colorful orchid tunic was *inside out.*

Exactly how Hilary would've whispered it.

Laura hurried from the register. Aggie, her new shop assistant, emerged from the back room where she'd been unpacking a shipment of iridescent silk threads. Laura touched Hilary's arm.

Hilary trembled.

"Would you watch the front for me please, Aggie?" No one else from the group had arrived yet. "Mrs. Munro and I are going to step into the back for a moment."

Aggie smiled and straightened a cockeyed sample hanging on the wall. Aggie was a godsend, enabling Laura to leave the shop every afternoon at three, meet the school bus, and fix dinner for the men in her life.

The men in her life . . .

Laura fought the urge to slip into pleasant daydreams, starring a certain Jon Locklear. Daydreams that, when indulged in, burned toast, narrowly dodged kamikaze squirrels on the road, and caused her to obliterate a hitherto undetected tower of Good Dog Hearty Chow at the Harris Teeter earlier today.

"What's wrong, Hilary?"

Hilary sank into the desk chair. The leather gushed air and groaned. Hilary held a snow-white handkerchief to her nose.

She was one of those — though not willowy — fluttery Southern females. In a crisis, hard for man, friend, or beast to resist. Laura had long ago seen the charm — the lure — Hilary must've aroused in the dapper Old Raleigh attorney, Nolan Munro, to defy class convention and marry the young beauty queen thirty years ago.

"I can't imagine what the children will think when they hear."

Laura knelt beside her. "Hear what, Hilary?"

"When they hear the Raleigh Police Department has requested a" — Hilary searched for the correct terminology — "saliva sample in regard to poor Renna's untimely demise."

Hilary's liquid-brown eyes, not unlike Buggs, filled with childlike hurt. "They're suggesting Nolan and Renna . . . Little Renna? My Nolan?" She choked off a sob.

A knot formed in Laura's stomach. This was her fault. She'd fed the police the names garnered from Patti's gossip.

"Probably not, Hilary. They're conducting a DNA dragnet, Jon called it, on any male who knew Renna. Renna spent time this winter in Nolan and Woodrow's law office."

Hilary stiffened. "They mean 'knew' in the biblical sense. As in fathered her child."

Laura stroked Hilary's hand. "That's one theory they're developing. That the father of her unborn child was Renna's killer. To stop blackmail or keep Renna from ruining a reputation."

Something flickered in those pools of brown.

"I'm sure they don't truly suspect Nolan. It's more a matter of eliminating persons of interest and narrowing the suspect list to the real killer."

The whites of Hilary's eyes mushroomed. "Why do they suspect blackmail?"

Laura wasn't sure why that idea popped into her mind or if indeed the police were looking into that angle as a contributing factor to Renna's death. She didn't ask for details Jon didn't have to give. She didn't want anything to rock the boat of their still tenuous relationship.

"Your worries are probably unfounded, Hilary. The police, I've been assured, are keeping every bit of evidence they unearth close to their Kevlar vests. Discretion is the word."

She patted Hilary's hand. "Especially with

so many lawyers involved who could, if falsely accused, sue the holsters right off the RPD budget."

Hilary lumbered to her feet. The chair rotated, knocking Laura off balance and into a stack of fabric bolts.

"Sorry to have bothered you. Tell Velma I don't feel up to the group today." Hilary floated toward the door and paused. "But don't tell them why I'm not up to it, okay?"

Laura hauled herself to her feet. "Of course not." She scanned Hilary's pinched features.

Something or someone had Hilary's panties — *Aunt Velma get out of my head* — in a wad. What exactly was Hilary so afraid of? And where there was smoke, there was usually fire.

Laura snatched at Hilary's caftan in an attempt to detain, delay, and distract.

Concern for her friend warred with an equally strong desire to find Renna's killer and bring this circle of violence that almost claimed her son to an end. Hilary Munro, usually as uncomplicated as a toilet bowl, either knew something or suspected something.

"Maybe we could step out and get coffee. Talk till you're feeling better."

Hilary shook her off, like Buggs after a

baptism with the water hose. "I've got errands to run. Things to check. Good-bye, Laura."

"Wait, Hilary."

The front door whooshed shut in Laura's face.

She returned to her Accounts Payable ledger. And thoughts of Jon.

Laura still shook with anger and fear at the memory of what could've happened to Ian. She quivered at the notion of how she could be attending a funeral for her son. It had taken the both of them to convince Ian to get to bed that night. Less than an hour later, Ian awoke screaming from a nightmare. So Jon spent the night.

On the couch with his ear tuned for any more night terrors from Ian.

Beard stubble darkening his jawline, Jon departed at the crack of dawn, apologizing that, once again, he'd compromised Laura's reputation.

She told him not to worry about it. She hoped God would understand Jon's overwhelming need to be there for his traumatized son. Not that God wasn't there with Ian, too.

But she believed God understood in the eyes of a child — or in the case of a freaked-out mom — sometimes only a father with "skin on" would do.

She and Jon decided to wait until after the camping trip this weekend to tell Ian about Jon's real relationship to him, allowing the relationship to grow and deepen on its own over the next few days. A future with Jon Locklear felt like something out of a longed-for dream.

A dream she'd never considered remotely possible. But in God's grace, a second chance.

"God," she raised her eyes to the ceiling. "Please don't let me blow it this time."

Because part of her, the part that believed in Murphy's Law, waited for the other shoe to drop.

The phone rang, jarring Laura out of her distraction. "Tapestr—"

"Aunt Velma says you need to come quick, Laura."

The voice sounded like . . . Tayla?

She glanced at the caller ID.

Jones, V. L.

What mess had her feisty aunt gone and gotten herself into now?

Since when did Aunt Velma have a cell phone? And somehow, over the course of constructing a needlework sampler and building a Facebook page for Velma, Tayla had gone from outright hostility to using the biracially affectionate term of *aunt.* Not the "ant" of Southern white folk, but the equally endearing "ahnt" of the Southern black community.

African American. Velma was right. This politically correct stuff was wearing.

"Laura?" Tayla hissed.

She snapped out of her reverie. "I'm here. Where are you? What's going on?"

"We're at Mrs. Stanley's house."

In the aftermath of the attempt on Ian's life, she'd forgotten about her promise to pay the old woman a visit. "Is Doris okay, Tayla?"

A significant pause while Laura tapped the end of her ballpoint against the counter.

"If by okay you mean alive? Uh . . . no."

"What?" Laura's voice rose in a shriek. Aggie scurried forward from the back.

Laura heard the sound of a hushed conference on Tayla's end.

"Tayla? Let me speak to my aunt. Tell her I said —"

"Aunt Velma said not to take that tone with her and for you to get your, and I quote" — Tayla cleared her throat — "fair-bottomed derrière over here. Now."

"You've called the police? What about the General?"

Tayla made a rasping sound. "Aunt Velma

will not call the police until you get here. The General will wreak World War Three on the unknown person who killed his wife if the police don't get here soon and restrain him."

Laura gasped. "Doris has been murdered? How?"

"Aunt Velma," Tayla whispered, "was afraid the General would hurt himself after the three of us found her body." Louder dictation from her elderly sidekick. "So get over here pronto so we can call the police."

The killer could still be on-site. That stubborn, foolish old woman endangering her life and Tayla's.

Laura clenched her teeth. "I'm on my way."

18

Clutching the white Char-grill bag containing his burger and fries, Jon slurped his milkshake as he made his way over to Ana. She waited for him at one of the picnic tables under the shade of the fuchsia crape myrtles.

She wiped a hand across her brow, beaded with sweat. "We couldn't meet somewhere with air-conditioning?"

He swung his leg over the bench and underneath the table. "A guy has to eat."

"You may not want lunch when I tell you what the lab has determined so far and" — Ana fluttered her lashes at him — "what old-fashioned detective work uncovered."

Jon took a bite from his hamburger. He knew she was dying to tell him.

"Turns out one person of interest recently acquired a pair of expensive running shoes."

He asked around a mouthful of fries, "The yak kind?"

She nodded. "I'll have a search warrant for his car, office, and house within the hour."

"Who?"

"Woodrow Ogburn, attorney-at-law."

Jon gave a low whistle. "DNA back yet?"

She sighed. "You know how long that takes. Budget cuts, understaffing, heavy case load at the SBI."

"But you're pushing it?"

"Your mama ever tell you a person can get more flies with honey than vinegar? I've got my connections over there at the State Bureau of Investigation." She preened on the bench. "I'm working those."

He resisted the urge to roll his eyes. "I'm sure you are, Detective Morales."

She gave him a cheeky grin and punched him in his bicep.

"Hey . . ." Dropping a handful of fries on the ground, he rubbed his arm. "Anything else?"

"Vic in truck is indeed our missing handyman, Zeke Lowther. Doc estimates time of death probably late Friday night or early Saturday morning. His wristwatch stopped at twelve twenty-five a.m. when the water swept in."

Jon's neck muscles tensed. "Mere hours from the time Renna died. Was he our murderer or an accomplice killed to wrap up loose ends?"

"Maybe Lowther witnessed the killing and was killed to silence him as a potential witness."

Jon mulled over that possibility. "If not, and Lowther turns out to be Sheldon's killer, what would've been his motive in killing the girl? Have you found any link between Lowther and Renna?"

"So far no connection between either of our victims. Except," she glanced away, "for their association with Laura Mabry."

His eyebrows bunched. "What about the attack on Ian? Laura had nothing to do with that. If Lowther was Renna's killer, we'd also better be figuring out who killed him."

Ana held up a hand. "Don't go ballistic on me. I'm inclined to agree with you about Laura's innocence. Doc found canine teeth marks on Lowther's leg. Corroborates her testimony about being attacked after stumbling across Sheldon's body. But are you sure your girlfriend is being completely up front with you? Not holding anything back?"

"Absolutely."

She rolled her eyes. "Whatever. You're why I don't do love. Makes you blind, deaf, and stupid."

Ana placed her hands on the table. "Doc

put a rush on it and the blood work came back on Lowther. Doc found traces of diazepam in his blood. High enough dose to cause dizziness, confusion, reduce coordination, and stimulate drowsiness."

Jon grimaced. "Just enough to impair Lowther while tying his hands and legs so his killer could whack him in the head."

"That's the way I call it. Then his killer put the truck in neutral, gave it the old heave-ho, and said 'bye-bye, Lowther.' "

Jon ran a finger between his shirt collar and his neck. "At least he was already dead when the water started pouring in. Although I'm feeling less sympathy for the creep after he tried to murder Laura."

"He was probably too incapacitated to prevent the blow to the head that killed him. I daresay he saw it coming and couldn't do a thing to stop it." Ana's shoulders lifted and dropped. "Either way. Pick your poison."

She grabbed an object at her feet. "Appreciate you collecting Lowther's tools from the Mabry yard." With a heave, she clunked the metal toolbox onto the table. "What do you see?"

"Phillips head screwdriver. Nails. Pliers. String. Level." He ducked his head to scope out the area beneath the table. Nothing more.

Jon closed his eyes, willing the memory of the scene to the forefront of his mind. "Wheelbarrow full of gravel. Posts on ground. Bags of concrete left in the backyard as if he just walked away in the middle of the job."

He opened his eyes. "Did patrol deliver the posthole digger Lowther left leaning against one of the finished sections of the fence?"

"Yeah. And I know you sorted through the gravel in the wheelbarrow and found nothing." Her eyes glinted. "Anything not in the toolbox that should be, though?"

He frowned. "That's everything I found in the grass — Oh. I see what you're getting at."

She nodded. "Like what we should've found in a carpenter's toolbox."

He narrowed his eyes. "A hammer."

"A hammer we've been unable to locate at either the Sheldon crime scene or Lowther's truck. Checked his trailer, too." Ana swiped a fry.

She stuck it between her teeth, crunching. "Doc thinks the handle of a hammer has a high probability of turning out to be our murder weapon for Sheldon and Lowther.

Same strike pattern. Same indentions of circumference and depth of wound. Matching slivers of wood in both vics' skulls. Just need to find the hammer to match."

Ana snagged another fry. "The hammer we took from Laura Mabry's garage isn't a match to the wood fragments found on our vics. Hers had a titanium steel handle. Not wood."

Maybe now Ana would get serious about the other suspects and leave Laura alone. "So you think Lowther's missing hammer killed Renna, and then was later used against him?"

"A definite possibility. And as far as the attack on your son, I'm checking rental car agencies and body repair shops for a black four-door sedan with damage to the front headlights and grille. No license plate, witnesses said."

His jaw clenched at the reminder of how close he'd come to losing Ian.

Jon touched Ana's hand. "You're the best."

She moistened her lower lip. "Apparently not, compared to Laura Mabry."

At his stricken look, Ana burst into laughter. "Just joshing you, Locklear. Try not to take yourself so seriously."

She flipped her tangled black locks over her shoulder. "I don't." Ana reached for his milkshake, moisture condensing on the outside.

"Feel free to help yourself."

Ana wrapped her lips around the straw. "Don't mind if I do. Thanks for asking."

He rolled his eyes this time.

She took a sip. "You want to accompany me on the search at the Ogburn residence?"

Jon pushed the remains of his burger across to her. "Don't mind if I do. Thought you'd never ask."

Ana smiled and sipped the remains of the chocolate shake.

The furnace effect of the June heat wave on her closed, parked car robbed Laura of breath. She fumbled to switch the air vents on full blast. Leaving Tapestries in Aggie's capable hands, she sped toward the Stanley residence.

Screeching to a halt at the curb behind Velma's Crown Vic, Laura wrenched open the door. Lunging out of the car, she charged up the bricked driveway.

Tayla rounded the corner of the white, gingerbread-trimmed Queen Anne. Her hand at her throat, Laura skidded to a stop.

"On the terrace. Aunt Velma has the General confined inside."

Following Tayla, she froze at the broken

form of the elderly Doris seated at a wicker table, slumped over a tea tray. Blood droplets from her caved-in skull dotted the white tablecloth.

"Oh, Miss Doris." Over the heavy scented gardenias, Laura noted the sickly coppery smell of blood. Fresh blood.

She swung toward Tayla. "Why are you and Aunt Velma here?"

"Aunt Velma volunteered to take Miss Doris to the needlepoint group so the General could get to a doctor's appointment." Tayla's eyes drooped. "Not many people know this — Aunt Velma did, of course — he's been diagnosed with metastatic prostate cancer."

Laura put a hand to her mouth.

"Asymptomatic until it was too late." Tayla shrugged her shoulders. "You know how some men are about regular health checkups."

Emerson's similar reluctance to address his high blood pressure led to the stroke that incapacitated Laura's father.

"Did Miss Doris know?"

Tayla shook her head. Her gold hoops quivered. "Miss Velma had been trying to talk the General into moving Doris over to Stonebriar Assisted Living where Miss Velma could keep an eye on Doris while he underwent chemo. The chemo would only prolong his life marginally, not cure him, but he was willing to do anything if it meant being around one more month for his wife."

The young girl cut a glance through the French doors into the darkened interior of the house. "When we arrived, the General walked us through the house to where Miss Doris was . . ." Tayla pressed her lips together.

Laura glanced around the terrace again, careful to keep her eyes averted from Doris's battered form. "Looks like a tea party."

She counted five teacups and saucers. "It's good you entered through the house and no one trampled the crime scene."

Tayla cleared her throat. "Not exactly."

"The cups were for you and Aunt Velma and the General?"

"Not exactly."

Laura frowned. "What are you talking about, Tayla?"

"Miss Doris liked to have tea every morning with her . . . her babies."

Laura's eyes widened. "Her babies? The Stanleys never had any children. What babies?"

"Miss Doris had doll babies. The kind little girls played with fifty or sixty years ago. They looked alike. Dionne kids, Miss

Velma said. Black hair. Rosy cheeks. Big brown eyes. Say 'Mama'."

Laura remembered the doll cases in the front entry of the Queen Anne on a prior visit. "So? Doris collected dolls."

Tayla placed a hand on Laura's arm. "These were not part of her collection. She believed they were flesh-and-blood babies. *Her* flesh and blood babies."

The Alzheimer's. Doris had called for one of those babies at Renna's funeral. Laura's mouth trembled.

She flicked another glance over the wicker tableau. The dolls were missing. "The General took them away, didn't he?"

Tayla nodded. "He said he couldn't bear to see her . . ." For the first time, Tayla's voice wobbled — "humiliated in the eyes of the world." She drew Laura toward the house. "Aunt Velma's found something she wanted you to see before we called the police."

Laura paused on the threshold, giving her eyes time to adjust to the darkness of the living room after the bright glare of the sun. After a few moments, she spotted the General. His posture rigid in a leather club chair, his face was as drawn as a corpse. Aunt Velma clutched Doris's needlepoint bag.

"Aunt Velma?"

Velma put her index finger to her lips and with her other hand motioned for Tayla to take her place on the sofa. In the distance came the faint wail of sirens. Velma dug her fingers into Laura's arm and yanked her into the adjoining kitchen. "You called the law on us, didn't you?"

Laura jerked free. "I most certainly did. Did you and Tayla ever stop to think the murderer could still be hanging around? What have you gotten yourself into this time?"

Velma stiffened. "I'm protecting the reputation of a dear friend."

"Reputation? What are you talking about? Who do you think you are, Miss Marple?"

Velma glared The Look that had reduced senior football jocks to jelly. "That sassy mouth of yours, Laura Bowen, you did not inherit from the Jones side of the family."

Laura's nostrils flared. "Wanna bet?"

"I need your help." Velma assumed a piteous expression. "It's rather beyond the scope of an elderly woman like myself."

Laura doubted the reinvasion of Normandy was beyond the ability of her aunt. She tapped her foot on the linoleum. "Not buying it. Try again."

Velma gave an exasperated snort. "Fine."

She reached inside Doris's sewing bag and withdrew several pieces of stationery. "I found —"

Laura's breath hitched, and she grabbed them. "Where did you get those?"

Velma balanced the bamboo handle of the bag over the crook in her arm, a puzzled look on her face. "You act like you already know what these notes say."

Laura scanned the notes. "Unfortunately, I do. Almost exactly the same messages as the ones I received."

Velma sagged against the granite countertop. "You've received notes, too? Oh, Laura. Why didn't you tell me?" Her aunt straightened. "Of course you didn't tell me. Same reason I didn't tell anyone about the notes I received over the last month. Why Doris, bless her heart, only told me in one of her more lucid moments yesterday about the three notes you hold in your hand. Hers appeared first in her needlepoint bag she carried everywhere with her. The second under the tea tray one morning on the terrace. The third slipped into the program at Renna's funeral."

"Aunt Velma?" Laura's voice squeaked. "Who's doing this? What purpose could there be in these notes?"

"No purpose. Except somebody crazy or

who thinks it's his job to punish." Velma touched the back of her blue-rinsed curls.

"Where did you find your notes?"

"In the hymnal in the pew I occupy at church. Another in my tote I carry to the quilt guild." Velma sighed. "And under the door of my room at Stonebriar last night." She handed Laura a crumpled pile of notes from the pocket of her white linen skirt.

The whirr of an ambulance drew closer. Tires squealed out front. Car doors slammed.

Velma pointed at the notes. "This changes everything. I didn't realize this went beyond two old ladies and long-dead secrets. If you're involved, you need to come clean and tell Jon." Compassion flickered across her face. "You haven't told Jon about your notes, have you, honey?"

Laura shook her head.

"Embarrassing, I know. Our dirty laundry hung out for everyone to see." She patted Laura. "Especially in front of someone whose opinion you care for so deeply. But we have to do it. You're right. Miss Marple we are not. In the real world, Miss Marple and her nosiness would've been dead in the first chapter."

Pounding on the front door.

"Aunt Velma?" called Tayla.

Velma sallied past Laura. "I'll get the door. Everybody stay put."

The front door opened with a squeak followed by the low rumble of voices. Men's voices, except for one sultry female tone.

Laura closed her eyes. That Morales woman. Great.

At the sound of shoes creaking toward the kitchen, Laura swiveled.

Grim-faced, Jon stood in the doorway.

Ana Morales shouldered past him. "Well, well, Mrs. Mabry. We meet again. You do have a habit of dropping into the most interesting places. Like where other people seem to lose their lives."

Unable to meet Jon's bewildered gaze and unvoiced suspicions, Laura bit her lip and traced the black diamond outline on the linoleum with the toe of her white-sandaled foot.

"So answer Morales's question, Laura. What are you doing here?"

Ana left him and Laura alone in the kitchen while the team secured the crime scene and began the interviews.

Laura refused to look Jon in the eye. Instead, she shuffled her feet and clenched her hand around something she'd hidden in the folds of her gauzy skirt.

Jon tried again, impatience warring with professionalism. "I thought you'd be at Tapestries this morning. I had no idea when Ana and I got the call —"

Laura's head snapped up. "You and Morales were together this morning?"

"At lunch when we got the call from dispatch. A call I understand you placed from Tapestries."

Her eyes darkened into a stormy navy blue. Zeroed in on his askew tie. "You and I were supposed to have lunch today."

Didn't she trust him by now? Know his heart?

Jon smoothed down his windblown hair and let out a huff of air. "I'd have been ready to eat again by then, too. We'd come from finding Lowther's body at the bottom of Glen Lake."

Her eyes widened. "Zeke Lowther's dead?"

"Stop avoiding the question, Laura. Why are you here?"

Through pinched lips, she told him about Tayla's call, her decision to call the police, and her headlong rush to rescue Aunt Velma and Tayla from imminent danger.

He scrubbed the back of his neck with his hand. "You ever stop to think you were putting yourself in danger, too? Did you think about Ian getting off the school bus this afternoon with no one to meet him? *Permanently.*"

She shrank back. Conversation in the living room died away.

He was doing it again. Bullying her. Garrett's modus operandi. Not a trait Jon wanted to share with Payne. But Morales was right. Laura was holding something back. He couldn't ignore his gut anymore.

So much for her declaration to adhere to the truth and the truth alone, so help her God.

He forced out an expulsion of air and prayed for patience. "What aren't you telling me? This is no time for playing games."

Blue fire sparked in her eyes. She thrust a wad of paper at him. The ivory note cards crinkled as he took them from her. "What's this?"

"Notes. Miss Doris received these from an anonymous tormentor."

He frowned at their creased appearance. "I'm afraid to ask how many people have handled these. Probably no hope of isolating fingerprints." One hand lightly holding the outlines of the stationery, with his fingernail he pried open the one on top.

I know what you've done. I'm here to make sure you don't get away with it.
Signed, The Accuser

"What had Doris Stanley done?"
Laura frowned. "I don't know. Read the next one."
He shuffled the first one to the back of the stack. "Any envelopes?"
"No. Read."
The second read:

You've deceived others but be you not deceived. Fornicators and adulterers will not inherit the kingdom of God.

The third.

All murderers and liars, like you, Doris Stanley, will dwell in the lake of fire forever.
Judgment Day cometh. Soon.

"Frail Doris Stanley is a murderer?"
Laura's finger shook as she pointed to the words *murderer* and *liar* underlined in blood red. "Those words were of special significance. Signed by The Accuser."
"These three were sent to Doris. Who received the others?"
She gulped and gestured for him to read

the remaining notes.

His eyes widened. "First one same message as Mrs. Stanley but addressed to Velma."

Laura folded her arms. She cupped her elbows with her hands. "Before you ask, I don't know what Aunt Velma could've possibly done either to inspire this sort of hatred."

He assessed the second. "*Fornicator* underlined on Velma's." He examined the third. "This one is altered from Doris's. *All immoral persons and liars* used instead of *murderer,* but both terms underlined in red."

She nodded.

He removed a plastic evidence bag from his pocket. "Is this all of them?"

"No . . ." Her voice sounded strained. "I've received three messages also."

White-hot anger lanced him. "When?"

She averted her face. "The first one on the night of Renna's murder. It was placed in the mailbox."

"The others?"

"On the windshield of my car behind Tapestries the next day. The last one . . ." She moistened her lips. "In my lingerie drawer on Monday night."

He slammed his hand on the counter. She jerked.

"Everything okay in there, Locklear?" Ana called from the den.

"Nothing I can't handle," he yelled back.

He loomed over Laura. "You and I . . . I thought we had an understanding. No more lies. You promised. Now this?"

Jon stalked over to the window. "Why, Laura? Why would you hide these notes from me? You endangered your own life, not to mention Ian's, by withholding evidence in a murder investigation. Ana would be within her rights to charge you with obstruction of justice."

Laura placed a hand on his shoulder. He shrugged her off.

"I didn't know until today that there were others who'd also received notes. That there might be a connection with Renna's death."

"And maybe Zeke Lowther, too."

"Zeke's dead?"

His face felt as set as stone. "Don't know you've given me any reason to trust you with information, Laura. Information, if in the wrong hands, could jeopardize this investigation."

Laura quivered. "You don't think I had anything to do with Renna or Zeke's death, do you?"

"What I don't understand is why you didn't trust me enough to show me those notes after we . . ."

Ana's accusations weighed heavy on Jon's mind. The mistrust of his previous relationship with Laura returned. Truth would trump chemistry — if that's all it was on Laura's part — every time. The barriers of self-protection dropped in place again.

Laura's mouth flattened. "The notes are in my purse for safekeeping. I left them in my car outside." She motioned toward the front of the house. "I'll go get them."

He seized hold of her wrist. "I'll make sure you get there and back safely."

She shot him a sharp look followed by something akin to misery.

He hardened his heart.

At her car, she retrieved the notes and waited, silent and brooding, while he read them.

"Identical," he observed. "But yours arrived in envelopes."

She remained rigid next to the car. "Similar messages except in the second one *fornicator* is underlined. And in the third, *immoral* and *liar* are underlined. Like Velma's."

Laura wrapped her arms around her body. "So you think this is part of the attempt on Ian's life, too? That if I'd spoken up earlier, he might not have been targeted?"

He heard the little-girl-lost note in her

voice, the mother guilt. "I don't know."

"Look in the first envelope. There was something else left inside the first one."

He withdrew a dried honeysuckle blossom.

"My nightgown had been sprayed with the scent when I found the third note." Her lips trembled. "No one ever knew about . . . No one knew the specifics except for —"

"You and me."

With a ragged breath, Jon dropped the petal inside the envelope. "You thought I sent those notes, didn't you, Laura? That's why you didn't say anything."

He gripped her upper arm. "You believed I actually hated you enough to do this? To torment you?"

"Ten years is a long time to be angry. Time to turn bitter. Especially after you found out about Ian."

His hand fell to his side. "But the notes began before I knew the truth. So you say." Jon crossed his arms. "I was angry. I was bitter. But for the grace of God . . ."

She touched his sleeve. "I considered the timing. I never could wrap my head around you being the author of something so poisonous. And after we reached an" — she threw out her hands — "an understanding, I was ashamed of the truth of those notes.

The truth of what I'd been." Her fingers splayed against his chest.

An understanding. That's how Laura viewed their relationship?

Jon stepped out of her reach. "But you still didn't trust me enough to tell me the truth about what was going on in your life." His eyes probed hers. "Is that all? Nothing else you're hiding for whatever self-serving, convoluted reason?"

Avoiding his gaze, Laura looked away down the tree-lined street.

Jon clenched his fists.

She was still holding something back, something she didn't believe he needed to know. He waited one more moment, hoping she'd change her mind, trust him, and come clean. His eyes scoured her shadowed face, begging her to tell him the truth.

But she didn't.

Doubts savaged him. He'd been a fool to think this would work. That there'd been a chance for them.

His gut instinct had been sound. Too much time had gone by. There'd be no going back. Not for them.

"Ana will want you for further questions."

No response.

Would closure, a proper good-bye, ever be possible with Ian ever and always between them? No way to gauge what might have been. Perhaps their destiny would be unwittingly to hurt and maim the other in countless small ways until the day they died.

Engulfed in a wave of sadness, Jon pivoted and walked away.

Before he said something he could never take back.

19

Laura, Velma, and Tayla spent hours at the station in interviews with the police. Jon made himself noticeably absent. He told her — not asked her — that he'd meet Ian's school bus and take him out for dinner until she returned home.

The General collapsed when forensics bagged Miss Doris's body. Admitted to Rex Hospital, his vital signs flagged. Another casualty of what the media dubbed "The Greenway Killer" since the Stanley property also abutted the recreational trail.

This supported Detective Morales and her team's working theory that the murderer killed the elderly woman via the greenway shortly before Tayla and Aunt Velma arrived.

Shaken, Velma looked every one of her seventy-plus years for the first time in Laura's memory. Following Tayla and her aunt to Stonebriar in her own car, Laura sent Tayla home.

Laura secured a cup of Lady Grey tea for Aunt Velma from the Commons Area and guided Velma to her suite. Clad in a baby-blue chenille robe, Velma finally emerged and joined Laura in her sitting room. Her feet encased in a pair of matching slippers, Velma brought with her a large book.

Velma curled into the wingback chair and tucked her feet underneath her. Laura hoped to be as flexible and spry at the same age.

"All right, Aunt Velma. Spill it. What's behind those notes?"

Velma cocked her head like a little bluebird. "Why are things tense again between you and Jon?"

Just like Aunt Velma to answer a question with a question.

"I didn't tell him about Doris's dolls."

Velma cleared her throat. "Ever since you found out about your father and Barbara, you've had trouble trusting. But, my darling girl, secrets have a way of coming out. And at the worst possible time. Take it from one who's been there, lived that." Her aunt's voice quavered. "Tell him the truth. Before it's too late with Jon."

Laura grimaced. "It's already too late with Jon. No surprise, I've blown it with him again."

"Sometimes it's hard to break old habits. God can help you, Laura, to put off the old and replace it with something new."

Laura stiffened. "Jon has his own issues." She shrugged. "Sure, well-earned issues of trust with me. But how can I trust this God of yours when every man I ever loved betrays me?"

"Except for Holt."

Laura's lips twisted. "He died, didn't he? In the end, he left me, too."

Velma's hand shot out, capturing hers. "Honey —"

"You want to tell me why Doris had dolls she . . ." Laura freed herself from Velma's grasp. "That she believed were real? Why she called the dolls her babies?"

Velma fingered the sash on her robe. "In the fifties, there were fewer options . . ." She examined a fingernail. "Less forgiveness for ill-advised behavior."

Laura heaved a sigh. "Does this story truly begin over sixty years ago?"

Velma poked out her lips. "Do you want the answers to your questions about Doris or not?"

Laura leaned against the yellow silk loveseat.

"The General was not always a general. First, he was a boy who received a commission to West Point. He and Doris, a Raleigh debutante, met his third year. They were forever smitten. When it was time for him to return to New York, Doris begged him not to leave her but to take her with him. The General has loved two things in this world," Velma's voice wobbled. "His country and Doris. He gave in, and they secretly married."

"Secretly? Did Doris's family not like the General?"

Velma shook her head. "No, it was nothing like that." She leaned forward. "West Point cadets aren't allowed to be married or they lose their commission."

"Okay . . . I think I'm following you so far, but what about the babies? I didn't think the Stanleys had children. Did Doris have a miscarriage or stillborn children?"

Velma raised her eyes. "No. Seventeen-year-old Doris discovered she was pregnant after Fred went back to school. She'd sworn their marriage to secrecy at the risk of his career."

"Her parents didn't know about it? And she didn't tell them about the baby."

Velma nodded. "So, without telling Fred, she found another solution to her dilemma." Her aunt swallowed. "I'm not saying what she did was right. Not a choice I would have made. But she was young and felt alone. She thought, Doris told me years later, there'd be plenty of time for children once Fred finished his schooling."

Laura felt a rush of pity for the young Doris.

"She found some quack." Velma scrutinized the carpet. "She suffered an infection afterward that she was too ashamed to have treated. As a result, Doris was left barren."

"How did the General react when he learned the truth?"

Velma tugged at the ends of her robe, pulling them tighter. "He was incensed she'd killed their child. Furious that she had made such a life-changing decision without him. But Doris believed she was saving him from losing his career. Almost cost her the marriage."

"That's why The Accuser underlined *murderer.* But who else knew about this besides you and the General?"

Velma frowned. "Don't go thinking the General was behind this. He's not mobile enough. Nor mean enough. He and Doris worked through things and came to regard Renna's mother, their niece, as a surrogate daughter. Spoiled her and Renna — too much, if you ask me."

"The dolls. When did that business start?"

"Just in the last few years. That's when the General realized something was wrong, and Doris was diagnosed with Alzheimer's. It's a funny thing about the mind. As I understand it, recent events are wiped first. But long-term memories aren't. At least, not for a while."

"I remember her being a lovely, trusting woman."

Velma's brow puckered. "Too trusting."

"You think in one of her rambling moods, Doris told someone besides you about her past?"

Velma spread her birdlike fingers across the armrest. "I do. Doris's circle isn't large, especially since the Alzheimer's. People became impatient with her. Pitying. Only the old friends at the Club, church, and Weathersby continued to visit."

She eyed Laura. "I appreciate your attempt to spare Doris's reputation, but tell Jon about the dolls. Doris is past caring, and the General soon will be. Nothing's worth damaging your budding relationship again with Jon Locklear."

That was the real issue. Laura wasn't sure exactly how to define their relationship. Doubts regarding Ana resurfaced. Was Jon playing her, as he believed Laura once played him? His version of payback? And then, there were those hateful missives . . .

Laura fretted the strap of her purse. "You still haven't explained why you think you received the notes, too."

Velma uncurled her feet and rested them on the needlepoint-covered stool. "Do you know why you're receiving the notes?"

Laura shrank back. "When Jon and I . . ." She gazed out the window at the water sprinklers keeping the green grass alive in the heat wave of June. "I lied about my baby. To everyone."

The grandmother clock in the corner ticked.

"I've always admired you for having Ian and raising him yourself. Admired you and Holt for ignoring the snide whispers and sidelong glances."

"Most people saw the three of us and assumed Ian was adopted." Laura cut her eyes at Velma. "You knew all along, didn't you?"

"I knew Ian Bowen Mabry bore a strong resemblance to the tribe I spent most of my adult life teaching in Robeson County. With a more-than-coincidental resemblance to a certain young man with whom you were so in love that summer."

Velma bowed her head. "The summer after Louise died, when I was so useless to you in my own grief."

Laura sprang off the couch. "Don't for a minute think any of this is your fault." She clasped Velma's hands. "Jon and I both understood the chance we were taking."

Velma lifted her chin. "And you didn't care . . ."

Laura dropped her eyes. "To my shame now, no, I did not."

Velma patted her cheek. "Always my honest girl."

Laura gave a bitter laugh. "Jon would hardly agree with that assessment of my character."

"You've always been honest with yourself, and that's what put the barrier between you and Holt. And God. In so many ways, you tried to leak the truth. Even in the naming of your son, you betrayed yourself."

Laura's eyes welled.

Velma's voice became brisk. "You and I are so much alike. Guilty of making the same mistakes."

"You and me? I don't understand."

"Doris wasn't the only one who made poor choices. I once loved a man." The corners of Velma's thin lips drooped. "I've never told another living soul since I shared my secret with my older brother and his wife, Nadine."

"I never knew you'd been in love, Aunt Velma."

Velma laughed, hoarse and raspy as fingernails scraping across a chalkboard. "Most people saw me as a dried-up old spinster no man ever took a second look at. But once, when I was twentysomething like you, I met a soldier at an Army ball at nearby Fort Bragg. We dated while he was stationed there. Then he was called with his unit to Korea. I followed my heart and not my head and . . ."

She took a deep breath and laid a trembling hand on Laura's head. "Your mother, Louise, wasn't my niece."

"What do you mean? You're saying . . ." Laura's eyes widened. "That would make you . . . my grandmother?"

"The hardest thing I ever did was put my baby, your mother, in Nadine's arms. She and my brother were unable to have children. In the fifties, there was no tolerance for unwed mothers. No future for illegitimate children. I wanted better for Louise. They gave her the life I dreamed of for her."

"What happened to your . . . the soldier?"

A faraway look entered Velma's eyes. For a moment, the years fell away, and Laura visualized what the young Velma must have been like to that long ago young man.

"He never returned from a battle historians call Heartbreak Ridge." Velma choked.

Laura squeezed her hand.

Velma quivered, but regained her composure. "Do you remember your grandparents?"

"A little."

"Nadine was one of the kindest souls I ever knew. She *was* Louise's mother. Her real mother. The one who held her head over a basin when she was sick. The one who sewed May Day costumes for the school play. The one to whom Louise confided the hushed secrets of puppy love. But Nadine always included me. Every Christmas, every birthday, I traveled from Mimosa Grove to Raleigh."

"You've always been there for all of us. Always a shoulder to cry on, or to dispense much-needed advice. Mom's beloved Aunt Velma. Mine," Laura stroked Velma's hand. "And Ian's, too."

Velma smiled, a plucky, never-say-die smile. "And so you see why our notes were almost identical."

Laura grimaced. "Those tortured images of judgment pronounced by The Accuser. Judgment I probably deserve. But who would do such a thing, Aunt — I mean — Grandmother?"

"Hush, child. I am and will always be your aunt. It's enough that you know."

Velma gripped her hand. "My saddest regret is I lacked the courage to tell Louise before she died. But it seemed so selfish at that point, though Nadine and my brother were long dead. So wicked to rock Louise's world. And yet . . ."

Laura flung her arms around the old woman.

"Don't wait till it's too late, my sweet girl, like I did." Velma's breath fluttered through Laura's hair. "Don't allow misunderstandings to separate you from those you love."

Fear ground its fist into Laura's belly.

Love was, of course, the problem. Over the last week, Jon never said he loved her. Just that he never forgot her. He'd only spoken of the desire to see where their new relationship could take them. No promises.

Just the chemistry between them at work again? Nothing more on his part?

Their kind of "love" never worked out, never ended well. Romeo and Juliet. Heathcliff and Catherine.

Obsessive and self-serving. Doomed. Hindsight always 20/20.

Laura stuffed the fear down deep once more. "I'll tell Jon about the dolls, I —"

Velma thrust Laura back and studied her

face. "I'm not only talking about Jon. I know about the bad blood between you and your father since Louise died."

Laura jutted her chin. "And since he told Jon about my pretend engagement to Holt. He was also responsible for framing Jon via another nasty note with th-that woman, so I'd believe the worst. If anybody deserves hellfire —"

"Is your heart so hard, Laura Lou," Velma's eyebrows rose, "you'd actually wish hellfire upon your father or Barbara?"

Laura reared. "How can I forgive him, much less Barbara, when I can't forgive myself? How can I expect Ian and Jon and God to keep forgiving me? Laws don't work like that, Aunt Velma. Neither man's nor God's."

"Why should God forgive me, Laura Lou, for what I've done? Forgive any of us for what we've done?"

Velma tucked her chin into her chest. "But there's a higher law of grace. I don't know why God would choose to offer me or anybody else forgiveness, but He promises He will if we ask Him to. When I fail Him, when I'm discouraged, I try to remember the words of Lamentations."

"Lamen-what?"

Velma's mouth quirked. "Lamentations.

Goes something like this. 'Because of the Lord's great mercies we are not consumed. His compassions never come to an end. Great is Thy faithfulness, O Lord.' "

Laura choked back a sob.

Mercies. It always came back to that.

Velma tilted her head, thinking out loud. "That note business with Jon doesn't sound like Emerson. The revelation about the engagement I can believe. Emerson tended to be more in-your-face with his attempts to control."

The old woman snorted. "More heavy-handed in his approach with people. Throwing his weight around and letting everyone know it. The floozy thing sounds too devious for him."

Her au— grandmother — reached into the side pocket of her chair and drew out an album. "Mimosa Grove High School Yearbook. The year your father graduated. I want you to understand him better. And Barbara."

Laura made a motion of protest.

Velma set her jaw. "I've had a hard time forgetting, much less forgiving, his betrayal of my Louise in those last days."

Her china blues, so like Laura's, sparked. "But I want you to understand and forgive. Not for their sakes, but for your own. Like

Louise did. Like her good mother, Nadine, taught Louise to do with life's hurts."

"But —"

"Promise me, Laura. Promise me you'll try. Your father doesn't have long to live. Doesn't want to live in that condition. I don't want you to have to live the rest of your life with regrets."

Laura nodded, unable to trust herself to speak.

"You were the delight of his life." Velma cupped Laura's face. "As you and Ian have been the joy of mine. When Emerson tried to warn Jon off with news of your engagement, I'm sure he believed he was protecting you. Protecting your future. Emerson always had high aspirations for himself and those he loved. He left Robeson County determined to reach the highest pinnacles of power. Did you know Barbara grew up with Emerson? Her father was the farm manager of the Bowen estate."

Velma sighed. "Lot of history between Emerson and Barbara. I taught them both. Her father was one of those awful sanctimonious, Bible thumping, makes-kids-want-to-do-crazy-things kind of fathers. I perceived a lot of things others didn't."

"Like what?" Laura's voice sounded hoarse, as if she'd been crying a long, long time. Or, storing tears instead.

"Barbara was plumb nutty about Emerson Bowen. Chased him without shame. Hard for any man, much less a boy, to ignore that kind of adoration." Velma shot her a sharp look. "Adoration best given to God and not any human being. And I'm not just talking about Emerson, Laura Lou."

Laura decided to let that zinger pass. "And Dad let her catch him, I'm guessing."

"Not for a long time. He was off to law school. He started his practice in Raleigh. Met your mother."

"Whose connections helped him get his seat on the bench."

Velma nodded. "But he cared deeply for Louise. I made sure of that. And when you were born . . ." She let out a tiny puff of air. "Barbara married a pig farmer the same age of her own father. She showed up in Raleigh one day. I think she caught Emerson in a weak moment on the campaign trail. Thereafter, blackmail, guilt, whatever you want to call it, he hired her as his personal assistant, set her and her boy Garrett up in a house . . ."

"How utterly sleazy of him."

Velma slumped. "We each have our addictions. For some it's alcohol. Others, drugs. Still more it's food or money or whatever."

She shrugged. "But the two of them, I don't excuse it, but I could tell when Barbara came to town, there was a change in him. Barbara was his addiction. And he was hers. A bitter roller coaster of shame and consequence."

She thrust the yearbook at Laura. "You have my permission to tell Jon these things about the notes if it will help locate Doris's killer. Too many secrets."

Velma reached for the cup of the now cold tea Laura had placed beside her elbow on the side table. She took a sip and made a face.

"I'll reheat it in the microwave. But I feel better. Always makes a person feel better to come clean. To tell the truth. Glad I've gotten that off my chest. You go home and think about what I said." Velma creaked to her knees.

Laura reached out a steadying hand, but recognized she was being dismissed. She feared, unlike Velma's soul-cleansing revelations, with Jon and her father there had already been too many lies to overcome.

"Where's my mom?"

Hostility radiated from Ian. It was a reaction Jon was unused to receiving from the boy.

"She's at the station, finishing —"

"Did you arrest her?" Eyes, dark as Jon's own, glared.

"No, I did not. She'll be home later. I told you that."

Ian kicked the leg of the chair at Mambo's. "I want to go home."

Jon sighed. "Why don't you finish your pizza first? I thought you liked Mambo's."

Over the intercom, Dean Martin sang his version of "Mambo Italiano."

He'd chosen a table where he could keep his back safe against the wall and his eye on the door.

Old habits, like old loves, died hard.

Hours after more of Laura's redacted version of truth, his chest continued to ache. And Jon hadn't for one moment forgotten how Laura cried out for her dead husband in this very shopping center. Holt Mabry — the only man Laura ever trusted. Maybe would ever trust.

Jon struggled to hide from Ian his anger at Laura. To not reveal how his hopes and dreams for them to become a family had been dashed. He should've known he couldn't trust Laura. Looking back, it wasn't like she'd ever made any declarations of love.

Same old Laura. Same song, different

verse. Same trust issues.

Once again, he let his heart overrule his common sense when it came to Laura. There'd never be a future with someone he couldn't trust. Jon glanced at the boy beside him. But a future with his son was an entirely different matter.

Ian took a sip of his Coke from the blue-tinted glass. "Can I ask you something?"

Jon tensed.

"Something personal?"

Jon's stomach clenched.

"Are you Indian?"

He blinked at Ian.

"I mean," Ian took a breath. "Native American?"

Suspecting there might be land mines ahead, Jon proceeded with caution. "My grandmother told me a long time ago if anyone asked me, to tell 'em I was American Indian. Doesn't matter which you call me. Native American or Indian." Jon held up his hands, balancing them like a scale. "Either or. As long," he poked Ian with his elbow. "As you remember to call me for dinner."

"What kind?" Ian fiddled with his napkin. "I mean, tribe?"

"Lumbee."

"I like Indians. You could tell that from

my room, right?"

Jon nodded and waited for the other shoe that always accompanied these heart-to-hearts with Ian to drop.

"What's it like to be an Indian? To be Lumbee? To be from where everybody, you said, is like you?"

Jon smiled. "It's good. It's a proud thing. Every Fourth of July in a town close to where I grew up, we have Homecoming Weekend. In Pembroke. Parades. A traditional powwow. Costumed dancers. Music. Lots and lots of food."

He rubbed his belly, grinning. "It's put on by the university Native student group. I went to school there a few years before I joined the Marines after 9/11. There're other powwows in nearby Lumberton to celebrate the Spring Moon and another one in the fall. Good times to visit with friends and family you don't see every day."

Ian laid his cloth napkin to the side of his plate. "I've never been to a powwow." He kept his eyes on a small stain of tomato sauce. "Do you think we could go this Fourth of July? You and me? Together?"

Jon's heart lodged in his throat. "Sure thing, bud. I'd be honored."

"You've got family there, don't you? A

mom, sisters, and a niece, my mom told me."

Oh, Laura . . . Would he ever fathom that woman?

Just when Jon was good and mad with her — with righteous reason — she did something that confused and delighted him. She was preparing the boy, their boy, for the truth. Jon phoned his mother this week about Ian. And Florence Locklear was chomping at the bit, as were the rest of his family, to meet this precious child.

"Sure do. In fact" — Jon reached over to the empty chair beside him and extracted a pine-needled basket from the briefcase he'd carried inside with them — "this is for you. Arrived today. UPS from my mother, Florence Oxendine Locklear, for you."

Ian took the small-lidded basket with both hands, his eyes huge and a look of wonder on his face. "For me? You told your family about me?"

Jon nodded.

"Can I open it now?"

"Be my guest."

Ian cradled the basket between his hands as if he held the Holy Grail. "Your mom is a famous artist, isn't she?"

"She taught your mother, Laura, to quilt. She's better known nowadays for her jewelry design. My sister, Yvonne, made the basket. My uncle, Leo Oxendine, made what's inside."

Ian lifted the lid off and drew out the carved green turtle.

"We're the People of the Dark Water, the Lumber river. A land of corn and soybeans. Farmland reclaimed from what was once swamp. The turtle's a symbol of the Lumbee."

"So's my pinecone quilt." Ian raised his eyes, a question there unasked.

Best to leave that alone for today.

"The turtle," Jon laid a finger on its cool, smooth surface. "Is a wish and a prayer for long life and well-being for you from my mother."

"Do the Lumbee have a special language?"

"We're unique in that our land was never taken forcibly from us. When the whites first came to the shores of North Carolina, legend says we drifted west out of their reach, joined ourselves with other decimated tribes, and took possession of land nobody else wanted."

Jon shrugged. "It kept us isolated, but at the same time protected us. For a while. When the first whites came upon our swampland, we were already dressing like Europeans, farming like Europeans, living in houses like Europeans, already praying to the Christian God. Some think we were wise. Others say that in being so quick to adapt to white ways we lost much of our heritage. We lost our language in mingling with other tribes, although a few words remain. But we were left in peace to farm and to raise our families."

Ian pursed his lips. "And survive."

"That's right. We're survivors. All of us with Lumbee blood in our veins can be proud."

Ian stuck his chest out. "I'd be proud."

Jon gave him a sharp look. This boy could worm secrets out of Al-Qaeda.

Ian returned his look with a smile that on a woman might've been described as a Mona Lisa smile.

His son bent his head over his straw. "If I was a Lumbee, that is."

"Ian —" The phone in Jon's pocket vibrated. He fished it out. A text from Ana.

Got warrant. Meet there in 30.

"You got cop stuff to do?"

Jon reached for the bill. "Your mom should be home by now. I'll drop you off on my way." The night promised to be a long one as the investigation heated up.

Ian pushed back his chair. It scudded across the heart-pine floor. He clutched the basket and turtle to his chest. "I enjoy these talks of ours. Learn something every time."

Jon bit back a laugh. So did he.

But he sobered as his heart pinged, thinking of Laura. Longing for the joy he'd rediscovered over the last few days. The sound of her laughter. The light in her eyes for him.

Gone.

As illusive and unreal as an early-morning mist rising and dissipating to nothingness over the swamp bottoms of Mimosa Grove.

Because when it came to Laura, Jon Locklear was apparently a slow learner.

20

Back home, Laura stretched on her sofa, a pillow behind her back. She rifled through Velma's yearbook to keep her thoughts from straying to Jon. To keep her mind off the emptiness threatening to swallow her whole. She wasn't entirely sure why she'd chosen not to tell Jon about the dolls.

Him spending time with Ana Morales had thrown her for a loop. Maybe with old insecurities resurfacing, she'd decided to beat him to the eventual punch. And self-sabotaged.

Or, perhaps Velma was right; old habits did die hard. But the lies, the omissions, the sugarcoated commissions were getting harder and harder to bear.

She paged to her father's senior class picture, his boyishly handsome face determined and a trifle arrogant even then. Pictures of him as the high school quarterback. On the Senior Prom Homecoming

Court with a girl from the cheerleading squad. His superlatives — voted Most Likely to Succeed, Most Likely to Rule the World.

Laura stifled a bitter laugh. He'd certainly tried to be king over everything in his world. Hometown boy made good. One of the brightest stars to come out of Robeson County.

She traced the outline of Emerson's face with her finger. They'd been best pals until . . . until she'd found him in the arms of the hateful Barbara Payne.

And a further estrangement happened that summer when he set out to drive her and Jon Locklear apart. He'd gone behind her back and yet, like Aunt Velma said, was "in-your-face" — Jon's face — with his revelations about the fake engagement. He'd played Jon's insecurities.

Maybe Velma was right about the other thing, too. That luring her and Jon to the motel fell outside the scope of Emerson's usual attempts to control Laura and public opinion.

Laura sighed. As with Garrett, her dad always had another election around the corner. Always a public to be wooed and won.

But what was done was done. She recognized Velma's wisdom in something else, too. She needed to iron out things with her dad before they were past mending.

Out of obligation to Aunt Velma, Laura flipped through the pages of the yearbook in a desultory attempt to locate Barbara. And Laura was surprised with what she discovered. The younger Barbara's face revealed a wide-eyed vulnerability. Different from the calculating home wrecker Laura knew.

Few pictures of Barbara adorned the yearbook. No superlatives. No cheerleading or band. A not-so-popular girl from all appearances. A girl, if Aunt Velma were to be believed, from the wrong side of the Mimosa Grove social tracks.

FFA — Future Farmers of America. An award for Best Senior Project in shop class. The Spanish Club. Home Economics Club.

The notion of the patrician Barbara in overalls, on a tractor, wasn't something Laura could wrap her mind around. Still, with her father as the Bowen farm manager, Barbara probably had 4-H–type experience. The only other photo of Barbara depicted her stepmother in a cap and gown. Salutatorian to Emerson's valedictorian.

Nobody ever accused Barbara of not having brains. Laura questioned Barbara's heart, yes. Brains, no.

But Barbara's pinched features in the graduation photo were a long way from the vulnerable senior picture taken at the beginning of her twelfth grade year. Her heavily made-up face, masklike, spoke of worldly wisdom, hard won. This last snapshot was closer to the current hard-bitten demeanor of Laura's stepmother. Somewhere during her senior year, life taught Barbara a lesson.

A harsh one.

Laura wondered if her father had a hand in that.

"What happened to you, Barbara Smith? How did you become Barbara Payne and Garrett's mother?"

Garrett never knew his father. A bitter memory Barbara refused to share with her son. A man, she told him when a teenage Garrett had pressed her, who disappeared from their lives one day and left them both to starve.

"Only one person going to take care of you in this life," Garrett said once in imitation of Barbara. "And that is yourself. You don't help yourself, nobody else will either."

Laura peered out the mullioned window as Jon's truck pulled into the driveway. Tucking the yearbook behind the pillow, she headed toward the door. Ian had hold of

Jon's hand, pulling him toward the porch.

She smiled despite the heaviness in her heart. A dream come true to see Ian with his father.

Again, Aunt Velma was right. Secrets became exponentially harder to bear, not easier over time. Laura tried to formulate a prayer, but no words would come.

"Mom bought this gadget thingy off eBay for the campout."

Jon stopped at the bottom step and loosed his hand out of Ian's. His eyes flickered to Laura. Anger simmered across the sharp planes of his face.

Her smile froze, and she ached with what might have been, except for her lies.

Always the lies between them.

The tension lay as thick as the blanket of humidity that weighed upon the city.

Ian, in a surge of momentum, was halfway up the steps before he realized Jon wasn't following.

Jon raised his phone as a reminder. "I've got to go, Ian."

"But Jon —"

She laid a restraining hand on her son's shoulder. "He said he had to go. Another time. I need to talk to Jon right now."

"It'll just take —"

"Do what your mother says," Jon barked.

Hurt crisscrossed Ian's face.

She nudged Ian to the door.

"Ian. Wait." Jon bit his lip. "I'm sorry. That came out way harsher than I meant."

"Forget it," Ian called over his shoulder. His voice tremored on the verge of tears.

"Ian, I'm sor—"

But Ian had disappeared into the house.

She rounded on Jon. "Just because you and I —"

"I'm sorry." He held up his hand. "I shouldn't have taken my anger at you out on him." He rubbed the back of his neck. "I'm new to this parenting thing. It won't happen again."

New because of her lies.

Guilt stabbed Laura. Time to choose truth. Was it possible, as unworthy a creature as she was, to put off the old as Aunt Velma claimed? To put on something new? Even with God's help?

This Christian thing was so hard. Not for the faint of heart. Not for cowards like her to take the easy way out. Would she always struggle with the entangling lies?

Forgive me again, God. Help me believe and speak truth. Always.

Laura took a deep breath. "I didn't tell you something at the Stanley house. I don't know that it has any relevance to the murder, but I was trying to protect Doris's memory and the General."

She'd also been in a snit of jealousy over Ana. Nudged by something Otherly, Laura needed to come clean with that, too.

"And I was —"

"What now?" Jon sneered. "Did you neglect to mention you found the murder weapon? Or perhaps you've ID'd the killer, but it's your best friend, and you don't want to see his face splashed all over *The News and Observer*?"

Laura's lips twisted, her good intentions fading fast. "It's not that big a deal. Miss Doris was having a tea party with her dolls when she was killed. The General didn't want the media learning about it, about Doris's illness, so he removed the dolls before I arrived."

Jon gaped at her, his eyebrows raised almost to his hairline. "Dolls? What are you talking about?"

"I know it sounds crazy."

Not holding back this time, she gave him the CliffsNotes version.

He sighed, a long, slow leak of frustrated air. "This means Ana will have to send someone over to bag and tag those dolls."

Ana again . . .

Irritation enflamed Laura's nerve endings.

Was Ana always Jon Locklear's first thought?

Overweening anger pulsated through Laura's veins. At the spiraling loss of control over her own life. The loss of control that began ten years ago.

She'd lost Jon once more through yet another example of her moral stupidity.

If — a big if — she ever really possessed his heart in the first place.

Hope, dangled like a carrot and then snatched away. Sandbagged by some perverseness by which Laura kept Jon at arm's length.

Laura clenched her hands on her hips. "Why are the dolls so important compared to catching the person who killed Doris and Renna? More important than finding out who tried to run down your son?"

The bloody sight of Doris's battered skull rose in her mind. A sight she'd kept at bay since that morning. Anger — at the killer, at the hit-and-run driver, Morales and Jon, at herself — seared Laura.

Jon's face contorted. "Nothing is more important to me than keeping my son safe." He glared at her. "But don't you dare try to excuse your behavior, Laura. Or your lies."

She lifted her chin.

Jon closed the gap between them. "You've

contaminated the chain of evidence. Obstructed —"

"I never touched those dolls." Her voice rose.

". . . and delayed an ongoing police investigation," Jon ranted as if she'd never spoken. "Withheld vital information —"

"Why don't you go ahead and cuff me right now, Detective? Get it over with." She thrust out both hands, wrists together. "Punish me for everything I've done."

He grabbed her wrists and encircled them with one hand.

She gasped as Jon yanked her wrists and placed them against his chest.

No longer at arm's length, she felt his rapid-fire heartbeat beneath the cotton fabric of his shirt. His muscles tightened underneath her palms. If she lowered her chin an inch to where he stood on the bottom step, their lips would be within a hair's breadth of touching.

"Maybe I will arrest you." His eyes flared. "Don't think I wouldn't like to."

Laura stamped her foot. "You make me so mad."

"You make me madder."

Heat scorched her body. And because she was a scab picker — because she loved to torture herself with what could never be hers — Laura rammed her lips on his. Her anger, her helplessness, her hope spilled across his mouth.

And kiss for kiss, he answered her back. Angry, relentless, starved.

Just when she'd expended her last breath of air, Jon moved away. He clamped his lips together. But his gaze lingered as if hypnotized by her mouth.

Her lips burned. Her skin felt bereft, forsaken without him. She swayed, wide-eyed with shock.

"J-Jon . . . I lov—" She trembled, biting off the words at the last moment. "I'm trying. Really I am."

And something akin to triumph — hope? — glimmered in his dark eyes.

He took her hands off his chest, but his hand remained wrapped around her wrists. "I'd love to stand here and argue with you all night, but I've got work to do." A muscle jumped in his cheek.

Without a doubt, they *argued* better than with anyone else she'd ever known.

Question was, could they trust each other?

She searched his face for answers he couldn't give her. Maybe answers he didn't know.

Laura pulled free and rubbed her wrists. "Well, go then. Nobody's keeping you here."

"You're not getting rid of me that easily." A lopsided smile followed his slow drawl. "I'll be back."

Please, God . . .

She hoped so. Oh, how she hoped so.

He gave Laura a stiff bow from the waist. "Thank you for telling me everything."

Jon cocked an eye at her. "You *have* told me everything?"

"Yes, I have. Any leads on the case?"

He angled, one foot already descending toward the ground. "Nothing you need worry about. Ana and I have a warrant to serve."

Laura sucked in a harsh breath.

Spending the evening with Ana.

Her stomach twisted.

"A hunting expedition that could snare a murderer." He waved as he headed toward the driveway. His step lighter.

Because of their "truce"?

Or because he was on his way to meet the sultry Ms. Morales?

"Be careful, Jon Locklear," she whispered as he backed the F-150 out of her drive.

And as she closed the door, she realized it to be a caution she should also heed concerning one particular Lumbee cop and herself.

She feared it was already too late for her heart.

Ten years too late.

Delayed by his confrontation with Laura — no, make that armed rapprochement — Jon arrived at the Ogburn residence well behind Ana and the team. The Spanish Moroccan–style two-story sprawled oddly out of place in the refined Old Raleigh neighborhood of oaks, magnolias, and green lawns. The same neighborhood, give or take a few blocks, as the Stanley and Bowen residences.

Lips tingling from his encounter with Laura, Jon parked behind several blue-and-whites in the half-circular drive. Uniforms fanned out across the property and out-buildings. Dodging busy colleagues, he dashed up the steps between terra-cotta urns filled with tall, spiky yucca toward the open door.

A row of shoes waited inside the entrance. A leather pair of men's dress shoes. Rainbow flip-flops. Assorted pairs of Sperry's and other deck shoes. In the sunken living room, he spotted Patti Ogburn lounging on a chaise, sleek as a Siamese cat, copper beads at her throat and her metallic toenails peeping out from underneath a filmy bronze tunic.

Her husband, an athletic, ruddy sort, stood stiffly beside a mantel in a loosened red silk tie, Oxford starched shirt, and navy-blue trousers. A slick customer and devious opponent in the courtroom on behalf of a client, according to Ana, for now humanized in his blue-stocking feet. Two officers, arms crossed, guarded the den and prevented the Ogburns from discussing anything among themselves.

At the top of the staircase, Ana held a neon-green running shoe in one hand and with the other, the printout of the shoe tread found at Renna's crime scene. Her lips parted in a wide grin.

"Got him." She beckoned for Jon to join her. He took the stairs two at a time.

"See the funny cut between the grooves of the print found in the mud? A rock, sharp stick or something made that deviation at one time."

Ana upended the shoe to let Jon see. "Experts will have to verify, but it looks like a match to me."

"Great work, Detective Morales."

She preened, a wiggle in her hips. "That's not all. Ross!"

A junior officer, mentored by Mike Barefoot, emerged from a bedroom.

"Show Detective Locklear what you found

in the garage."

"Yes, ma'am."

She rolled her eyes. "You polite Southern boys make a woman feel so old."

Reddening beneath the collar of his starched uniform shirt, Ross produced an evidence pouch.

Jon's lips curved into a smile. "A hammer."

Excitement filled Ross's face. "And you noted the trace amounts of blood and hair on the wooden end?"

Ana frowned. "Don't believe I heard about you making detective yet, Ross. Seems like those exams are at the end of summer for you."

Ross took a step back. "Yes, ma'am. Sorry, ma'am."

She snagged the plastic bag from his hand. "Stop ma'aming me, and get back to your search."

"Yes, ma'— I mean, yes, sir — I mean —"

Jon folded his arms across his chest. "Play nice with the younger kids, why don't you, Morales?"

Ana heaved a sigh. "You suck all the fun out of being a senior officer, Locklear."

She shooed Ross. "That's 'yes, Detective Morales,' to you, Ross."

Ross opened his mouth, thought better of it, and backed into the bedroom.

She leaned over for Jon's ears only. "He's going to make a great detective. I've got dibs on him when he's assigned a partner."

"Although," she took a parting look down the hall. "He's right good-looking. Maybe I'll suggest he be transferred to another department so there's no conflict of interest."

Jon snorted. "A little young for you, Morales."

She smiled and moved past him to the stairs. "Help me interview the Ogburns. And my motto is, get 'em young, train 'em right."

Resisting the urge to laugh, he updated Ana on the dolls that had been removed and explained Velma's take on the notes.

Ana gave him an aggrieved sigh. "You better keep that girlfriend of yours on a short leash, Locklear, or I'll have her locked up just for practice."

"I know. I'm sorry. Laura operates in this tight little social circle with misguided loyalties. I appreciate your forbearance."

Ana descended the stairs, one hand resting on the curled iron balustrade. "Only for you, Locklear. After we talk to the Ogburns, I want you to go over to the Stanleys' and see if you can salvage any evidence."

Face-to-face with the Ogburns, Ana presented the evidence she'd found. "Can you explain, Mr. Ogburn, how this exclusive shoe of yours matches the print we found at the Renna Sheldon crime scene?"

Woody Ogburn jutted his chin. "Without my lawyer present, I don't have to answer your questions."

Ana threw Jon an exasperated look. When the canny Mr. Ogburn lawyered up, their options for questioning him would be severely limited.

Patti tilted her head. "I'm sure Woody would be happy to clear up any matters that he can in this tragic case, though, won't you, honey?"

Woody's face turned ruddier. He threw a glance at his wife. "Yes, of course. I can't explain why the print you found matches my shoe. Patti gave me those shoes for my birthday in April. I've only worn them a couple of times."

"How well did you know Miss Sheldon?"

Woody flushed and fiddled with his hands. "I don't like your insinuations. Until the DNA test comes back, you know I can't prove what I've been telling you. Renna was a student of my partner, Nolan, and spent time in our office."

"Do you have an alibi for the afternoon Renna Sheldon was killed?"

"No. I was on my way home from a seminar in Greensboro. Stuck in rush-hour traffic on I-40 at RTP to the best of my recollection."

Ana brandished the hammer in the pouch. "How do you explain this?"

Quizzical frown lines formed across Woody's brow. "It's my hammer, I guess. What do you mean?"

"The only reason we haven't charged you with murder right now, Mr. Ogburn, is we're waiting on the test results for this weapon we believe you used against Renna Sheldon, Doris Stanley, and Zeke Lowther in a lethal manner."

Patti leaped from the couch. Her bejeweled hand clutched at her throat. "Doris is — ?" She tore at Woodrow's sleeve. "What did you do?"

Woody shook her free like an angry bulldog. "Shut up, Patti. I'm not saying another word."

He jabbed a finger in Ana's face. "You're not going to pin this on me."

Jon and the two officers took a precautionary step toward him.

Woody stepped back. "I had nothing to do with any of those murders. I had no idea until now anything had happened to Mrs. Stanley or Lowther."

Ana gazed out the French doors. "If I'm not mistaken, your property adjoins the greenway, too. Less than half a mile from the Stanleys' in fact."

Patti buried her face in Woodrow's back. "He'd never hurt a helpless old woman. Woody was horribly jealous — without cause — of Zeke working here. He and the General had their differences, but —"

"Shut up, Patti!" Woody roared.

Patti backed toward the chaise.

"How do you explain what's obviously blood on the wooden handle, Ogburn?"

Woody's red-gold brows bunched.

"Oh," he pivoted toward his wife. "Last month, you remember, Patti? You asked me to fix that loose board on the deck off the garage."

He shrugged his shoulders. "I'm not handy. Don't know why she didn't pay that good-for-nothing lothario she was so fond of to do it for her."

Ana flicked Jon a look.

Woody caught the unspoken innuendo. "I smashed my thumb, and it bled. Nothing serious."

The attorney plastered a smile across his cheeks. "You guys" — Ana coughed — "You *people* know how it is with women."

All four members of the RPD tensed.

Woody sank beside his wife. "Our arrangement has always been I make the money, and she gets to spend it. You remember the deck, honey?"

He slanted an eager look at his wife. "That day I busted my thumb. That's how the blood got on the hammer, Detective."

Patti frowned. "No, Woodrow. I don't remember. I would've asked Mr. Lowther to fix that for me. Not you. You're not good with your hands."

She turned a frightened face toward Ana and Jon and then back to her husband. "But if you want me to remember that — say that — for you, Woody," she whispered *sotto voce,* "I will. I will."

Woody jerked to his feet. "Say that *for* me? What are you talking about, Patti? Tell them what happened. That you asked me to fix it. You were the one who bandaged my thumb."

Patti's fingers twisted her copper beads. "I'm sorry, Woodrow, but that just didn't happen."

Woody grabbed hold of Patti's shoulders, shaking her. "Why don't you remember? Tell them. Tell them —"

Patti screamed.

Jon and the two male officers pried Woody's hands off Patti and wrestled his arms behind his back.

Ana straightened. "Woodrow Ogburn, you have the right to remain silent. You have the right to —"

"You can't charge me," he yelled. "I haven't done anything. You can't prove any connection between me and that hammer and those deaths."

Jon cuffed him. "Not yet, Mr. Ogburn."

"What I can charge you with," Ana countered, "is assault. On your wife. And resisting arrest."

The attorney went limp as Ana Mirandized him. As the officers led Ogburn out, Ana placed a hand on Patti as she wept.

"Mrs. Ogburn? I'm afraid I'm going to need you to come to the station and file a formal complaint against your husband."

Patti's head snapped up. Her brown mascara ran in streaks down her face. "Against Woodrow? But I couldn't. He didn't mean it. He gets upset like that sometimes."

Ana cut her eyes around to Jon.

"Woody's always so sorry afterward."

"Mrs. Ogburn, you were a good friend to Doris Stanley. Same needlepoint group. If there's any chance your husband got angry with that defenseless old woman and . . ."

Patti bit her lip. Hiccupping sobs jolted her body. "I suppose when you put it that way." Her eyes filled with tears. She cast Jon an imploring look. "I have to this time, don't I? I have to?"

Jon took Patti's hand and helped her stand.

Ross poked his head around the door. "Detective Morales?"

He lifted a brown bottle with a white screw-on top. "Found this at the bottom of the trashcan in the home office."

Ana crossed the room. "Empty?"

He nodded. "The label reads Valium. Prescribed to Mrs. Ogburn."

Patti lurched forward. "Empty? I don't understand. I had that prescription refilled as you can see from the pharmacy date two weeks ago."

"Get forensics to check the pipes and drains for every sink on the property." Ana glanced at Jon. "He didn't use the whole bottle to disable Lowther. Must have tried to pour it out and get rid of the rest of the evidence."

Jon shrugged. "Unless he disposed of it on the lawn."

"Ross," barked Ana. "Comb the yard for any sign of a liquid substance being dumped on the ground."

"Why?" Patti clutched Jon's arm. "Why would Woodrow do something like this?"

Her mouth tightened. "Do you think he was the father of that poor girl's baby? That he killed her to shut her up? Killed Miss Doris because she knew something? And then Zeke Lowther because Zeke had seen him?"

"We're not going to give up until we answer those questions to our satisfaction, Mrs. Ogburn."

Ana's eyes narrowed at the sight of Patti's fingers curled around Jon's arm. "Why don't I escort Mrs. Ogburn to the station? Detective Locklear has a follow-up assignment at the Stanleys'."

Prying Patti's fingers free of his arm, he transferred Patti's hand to Ana.

Ana looped an arm around Patti and started for the door.

"Wait. My shoes." Patti stuffed her bare feet into one of the several pairs of shoes that lined the entrance.

Jon mouthed a silent thank-you over Patti's cinnamon curls to Ana.

She gave Jon an insolent wink over her shoulder. "Any time, Locklear. Any time."

21

Laura watched as Ian circled the cul-de-sac with Buggs for an abbreviated evening walk. His lips were fixed in a grim line, highly reminiscent of a certain detective she knew.

And when he and Buggs returned, "Why can't Jon and I go to the campout tomorrow?"

She tucked strands of hair out of her face. "With everything that's happened this week, I don't think it's a good idea for you to be away from home alone."

Ian wrapped the leash around his fist. "I won't be alone. I'll be with Jon. You don't want me to spend time with him because you're mad at him."

She let out a huff of air. "That's not true. I don't think it's safe."

Buggs made himself comfortable on the asphalt.

Her son snorted. "Safe? How much safer could I be than with a former Marine and a police detective? You want me in your sight, under your thumb, every moment, every day."

Ian made Laura sound like . . . her father.

"That's not true. I —"

"Why are you trying to ruin my life, Mom?" Tugging Buggs upright, Ian stalked up the driveway.

Laura scrubbed her forehead. That hadn't gone well.

As a teenager, she'd been convinced that her father had been out to ruin her life. Rightly so, as events unfolded that summer in Mimosa Grove.

But that cursed honest streak grappled with the fears that led to the lies, and wouldn't allow Laura to leave it there. True, Emerson had complicated matters, but in the end, it had been Laura's choices that set in motion the current course of her life.

Pressing the button to lower the garage door, Laura experienced an acute longing for Holt's SUV to fill the empty spot in the two-bay garage.

Was it right to blame everything that transpired that summer on her father? Despite the wrong choices she'd made — in believing her father's lies, not trusting Jon, and corralling Holt in her deceit — had her life been ruined?

Laura recalled Holt's kindness during her pregnancy, and his patience in the years that followed. How he encouraged Laura to finish her degree. How Holt encouraged her dream of opening her own shop. How he'd loved — without reservation — another man's child.

And she'd been the woman screaming his name, calling for Holt when Ian's life had been in jeopardy.

Because deep down, she'd always known Holt loved her. Unconditionally. Without reservation.

Like God loved someone as unworthy as Laura Bowen?

Both gifts of love Laura could never repay. Both givers Laura could never outgive.

So many twists and turns in the path her life had taken. A path Laura never envisioned. Yet through it all, she'd relied on Holt's abiding strength and grace.

And now, with new eyes, she also recognized God's abiding faithfulness and grace. Despite her indifference, His hand had been upon Laura through every curve in the journey. Bringing good out of wrong. Everything sifted through His fingers of love.

"Mom!" Ian shouted.

Jerked out of her reverie, Laura skidded into the kitchen. She dashed out to the screened porch where Ian stood over Buggs lying on his doggie bed.

His eyes wide, Ian pointed. "Look what Buggs found in his toy box."

Laura knelt beside Buggs, whose body almost, but not quite, obscured the plastic figure of a doll. His drooling mouth chewed on a leg. Bringing to mind a less pleasant memory of a purple Converse sneaker. Her lip curled, Laura reached for the doll's other leg and pulled.

Buggs growled.

"Let me, Mom."

Sinking to his haunches, Ian waved a canine treat in front of Bugg's nose. The black triangle of his snout sniffed at the air. His tail thumped.

"Here, boy." Ian held the fake bacon out of Buggs's reach. "You know you want it. You know you do. Let go of the doll."

Ian pulled at the doll clamped between Bugg's powerful jaws.

Buggs whimpered, his hindquarters wiggling. But he opened his mouth and lunged for the bacon.

Ian yanked the doll free. "Here, Mom."

He thrust the drool-soaked doll into her hands. "Dolls are for girls, Buggs. Let's find you a more manly toy."

Manly? The word brought an incongruous

flashback to the pool earlier in the week. Something manly that didn't fit.

As Ian dug through the wooden toy box Holt had built for Buggs, Laura examined the doll.

Black hair. Big brown eyes. Rosy cheeks. Little bonnet, panties, and pinafore.

Except for the teeth marks on one leg, an exact replica of the dolls Tayla described at Miss Doris's tea party. Tayla's words registered. The Dionne kids.

Tayla probably meant the famous set of quintuplets from Canada in the 1950s. Laura racked her memory, straining to recreate the tea party tableau in her mind. Miss Doris plus four chairs. Miss Doris's teacup and saucer.

Four other teacups and saucers. For the four dolls. But there had been five Dionne sisters — quints.

Was this the missing fifth doll? The one Miss Doris cried for at Renna's funeral? The one Miss Doris said . . . What had been Doris's words?

Renna not being a good girl. Something about a pinky swear? Renna hurting Doris's babies. How had this doll ended up in Buggs's toy box?

Had Renna taken one of Doris's babies? If so, why had she hidden it at Laura's house? She'd been manning the store last Friday when Laura left to drop Ian off at the Prescotts'. Laura and the police assumed Renna left the store for a rendezvous on the greenway with the father of her child.

But had Renna actually been on the greenway because she stashed this doll at Laura's house first? Had Renna been on her way back to the store when she encountered her killer? What was so important about this doll?

Perhaps Zeke observed Renna entering the empty house. Maybe he questioned her. But what possible reason would Lowther have for killing Renna?

Jon speculated once that Renna might have been trying to tell Laura something before she'd met her death. But Renna had known Laura wouldn't be at home that afternoon. Maybe she'd counted on Laura's absence, taking the opportunity to hide this doll right under their noses — make that Buggs's nose.

Ian plopped beside Laura. The air in the foam cushions gusted. "What's going on, Mom? Who put that doll in Buggs's box?"

"I think Renna left it here."

His eyes grew enormous. "Maybe she hid something inside the doll. Something she wanted you to know. Something" — he gulped — "that got her killed."

The hair on her arms prickled. Laura untied the bonnet. The doll's face and head seemed intact. She pulled off the panties.

Ian bolted. "I'm outta here. This is too gross." He pantomimed gagging. "Too girly. Like a creepy game of dress-up. I'm going inside."

Girly? Manly? Something wavered on the edge of Laura's memory. She held her breath.

Nah . . . still nothing.

She unsnapped the rivets holding the doll's pinafore in place. The doll appeared normal. She rotated the doll onto her face and discovered a slit in the plastic skin of the doll's spine.

A three-sided, hinged slit hacked into the doll's plastic body. With an X-Acto knife from Tapestries?

As she folded back the flap of plastic, Laura's breath hitched. A rectangular-shaped device about the length and width of her thumb lay tucked inside the doll's belly. A thumb drive.

Laura remembered Doris's confused comment about a pinky swear — not pinky. Doris stared at her hand that day in front of Renna's casket. Doris had realized pinky wasn't correct, but lost the train of thought before identifying the correct digit: her thumb.

Laura should call Jon or Morales right away. She'd be contaminating evidence again. But Renna had left this in her house. For Laura or Ian to find. Why?

What was so important about this drive that Renna had paid for it with her life? Had the police, herself included, been wrong to assume Renna died because of her unborn child? Or, perhaps evidence on the drive implicated the father of the unborn baby in such a way that he was willing to kill Renna to hide any traces of his involvement. How did Lowther fit into this murder?

Driven by something she couldn't define, Laura hurried to her computer. Upstairs, the floorboards creaked as Ian rummaged in his room. She slipped the thumb drive into the USB port.

Seconds passed. Whirring, the machine sprang to life and retrieved the data. Hitting keys, she squinted as several folders popped onto her screen. Laura clicked to open one.

Bank deposits listed. Her eyes bulged. Huge amounts for a college girl whose only legitimate source of income was from a part-time job at Tapestries. Blackmail money?

Renna had been blackmailing the father

of her child.

The police would be able to trace this to withdrawals from someone else's account. The baby's father had made a half-dozen payments. Then decided to once and for all end the financial drain?

An awkward conversation replayed in Laura's mind between her and Hilary Munro. The baby's father could've killed Renna.

Or . . .

Laura closed her eyes at a horrendous thought. Maybe his wife had, desperate to keep reputations and her marriage from ruin.

"Oh, Hilary."

She recalled Hilary's devastated countenance earlier at Tapestries. Haggard. With guilt? Shame?

Laura knew firsthand how those emotions could change a person, alter thinking processes, and produce irrational behavior.

Hence, her relationship with Garrett over an unrequited love she'd never be able to return.

The evening sky split with razor-sharp light. A boom rattled the panes in the windows. Laura jumped. Her screen wavered.

She glanced out the multipaned windows

at the black horizon above the tree line. A summer thunderstorm. The wind whipped the top of the trees with crescendoing frenzy.

Laura needed to unplug the computer before she and the machine got fried. Surge protection in these kinds of storms, Holt learned the hard way on his laptop three summers ago, were no guarantee. She closed out the file, removed the drive, and shut down her laptop.

Unplugging the Mac, she grabbed her cell phone. Not a great time to make a call either, but something she needed to do before she lost her nerve. Her flesh crawled at how the thumb drive made her and Ian targets of a murderer. She dialed the station, impatient to get this device out of her house.

It took an agonizing fifteen minutes of elevator music before the dispatcher reached Morales — not Jon — somewhere in the bowels of the RPD.

"What do you want, Mabry?" Morales's abrupt voice shattered the calming elevator music.

Laura's mouth twisted. Ana Morales would never be a candidate for Miss Congeniality. Her heart plummeted at the thought of her friendship with Hilary and yet where her duty lay.

She relayed how she and Ian had discovered the thumb drive. And voiced her speculations concerning Renna's final intentions. Laura, grudgingly, shared her conversation with Hilary.

A silence.

"You had to open that file and take a look-see for yourself, didn't you, Mrs. Mabry?"

And abandoning professionalism, Ana, in a brittle tone, murmured something uncomplimentary about Laura's heritage, a heritage that slurred Buggs and his kind, too.

"I ought to throw your sorry" — Laura cringed at the expletive — "in the county lockup. See how an orange jumpsuit complements your delicate, debutante complexion."

Laura decided discretion — silence — was the better part of valor. And the quickest way to shut Morales up and wind her down.

Morales ranted for a few more moments.

Then, "Fine. Thanks so much for calling." Her voice laced with sarcasm. "I'll send the nearest patrol car to pick it up. Did you stop to consider now you, too, possess info that could get yourself killed? And your son?"

That was shouted.

Laura held the phone away from her ear.

"Not that I care about your demise, Mabry. But Jon would. And he doesn't deserve to have his heart broken a second time. Don't go anywhere. Don't talk to anyone. Don't do anything else stupid. You got that?"

A click and the phone went dead.

Laura gritted her teeth.

It would've been so satisfying to slam the instrument down in Morales's ear. First.

Nostrils flaring, Laura comforted herself by slamming the cell onto her desk. Something vital cracked, and the power light died.

"What're you doing?"

At Ian's voice, she convulsed, her hand over her heart. Laura hadn't heard him come downstairs. She pivoted.

He crossed his arms over his Skywalker pj's. "That" — he pointed at the ruined remnants of twenty-first-century technology in her hand — "was a hissy fit, wasn't it? I'm gonna tell Aunt Velma."

Laura rolled her eyes as he smirked. "Nobody likes a tattletale, Ian."

A serious look creased his face. "I'm sorry for earlier, Mom. But Jon is . . . m-my friend." His voice quavered as his eyebrows bunched.

She leaned her face against the lightsaber etched on his T-shirt. "I know Jon is important to you." She sighed. "He's important to me."

Laura straightened and clenched her jaw.

No wonder Jon had practically run from her on the steps this afternoon. Run toward sane, logical Ana Morales, undamaged goods. Laura was an emotional seesaw, a crazy person. She'd have run, too.

And in a moment of clear illumination as sharp as the jagged streaks of lightning splitting the sky, Laura understood why she'd held back from Jon before. Why fear paralyzed her trust in him. Paralyzed her ability to open herself, to be vulnerable with him.

Her greatest, unspoken fear?

That she wasn't as important to Jon as he was to her. That even now, he only wanted to make love to her, not *love* her. That Ian alone drew him to her doorstep.

That despite being one-time lovers, to Jon she was unlovable.

Laura traced the outline of the Starfighter spaceship on Ian's pj's. Ian's belly rippled at her touch. He swatted her hand away.

The mother of a son may not know the difference between various American Girl dolls, but she did know the proper Latin names for dinosaur species, names of big equipment rigs, and Star Wars trivia galore. Laura knew Ian's ticklish spots. And she knew his heart, the source of *his* greatest unspoken fears.

"Jon will always be part of your life." She cupped Ian's face between her palms. "No matter how things work out between him and me, Jon is here to stay. If not this campout, there'll be another one."

Ian's dark eyes studied her. "You promise?"

She nodded. "Did you know Jon attends Redeemer Fellowship?"

Ian shook his head.

She attempted a small smile. "We'll see lots of him there."

"We?" Ian stiffened. "You going to stop hiding out in the parking lot every Sunday?"

She gave a tiny gasp. He'd known. Ian somehow had known of her reluctance to face what in her mind had been a vengeful God full of retribution. Not the God Laura rediscovered this week. The God, Aunt Velma insisted, whose compassions never ceased.

Not unlovable to God, Laura reminded herself. But graced by forgiveness. Mercy's recipient.

She didn't have to live in the fear anymore. Or operate in the lies that spun out of self-protection. Because despite the way she'd lived her life up to this point, Laura didn't need Emerson, Jon, Holt, or Aunt Velma.

Peace seeped into her soul as Laura finally

understood what Velma had tried to impress upon her earlier. Laura didn't need any man or woman or hobby or career to satisfy. Which was what she'd truly been looking for that summer after her mother died. For only God Himself could fill that kind of emptiness. Only He satisfied the innermost longings of the human heart.

A truth Holt spent the better part of his life trying to show her.

"I think it's time for us to find our way home, Ian."

He nodded. "Like Dad would want."

Time for a new beginning. But they'd both, Laura realized with a pang, miss Holt Mabry until the day they died. And joined him once more.

Love and gratitude surged through her.

And with it, deep sadness for everything she underappreciated. Her eyes filled. Laura gazed mutely at the fury unfolding outside the safety of their cottage home.

Too late Laura apprehended her life wasn't about the love she missed, but the love she'd gotten instead.

Gone but never lost. Right, Holt?

Her lips curved into a faint smile. Love not lost, but waiting. For its own time and place.

Someday . . .

Ian hugged her. She buried her face in the little-boy smell of his body, a smell of Buggs, outdoors, and the few licks of Ivory soap he slapped on himself in concession to mother demands.

She had holes to mend in the fabric of her relationship with Jon. If Jon could once again find it in his heart to be merciful.

With or without Jon, life's sweetness was meant to be savored. Maybe this time and place were meant for her and Jon to be together.

But maybe not.

And there'd always be more hills and valleys to overcome, if she lived long enough.

This time, though, Laura wouldn't travel alone. This time she'd travel hand in hand with Someone better than Holt or Jon. Someone whose mercies would never allow His precious child to be consumed, as her sins deserved.

Jon sat at his desk at the station, his finger on the rewind button, going forward slide by monotonous slide through the security video from the Village shopping center. He zoomed in on the frame of Renna leaving Tapestries and the object tucked underneath her arm.

Ana, lines of weariness etched across her

caramel features, approached. She leaned over him to peer at the screen. "So now we know what Miss Sheldon was carrying."

"Toxicology report come back on the hair and blood from the hammer?"

She straightened. "Blood matches Renna. Another type smeared into the handle farther up. Matches Lowther. His fingerprints on the metal head of the hammer."

Jon gave her a sharp look. "Lowther's fingerprints aren't on the wooden handle? But on the top where her killer would've gripped the hammer as he bashed in Renna's head."

"No other fingerprints on the metal to tell us who bashed in Lowther's skull. His killer probably wore gloves. Only Ogburn's on the wooden part, as you'd suspect, since the hammer belonged to him originally. The part where most people repairing a loose board would place their grip on the hammer."

The confusing mix of evidence. Contradictory. Like his conflicted feelings for Laura.

"Any trace of Doris Stanley on the hammer?"

Morales shook her head. "Slivers of walnut found in her head wound. Not the hickory handle of the hammer in the evidence locker. No evidence that hammer was used in Mrs. Stanley's murder."

He frowned. "That doesn't make sense. You don't suppose — ?"

Ana gave a long sigh. "I don't suppose anything at midnight, Locklear. Maybe Ogburn cut his thumb like he said, or maybe he hurt himself bludgeoning our vics to death. The hammer definitely ties Ogburn to the murder weapon and the murder victims."

His fingertips touched his chin, steepled as a church. "Two of the murder victims."

She nodded. "The thumb drive your girlfriend unearthed has proved to be highly enlightening as well."

"Did you trace the account from which the funds were withdrawn?"

Her eyes glinted. "Two accounts."

Jon pushed back in his chair. "Two accounts? As in two separate people?"

She pursed her lips. "Miss Sheldon had quite the thriving blackmail business. Cyber team has linked the funds from Ogburn's account and Nolan Munro's account."

He whistled. "Little Miss Sheldon did get around. Which one do you think was the baby's father?"

She shrugged. "Doesn't matter which one. Murderer was whoever believed it and decided to put an end to the blackmail. Or"

— she tossed her hair over her shoulder — "maybe a missus acting on his behalf."

"Any connection between Hilary Munro and Lowther?" Jon wondered out loud. "Ross said forensics also found trace amounts of Valium in the garage sink pipes at the Ogburns'."

She grimaced. "Only Patti's fingerprints found on that. As you'd expect, seeing as it was her prescription. But why wipe his fingerprints off the Valium bottle and not the hammer? Not very smart of our attorney suspect. But hey, if criminals were too smart, we'd never catch them."

"Maybe he didn't realize we could lift prints off wood. So we've got Ogburn with the Valium and the hammer for the murder of Renna and Lowther."

"Ogburn's cooling his heels in a holding pen. DNA will prove whether or not he or that Munro dude was the father. Probably Renna told both of them they were the father to increase her revenue. I've got Munro and his wife in separate interview rooms."

He lifted his brows. "Really?"

"Just trying to make sure I tie up the loose ends. Dot every 't'. Cross every 'i'."

He grinned. "I think you mean dot every 'i' and cross every 't'."

Ana clapped Jon across the shoulders. "Don't get technical on me. I told you I'm tired."

"It's going to be a long night," Jon agreed. "You want me to help you interview one of the Munros?"

She dug her fingers in the pockets of her navy slacks. Looked like the sergeant had gotten around to the dress code chat.

Ana's eyes narrowed at his scrutiny. "Sure. But first, if you can spare the change, I need caffeine."

Jon opened the middle drawer of his desk and withdrew a handful of quarters. "Here. It's on me."

"Thanks." She flashed him a wicked smile. "But don't think that makes us even. Someday I'm going to collect the IOUs you owe me from not slapping your girlfriend into a cell next to Woodrow Ogburn."

His lips quirked. Payday would come. And knowing Ana, it'd be a big one. "I appreciate your generosity of spirit, Morales."

She waved a hand. "Think nothing of it. Until I collect, that is. Why don't you tackle Mrs. Munro? I'll corner the husband. You know, you and I would've made an awesome team, but you got it bad for the Widow Mabry, Locklear. Real bad."

Jon rolled his chair away from the desk.

He touched the sleeve of Ana's hibiscus-orange blazer. Dress code correct, but still so Ana.

"You are something else. My loss, Morales. Someone else's gain."

"Locklear, I could say the same about you. I sure hope Laura Mabry realizes what a lucky woman she is."

Remembering his last conversation with Laura, Jon sincerely doubted Laura would agree.

God, why couldn't I have fallen in love with Ana Morales? So simple, so easy.

He deflated into the chair. Although, upon second thought, Ana wasn't exactly uncomplicated, either. Maybe that was the trouble.

Maybe all women, not just Laura, were marvelous enigmas, and he was too simple-minded to unravel the code. He rubbed his hand over his face. What was he going to do about Laura?

Time to call it quits?

He'd shown her, all right, on the steps of her house. Shown her how done he was with her — in between his impassioned displays of affection. All over her mouth.

Ana's cell trilled. She glanced at the caller ID. "Ross. I thought that boy went home hours ago."

She punched talk. "What you got, Ross?"

Her brown eyes grew enormous. "Oh, really? You don't say. Bring it in, Ross. We'll take a look. See if anything new pops up."

She held her hand over the receiver and whispered, "Ross, bless his hound dog heart."

Jon had a sudden, humorous image of Buggs clad in an inverness cape and deerstalker hat of Holmesian fame.

"Ross decided on his own time to reinterview the shop owners at the Village. Seems like that Mr. Wangchuk, the Buddhist dude, came clean with a secret video camera he installed to catch a bunch of juvies who've been tagging the side of his florist shop with spray paint."

She spoke into the phone again. "Oh, and by the way, good work, Ross."

Ana clicked off. "That boy, unless I decide to date him, is definitely going to be my next partner."

"Why didn't Wangchuk tell us about this earlier?" Suspicion coated Jon's voice.

She sighed. "Where Wangchuk comes from that kind of surveillance is only done by the secret police. The gang has been targeting him and his little Buddhist band with racial slurs. He and his people are leery of the police. He wanted to handle it himself."

"And what was he going to do when he captured images of the perpetrators?"

"Better not to ask questions you may not want to hear the answers to. Best thing though, the camera was mounted, Ross says, on the back corner of the shop. Facing where the greenway section of Woods Edge begins."

She rubbed her hands together. "Finally. Maybe we'll have enough solid evidence to keep our greenway Killer behind bars for good."

22

On Friday, Laura waved good-bye as Ian stepped aboard the yellow bus for the last day of the school year.

Hello, summer. Here we come.

She welcomed freedom from homework — always a joint effort at Ian's age — lunch boxes, and routine. Memorial Day was a sweet teaser to pool time, baseball games, cookouts, and catching fireflies in the long evenings of summer. When, as the songwriter said, the living gets easy — or easier, at any rate.

Laura backed her Lexus out of the garage and hurried through the winding streets of Woods Edge toward Tapestries. She restocked and hummed as she did a quick dusting of the shelves. Around eleven, she received a call from Aunt Velma.

"Have you heard?" Velma didn't give Laura room to reply. "The RPD charged Woodrow Ogburn last evening with Renna's murder."

Laura gripped the phone. "Was he the father of the unborn baby?"

"Don't know. But Patti is, of course, devastated. The needlepoint group's bringing food."

Southern comfort at its finest. Hospitality a cultural norm, not a myth.

Velma cleared her throat. "Patti has always been . . ."

Laura's lips twitched.

Patti had always been one who liked to not just color outside the lines, but do everything outside the boundaries of what was considered polite behavior for a well-brought-up Southern woman.

"But despite everything, Patti's never been a hypocrite." Velma's voice dropped to a whisper. "It sounds like a circus over there. Can you come help?"

Laura glanced around her store, where three or four customers browsed. "Patti's been a good client since Holt died. I'll come as soon as Aggie arrives."

"Don't worry about bringing anything. Lula made enough for ten of us. Tayla and I are picking up Hilary on our way to Patti's. She was released from police custody in the wee hours and needs our support, too. Patti says for everyone to avoid the reporters and slip in from the greenway."

A lingering feeling of dread from her last encounter on her home stretch of greenway made Laura wish she could renege. But loyalty to her friends, especially when they found themselves in trouble, was a quality she prized.

No matter what Velma said, Velma was her grandmother. A grandmother Laura knew far better than the distant memory of Nadine, who died when Laura was only a small child. She fingered the silver loop dangling from her earlobe.

So many of her relationships were in transition.

Her relationship with her father. With Jon. With Ian.

An hour and a half later, she parked two streets over from the Ogburns'. Cutting through the clipped boxwood hedge of a fellow Weathersby quilter, Laura accessed the greenway amid the chatter of birds and enjoyed the immediate, cooling shade on her sun-baked skin. The tangy smell of pine evoked bittersweet hopes no longer of what might have been, but instead of what might be.

With temps in the low nineties, the dew points hovered in the mid-seventies. Real feel? The radio announcer had mentioned one hundred and seven.

Another hot, humid, sticky day. And, despite the thunderstorm last night, no hope for a break in the heat, barring a tropical storm at best or a hurricane at worst.

Leaving the shelter of the glade, Laura entered the property through the stone pillars. She unlatched the scrolled iron gate and emerged into the Ogburns' yard. The plaintive cooing of mourning doves dogged her steps. A random thought, one of those useless bits of knowledge accumulated over the years, filtered through the cloud of anxiety gripping her mind about how mourning doves mated for life.

Not to be her fate no matter how hard Laura tried.

Approaching the red-tiled patio, she wiped her brow beaded with sweat and adjusted the folds of her robin's egg–blue dress. But her skirt wrapped between her legs and stuck to her skin. Shaking her doleful thoughts, she picked her way among the clusters of similarly clad, well-heeled Southern matrons.

Some waved as they sipped sweet tea and munched from china plates holding pimiento cheese sandwiches, deviled eggs, and various combos of fruit and pasta.

Others stopped to inquire as to her and

Ian's health. Many of the women had known and loved Laura's mother. Taking a peek through the French doors, Laura stifled displeasure at the sight of her stepmother, Barbara.

Laura navigated around the flip-flops and deck shoes that littered the patio. But as she entered the coolness of the interior, Barbara's ice-blue eyes narrowed. Patti held court on the chaise like Cleopatra receiving her subjects. And Garrett held Patti's hand.

She shouldn't have been surprised that Garrett would be there, although the only male in evidence. The Ogburns had been what Garrett called "serious" supporters of his campaign from the beginning. Barbara and Patti were longtime friends.

Glimpsing Laura, Garrett's face went rigid.

An awkward tension vibrated the air between her and the trio. But Aunt Velma materialized and broke the current, snagging Laura's arm.

Velma plastered a big, fake smile on her face as she propelled Laura toward the kitchen. "Laura's come to help with lunch. She'll be back to say hello."

Laura allowed herself to be pushed into the relative safety of Patti's Mexican-themed kitchen with its terra-cotta floor tiles and hand-glazed Talavera backsplash. Here, amidst heaping trays of food, Miss Lula reigned supreme, issuing orders to the white doyennes of Raleigh society.

Love, Southern style.

"Salad bar needs replenishing in the dining room," barked Lula at the wife of a former lieutenant governor. "More sugar in that tea," she directed another woman, the past president of the DAR. "Sugar's good for shock."

The only one in shock was Laura after seeing the unholy alliance gathered in the living room.

"Hey, Laura." Lula stirred a pot of something delicious on the stainless steel, commercial-worthy stovetop.

Tayla and the others fluttered their fingers. Hilary slumped despondent on a bar stool.

Laura jerked her head toward the living room. "Did I miss something out there?"

Velma's eyebrows arched. "Patti's already working on her next husband. A girl has to move on, you know." She rolled her eyes.

Laura blinked. "Isn't Patti a little . . . ?"

Velma laughed. "Do you really mind?"

Laura sniffed. "Hardly. She's welcome to him and him to her. Good luck, I say, to anyone with that witch for a mother-in-law.

And *witch* isn't the most apt word for Barbara."

Velma handed Laura a stack of cherry-red Fiestaware plates. "Patti and Garrett go way back. Two of a kind."

Laura's eyes widened. "You don't mean . . . ?"

She and Aunt Velma exchanged meaningful glances.

Laura followed Velma into the packed dining room. A bevy of ladies, with plates and utensils in hand, circled the oval mahogany table. "How Mrs. Robinson of her."

"Quite." Velma set the trifle upon the groaning sideboard. Her aunt filled Laura in on Woodrow's arrest, the evidence against him, the charges.

"Why didn't you warn me about . . . ?" Laura lifted her shoulders and dropped them. "About Garrett and Patti?"

Velma's eyes glittered. "I believed it was old news. And you know I don't gossip."

Open-mouthed, Laura stared, edging a few inches away in case lightning struck.

Velma snorted. "At least not about stuff I don't know for sure. I put no stock in rumors from unreliable sources. But I knew eventually you'd come to your senses, and see that *politician* for what he is. Especially after a certain Lumbee detective arrived on the scene."

"Rather fortuitous, Aunt Velma, Jon's job here." Laura jabbed her thumb in the direction of the back of the house. "I could've married that jerk —"

"I think not, Little Miss Thinks-She-Knows-Everything. I've kept in touch with Florence Locklear for years. Who do you think put a bug in Mike Barefoot's ear about a job opening in the RPD and a certain police detective employed in Baltimore? I've got my connections."

"Well, if I think I know everything, and I don't," Laura countered with a pointed look. "I know now where I got it from."

A pleased smile flitted across Velma's mock-stern features.

Laura stepped aside as Lula and Hilary lumbered into the dining room. Miss Lula draped a comforting arm across Hilary's shoulders. "You haven't had anything to eat in days. Starving yourself won't help Nolan or your children."

Tears welled in Hilary's hurt-beyond-belief puppy-dog eyes. Laura cast Velma a questioning look. Everybody probably assumed Jon kept her in the loop.

If only they knew how wrong that assumption was in reality.

Velma straightened, the English teacher

back in play. She thrust a plate into Hilary's hands. "What's done is done, honey." The last part added to lessen the sting.

But Velma resumed a brisk, no-nonsense tone. "Nolan's going to have to answer for what he did. And what can't be cured, must be endured."

Miss Lula rubbed Hilary's arm. "You hold your head high. Men are . . ."

"Pigs," the former DAR president interjected, her nose wrinkling.

"Bovine." The lieutenant governor's wife looked as if she knew whereof she spoke.

Heads nodded. And there followed a chorus of well wishes and support. Southern women might have big ears. They might possess big mouths. They did love to talk — more than one lady bearing the moniker "Mouth of the South" for good reason. But Southern women also possessed the biggest hearts.

Hilary's lips quivered, but she reached for the spoon in the chicken salad. There were genteel, ladylike claps and cheers. Pearl-white teeth flashed above pearl chokers.

Velma's gaze flicked to the Palladian window. She elbowed Laura.

Laura glanced at her and then toward where Velma's chin jerked.

The voices quieted as one by one the

ladies observed the blue-and-white police cars block the street, and the officers pour out of their vehicles. Hilary froze. Patti's wedding china Limoges plate would've landed on the Persian carpet except for Miss Lula's quick save.

"Oh, no." Hilary's lips had gone as white as paper. "They didn't believe me."

Her head swiveled from side to side, frantic for a means of escape. "I didn't have an alibi. You know how I lose track of time. I couldn't be sure if I was shopping, or curled up with a good book, or napping when Renna died that afternoon."

Winnie, the Greek-American woman who ran the Weathersby gift shop, rounded the table and held Hilary close. The other women joined them on either side. A sea of pink, blue, and yellow linen, pearls on each earlobe, closed ranks against the invaders.

Pounding on the door set Hilary aquiver. Miss Lula gripped her hand.

Velma spoke. "You go, Laura."

Laura raised her eyebrows. "Me?"

"They know you. Let them in. We'll stand with Hilary."

Laura swallowed. "Yes, ma'am."

She headed for the entry hall, reached for the knob, and swung wide the door. Ana stepped back. Jon's eyes widened and then rolled.

His lips narrowed into a thin, straight line. He wasn't pleased to find her here. A cordon of officers spread themselves across the front lawn. A disheveled Woodrow Ogburn stood off to the side.

"Must be nice to be independently wealthy," Ana mocked as she brushed past Laura. "I for sure wouldn't know. Some of us work for a living."

"What are you doing here, Laura?" Jon hissed.

He and Ana paused only long enough in their trek across the foyer to take a quick, rubbernecked gander at the occupants of the dining room.

Laura backed away from Jon's ire. Instead of sweeping into the dining room, though, Ana and Jon halted on the threshold of the living room. Meek as mashed potatoes, Woodrow joined them.

Ana flashed her badge. "Mrs. Patti Ogburn?"

Patti shrieked as she caught sight of her husband.

"You are under arrest for the murders of Renna Sheldon and Zeke Lowther. You have the right to —"

A cry rang from the dining room. Laura

swiveled as Hilary sagged against Winnie and Lula.

"Not me. Not me," Hilary whispered. "They believed me. I never . . ." She turned anguished eyes upon Velma. "I never knew about Nolan and that girl. Or the money that went missing from our account these last few months. Call me a fool for believing the lies. But I never would've hurt Renna, even if I'd known."

Velma patted her cheek. "Of course you wouldn't, Hilary. Your friends knew that about you."

Laura exhaled.

Not Hilary, the one who helped Alison Barefoot survive financial chaos following the murder of her first husband several years ago. Not Hilary, the woman who cajoled Ian to life with Rice Krispies treats at Holt's wake when the rest of the grownups ignored him.

But Patti?

Something wasn't right here. Ana and Jon must have gotten something wrong. Laura tiptoed into the living room. Mike Barefoot's protégé, Officer Ross, handcuffed Patti, who was spitting fire. Garrett advised the police of his client Patti Ogburn's rights.

"Don't say a word, Patti," he shouted. "Not one word without me present."

Barbara faded against the Mission-style desk, clutching her Prada handbag. A wild look glazed her arctic eyes.

A crowd of faces gawked on the other side of the French doors. Ana gestured to several officers. One headed for the stairs. Another moved toward the desk.

"You can't search my house without my permission," screamed Patti.

Ana's mouth quirked. "Actually, I can. The search warrant you were served with yesterday has a date that doesn't expire for twenty-four hours."

Laura tugged at Jon's sleeve. "What's going on? Didn't you arrest Woodrow for Renna's and Lowther's murders?"

Jon pulled Laura into the now-empty kitchen. "We did. Just like Patti wanted us to do."

"What do you mean like Patti wanted?"

Jon rubbed the back of his neck underneath the collar of his white shirt. He longed to be in a short-sleeved T-shirt on a summer day like this. Not in a tie and blazer.

"She set Woodrow up to take the fall for her murders." He shrugged. "Or at least the murders she engineered."

"I don't understand. Don't the hammer

and the shoe prove Woodrow's involvement?"

His eyes narrowed. "How do you know about — ?" Jon sighed, casting a look around at the platters of food. "Never mind. I can guess. Raleigh is as small town as Mimosa Grove when it comes to stuff like this. Ross found a secret video Mr. Wangchuk —"

"The florist?"

"Yeah. A video he made of vandals. It not only caught Renna heading into the greenway with that doll, but twenty minutes later showed another person, talking on a cell phone, enter as well. We reexamined the footage we obtained from the shopping center and spotted Patti Ogburn's car parked several stores down from Tapestries the whole time. She came out of the store, sat in her car, probably unobserved, as Renna made her way toward the greenway."

"Patti admitted to being the last one to see Renna alive when she bought something at Tapestries that afternoon."

"To cover her butt in case someone spotted her there. But the tape doesn't lie. Her car remained in the same spot for a half hour. Renna never emerges again. Patti Ogburn does. One guess as to what Patti wore on her feet and the first guess doesn't count."

Ross's voice boomed from the den. "Found it, Detective Morales."

Jon and Laura poked their heads around the doorframe of the kitchen. Ross gripped Patti's needlepoint tote in one hand. And with the other, he lifted out a pad of stationery.

Ivory note cards.

Laura gasped. "Patti sent those horrible notes? Why? How could she have known those things about us?"

Patti issued a vitriolic stream, most of it obscene, against the police and her husband. "I don't know what game you cops are playing. I have no idea where that stationery came from or what it means. I didn't put those note cards in my bag. Someone's trying to frame me."

Ana snickered. "Like you tried to frame your husband."

"Patti, calm down," Garrett yelled above Patti's threats.

Laura's forehead wrinkled. "Why would she kill Renna? The baby —"

"That baby." Going rigid, Patti spun toward Laura. Something akin to crazy flashed in Patti's eyes. "Woody and I had an understanding. I never wanted children. The grubby, nasty brats. We agreed to do as we pleased. Gather whatever rosebuds while we may. No harm, no foul."

"Be quiet, Patti," growled Garrett.

"She can't be quiet without her Valium," Woodrow sneered. An ugly red flush crept from Ogburn's open shirt collar. "Used it up when you subdued and murdered your lover accomplice Lowther, didn't you, Patti?"

Patti lunged at him. Ross dropped the needlepoint tote and came to the assistance of the lone officer holding the cuffed woman. Ana stepped between Woody and his wife.

"Only your fingerprints were found on the bottle, Mrs. Ogburn. A big mistake. We talked with your doctor. Your prescription was usually for pills. This time you asked for the liquid form. The faster-acting, more virulent form with which you incapacitated Lowther to whack him with the same hammer he used to kill Renna Sheldon. Then you shoved him and his truck into Glen Lake, hoping he'd never be discovered."

"I never murdered Renna," screeched Patti. "You'll find none of my fingerprints on that hammer. You can't prove any of this."

Ana leaned against the baby grand. She

crossed her feet at the ankles. "No, that's right. Because you got Lowther to do your dirty work for you. But we have evidence you were present at the kill."

Laura wilted against Jon. "It was Lowther who attacked me?"

"I'm afraid so. We believe Patti planned the confrontation with Renna at Tapestries that afternoon. A teller remembers Patti Ogburn making those withdrawals we traced from Renna's blackmailing scheme."

"Renna was blackmailing Woodrow *and* Nolan Munro?"

"We believe, while working on your fence, Lowther called Patti when Renna entered your house. Maybe he didn't see the doll."

"Why did they care if she had something to tell me or not?"

"You didn't examine all the files on the thumb drive, did you, Laura?"

"No, there was a storm. I had to get off the computer."

Jon grimaced. "Renna had records involving illegal campaign contributions funneled through nonexistent political action groups to Garrett by way of Patti Ogburn. Garrett's going to have questions from the Justice Department to answer. Maybe, as your friend, Renna wanted to warn you against a growing relationship with a man she'd discovered was corrupt."

He unsuccessfully attempted to keep the satisfaction from coating his voice. "We think Lowther called Patti while she was still parked at the Village. And Patti told him to stop Renna."

"So he grabbed his hammer."

Jon shook his head. "Actually, the footage shows Patti bringing the hammer to the greenway herself. Wearing gloves, of course, suspicious in the midst of a Carolina heat wave. I think she'd already set up Woodrow for his fingerprints to be on that hammer by asking him to fix a deck board earlier. A claim she later denied to make him look guilty."

"But why attack me?"

His lips tensed. "You showed up at the wrong place and the wrong time. Lowther used the murder weapon against Renna on Patti's instructions. The same weapon Patti later used against him."

Laura frowned. "And the shoe print?"

"Patti has a bad habit of wearing whatever shoes are available at any given moment."

"The deck shoes . . ." Laura nodded. "Manly."

"What?"

"The other day at the pool, Patti wore these manly shoes. I didn't catch it at the time, but it stuck in my brain."

Jon widened his stance. "Patti and Woodrow are the same height. Wear the same shoe size. The sneakers were bought for Woodrow and matched the shoe print at the crime scene on the greenway. We found copper metallic flakes of toenail polish inside the tip of the shoe."

"So Patti stood there and watched Zeke kill Renna?" Laura shuddered. "Hid and watched Lowther when he tried to kill me?"

A muscle ticked in Jon's jaw. "Then, deliberately, left the print implicating her husband."

Scuffling erupted in the den.

Ross lugged Patti toward the foyer. Her bare feet skittered across the hardwood floor. Ross allowed her to pause long enough to slip her wide feet into a pair of low-heeled flats.

"Why, Patti?" Woodrow Ogburn huddled against the iron balustrade of the staircase. "Why set me up? You never minded about my woman friends before." Ogburn flicked a contemptuous glance at Garrett. "As I never minded about Lowther and the other men in your life. Why kill Renna?"

Patti ground to a halt. "That stupid, greedy, little . . ." Her face twisted. "She was the only one you ever got pregnant. The only woman who gave you what I wouldn't. A child."

Garrett moved to intercept her.

Patti shrugged him off, her words targeting her husband. "She said you promised to leave me for her and the child. Renna had high ambitions of taking my place. I love you, Woody, and I may be a lot of things, but I'll never allow any man to make me the fool in front of all of Raleigh."

Ogburn lifted his hands. "It wasn't true, Patti. I wasn't the father of that baby, I swear. She was goading you. You know what a child Renna could be. I took precautions. Always."

Patti's face contorted. Stricken, her shoulders slumped. "Not you? But I thought . . . ."

Ross and another officer grabbed hold of Patti as she sank toward the floorboards with a moan.

Laura shivered.

"Why, Patti?" Woody Ogburn dropped his head between his hands. "Why? I loved you, Patti. Always. In my fashion . . ."

Patti wailed as the officers dragged her toward the police car.

Jon drew Laura toward the French doors where, true to form, the crowd had vanished at the first hint of scandal. The hazy, soupy air felt warm and comforting after the suffocating chill of the Ogburns' twisted version of love and marriage.

"He loved her?"

Jon clenched his teeth. "In his fashion."

"And she orchestrated Renna's murder, would have allowed Lowther to kill me, and then silenced her accomplice because . . ." Laura lifted her face. "Because she loved Woodrow?"

"Sick and selfish, and did I say, sick?"

"All because of lies. Renna to Patti. Patti and Woodrow to each other." Laura blew out a breath. "It's over. Our lives can return to normal."

"Can they, Laura?" His heart hung in his throat. "This . . ." Jon cast his eyes about, searching for the right words. "This thing we've felt all these years. It's not going to go away, is it?"

She quivered. "I promise you I'll never keep Ian from you again. He's your son, Jon."

"What does the new normal look like for us?" Jon took hold of her arm. "This has nothing to do with Ian. I love you, Laura."

He'd said it. What had always been in his heart for Laura.

Tears trembled on the brink of her eyelids. Her pulse throbbed in her neck.

"Whatever we want it to look like for us,"

she whispered. "I know you're angry with me. I'm sorry for not trusting you and for keeping things from you. Could you . . . ?" Her eyes dropped. "I don't deserve it." Laura's voice broke. "But would you forgive me? Again? I'm no better than Renna or —"

He put a finger to her lips. "I'm not going anywhere. You're nothing like Renna or Patti. What do you want to happen next, Laura?" He brushed away a tear from her cheek.

She closed her eyes, her forehead touching his. "I'm afraid of what I want. Afraid of loving and losing again. Afraid not to love again. I'm a big mess, in case you hadn't already figured that out, Jon Locklear."

Jon seized her face between his hands. "You and me both. We'll be messes together and figure this thing out one day at a time with God's help, I promise."

"I know there's so much God needs to change in me, Jon. But I'm determined to make a new start. With God first."

Jon nodded. "No pressure from me. No expectations."

Her laugh wafted like a welcome afternoon breeze. "Too late. I already have a few of my own expectations."

She planted a light kiss on his lips. Her

hand quavered as she feathered his tight curls with her fingers. His pulse quickened as he waited for words a decade in the making from Laura's lips.

But the seconds ticked by in silence.

Jon drew a slow, deliberate breath. "Expectations such as?"

She twined her arms around his neck, reaching on tiptoe. "Such as a little R and R on a certain porch swing with Buggs as a chaperone after Ian's wrestled to bed every night."

"Anyone in mind for Buggs to chaperone?"

"One guess." She leaned in with another kiss.

This one lasted longer. Not long enough, though, from Jon's perspective. His heart melted at the expression on her face.

Laura caressed his cheek with the pad of her thumb. "If we hurry we can meet Ian's bus and get you both packed in time to make that all-important father-son camping trip." She smiled.

The smile that captured his heart ten years ago. A smile that haunted his dreams. A smile that beckoned a new beginning for all of them.

Laura . . . always his Laura. To cherish. To protect.

Joy exploded inside Jon, and his arms tightened around her waist. "I'd like nothing better."

She gave him a tiny tap on his bicep. "And, by the way, how good are you with a posthole digger? Looks like I'm going to need the services of another carpenter to finish the fence."

With an effort, Jon copied Laura's studied, playful tone. "For dinner and some sweet stuff, you got yourself a deal."

"Is that all it takes to engage your skills, Detective Locklear?" She fluttered a hand at him, a teasing smile on her face. That silvery laugh again. "What sweet stuff are you talking about?"

Not everything he longed to hear. Not by a long shot. Despite what she said to him that afternoon in her kitchen, did the shadowy Holt Mabry even now stand between them?

Would Laura ever love Jon the way he loved her? One day would she trust Jon with the words he'd die to hear? Could a true union of heart, mind, body, and soul be possible without those words?

Exquisite agony and sweet ecstasy. The coil in his stomach refused to loosen. He'd waited so long . . . But for Laura, he'd wait forever.

Jon captured her hand and raised it to his lips. She vibrated at his touch. His eyelids heavy, he gave her a lazy smile. "Whatever you can offer, I'll be there."

23

In a whirlwind of packing, Laura assembled a batch of Rice Krispies treats, Ian's favorite, for the journey. And Jon looked forward to uninterrupted time this weekend to get to know his son.

His favorite color, his favorite TV shows and movies. His favorite Bible verse, how Ian had first come to love and trust God.

Uninterrupted time to get to know each other better and make new memories.

Ian's delighted grin when Laura announced the on-again camping trip would stay with Jon for a lifetime. As would Ian's tight embrace around his waist, his face buried in Jon's shirt. A lifetime of possibilities to savor.

God was far better than Jon deserved.

He and Ian drove in his truck to the meeting place for the other scouts and their fathers. The state park lay less than an hour from the hustle and bustle of the capital city, but a world away from the hectic pace of civilization. Stephen Prescott, a friend of Holt Mabry's, welcomed him to the group. Ian gave Prescott's son, Dillon, a huge thumbs-up.

The other dads also welcomed Jon into their circle with few questions but ready handshakes. The difference — remembering the hen party at the Ogburn house — between men and women, Southern or not. Those women would've pried Jon's life history out of him between bites of coconut cake. Nazi interrogators could've learned a trick or two from those genteel souls.

Jon snorted. Those magnolia-skinned matrons were about as gentle as a bur hidden beneath the soft, sandy soil of his homeland.

"I suck mosquitoes up my nose by accident sometimes, too," Ian offered in an effort to be helpful about the sound Jon made.

Jon choked off a laugh. Leaving his thoughts of Southern women, Jon directed his attention to his boy. Ian held the tent line in place while Jon walloped the peg into the ground.

"When do you reckon you and Mom will feel comfortable enough to tell me the truth?"

Jon paused, mallet in midair.

"I'm not a baby. I can take the truth." Ian gave him a frank, all-wise look. "I've always lived by the philosophy it should be the truth in everything, the whole truth" — he struck a pose — "so help me God. Truth sets people free."

"Oh, really? Lived by this philosophy your whole, entire lifespan of ten years?" Jon fought unsuccessfully to keep the grin off his face. "Wow. You amaze me."

Ian crossed his arms and widened his stance, his feet even with his hips. A stance Jon recognized, with a surge of gut-level pleasure, as his own. "I understand how things get confusing sometimes between men and women."

Jon's eyebrows rose. "You do?"

Ian nodded, serious as a heart attack. "Yeah." He waved a hand. "I go to public school. And ride the bus."

"And in your vast level of experience, combined with sophistication," Jon bit the inside of his cheek, "what have you learned?"

"Sometimes things don't turn out how you wanted or intended, and you get tangled in stuff you don't know how to get out of or make right."

Tangled. That sure described his relationship to Ian's mother and Jon's crooked path to this reunion with his son.

Ian tilted his head. "What I'm saying is we all could use a little help in getting untangled, getting free. And I'm offering to do what I can."

His son rounded his eyes at Jon. " 'Cause I'd love it if you and my mom could tie the knot by Christmas. Scouts offer a family backpacking trip on the Appalachian Trail come Spring Break. And if anyone could convince my mom it's okay to use the toilet facilities only nature provides, it'd be you."

"I appreciate your vote of confidence, but things are rarely that simple —"

"Let me" — Ian pointed from his chest to Jon — "make it simple. Mom thinks I don't know how to use a comb, but I do know how to use a mirror. And I've got eyes and brains in my head. I realized the first day I saw you and Mom up against the vines, you must be my real father."

Jon's throat went dry.

He tugged Ian into the perimeter of the forest.

"Ian, I don't know what to say. Your mom and I wanted to talk with you after we returned to Raleigh this weekend. How do you feel about . . . ?" Jon swallowed past the boulder-sized lump in his windpipe. "About me?"

A smile curved Ian's lips and stretched to the corners of his eyes. "I figure how blessed could a guy be to have not just one great father in a lifetime, but two."

Jon's arms went around the boy. "I want you to know how proud I'd be to have a son like you, Ian. A son I never in a million years imagined I could ever call my own."

Ian returned his hug.

God was so good.

Ian's nose scrunched as he sniffed the air. "Looks like they got the hot dogs roasting. This gut-sharing business makes a guy hungry."

He peered at Jon. "How do the girls do it, day-in day-out, with their BFFs?"

Jon ruffled his son's hair. "Let me clue you in on a well-known but little publicized fact between us guys. Don't be fooled by pretty faces and sweet-tea pushers. Those itty-bitty Southern belles are the ones with real guts for garters."

"Uh, Jon? What's a garter?"

Jon laughed as they headed to claim their spot by the campfire.

Hours later, unable to sleep, Jon crawled out of the tent into the open air, careful not to disturb the slumber of his boy.

Jon gazed at the darkening night sky. Something nagged at the fringes of his mind. Something on the edge of his consciousness. On the tip of his tongue.

Something Laura said when they arrested Patti Ogburn. She asked in shock how Patti could've written those notes. Not incredulity at the viciousness of human nature. He'd seen far too much to ever be surprised at anything human beings could and would do to each other.

But the heart of Laura's shock lay in how Patti could've known those things in the notes about her and Jon. He frowned. A pair of unidentified prints lifted from Laura's notes didn't belong to Patti.

Women talked to each other. Raleigh, though a city of a half a million, was still a set of little villages. People knew things about each other. Especially the ones who spent their whole lives together.

Nothing remained as secret as people liked to believe. Sure, Patti could've learned of Doris's abortion. She'd been good friends with Renna's mother for years. No doubt Patti's long association with Barbara Payne could've revealed Velma Jones's deepest and darkest secrets.

Velma and Barbara were both from Mimosa Grove. Nothing there was secret for long. If Jon probed his mother's memories, and Florence Locklear wasn't one to gossip about county neighbors, she'd probably recall talk of an unexplained leave of absence by the then-young English teacher.

But the notes to Laura? The pond. The honeysuckle.

Patti could've conceivably planted the first two notes in Laura's mailbox and on her windshield at Tapestries. But how had she gained access to Laura's bedroom? Who had access to Laura's home on such a regular basis that a hound dog wouldn't question their presence in an otherwise empty house?

The only possible answer drove Jon to his feet.

And there remained the matter of the attack on Ian. Despite the RPD's best efforts, Ana had been unable to locate a vehicle that bore the marks of the collision. No damages sustained by any rental cars in the area, but maybe to an unrepaired sedan someone kept out of sight.

What about the murder of Doris Stanley? The wooden slivers didn't match the slivers found in the head wounds of either Renna or Lowther. A different weapon.

Did that compute to a different murderer? For different reasons having nothing to do with unborn babies and blackmail?

He had a bad feeling the case of the greenway killings wasn't as closed as he or Ana hoped. That the murderer of Doris Stanley might not yet be finished with their macabre trail of death.

The Accuser, the notes were signed.

What game was that psycho playing?

The Accuser was a pseudonym in the Bible. Used only once, if Jon recalled correctly. Used in the book of Revelation. A pseudonym for Satan, the accuser of the brethren.

An accuser was, at his core, a prosecutor. Someone capable of sabotaging Holt Mabry's brake system on an icy winter night. So much had happened in the span of a week. Jon's emotions had soared and plummeted like a roller coaster. Threads Jon should'vc followed up on before now.

If now wasn't already too late.

His heart beating like a drum at a powwow, Jon fished the cell phone out of his cargo shorts. "Come on, come on," he hissed as it powered to life.

For a second Jon feared there'd be no service out here in the woods, but he breathed as his phone hummed to life, albeit slowly. Luckily they weren't too far out of the bounds of the transmitter that kept Raleigh and its citizens on the grid.

He rang Laura's number first. No answer. Her lilting voice came through voicemail.

This is the Mabry residence. Ian is unable to take your . . .

"Pick up, pick up. Where are you, Laura? You said you'd be home all — Hello?" His voice sounded just this side of full-blown panicked. "Laura, if you're there, pick up. I need to speak with you immediately."

A thought occurred. "Everything's fine with Ian, but it's important we talk right away." If she was okay, had stepped out to walk Buggs, Jon didn't want Laura to receive this message and worry.

But what if she wasn't okay? Was someone there, in the house, making sure Laura couldn't answer her phone?

"I'm calling Ana. She'll send someone by to be sure you're okay. Sorry to be such a worrywart but" — Jon's voice broke — "it's my job to worry about people I love. Be safe," he whispered. "I'm on my way. Something about this doesn't feel right to me."

Jon disconnected.

Ian popped his head out of the tent. "You think someone could still be threatening Mom?"

The boy did have the ears of a hawk.

"I'm sorry about this, Ian, but I —"

"Don't worry. You go. I'll wake Dillon and Dr. Stephen and let them know you had to leave."

He enfolded the boy into a tight hug. "I'm sorry."

Ian gave Jon's arm a shove. "Go. Keep Mom safe. There'll be plenty more campouts. Spring Break, remember?"

Jon nodded, his mouth grim. "I remember."

To lose Laura now with the fulfillment of his hopes and dreams so close at hand . . .

God, keep her safe. Show me what to do.

He had Ana on speed dial before he reached his parked truck.

"Could I entice you over to Stonebriar to share a belated dinner with me of pimiento cheese sandwiches, deviled eggs, and pecan pie?" Velma's call had come as Laura waved the guys out of the driveway.

Her guys.

A rush of pleasure at that thought. Far more than she deserved. God was good.

She cradled the kitchen phone against her neck. "I take it you took home some of Patti's bounty."

Velma gave an unladylike snort. "Honey, over the years a lot of Raleigh took home some of Patti's bounty." She laughed. "But in this case I'm referring to the food. After the hullabaloo died down."

Laura dreaded a future that didn't include

the Depression-born, World War–tempered generation of Velma Louise Jones. "Aunt Velma, you're something else."

"Truer words, Laura Lou, were never spoken."

Much later, after her visit, as violet streaks merged to indigo above the tree-lined horizon, Laura pulled into her driveway. With the setting of the sun, the air had cooled. A smidgeon.

She hurried into the kitchen, balancing the plates Aunt Velma insisted Laura bring home for "the boys" to enjoy. Aunt Velma swore she couldn't let another bite pass between her lips, or she'd never attract the attention of that handsome octogenarian down the hall.

Love.

It do make the world go 'round.

Laura resisted the temptation to snag another deviled egg as she deposited the plates inside the refrigerator. She'd never met a carb she didn't love. Problem with being five foot four inches, she reflected not for the first time. No room to grow without expanding in ways frowned upon in her culture.

Now, the Lumbee, on the other hand . . .

Laura smiled and looked forward to getting reacquainted with Jon's mother and sisters. The Lumbee didn't mind a little meat on their women.

She patted her hips, no longer as slim as her former twenty-year-old self. She hoped Jon, true to his heritage, wouldn't mind, either.

As the refrigerator door swung shut, a disturbing thought intruded upon her contentment. How had Patti known about the pond in little Mimosa Grove ten years ago?

Velma's earlier comment followed on the heels of that question. Her aunt said something to the effect that Patti was no better than she ought to be, but she'd never been a hypocrite. The notes were so not Patti's style. As another note, long ago, had been out of character for Laura's father.

A feeling akin to the willies raised the hair on the back of Laura's neck.

But the stationery was found in Patti's needlepoint tote. The type of legal stationery that Woodrow Ogburn would possess. Like former Judge Emerson Bowen probably still had lying around the house that had become a travesty of Laura's childhood home since Witch Barbara ascended the throne.

An image of the last time she'd seen her father in his study worried, like Buggs with a bone, at Laura's mind. Something hadn't been right. He'd been seated in his wheelchair at his desk. The wall behind Emerson lined with his awards, degrees, and accomplishments.

Unable to resolve the nagging feeling something vital had been missing, Laura returned to the puzzle of how and why Patti Ogburn would launch such a nasty attack upon her.

With niggling feelings of unease, Laura stepped into the living room to erase the cobwebs from her brain. Turning on the lights, she settled into her favorite wingback chair by the diamond-paned casement window. The cul-de-sac lay dark with Laura's neighbors scattered among beach, lake, and mountain vacation homes this time of year. The question remained not only how Patti had known but also how she'd been able to place that note in Laura's bedroom drawer.

Was Patti truly The Accuser, or had someone planted the stationery on Patti? Someone with access to both Laura and Patti's homes?

Laura's heart wrenched.

Someone like Garrett, with similar stationery from his law office. As for access to Laura's home? A privilege she'd facilitated for Garrett over the last few months. He had retrieved the mail from her mailbox the day Renna was killed when the first note appeared. He'd have had no trouble placing the second note under her windshield in the alley behind Tapestries where no one could spot him.

And the third note mixed in with her lingerie?

Laura's skin crawled. Last Friday, she'd jumped into the shower after the attack, and Garrett had been left alone to roam her house at will. And he later insisted she set the security alarm before he departed, watching her punch in the numbers.

Memorizing the code to return at his leisure?

Laura shuddered at the image of his hands rifling through her private things.

She recalled the strange feeling she had on several occasions that something in the air felt disturbed at Tapestries and in her home. Had he been looking for the thumb drive that contained incriminating evidence of his corrupt campaign?

There'd also been Garrett's fanatical insistence upon an engagement and a swift wedding. The intensity in his face and voice. His increasing efforts to manipulate and browbeat Laura into acquiescence.

Why, if not to ensure damage control was at a minimum with her as his wife?

Laura surged to her feet. Hastening into the kitchen, she grabbed the phone only to discover no dial tone. She stared at the dead instrument for a moment in disbelief. She'd used this phone not two hours earlier with Aunt Velma.

Had someone else been here then, listening, waiting?

Laura groped for the familiar lump of her cell in her pocket. She chewed the inside of her cheek. Not there. Because she'd destroyed her phone in a fit of pique with Ana Morales yesterday. And with the momentous turn of events today, Laura never got around to replacing it.

Icy shivers of fear crawled up Laura's arms at her isolation. She wrapped her arms around her body. Laura's eyes darted around the familiar contours of her home.

Think . . . think.

No need to panic. Laura shook off the fear and lifted her chin. Just get Buggs, get in her car, and drive to Detective Morales with her suspicions.

Laura stepped onto the screened porch. "Buggs . . ."

No answering bark greeted her call.

The dog's pallet lay empty. Instead of Buggs's wet doggy odor, the cloying scent of honeysuckle teased Laura's nostrils. Her eyes fastened on a trail of blossoms, leading out the open screen door. The petals meandered across her lawn and disappeared into the dark tangle of vines adjacent to the greenway.

Her heart thudded.

"Buggs!"

Only a distant, mournful baying echoed through the still, sultry night.

Shaking, Laura backpedaled. Reaching the kitchen island, her hand groped for the keys where she always tossed them out of habit. But she came up empty.

Laura whirled. Her eyes skittered across the smooth, granite countertop. Nothing.

Had she carried them into the living room? She'd been juggling plates. Laura stepped away from the island.

She could've sworn —

The house lights plunged into darkness.

On the other side of the garage door, the wooden steps groaned.

Whipping around, Laura stifled a cry. The doorknob leading to the garage — and the circuit breakers — rattled.

How had he . . . ?

She'd lowered the garage bay, Laura was sure. This entry door to her home via the garage was never locked. And even if Laura had possession of her keys, he now blocked her only way to the car.

The hinges she'd been meaning to oil creaked as the door swung inward. In the space of a split second, Laura measured her chances of making it to the front door, unlatching the chain, and disengaging the dead bolt before Garrett would be upon her.

The baying started again, frantic and growing more distant.

Buggs must have gotten free when Garrett entered the house. Buggs would protect Laura as he had once before when Lowther attacked her. Holding her breath, Laura edged once more toward the screened porch.

Her only hope lay in reaching Buggs, getting to the Village, and to the safety of other people.

24

Laura raced out the screen door, now her only exit to escape. A low-throated laugh sounded behind her, too close. She plunged into the darkness and barreled across the grass toward the vines. She lost one of her flip-flops, but she didn't stop.

The vines slapped her face. Briars caught at her hair as she struggled to wriggle through the entangling creepers. Breaking free, Laura kicked off the other flip-flop. Better to be completely barefoot on the pine-needled path. Better for running.

With the half-moon hidden by the canopy of trees, Laura stumbled over a root. She pitched forward, catching herself. "Buggs!" she hissed.

But the baying had ceased. Was the basset hound cowering nearby and too scared to respond? Or had Garrett hurt Buggs?

On the footbridge, the wooden boards creaked beneath her pounding feet. Laura winced at the sudden, sharp jab of a splinter into her heel. Stopping to listen for sounds of pursuit, Laura positioned her weight over her uninjured foot.

But there was only silence, except for the humming of insects.

Laura knew the greenway better than Garrett. He'd be unfamiliar, especially in the dark, with the terrain. Her mother, Louise, grew up here. And Laura and Ian had spent countless hours counting tadpoles in the creek below the embankment since moving into Woods Edge. Together, they'd learned to identify the trilling song of the forest birds. Once, they even spotted the great blue heron, who called this stretch of wilderness home.

Something small scurried off to her right. A whisper of sound. Leaves rustled.

Laura jerked when Buggs's baying resumed. She leaned against the bridge railing to massage her foot. Not too far from where Renna . . .

She trembled in the steamy sauna of the June night.

Ian would be inconsolable if anything happened to Buggs. Laura's chest heaved. He'd be more inconsolable if something happened to his mom. If she could reach the Village —

Twigs snapped behind her.

Bolting, Laura ran.

She dashed beyond the site of Renna's murder. Stubbing her toe, Laura bit her lip to keep from crying out. But she kept going. She couldn't — mustn't — stop. Her side knotted with pain.

Inhale . . . Exhale . . .

A dog howled. Buggs?

The noise originated off trail in a tangle of underbrush not far from the trailhead at the Village.

Panting, Laura ground to a halt.

Was Buggs injured? Bleeding? Dying?

Laura recalled there used to be a shack in that approximate location. A shed where the Park and Rec guys once stored their maintenance equipment. Ian and his cohorts often used the dilapidated structure for reenactments of Death Star battles of epic proportions.

Now the kudzu enshrouded, consumed, and devoured what remained of its original form. The vines had reclaimed the land that once belonged exclusively to nature, destroying inch by inch what man had the gall to superimpose.

Here, honeysuckle ran amok.

Sparing only a thought for the chiggers, thorns, and ticks lying between her and the hut, Laura muscled her way through the tapestry of vines lining the deer path. She tried not to think at this time of the year about the water moccasins . . .

A whimpering replaced the howls.

"Buggs," she whispered.

Wading in deeper over rotting logs, she yanked the ramshackle door, hanging half on, half off its hinges. The shaft of moonlight illuminated Buggs amidst the shadowy interior. He lifted his snout as if to yowl again.

His tail worked in a feverish frenzy. Floorboards sagged as Laura hurried forward with her hand outstretched. Buggs lunged toward her.

A leather leash snapped Buggs in place. A tanned, well-muscled hand tightened its hold.

Behind Laura, acorns crunched. With a screech of hinges, the door swung shut.

"You've come." Garrett smiled in a sudden glow of his flashlight. "Just as she said you would."

Blinded by the glare, a woodsy scent of greenway bracken teased at Laura's olfactory memory. The scent she'd been unable to identify that day at Tapestries. Laura's eyes struggled to adjust to the spotlight Garrett beamed into her face.

Then Garrett focused the light over Laura's shoulder. "Did you leave the car parked in the alley?"

Laura wheeled.

"Hello, Laura, my dear." A satisfied smile lifted the corners of Barbara's mouth.

In her hand, Barbara held the one thing Laura had subconsciously missed from the wall in Emerson's study that day.

Similar in diameter to the hammer handle used against Renna and Lowther — the gavel used against poor Doris.

Chilled despite the humidity, Laura swiveled between mother and son. "I don't understand, Garrett. What's going on?"

Barbara's eyes glittered. "Let Buggsby return home now, son."

Released from the leash, with his tail wagging, Buggs sidled to Laura's side. He licked her hand and whimpered.

Barbara motioned. "Here, boy."

And, ever eager to please, Buggs trotted over to Barbara. She opened the shed door. "Go home, doggy boy. I've left you some lovely treats."

The dog hesitated.

Barbara nudged his backside with her leg. "Go now, Buggsby."

Still Buggsby remained.

Her stepmother's voice hardened. "Tell

him to go, Laura. For his own good. Your boy will need his dog."

Quivering, Laura cleared her throat. "Go, Buggs. It's okay. Go home."

With one last look at Laura, Buggs trotted out the door and disappeared into the night.

"So many dogs over the years on your dad's childhood farm." Barbara sighed. "I've always loved dogs. We'll have to get one, Garrett, once we're settled."

Laura angled to keep both mother and son in sight. "Why the notes, Garrett?"

Barbara tapped the gavel into her palm. "Buggs and I became fast friends when Garrett and I slipped into your house one afternoon looking for the thumb drive. Garrett didn't leave those notes. In fact, he has no idea what you're talking about. But then I'm not surprised you were too stupid to figure it out."

Garrett directed the light at their feet. "What notes, Mother?"

Barbara waved the walnut gavel. "Old business. Loose threads needing to be tied. To bring us to where we are today. For our end goals to be accomplished."

"Which are?" Despite a tremor that threatened to bring her to her knees, Laura fought to keep her voice collected. Lest Barbara, her Accuser, exploit any sign of weakness.

Her stepmother shrugged. "We'll get to that soon enough. So nice of Patti on her own initiative to solve our little blackmail problem with Renna."

Barbara cut a look at Garrett. "Patti would've been a much more suitable consort for you, dear, in the scope of our ambitions."

She brandished the gavel in Laura's direction. "But you were always so fixated on this little strumpet."

Anger stirred Laura. "That's rich coming from the Queen of Home Wreckers."

Barbara's mouth twisted. "Are you going to stand by while this trollop speaks to your mother that way, Garrett?"

He bristled. "I'll kindly ask you to refer to my bride in more respectful tones hereafter, Mother."

Bride? What was Garrett talking about? They'd — he'd — broken off their engagement.

Laura turned, facing Garrett. "I'm not your —"

The gavel whistled in a downward arc. Pain exploded in the back of Laura's head. Darkness descended.

25

Laura woke with a blinding headache. She tried moving, but with devastating results. Fighting nausea and the urge to moan, she waited for the queasiness to subside.

After a few moments, Laura dared to touch her fingertips to her head. She flinched when she encountered a goose egg–sized lump. She probed for the sticky residue of blood but found none. As her eyes gradually adjusted, she took stock of her present situation.

She lay across the backseat of a moving vehicle. Barbara's green Jag. Laura tilted her head and wished she hadn't when dizziness overtook her once more. In front, mother and son argued.

He reached for the button on his visor. "You had no right to hit her, Mother. Laura's my responsibility, not yours. I will handle things with her my way."

Gears grinded.

Overhead, a garage door rolled upward. A motion light sprang to life.

Garrett pulled to a stop. "You don't understand in the least how to deal with her. She'll come around, but Laura can't be rushed or coerced."

Barbara snorted. "Like you handled her so well this week? Weren't we supposed to be celebrating your nuptials tonight at Carolina Beach?"

Garrett's mouth tightened.

Digging her elbow into the leather cushion for leverage, Laura craned her aching head, neck muscles tense, to peer out further.

It was her old home, Barbara and Emerson's home.

Laura sucked in a breath at the sight of a black sedan parked next to the Jag. The sedan's front bumper was damaged. Garrett pressed a button and lowered the garage door. He shut off the ignition.

"We've no time to lose." Barbara groped for the door handle. "Get her out of the car and put her with Emerson. Then load the suitcases into the trunk."

Jerking open the car door, Garrett reached for Laura. She swatted at his hands and shied away, but he caught her arm and tugged her forward. Garrett cradled Laura's head in his hands. "Laura, honey? Are you all right?"

He scowled at his mother. "See what you've done. You've made her afraid. Of me."

Garrett leaned over Laura's rigid body. He smoothed a tendril of hair out of her face. She cringed.

"No need to fear, my love. Everything is going to be okay now. As you and I were always meant to be."

"Garrett . . . no . . ." Laura choked.

He scooped Laura out of the car. "You'd better not have permanently harmed her, Mother."

Laura's head swam. She swallowed and willed the bile down her throat. Her head lolled onto Garrett's shoulder.

Following Barbara into the darkened house, Garrett kissed Laura's head. His lips loitering, he inhaled the fragrance of her shampoo. An involuntary shudder streaked through her.

Help me, God.

Garrett nudged open the door of the study with his knee. Only the green banker's lamp atop Emerson's desk lit the room. Her father slumped in his chair. His hands rested on her mother's Bible. Raising his head, Emerson's eyes pooled at the sight of Laura clasped in Garrett's arms.

Emerson struggled to move his atrophied legs off the footrest. "No-oooo . . ."

Barbara clamped a hand on his shoulder. "Calm down, Emerson. Getting upset about what can't be avoided does no one any good."

A sheet-shrouded body lay on the Persian rug.

Garrett settled Laura upon the leather sofa at right angles to her father. "A few minutes more and we'll be off."

Laura moistened her bottom lip. "Off where? Garrett, I don't understand."

Barbara flicked a hand at her son. "The suitcases, dear. And don't forget to light the conflagration. Start in the kitchen."

A sick feeling welled in the pit of Laura's stomach.

Garrett ran his hand down her arm. "Don't worry, darling. We just have to cover our tracks."

Laura's mind whirled in a desperate attempt to make sense out of the nonsensical. "That's crazy. Everyone will know Dad and I have gone missing. There'll be a search."

Garrett gave her a patient, patronizing smile. "That's why Mother had the foresight to supply a few bodies from the homeless hangout under the Beltline bridge. The bodies will be unrecognizable due to the flames. By the time DNA results come back, we'll be far away."

He patted her hand. "Mother's hired a private plane to take us to friends in Cuba. No extradition there. By nightfall tomorrow, we'll be beginning our new life together."

Shivers of fear skittered across Laura's arms. "You won't ever get away with this. It's insane. You're both insane."

Jon would search to the end of the earth for her. He'd never give up.

Barbara jerked her head toward the door. "The fire, Garrett."

He departed with a long, smoldering look at Laura.

"So much you've never understood." Barbara glanced out at the night. "Neither you nor your mother or your snooty aunt. Always thinking you were better than me and Garrett."

Laura suspected if the duo succeeded in removing her and her father from the house, they'd never be found again. She sent a silent plea to heaven, for Jon or Ana or somebody to wonder where she was. All she could do now was trust that God would make things right.

Trust . . . always it came back to that.

Until then, she'd stall and delay their

plans as long as possible. "Why kill Doris? She was an old woman. She couldn't possibly have posed any threat to you, Barbara."

"I overheard what she said at the funeral. Doris's remark about the doll made me wonder. Renna had taken photos of sensitive documents at campaign headquarters. Renna boasted she had enough info on a thumb drive to discredit Garrett's campaign and possibly send him to jail. I searched Doris's house the day after Patti murdered Renna, when all of you gathered for your needlepoint group. Garrett's knowledge of your security code allowed us to search your home later."

Barbara sniffed. "Doris's death was inevitable. I couldn't be sure what else Renna had told her about Garrett."

Her stepmother cocked her head. "And someone had to teach Doris a lesson about what happens to baby killers. How unfortunate we didn't find the thumb drive that day. Perhaps none of this unpleasantness need have occurred. You and Garrett would be on your way to wedded bliss."

Laura stiffened. "That wasn't going to happen. Ever."

Barbara's mouth contorted. "Oh, it would've happened all right if that Lumbee" — an expletive — "hadn't intervened once again in our plans." She laid the gavel in Emerson's lap, atop the Bible.

Grabbing hold of the armrest for support, Laura stumbled to her feet. "What do you mean 'once again'?"

Barbara fondled a cut-glass spray bottle on the edge of Emerson's desk and inserted herself between Laura and her dad.

Garrett slipped into the room.

Barbara's look of sheer malice gave Laura a split-second of warning.

Throwing up her hand, Laura averted her head and prevented the liquid from hitting her eyes full force. A sweet scent of decaying honeysuckle drenched her hair and blouse. Emerson gave a hoarse cry.

Laura screamed and recoiled at the burning sensation. She clawed at her eye. She writhed on the sofa.

In two strides, Garrett knocked the bottle out of Barbara's hand. Spiraling, it shattered against Emerson's trophy wall. "What're you doing? You'll blind her, Mother."

"I'm sorry, darling." Garrett grabbed a water pitcher from the side table. Dabbing a handkerchief into the water, he pried Laura's hand free and held the waterlogged cloth to her eye. "I won't let her hurt you again."

Barbara stamped her foot. "You're the blind one, Garrett. She's nothing but a liar. She's strung you along all these years. She's hurt you over and over again. And yet, you keep coming back for more of the same. Like some stupid, abused mutt. She deserves this and more."

Tears flooded down Laura's cheeks. She blinked rapidly, desperate to ease the stinging.

Laura swabbed her eye with the handkerchief. "Just like in the note. My part in the fire, right, Barbara? Tell your son what you really intend for me."

Garrett straightened. "What's she talking about, Mother?"

Laura gripped his sleeve. "There's only one body under that sheet, Garrett. Can't you see? She's taking Emerson. Not me. I supply my own body to the flames."

"No." Garrett yanked back the sheet. A ragged, elderly man lay face down on the floor.

He spun to face Barbara. "You lied, Mother." A muscle throbbed in his jaw. "You said everything Emerson had would be mine, including Laura. That he owed you and me both for the shame and heartache."

Garrett curled his hands into balls. "After all the empty promises he made to you in

Mimosa Grove. You'd take him" — he jabbed his finger at Emerson — "and not my Laura?"

Laura lumbered to her feet. She pressed the water-soaked handkerchief to her eye.

"You're a fool." Barbara flicked Garrett a contemptuous look. "A fool, like your father. You want to talk about shame? All right then."

Her bejeweled fingers clawed into Emerson's shoulder. "Emerson left me for the university and better things than raising hogs and chickens."

Emerson hung his head.

"Left me 'deflowered and ruined,' so my father informed me in his wrath." Barbara's mouth pursed. "He beat me and forced me to marry one of his sanctimonious cronies, who nightly made it his business to teach me how a good, docile wife behaves."

Barbara glanced away. "But later, rat poison slipped into sweet tea got us away from that dirty cracker."

Garrett reeled like he'd taken a sucker punch to the gut.

"And you found my dad in Raleigh and insinuated yourself into our lives." Laura squared her shoulders. "You wanted me to discover your relationship with him that day before my mother died."

Emerson's mouth trembled.

Barbara folded her arms. "You were always meant for Garrett." She shook her head. "But you headed off to Mimosa Grove on that internship instead of finding consolation in Garrett's arms after your mother's death."

"How did you know" — Laura took a breath — "about Jon and me and — and the honeysuckle?"

"Did you imagine you two were the first young people in Mimosa Grove to appreciate the possibilities of that isolated location?"

Laura's eyebrows arched. "You had me followed? Spied upon?"

"I needed to keep track of you."

Barbara cut her eyes at Garrett. "He had his pick of Raleigh's finest by that point. It's along the lines of a Shakespearean tragedy that the only woman Garrett ever wanted was someone he couldn't have."

Garrett planted his hands on the edge of the desk across from his mother. "Laura and I will still be —"

"It wasn't you, was it, Dad?" Laura bent over her father. "Barbara sent the notes and arranged the motel room in Jacksonville."

Barbara rolled her eyes. "So slow on the uptake. That's what comes" — she patted

Emerson's arm — "from dipping into stupid debutante gene pools, my darling."

Emerson pursed his lips. "Not-t-t mmmm—eee."

"Oh, Dad." Laura took a step. "I'm sorry for believing Barbara's lies. For everything I said and —"

Emerson waggled his head from side to side. "M-m-m-eye f-fal-l-l—t-t-t."

"It's not your fault, Emerson." Barbara wheeled. "Stop upsetting your father, Laura."

Barbara's glacial eyes narrowed. "You were supposed to turn to Garrett then, too. Who could've predicted you'd rebound with Holt?" She lifted her shoulders. "But I took care of that situation, eventually."

Laura clutched her throat. "*You* sabotaged Holt's car?"

And she recalled the incongruous high school club memberships of the former farm girl turned court justice wife.

Laura's lips tightened. "Did you help your mother unclamp the hose on Holt's car, Garrett?"

Garrett grasped her upper arms. "No, but it was all for the best. Don't you see, Laura? We belong together. Always have. Once we get to Havana, you'll forget the Lumbee once and for all. We'll have other children.

Ian will be safe in the arms of his father's family and with his own kind." He hugged her close.

Laura fought her repulsion. Garrett remained her only ally, albeit twisted against the real threat of Barbara's murderous intent. She had to do something to alter the situation so she and Dad could escape.

Emerson coughed. Smoke filtered from underneath the door. Flames crackled in the distance. The room grew hot, the air stifling.

Barbara removed a gun from the desk drawer. "We don't have time for these histrionics. Step away from her, Garrett."

Laura sagged into him. "Barbara will never allow me to leave this house alive. She's never had your best interests at heart unless they aligned with her own. It's her interference that kept us apart."

She focused on Garrett's face. "She staged my discovery of her affair with my father, which led me to apply for the internship. She split up Jon and me when I was pregnant and vulnerable, which drew me to Holt while you were at law school. The notes show how she hates —"

"She's a liar," hissed Barbara. "Don't believe anything that tramp has to say."

Uncertainty coated Garrett's features.

"Don't let your mother separate us now." Laura took a breath, "Not ever again, darling."

"No," growled his mother.

Garrett tensed at the menace in Barbara's voice.

Laura captured his face between her hands. "Garrett, if you've ever truly loved me. Please."

To come so close to the life she'd always dreamed about with Jon and Ian . . .

If only she could fool Garrett. Say the words she never spoke to Holt. Her insides wrenched at how she failed to say what she felt to Jon, too.

Why had she withheld the words from Jon? He'd never know now how much she truly did love him. Why hadn't she the courage to tell him the truth of her heart?

The heat intensified. The fire ambulated, rippling, curling, and popping. Smoke poured from underneath the door. Emerson wheezed. Laura's irritated eyes watered.

She'd promised — God, Jon, herself — not to lie again. Not to control, but to trust.

Just one more lie. Surely God would understand this was the smart thing to do. The only thing to do. To save her skin. To ensure she lived to love Jon and Ian another day.

But the lies had landed her right where she stood now. Laura couldn't shake the conviction of her vow to lay aside the lies. Her mouth opened.

Her lips parted and formed around the words. "Garrett, please help me. Help us. I" — she swallowed — "I lov—"

But she couldn't.

Laura turned her face away.

No matter the cost, she couldn't lie any more.

Because she'd learned — too late — there was always a cost to the lies. For better or worse. A cost she would pay today for the truth. A cost somebody always had to pay.

A grace already paid for the lies, the sins . . . As her mother had tried to tell her. Holt, too.

With a prayer for courage, she readied herself to face the consequences for truth. Consequences — because of something more precious than her present life — she'd never willingly faced before. Something more important than a future with Jon and Ian. Time to trust God to do in Garrett's heart what she wasn't willing any longer to manipulate into being.

"Laura . . ." Garrett breathed.

"Garrett, I won't lie to you like your mother. I'm sorry I can't say the words you want to hear. But I promised God I'm done with lying to everyone, including myself. To lie to you would do you no favors. Despite everything, I think you know you could always trust me. When no one else was your friend, I was."

He closed his eyes. An infinitesimal sadness scrunched his boyishly handsome features. When Garrett opened his eyes, he held Laura's hands to his lips and brushed a kiss across her knuckles.

Barbara slammed her hand upon the desk. "Step away from her, Garrett. Now."

Uncoiling like a copperhead, his eyes blazed with raw fury. He whipped a small pistol out of his jacket. "Way I see it, we need one body more. Or, one body less for this scheme to work. And my vote is to take Laura." He fired two slugs into Emerson's chest.

Laura and Barbara screamed.

Laura ran to her father's side. Emerson raised his head to meet her eyes. Blood gurgled from his chest.

Barbara pointed her gun at Garrett, a near-demented look darkening her eyes. "You shouldn't have done that. No one hurts Emerson."

She pumped the trigger. In a burst of sound, several round holes materialized in the center of Garrett's blue polo shirt. Laura froze.

His eyes widened. Garrett staggered and gripped his chest as pools of red widened beneath his fingers. "Laura . . ." He collapsed onto the carpet. "Don't let her win."

Garrett flung the gun. It skidded across the hardwood where it came to rest inches from Laura's feet.

He flashed Laura the old vote-getting smile, which won female hearts from Murphy to Manteo. "I love —"

Garrett choked. A frisson of pain cramped his body into the fetal position.

And he went still.

The color drained from Barbara's face. "Nobody hurts Emerson," she whispered again. The gun wobbled in her hand.

Breaking free of her paralysis, Laura scrambled for the gun on the floor. Her fingers tightened around the cold steel. "Nobody but you, Barbara."

Laura jumped to her feet and aimed the gun at Barbara. "It's over. Drop the gun and wheel my father out of this inferno. I'll be right behind you."

Sirens pierced the night.

Laura jolted at the long, undulating wail of fire trucks followed by the shorter whirrs of the RPD.

An ugly look creased Barbara's face. Her hand steadied, and her stepmother's finger tightened on the trigger. "You're not going anywhere but hell."

With his good hand, Emerson gripped the gavel. Weak and wildly aimed, he knocked the gun out of Barbara's hand. The gun bumped and landed on the other side of the desk. His strength expended, Emerson sprawled half in, half out of his chair. His arm draped over the side.

Hammer blows pounded the door.

"Laura!"

The front door shook with the full force of Jon's weight thrown against it.

Laura pivoted toward Jon's voice. She lowered Garrett's gun.

Barbara seized the other gun lying on the mahogany surface of the desk.

Laura tensed, in that split-second too late to regain her advantage.

But Barbara pressed the steel against her temple.

Laura lunged. "No, Barb—"

Barbara's finger squeezed.

Laura closed her eyes.

The gunfire syncopated with the sound of wood splintering in the entryway.

Laura's eyes flew open. Her stepmother lay on her side. A portion of her head blown away, Barbara's glacial eyes gazed into nothingness.

Or did they?

Laura flung herself toward Emerson, whose face was paper white. "Dad?"

Shouting her name, Jon burst through the study door, his shirt on fire.

Laura rushed to him.

He wrested away from her. "No, not your hands."

Jon threw himself on the Persian carpet and rolled.

The flames out, Laura helped Jon to his feet. Angry red blisters showed through the fire-blackened holes peppering his shirt.

Jon's eyes darted to the bodies. "We've got to get out of here, now, Laura."

Orange flames consumed the doorway. Tongues of fire, like lies, searched for something new to devour.

She bent to unlock the brakes of her father's wheelchair. "We have to get Daddy out first."

Emerson flapped at her hands. "No—o-o-o."

Jon lifted her father from the chair and cradled him.

Emerson pushed the book at Laura. "S-sorree I b-bleave h-her l-lies." His chest labored for each breath as the smoke rose.

"Find something to cover him and yourself, Laura." Jon jerked his chin to the throw on the back of the sofa.

Laura grabbed the afghan and adjusted the folds around her father and Jon.

"We've got to go now." Jon eyed the curls of fire engulfing the corners of the room. "Cover your head, Laura. We've got to make a run for it."

Laura yanked the embroidered runner off the Queen Anne table behind the couch.

Jon bent his head protectively over Emerson. "Close your eyes, Mr. Bowen," he yelled over the din of the licking, greedy flames. He tightened his jaw. "Stay with me, Laura. Don't stop."

She nodded, her lungs burning from the superheated air.

Jon made a dash for the hallway. She followed, ducking her head as she passed through the smoking doorframe. Searing heat scorched the skin on her exposed arms as she held the runner over her head and shielded her mother's Bible.

"Ready?" Jon glanced back at her from the enflamed front door.

Laura's head bobbed, the intense heat burning her cheeks.

Clutching Laura's dad, Jon vaulted through the door. Laura held her breath and jumped. Jon rolled off the porch and angled to cushion Emerson's fall into the grass. Laura collapsed into a nearby heap.

Bolting upright, Jon settled Emerson on the ground then swatted at the cinder in Laura's hair.

A harsh rattling emanated from her father's throat. Emerson's gnarled finger touched the book she clutched. "You b-bleave b-book?"

Tears, not just from the smoke, streamed from Laura's eyes. "Yes, Daddy. I do believe the book." Her eyes darted to Jon. "Do something. Help him."

Jon frowned. "He's dying, Laura."

Her gaze swung to Emerson. "Hang on, Daddy. I love you. Don't leave me."

A smile creased Emerson's slackened features. "M-me Oh-k-kay." He patted the book in her arms.

Once. Twice. He closed his eyes.

And then, through bloodless lips, a sigh emanated from the core of his being. Like the whisper of autumn leaves letting go of the life-giving source of the tree.

"No, Daddy . . ." she wailed. "Come back." She strained forward.

Jon wrapped his arms around her. "He's gone, Laura. I'm sorry."

But dignity lingered on her father's face.

A peace he'd been unable to attain in life.

Truck doors slammed. Voices called. Men in helmets with fire hoses appeared. Jon called out terse instructions.

"Laura? Are you all right?" Jon gathered her closer. "Honey . . ." He brushed tangled strands of hair out of her face.

She sobbed onto his shoulder as firefighters made a vain attempt to save her childhood home. "How did you know where to find me?"

Jon coughed. "Buggs. I had a bad feeling at the campsite. I found your house deserted but when I spotted the honeysuckle . . ."

His voice roughened. "Buggs burst out of the greenway. He led me to the hut, but the trail stopped cold. You weren't at Tapestries. And then I recollected how the greenway connected Woods Edge with your father's neighborhood. My last hope was that Garrett had taken you there. I didn't know where else to find you."

"It was Barbara." Laura fought to clear the smoke inhalation from her lungs. "The notes. Doris's murder. Holt. Everything. She killed a homeless guy you'll find inside. And Garrett, too, after he shot Dad. Garrett had this obsessive notion he and I would be together. His mother fed on that and manipulated him like she did my father."

Jon's arms tightened around her. "I almost lost you tonight." He shuddered. "Ian almost lost you tonight."

It was God's mercy she hadn't been consumed as her sins deserved. A mercy new every morning. A mercy that ought not to be wasted.

Before Laura, a second chance with God. With life. With Jon.

She cupped his grimy, soot-darkened face. "I love you, Jon Locklear. I've always loved you. We misplaced each other for a decade. But after tonight, I never want to lose you again."

And Laura beheld something tightly bound loosen in Jon's eyes.

Something wonderful. Something that took her breath and flooded her heart.

"I love you, Laura. So much. For so long. For always."

His lips, dry and cracked, touched hers. "Do you know what 'Locklear' means?"

She shook her head, captivated by the love in his eyes for her.

Love for me . . . Thank you, God.

Jon traced the pattern of her face in the reflected glow of the burning home. "Locklear means to 'hold fast.' And this promise I'll never break so long as I live. To hold fast to you and Ian and our Lord forever."

Epilogue

Laura waved to Florence Locklear, Jon's sister, Yvonne, and his niece, Cami, on the Homecoming Court float winding down Third Street in the hot July sunshine. Florence was a former Senior Ms. Lumbee, Yvonne a former Miss Lumbee, and Cami, a Mini Miss Lumbee. In colorful turquoise, purple, and green calico, their trident-shaped crowns topped their brown, pulled-back hair.

The dresses were heavily embroidered at the hem and sleeves. A pinecone quilt motif emblazoned their white pinafore aprons. The Lumbee were big on their beauty queens. Current queens waved Queen of England–style from convertibles ambling down the parade path.

Under the umbrella shading them from the early morning sunshine in Pembroke, Velma lounged in a red canvas chair. Condensation dribbled down the sides of the plastic glass of sweet tea Aunt Velma gripped. Velma estimated half of the fifty-five thousand Lumbee members, scattered over the continent, would find their way back to their roots during this Lumbee Homecoming weekend.

Laura scooped her hair off the nape of her neck and fanned herself. Jon had taken Ian and Tayla over to the craft and food vendors lining Prospect Road and the Town Park. Jon wore a white T-shirt that read,

American by Birth.
Lumbee by the Grace of God.

Ian sported another one that said,

I Didn't Ask to Be Born Lumbee.
I Was Just Born Lucky.

With his hand resting on Ian's shoulder, Jon stopped every few feet to introduce "My wonderful son" to another cousin, former classmate, or elder friend of his deceased father. Black, white, or Lumbee — you were nothing and nobody without your people.

Laura's eyes watered. She and Ian were where they belonged. With all their people.

They had arrived yesterday afternoon for the Pageant festivities, held in the Givens

Performing Arts Center at UNCP. Ian applauded wildly when his new first cousin, Cami, was pronounced Mini Miss Lumbee. A 5K run inaugurated the festivities today.

It felt good and right to not be running from something, but instead running toward a new future. Her eyes misted over at the depths her relationship with Jon had grown during the three weeks since the fire. It was everything she'd dreamed love could be.

And in the truth of God's sacrificial, consuming passion for her soul, more than she ever imagined possible.

Velma — Grandma Velma, as Ian had taken to calling her — had been right as usual. No need to tell her that, though. Didn't want to swell her fluffy, bluish-white head any more than it already was.

Not that anyone would ever accuse Velma Louise Jones of lacking self-confidence.

She and Velma watched the Shriners careen down the street followed by the high school band, whose epaulettes gyrated to a grooving beat. Laura was so glad she'd made her peace with her father before it was too late. His funeral had been bittersweet. Laura remained sad for her and Ian's loss. But she rested content in the knowledge Emerson was free from the prison of his own making and safe in the arms of God.

"Miss Jones! Miss Jones!"

The distinguished Grand Marshal gestured from a silver convertible, trying to capture Velma's attention. The middle-aged man, a native Lumbee, was being honored this year for his contributions toward bringing social justice to the tribe.

Velma waved back. "Well, I do declare, if it isn't Brayboy himself, grown up."

The old woman had been virtually mobbed earlier, surrounded by her former students. Their faces wreathed in smiles, many who swore they wouldn't be half of who they were today without the influence of "the hardest, fairest teacher I ever had."

As the Grand Marshal rode past, Velma leaned over. "That child was destined to spend his life in a courtroom. Either side of the bench, if you get my drift." Velma shrugged. "Coulda gone either way."

Laura placed her hand on Velma's arm. "Something I still don't understand. Why did Barbara feel qualified to be anyone's accuser?"

Velma sighed. "You didn't know her father. A miserable, self-righteous man who judged everything that girl did for years, waiting to pounce on any mistake. She absorbed enough of his out-of-context Bible threats to be dangerous. A small step, as it is for some, from judge to executioner."

"And Barbara admitted to killing Garrett's father."

Velma sagged in her chair. "It probably made her feel justified in her own eyes that she wasn't as bad as Doris or me or you. She killed her abusive husband — from her viewpoint, a matter of self-preservation. She believed your mother stole Emerson from her, and this self-delusion embittered her against Louise and you. You and Garrett were a twisted way of getting back her own from Louise."

"Holt became her victim, too."

A *V* furrowed her aunt's brow. "I imagine Barbara exonerated herself from her own sins because, unlike Doris — unlike me, who gave my baby away — she didn't abandon Garrett to his brutish father. She took Garrett with her when she fled Mimosa Grove. Her success through Emerson's patronage was Garrett's success, too."

Laura frowned. "That's convoluted reasoning, even for Barbara."

"Barbara's not the first, nor will she be the last, to run from the truth."

Velma patted Laura's hand. "I'm so happy for you and Jon and Ian. My fondest dreams for you came true. Don't let anger at what's been lost taint the possibilities of what lies ahead, Laura Lou."

"I plan to cherish every moment now that I understand how truly fragile life and love are. I've been meaning to tell you about something I found in Mother's prayer journals. Something I didn't realize at first, but over the last weeks I've had time to study them and ponder what Mother meant."

Velma had given Laura and Ian so many gifts of love over the years. Time to give her beloved aunt, now her grandmother, one as well.

Her aunt's china blues gazed at her, puzzled.

"For the last year of her life, Mother listed her prayer requests. For me, for Dad," Laura heaved a breath, "even for Barbara." Laura peered at her sandaled feet. "I'm nowhere near that forgiving."

"Death" — Velma took hold of Laura's hand — "has a way of burning away the unimportant. And for those who look to Him, to those who long to come Home, a way of honing us onto the eternal."

Laura twined her hand through Velma's smaller, bony one. "Every week she listed those names and one more. She prayed for her mother."

Velma blinked. "Louise prayed for her

mother? Nadine died when you were six. She'd have been dead almost —" The old woman's breath caught.

Tears trembled on the edge of Laura's eyelids. "I don't know how or when. But she knew. Mother knew the truth about you, Velma. About who you were to her. She understood, and she loved you."

Velma swung her gaze to the military veterans as they marched past, sweltering in their too-tight uniforms of days gone by. Old men, with their heads held high and their shoulders back.

"Life and love," Velma whispered. "Infinitely precious and not to be taken for granted."

She and Velma sat hand in hand for a moment. They listened to the cheers of the crowd. The big band sound receded down the street. Together, they revisited the memories of those who'd loved them so well.

Laura squeezed her aunt's fingers. "How's Hilary doing?"

The DNA test had come back. Nolan Munro turned out to be the father of Renna's unborn child. The homeless man, Texas Pete, ID'd Nolan's voice as the man he'd overheard arguing with Renna behind Tapestries.

Velma shot an amused, affectionate look at Laura. "Hilary is stronger than she believed possible. The jury's out on whether that marriage will survive or not. Hilary knows either way she's got her friends, and she'll never be alone. She's offered to bring me to Redeemer every Sunday once Tayla returns to school in the fall."

Laura nodded. "She'll love Redeemer. And Redeemer will be good for Hilary. I hope there, like me, she'll learn she never has to be alone, even when life's at its loneliest."

Velma cleared her throat. "Life goes on with or without our permission. Come hell or high water." She grinned. "And I expect to be dancing at your wedding soon."

"Can't be soon enough for me." Jon ducked his head under the awning.

And smiled that slow, country boy grin that always turned Laura's insides to mush.

How she loved — loved, loved — that man. Loved him for his strength, emotional and spiritual. Laura loved his gentleness, his grin, and ready wit. Most of all, she loved Jon for his willingness to walk through the hard places of the past with her.

Ian and Tayla followed on Jon's heels. Ian's face bore the telltale tufts of pink and blue cotton candy. Jon came around, giving

Laura a peck on the forehead. The light in his eyes mirrored her own.

Tayla laid the paper plate on the armrest next to Velma. "I got that sticky bun you wanted, Miss Velma."

"Thank you kindly, dear heart." Velma patted Tayla's hand, keeping her eyes peeled on the Lumbee world passing by.

Laura gave Tayla a quick hug. Tayla and Velma had already planned tailgate football parties come autumn. Velma was considering piercing her ears and taking up hip-hop.

God help them all.

As Tayla told Laura last week, "Always been this cultural divide between our people in the South. Bad history. Bad blood." The college coed frowned. "Maybe always will be. But one thing I learned this summer from studying my grandma and Miss Velma."

"What's that?" Laura asked, not sure what she'd hear.

Tayla's dark eyes crinkled. The corners of her mouth turned up. "To respect those with the courage to reach across the divide, those who try to bridge the gap."

Amen.

"Miss Jones! Miss Jones!" Voices trilled from the street.

A rotund woman in her mid-forties led a

group of baton twirlers, each outfitted in white tennis shoes and sparkly blue-sequined leotards. Like a drum major, the woman flourished a long baton.

"Come join us," beckoned the woman.

"Lord-a mercy. That's Odella Jean Britt, all grown up." Velma cocked her head at Tayla. "And, bless her heart, grown out, too."

"Your fans are calling." Laura nudged Velma's arm.

Velma grasped the armrests. Tayla cupped Velma's elbow to help the old woman to her feet. "When you put it that way, Laura Lou, it becomes my civic duty."

Gaining her balance in her hot-pink Nikes, Velma smoothed a puff of blue hair and ran a hand down her chambray jean skirt. "I always say, 'Life may not be the party you hoped for. But while you're here, you might as well dance.' "

Velma sashayed past Jon and Ian. Reaching the curb, Odella Jean tossed her the baton. Laura flinched, but with a deft twist of her wrist, Velma caught it.

Joining Odella Jean at the front of the line, Velma raised the baton high over her head and gave a whoop. Hips swinging, high-stepping Nikes flashing, Velma strutted her stuff down Third.

Eyes popping, Ian and Jon craned their necks as she passed, marveling in her magnificent wake.

Jon scratched his head. "You say she's seventy-five, Laura?"

Tayla crossed her arms. "No disrespect meant. But that is one crazy white woman." She laughed, a look akin to hero worship on her face.

Laura slipped her hand in Jon's. "Isn't she, though? And I hope one day to be just like her."

The morning light danced on her ring — the one Jon intended to give her so long ago. The one he wanted to replace with something bigger now. An offer she refused. This symbol of their never-ending love Laura intended to cherish for the rest of her days.

Jon leaned in. His lips brushed her neck above the collar of her yellow blouse. "Lord, save us."

His breath mixed with hers and warmed her cheek. "I love you, Laura Lou, just the way you are."

Jon draped his arm around her shoulder. He placed his other hand on Ian's back.

So right. So natural. Her Jon. Loving their son. Loving her.

Laura snuggled into the shelter of his

embrace. She sent a grateful prayer heavenward through the steamy July sky for second chances. For grace.

And for love found again.

GROUP DISCUSSION GUIDE

1. Have you ever done something that, like Jon or Laura, you regretted?
2. Have you ever felt Laura's kind of despair that, because of your sin, nothing could make things right between you and God? How did you deal with it?
3. Laura wasn't the only one who struggled with entangling sins. What did Jon struggle with? What entangling sins do you struggle against?
4. What lies do you tell yourself? What lies do you believe about yourself? How have the lies affected you and others?
5. What stopped Laura from telling the truth to Jon when she first realized she was pregnant?
6. What stopped Laura from telling the truth to Jon ten years later until she was finally forced to tell him the truth?
7. What motivates people to hide the truth?
8. In what ways have you experienced the

consequences for actions you regretted?

9. What tangled webs, as Shakespeare puts it, were created by the lies of: Laura, Aunt Velma, Doris, Patti, Emerson, and Barbara?
10. Have you ever felt unworthy of God's mercy and grace? Why?
11. Have you ever had to forgive someone, like Jon did, who'd clearly wronged you? Did you forgive? How did you handle it?
12. Which is harder for you? To forgive others or yourself? Why?
13. Like Laura, Jon, and Aunt Velma, have you ever been haunted by the "what might have beens"?
14. How did God weave Laura's choices — failures included — into the tapestry of her life to His ultimate glory? How has He woven His mercy and grace into yours?
15. Has God ever given you a second chance? What did you do with your second chance?
16. Have you ever extended a second chance to someone else? How did he or she respond?

ABOUT THE AUTHOR

Blending Southern and Native American fiction, **Lisa Carter** is the author of romantic suspense novels, *Carolina Reckoning, Beneath a Navajo Moon, Under a Turquoise Sky,* and *Vines of Entanglement;* and also *Aloha Rose,* a contemporary romance in the Quilts of Love series. She and her husband have two daughters and make their home in Raleigh, North Carolina. A member of ACFW, RWA, and Sisters in Crime, when she isn't writing, Lisa enjoys traveling, quilting and researching her next romantic adventure. Visit her online at LisaCarter Author.com.

The employees of Thorndike Press hope you have enjoyed this Large Print book. All our Thorndike, Wheeler, and Kennebec Large Print titles are designed for easy reading, and all our books are made to last. Other Thorndike Press Large Print books are available at your library, through selected bookstores, or directly from us.

For information about titles, please call:
(800) 223-1244

or visit our Web site at:
http://gale.cengage.com/thorndike

To share your comments, please write:
Publisher
Thorndike Press
10 Water St., Suite 310
Waterville, ME 04901